The Thief of Solarrhia

Lauren Benson
&
Katie Speake

Cover design by Andrea Sanderson at Andrea Lamb Designs

ISBN 978-1-7906-6263-0

To our beautiful tropical Beta fish. You know who you are.

ACKNOWLEDGMENTS

There are so many people (and animals) who were involved in the making of Solarrhia, and we are so grateful for the support. First of all, thank you, Jesus, for creating us to create, and for providing the horses who live on through this story. Thank you to Scout, Country, Jem, Pistol, Comet, and to all the other horses who inspired us to "do better" every day. Thank you, JK Rowling, for the Weasley twins because, without them, our first conversation would have looked very different...less bonding, more silence. Thank you Parks and Rec for endless laughs and Tammy Two cackling. Thank you, our dear Samm, for reading all the versions of this story and for believing in us from the beginning. You are a star in the dark. To all of our friends and family who encouraged us, thank you.

PROLOGUE

"Stop, thief!"

Had Steele been new to this life, she might have frozen from fear—or maybe taken off running—but years of experience had taught her to fight against those instincts. The boy next to her, however, looked to be a novice. His hands flinched at his sides, probably toward what he had stolen, and he ran his fingers over his pockets. Silently, she gave him advice, knowing the inner debate going on in his mind. *Don't run. You belong here. He'll never see you.*

The boy leapt forward and pushed through the crowd. She frowned as she watched him run, drawing attention to himself.

The merchant's gaze snapped onto the fleeing figure. "Guards!" he shouted.

The boy stopped running and swiveled about, his eyes desperate for an escape. But it was too late. A palace guard was already upon him and wrapped his thick hand around the boy's small wrist. No matter how the boy yanked and wriggled, he was caught.

The buzz of the crowd waned, and Steele sighed. She knew what came next, and she didn't want to see it play out. She turned away as the guard forced the boy to his knees. The terrified sobs of the boy filled the street for a moment before the people resumed their business.

A horrible *crack* sounded, and Steele's stomach flipped. She imagined how one of the boy's hands lay crushed by the wooden and metal club that the guards of Asha always carried. Another popping crunch and the boy's wails rose a pitch. She hoped he would pass out and not feel the continued disfigurement of his hand. He would forever be marked as a thief, now.

"You!"

Her eyes widened as a hand pointed in her direction. The apple vendor.

"You were with him!"

She almost protested, but she'd been so distracted by the boy's capture, that she had not tucked the evidence away.

"Guards! My apples! This one, too!"

As he continued to yell, Steele whirled around, buffed the bruised apple on her dust-colored trousers, and threw it at him. His hand closed around the squishy side and bits of it splattered on his face. He grunted in disgust. She couldn't help but smirk as she ducked to the right, stepping behind a heavyset man arguing with a vendor over an overpriced oil lamp.

She glanced back at the apple merchant who was wiping the overripe pulp from his cheek. She adjusted her green hooded overcoat to better conceal her face and melted into the throng of people before any guards caught sight of her.

Steele had never been able to steal food without feeling guilty about it. Any time she couldn't rely on people's leftovers or garbage and needed to give in to her stomach's pleas for food, she could feel the weight of her father's disappointed look telling her that she hadn't earned that food. Now, when she had to filch something, she reasoned that it was fine if the food was partially or nearly spoiled. No one willingly purchased food that was going bad.

A stabbing pain in her middle stopped her in her tracks. She bit back a groan and risked a glance back toward the apple cart. True, a piece of fruit wouldn't have done much to give her nourishment, but it would have at least satisfied her empty stomach for a moment. And she could have fed the spoiled part to the horse.

She weaved through the busy street, bumping into a tall man who returned her apologies with a glare. "Watch where you're going, boy."

Steele kept her head down so he would not realize his mistake and told herself it was the trousers and not her face that had made him think such a thing.

She ducked down a narrow alley, leaving the buzz of the crowd behind. The constant chatter was giving her a headache, so she sat down, resting the back of her head against the wall. The coolness of the stone seeped through her hood, relieving some of the ache in her skull.

However, as the pain in her head dulled, her stomach wrenched uncomfortably. It had been too long since her last meal, and since she had failed to steal the fruit, she faced another night without food.

Steele closed her eyes for a moment in the hush of the alley and thought of her hometown as she often did when she traveled through Asha. She was from the capital of the Solarrhian Kingdom, called Rhia by the locals so as not to confuse the city and the kingdom. While the two cities had their differences, they were alike in many ways. There was a main market for trading and bartering, twisting narrow streets, clotheslines strung between windows, and a light coating of dust that blew in from the nearby Nasshari Desert. Asha was much flatter than Rhia, which sat closer to the Farest'Del Mountains, and was home to the Zhanbolat Palace.

Steele wished she could return there for good someday. After her parents died when she was twelve, her mother's friend, a woman named Tazmeen, had informally adopted her. Tazmeen and her son, Ali, had become like family to her, and she missed them terribly. It had been almost a year since she had seen them, and she was anxious to go home—something she wouldn't be able to do if she couldn't get her hands on some food.

She needed a new plan. She pushed back her hood and massaged her temples, allowing her dark braid to fall over her shoulder. As she undid the plait, she fluffed the dark mess, hoping to achieve the waves she had seen on some women. She removed her coat and turned it inside out, green becoming an ashy gray. Her fingers twitched at the hood, instinct telling her to cover her face. It was a risk to expose her face when more than just a merchant was after her, but it was one that she must take. She squared her shoulders and prepared to venture into the streets.

The slap of feet against stone brought her eyes up, skin prickling with anxiety. She tensed, and her hand reflexively twitched toward her belt knife.

A man was watching her, but he wasn't the apple vendor or a guard. He was more a youth than a man, she reassessed. If she had to guess, she would say he was younger than her sixteen years, maybe fourteen. He dressed simply and much like her in a vest and trousers. Although, instead of a hooded scarf, he wore a red cap that stood out against his dark hair. He looked as thin and raggedy as she did, but she still regarded him warily. A thief was a thief, and while there was an underground market for criminals and pickpockets who worked fairly well together, there were very few she trusted herself.

"You look hungry," he said, slowly approaching her. He clutched a loaf of bread in his hands, and he broke it in half. "Here, take this." He held half the loaf out to her.

Steele crossed her arms over her chest and studied him. "Why?" As much as she tried to avoid looking at the food, she couldn't help her nose. A sweet, grainy scent wafted toward her, and her stomach growled.

"Look, I saw you in the market. Something tells me you didn't steal that apple as some game no matter what that merchant was grumbling about." When she made no move for the bread, he shrugged before taking a bite out of the half he had extended to her.

He chewed, staring at her, and she raised an eyebrow. "What are you trying to prove?"

One side of his mouth turned up in a tentative smile, and he swallowed. "There. Not poisoned."

5

"What do you want from me? I don't have anything for you to steal."

The boy chuckled and threw the bread at her. She caught it and held it out, still hesitant to take a bite.

He grinned. "Street urchins have to look out for one another, right? Can't let the upper class be right about us being equal to the rats and all."

"An urchin? I haven't heard that one before," she said with a laugh. Her body relaxed, though she still looked at him with suspicion.

"Just the latest description I picked up from the guards," the boy smirked. He turned to walk down the alley, but paused, adjusting his red cap. "By the way, the name's Dal. If you're ever in these parts again, look up the Crescent Moon Inn. It's a sort of safe haven for people like us. I hope you have better luck next time."

Steele gripped the bread and smiled at him. "Thank you."

As Dal turned to leave, he paused to look at some papers stuck to the wall. He laughed once and tapped one of the pages. "This you?"

Steele made her way over to the paper and frowned as she usually did when she saw a sketch of her face. It wasn't awful; the artist got her dark eyes and hair, cheekbones, and narrow face right. She thought, however, that her nose looked too straight, and she didn't think her lips were that thin. But it had also been a long time since she had seen her reflection. Thankfully, the artist hadn't thought to include her father's phoenix feather she had braided into her hair. She never went anywhere without it.

"I take that frown as a yes?" Dal asked, tearing the paper from the wall.

"Unfortunately," she admitted, eyeing the paper in his hands, heart jumping. He could easily alert one of the guards.

"Well, in that case, I'll make sure no one else sees it," he said, tearing the paper into thin strips.

"Thank you." She felt the tension in her chest ease as the bits of paper fluttered to the ground, and she offered him a smile. "If I see your face anywhere, I'll do the same."

Dal grinned widely back at her. "So what'd you do?"

"Something against the law," she said evasively. "But I didn't think Asha would know of it." She frowned. The fact that the town had her face on record was all the more reason to keep moving. "Thank you again for the bread, and for that," she said, motioning to the shredded sketch on the ground.

"Okay, maybe you'll tell me next time," he said.

She gave him a small wave before walking back toward the market. As she neared, she took a deep breath and bit into the fresh bread, savoring the way it almost melted in her mouth. She considered the way Dal spoke. His words ran together quickly, similarly to how the apple vendor had talked, and she made a note to adjust her accent and tempo for conversation.

The market was still full. Every day and every market was different, depending on the size of the town and which season it was. Solarrhia was quickly approaching its warmest temperatures, and the people living close to the Nasshari Desert would be stocking up on what they could store away to avoid the markets during that time. No one wanted to be maneuvering through hundreds of people in such proximity as the sun beat down on their backs, no matter how familiar with the heat they were.

A man with a large set of lungs sold melons just ahead. His raised voice drew her attention, and she watched him as he occasionally sputtered rudely at the people passing by his cart.

Approaching the man, she offered him her most charming smile. "Good afternoon, sir."

The man glanced up at her and smiled toothily back. "Are you interested in buying some of the sweetest, juiciest melons in all the land? You won't taste their equal anywhere else."

"They certainly look delicious." Speaking as quickly as Dal had was strange, but Steele thought her accent was passable. "Do you mind if I feel some of them?"

The man nodded, and she reached for the fruit as a couple of children ran by. She lurched forward, as if bumped by the children, and knocked several melons to the ground. Apologizing, she bent to help with the mess, but the man was too busy yelling at the children to give her notice. While he was distracted, she slipped two melons into her bag hidden by her cloak and placed the last few back on the cart as the man was turning around.

"Those children run around as if they are wild," he said gruffly.

She nodded once, backing away from the cart. "If you'll excuse me, I'm going to look at some of the other vendors before making my final choice. My da wants just the right kind for his dinner party." The man grunted a response, and she turned away quickly.

She made her way down the end of the road, and, just in case the melon vendor might be watching, briefly paused at a few vendors, taking special care to glare at the women who suggested she fix her crooked nose. A man held a small iron cage in front of her face, forcing her to jerk back. Behind the bars sat a creature that looked similar to a human except for the blue-hued skin and pointed ears. And it was only the size of her hand. Though the creature gave her a defiant look, Steele thought she saw a hint of sadness about its shoulders, and she grimaced. Another caged being.

"Every lady needs a fairy! The great legends swear fairies bring husbands and riches. Only ten silver pieces for this one!" The vendor smiled, gaps surrounding most of his yellowed teeth.

Behind him were numerous cages, each filled with one or two pixies. As she studied the cages, she hoped people wouldn't fall for this trick. Fairies were supposed to bring good luck and be helpful servants, but a pixie would do just the opposite and probably steal your clothes off your back, too. Fairies and pixies looked somewhat similar to each other, but there *were* differences-the most obvious being the pixies' blue skin.

"How stupid do you think I am?" Steele turned to the taller woman standing beside her who was studying the same cage, and she pointed. "That's not a fairy! Pixies will kill you and take off with the money and your husband!"

The woman's eyes widened then narrowed at the vendor. Having protected the woman from a disastrous scam, Steele silently backed away from the woman. She turned toward the sparse forest on the outskirts of town, smirking as shouts escalated behind her.

Three girls bumped into her as she squeezed through the people.

"Excuse me," she said, but two of the girls didn't seem to notice the collision at all. Their friend, a girl with chocolate colored skin, gave her an apologetic smile before joining her friends. Steele took in their fine, colorful clothing with raised brows. Those girls were either high nobility or extremely rich. All three were adorned in fine linens, their faces covered in the half masks only the wealthy bothered to wear. Once the masks' purpose was a way to block the sun from burning people's skin, but only the rich had bothered to spend their money on the fabric. Now it was more of a fashion statement than anything Steele could think of.

The girl with flame colored hair giggled. "Avi, did you hear that woman say the princes are on their way to the market?"

Her companion nodded, blond hair blowing in the breeze. "What are they doing outside of Rhia?"

The princes? Here?

They must be heading to the northern kingdom of Hamonsfell to visit their grandfather, King Ferdinand. Steele didn't know much about Prince Hadrian and Prince Aldair. It was said that twenty-two year old Prince Hadrian, the oldest and heir to the throne, looked just like his father. She knew many women in the area found the sons of King Ax and Queen Marian to be ruggedly handsome with their dark brown hair and tanned skin. She'd never been close enough to get a good look at their faces, but she'd heard enough comments to believe the rumors.

Steele spotted an opening in the crowd, and as she moved toward it, two soldiers stepped in front of her. Her feet paused along with her heartbeat, and she stared wide-eyed at the men for a moment too long. One of the soldiers glanced at her, revealing brilliant blue eyes that reminded her of the ocean—or at least what she thought the color of the ocean was based on one of her mother's paintings. A fresh gash ran down the right side of his cheek and a crimson sash crossed his uniform, identifying his high rank. Ducking her chin, she rushed past him, hoping he hadn't recognized her. She needed to get out of there before more security for the royal sons appeared.

Still...

Steele glanced behind her and observed the man with the aqua eyes wading through the crowd, slowly disappearing from sight. She had only seen the Zhanbolat princes from afar, even though she had grown up just outside the palace, and like those three girls, her curiosity had been piqued. She looked around for a good place to hide and spotted a building with a stone replica of a dragon affixed to the edge of the roof. She could easily climb that.

She scaled the wall and hauled herself onto the ledge. Securing her bag against her body, she crept forward to conceal herself behind the dragon's wing.

She looked down on the market as two men were riding in, one upon a gray horse and the other a black horse. The people respectfully parted, bowing as the riders passed through. The prince on the black horse rode taller, engaging with the crowd and smiling. His brother sat more relaxed in the saddle, one hand resting on his horse's withers. By now, groups of girls had gathered along the roadside to catch a glimpse, and as he rode past one group, he leaned down. With a flick of his hand, he revealed a golden flower and tucked it behind a girl's ear. She hid her mouth behind the back of her hand while her friends stared on at the prince, probably hoping for tokens of their own. When he turned away, one of the girls frowned and crossed her arms.

The prince rode on a few more steps before reining the horse to a stop. This time when he reached toward a girl, she grasped at his fingers, and he appeared to kiss the top of her hand. When he released her, she sagged back against her friends for a moment before turning toward them and gesturing wildly. Steele rolled her eyes. Other sixteen year olds may have fallen for the smile or a gift from a handsome Zhanbolat prince, but she had other things to worry about, like staying alive and not getting arrested.

She flicked her gaze away and watched the other prince who had also stopped. Instead of focusing on the women, however, he was attending to a small child. The child bravely strode up to the tall black horse before being scooped into the arms of an older man. The prince gestured to the man, and the child reached out to pet the horse's neck. Steele smiled, heart warmed by the scene, and she hoped this was Prince Hadrian. The people of Solarrhia needed someone who would notice them. *And not for their pretty smiles.*

Her curiosity faded as the crowd swarmed the men, and she lowered herself onto the wall, cursing when her foot missed a hold. Carefully, she descended the rest of the way and hopped to the ground. Speckles of dirt swirled around her ankles, and she brushed her hands together. With one last look over her shoulder at the crowd, she turned toward the street leading away from the market.

Steele didn't stop walking until she was confident that no one had followed her out of the city. A large tree offered her shade so she sank down against it and pulled out one of the stolen melons. For a moment, she stared at it in her hands, her conscience prickling at her heart. The markings on the melon looked too much like a pair of eyes. Accusing eyes. Her stomach grumbled in protest, reminding her why she'd stolen in the first place. She took her knife and peeled away the rim of the fruit. She popped a bite sized piece into her mouth, and flavor exploded on her tongue. Her middle rumbled again. Despite the bread from earlier, she was still hungry.

"Thank you, Mister Melon Man," she muttered.

She ate the entire fruit and licked her fingers clean of the juice. Resting her head against the bark of the tree, she sighed. Day vendors from the town would be heading this way soon, and as much as she relished the rest, it was time to get moving.

As she secured her cloak around her shoulders, a couple of carts squeaked and groaned through the gates. A loud, angry voice rose above the noise and she grimaced, wondering if the melon vendor had realized there was missing produce. Not wishing to find out, she hurried toward the forest. A two day journey lay before her, and those two days would not pass quickly enough.

She made her way a little farther into the woods where she found the horse, Arrow, hobbled exactly as she had left him. The stallion nodded his head at her as she approached, and he stretched his wings out. His grumbling whicker brought a smile to her face.

"Now, now. No complaining. You'll get your food." Steele pulled out the other melon and banged it against a rock. The fruit split, and she fed it to the horse.

The animal chomped into the melon and chewed messily, sending juice from the fruit running down her fingers—and a little flying at her face. Ignoring the sticky liquid, she ran her gaze over the animal, making sure nothing had happened to him while she had been away. While she was occupied, Arrow grabbed the rest of the melon from her palm and quickly finished it. She wiped her hand on her trousers, then reached into her saddlebag to retrieve a brush. She gently groomed the stallion and began to hum a lullaby her father had used to soothe her to sleep. Arrow leaned into the brush and sighed.

He looked as if he belonged in the forest. His body blended in with the soft soil of the earth and the dark bark of the trees, and she could not help noticing how beautiful he was, especially now that he had some weight on his ribs. His hip bones were not as prominent as they once had been either. Her eyes traveled down the reddish brown of his hips to the stocking of one of his black legs. The color of his body contrasted beautifully with that of his legs, mane, and tail. The brown dissolved into black at the base of his wings, too, but it reappeared along the edges. His strange coloring puzzled her as it did not follow the uniform of a typical bay horse, but then again she had not seen many fliers in her lifetime.

The stallion's hair shone after the brushing, and she whispered promises of a better life to him while unhooking the hobbles. He stretched his legs as she grabbed her blanket and saddle that lay nearby and gently placed both just behind his withers. He looked at her while she tightened the girth behind his wings, and he blew air out his nose. She attached the chest piece Tazmeen had given her the last time she had been home and took a step back to look at him.

Arrow snorted, stretching his nose toward her, and she sighed. It was a shame he wasn't hers. She shouldn't have named him because it made it that much more difficult to give him up. But she knew she couldn't take care of him the way he deserved. Her fingers brushed over the large, bumpy scar on Arrow's shoulder, and she scowled, cursing the trader from whom she'd freed the horse. The scar was deep enough that she was sure he'd carry it with him the rest of his days.

Most would say she had stolen the animal, but she didn't like to think of herself as a thief when it came to horses. She only took horses who needed to be rescued from abusive situations and gave them to people who would properly care for them. Unfortunately, the law didn't seem to care about the creatures who gave their all to these ignorant—or worse, completely unfeeling—owners, receiving only starvation or injuries in return. The kingdom viewed her as a criminal, no matter her intentions, and wanted her to repay her so-called sins with blood.

As she put the brush away and gathered the rest of her supplies, she thought about Dal, her fellow street urchin. She wondered if he was disappointed that she had not returned the gesture by giving him her name. Names were powerful, particularly in the underground. It was vital that people wouldn't be able to track her in case they had connected her name with the wanted posters that displayed her face.

And Steele wasn't a name one easily forgot.

CHAPTER 1

The stable looked dark, but still Steele waited. Her heart beat so loudly she was sure the stable master could hear her. After all this time, she wondered if the nerves would ever disappear. She would have thought eight years would have been enough time to get used to the uncertainty of what these nights could bring. She always planned everything beforehand, considering multiple scenarios, and was ready for anything that might come her way. Yet, every time, the moment before she stepped inside a barn or a pasture, it was as if she were fourteen again, breaking into that first barn to free the horse that changed life as she knew it. Releasing a shaky breath, she adjusted her pack over her shoulders and moved out of the shadows, finally convinced it was safe to enter the stable.

Steele unhooked the latch, not daring to breathe as she eased the door open. She took a moment to thank the Creator for the lack of guard dogs around and slipped inside. She took in her surroundings. A cart with mud-caked wheels was stowed on the left, a long whip and bridle resting on the seat. To her right, a bag of grain lay on its side. A few kernels had spilled out where it looked like a mouse had chewed a hole. And in the back of the small stable stood the powder gray stallion. His ears twisted about anxiously, as though he knew what was about to take place.

A ragged snore and low mumbling froze her in her tracks. *And this is why those nerves are good*, she reminded herself. Someone was inside! But where?

Heart slamming against her ribs, she searched the interior of the stable until she spotted a lump of a man in the left hand corner. His body lay draped over a chair, drool oozing out of his open mouth, and a half-empty bottle hanging loosely from his fingers.

She swallowed and hoped that being so obviously drunk would make him a sound sleeper. Still, a liquor-induced coma did not make a man deaf. How was she to get the horse free without waking him?

Steele took a couple deep breaths and crouched low. She watched him for a moment, and then she flicked a glance at the horse who was watching her, his neck arched as he pawed at the ground.

Steele licked her lips and picked the bridle off the seat of the cart. She approached the horse, silently pleading with him to be cooperative.

The horse hung his head over the gate, and Steele slipped the bridle over his ears. He took the bit in his mouth willingly, and she hoped that was a good sign since she had only ever seen him pull a cart. He could easily decide to buck her off the moment she sat upon his back. A risk she was going to have to take.

Her pulse raced as she fingered the latch on the stall door, sliding the bolt over. She winced at the rusty screech that sounded when the bolt released. The man coughed mid snore, and Steele pushed the gate open fully. Quickly, she leaped onto the horse's back. She barely managed to balance herself before he lunged from the stall, hooves clattering against the ground.

She saw the man sit up and rub his eyes. It took him a moment to focus on Steele righting herself on the back of the horse. He blinked, and then his eyes unglazed, clarity sinking in. "Hey! What are...You!"

Steele heeled the stallion in the ribs, and he gladly sped out of the stable. From over her shoulder, she saw the man reach for the reins, but the horse snaked his head around, nipping at his fingers. He swore and threw the bottle at them, regret immediately flashing on his face as it soared in the air toward her, liquid leaking out the top. Alcohol splattered across her cheek, and the bottle bounced off her shoulder, rolling down the horse's neck. Mid-trot, the horse swiveled to the side, arching his body away from the attack.

Defeated, the man screamed, "Thief! Thief!" as he stumbled behind them out of the barn.

Steele looked ahead, and the horse broke into a canter, hunching his shoulders and kicking his hind legs out behind him. Steele grunted but held on, and when she pressed her calf tight against his side, she was pleased to see him swerve to the right.

They barreled down the road, the unintelligible shouting behind them fading into the distance. Steele preferred not to use the road, but speed was key tonight. The closer she could get to Azubah, the better. She applied pressure to the reins, willing the horse to slow his mad gallop down the road. His pace only eased a fraction as she searched the side of the road for the break in the trees. It was the only indicator of a shortcut she'd discovered years before.

It came upon her sooner than she'd anticipated, and she sat back and pulled hard on the reins. The horse resisted at first but finally obeyed, throwing her an opinionated look as he slowed to a trot.

"I know, I know." Steele held the reins in one hand while patting his neck with the other. She turned him around, angling him toward the trees, as she listened for sounds of the man or anyone from the village pursuing them. Only insects chirped and hummed. The branches swayed in the light wind.

The path narrowed and weaved through the trees, constantly twisting, but with the moonlight breaking through the branches above her, she could make out the trail easily enough. She kept the stallion at a ground eating trot until her legs screamed and her arms ached. Finally, she asked him to stop, and when she slid from the animal's back, her knees buckled.

The horse was breathing heavily, sweat darkening his light gray coat, but his eyes were bright. He took in their surroundings with pricked ears. "Sorry for all the excitement," Steele said, running her hands down his face to stroke his nose. He snorted, wafting warm air over her fingers. "But I wanted to rescue you from that horrible man."

The horse nibbled at her fingertips, and she thought about how he had tried to bite the man as they were leaving. "I think I'll call you Snap."

The horse bobbed his head as if in agreement, and she scratched his forehead. She had not grabbed any grain from the stable, but there were some patches of grass along the trail for Snap to eat while they rested for a moment in the comfortable seclusion the forest provided.

She was taking Snap to the town of Falu, and even with the shortcut, it would take them over a week to get there. At least she could use those days to train and test Snap. If they made good time, she hoped to stop for a meal with Dal in Asha along the way.

"The place I'm taking you is wonderful," she said, running her hands along Snap's neck. "You'll have a family who will smother you with love and carrots, and there's a young girl who needs you to be her friend. If you get to meet *my* friend Dal, I apologize in advance for not letting you stay with him. He's wonderful, too, but Asha is just a little too close to here."

Snap shifted away when her fingers reached his shoulders, and she sucked in an angry breath. A handful of welts peppered his flesh, some scabbed over, others ringed with drying blood.

She pressed her hands against his sides and under his belly, checking for soreness or tension. She hadn't had time to earlier, but she didn't want to cause any further pain. He paused his eating, but after flicking an ear in her direction, he went back to munch on the grass. While he ate, she searched for something to use as a lift. While she wasn't terribly short, Snap was a tall horse, and sheer adrenaline had boosted her onto him in the stable. She wasn't sure she could do it again. Snap pawed at the ground, arching his neck, and she eyed his back nervously. She had had her fair share of falls, but it had been a while.

The trail was narrow and frustratingly flat, save for a couple of low-sitting boulders and too-high branches. Rolling her shoulders back, Steele led Snap to one of the boulders. With steady breaths and the rock as a boost, she swung onto his back before she could change her mind. The stallion went rigid as she gathered the reins and let her legs hang loosely along his sides.

"It's okay, Snap, I'm still here. Just like before. Nothing has changed, except no one is throwing bottles at us. So please don't buck me off. That wouldn't be a nice way to thank me for rescuing you." The words tumbled from her mouth as she ran a hand along his neck. His dark tipped ears swiveled back to her, and she felt his muscles relax beneath her fingertips.

Steele continued to speak as she pressed her calves into his sides, and he stepped out stiffly at first, little by little becoming more comfortable as they moved down the path. Gathering her courage, she asked him to trot, and he eagerly broke into the faster gait. His trot was smoother than she had imagined it would be due to his lack of training, and she smiled. It seemed he agreed with her that his long, slender legs were made for running free, not pulling carts under that man's cruel whip. Giving Snap some slack, the horse shifted into a slow, rocking canter, and Steele grinned as the fear of being caught lifted from her shoulders and fell along the trail behind her.

CHAPTER 2

Steele exhaled, relieved as the patrolmen turned the corner without noticing her. She was most comfortable in the shadows and confident in her ability to blend into them, but only fools believed they were invisible.

Just around the corner was the Crescent Moon Inn, and she was anxious for a hot meal. And to see Dal. Smiling to herself, she slinked alongside the building, recalling their first meeting six years prior. She had been so suspicious of him and never would have dreamed he'd turn into such a good friend.

Her thoughts paused over the word *friend*. She didn't have friends, not really. At least not in the normal sense of the word. There were a few people she knew and trusted, but she saw them so infrequently. Dal and two other grinning faces danced in her mind. Twitch and Spar. She'd met the brother and sister not too long ago, but she'd connected with them instantly. Those were her friends, she supposed. Friends who knew only the basics of each other's lives, that they were all orphans and thieves and in need of allies in a world where people would rather steal the pack off an unsuspecting shoulder than speak to the pack's owner. Sure, over the years she had found places where people let her be, but she could never count fully on honor among thieves.

Thinking of Twitch and Spar, she pulled a small, misshapen magi gemstone out of her pocket. Dal had cleverly lifted four of these stones off a merchant the previous year. He had been so excited, thinking they'd be worth at least a pouch's worth of gold, maybe even more. Magi used magically linked stones to communicate with one another. Occasionally some of them ended up in the human markets, and for their beauty and rarity, they always sold for a high price. She had snapped up one of the stones then, filled with curiosity. She and Dal had fiddled with them until Dal had managed to push a trigger on one, turning three out of the four stones the same color.

"They're linked!" she had exclaimed. "Well, except for that one."

They'd stared in awe, immediately looking for all the ways the stones could work.

"They'll be worth even more now!" Dal had sung with glee. He'd stopped then, pressing another section of the stone. All three linked stones turned red. "You know, we could use these as a way to communicate with each other. It's been almost a year since we spoke. I was starting to wonder if you'd been caught."

They had worked until they'd managed to turn the stones five or six different colors. Dal had been disappointed they couldn't do more, knowing there were other ways to use them, but the wheels had turned in Steele's head until she had come up with a color scheme for the towns and areas she and Dal frequented. They'd agreed to keep the stones, Dal graciously giving up the third so that Steele could pass it along to Spar and Twitch. She wondered how much the fourth stone had sold for, though she would never ask Dal for that sort of information. The stones were a crude but effective way to communicate and allowed Steele the ability to keep her strange group of friends.

Pushing a corner of her stone, she watched as gray dissolved into green, her palm warm from the magic. She hoped Twitch and Spar would be able to meet with her at the Valley of the Thieves. The mischievous siblings always managed to lighten her heart.

Steele pushed open the door to the inn and glanced around. Dal sat in a corner, and he grinned when he saw her, beckoning her over. She recognized a few of the people seated around the room. As she made her way to Dal's table, she dipped her head to a few of them, receiving nods in return.

Thieves mingled more openly in this inn, than anywhere else Steele knew, though there were always customers who never knew they were surrounded by criminals. Still, in their own slang, thieves shared their exploits, what they'd done and what they'd taken, but Steele could never be so free with her words. The less people knew about what she did, the less they could hold against her.

The first genuine smile in weeks stretched across her face the moment she sat across from Dal.

Rescuing Snap, though successful, had taken a long time, and she was tired. She hoped seeing Dal and eating a decent meal would give her the energy to complete her mission with the stallion.

As she pulled her scarf down off her head and away from her face, she studied the boy across from her. Dal had grown in the months since she'd seen him last. His black floppy hair was longer, falling just past his eyebrows, and scruff dusted his cheeks.

"I already ordered us food," he said. "I hope the steak-and-potato stew is okay."

Her mouth watered. "That sounds wonderful."

Dal grinned. "So what have you been up to? Running around on all your *secret* missions?"

She rolled her eyes. He found it extremely entertaining how reserved she was about her lifestyle, even in little havens like this place. "Yes, yes. I've been busy. Trying to stay out of trouble mostly." She gave him a sharp glare. "I hope you can say the same."

"Yes, *Mother*," he said sarcastically. "I'm eighteen. Not a child, despite what you think."

She scoffed and gave him a flat stare.

"I haven't been in trouble in several weeks," he said, mirroring her stare. "And anyway, it's not like I can't outrun and outwit the guards. Many of them are fat and slow."

Steele laughed in spite of herself.

A barmaid brought them their food, and they fell silent as they inhaled the stew. It wasn't much, but the mushy potatoes and stringy meat was the best meal she had eaten in weeks. She savored the flavor, and the taste instantly reminded of her last sunrise at home. Tazmeen had looked so beautiful standing in front of the fireplace stirring the same kind of stew Steele was eating now. The sun's rays had pierced through the small window above the wooden counter that Steele's father had made for Tazmeen shortly before the accident. From where Steele had been sitting at the small table in the corner of the kitchen, the rays completely covered Tazmeen's body as if she were light itself.

An unusual wave of homesickness washed over Steele. How many months had it been since she'd last seen the mountains, the beautiful view of the palace, and more importantly—to her at least—the cozy place she'd learned to call home after her parents had passed?

Steele was glad this journey would eventually lead her back to Tazmeen. And seeing her adopted younger brother, Ali, wouldn't be so bad, either. She glanced at Dal and had to smile. He reminded her so much of Ali sometimes. Ali, who was growing up much too quickly. He would have just turned sixteen, and it seemed like only yesterday that he had been a child, following her around and begging for attention.

"Do you ever think about leaving Asha?" She asked, wondering if Dal had anything tying him to this town. He had no family as far as she knew. She had never asked, and he had never offered her any details.

He shrugged one shoulder. "Sometimes. I think it would be nice to go to the sea!"

She grinned. "The sea to the south or the sea to the west?"

"The west of course," he said with a laugh. "Haven't you heard the stories about King Eram's land?"

She shook her head. She'd never ventured south before, or at least not far enough to set foot in Eram's kingdom, Oakenjara.

Dal leaned forward and whispered, "They say the land is cursed by magi. They say that once there was a war or something, and the magic that was used left its mark all across the lands."

"I'm sure that's just a story," she said. "I bet the sea is nice in the Barrowlands *and* Oakenjara."

"Maybe, but the Barrowlands doesn't have stories involving cursed land. At least not that I've heard. So. Let's say we leave this area and head there. What do you think Queen Evelind's treatment of thieves is like? Would we be thieves there as well? Stealing boats and fish and whatever else they have by the sea?"

"Hmm," she mused, "I think we could try for honest work. You'd make a good fisherman, and I could make nets and patch sails?" She laughed. "Is that what people do there?"

Dal laughed and shrugged again. "I have no idea. I'm just going off of stories I hear."

"Since I don't know that much about the sea folk, and I'd rather not cross the Nasshari Desert to get there, I think I'd be better in the mountains," she said, closing her eyes to picture the towering peaks she'd only seen from far away.

"Wouldn't you have to cross the desert to get there?" he asked skeptically.

"No, if you go north from here, it's a straight shot to the Wolfkiel Mountains. I've taken a horse up that way before."

"I hear it's cold. You'd probably turn back after a couple freezing nights," Dal said dryly. "I know Solarrhia is near enough to the Nasshari that you're used to the warm."

"The Farest'Del Mountains are close, too, though," she protested.

"Yes, but are they as tall and wild as the Wolfkiel peaks? Or even Oakenjara's Gilded Alps?"

She wrinkled her nose. "Supposedly there are dragons. And you can't bring the Gilded Alps into this. I thought Eram's land wasn't an option since you're scared of stories about magic."

"I'm not," he said quickly. "I've also observed the people from the south seem less happy than other people, and I blame their king for that. He must be a horrible ruler."

"Stop it," she laughed. "You can't know that for sure."

"All right, true, I don't know that for sure. But I'd still rather go west."

"And I'd rather go north, even with the cold. So whenever we decide to leave this part of the world, I'm glad we've figured out where we're going."

Dal grinned. "It's like a weight has been lifted from my shoulders."

They fell into a comfortable silence until Dal laughed to himself. She raised an eyebrow at him, and he sniggered. "Since we're doing all this future planning I have to ask, when are you going to marry some rich man so I won't have to be a thief anymore?"

The question was so random that she laughed once and stared at him, waiting for him to finish his joke. When he stayed silent, she sighed. "You think that if I marry a wealthy man you'll be set for life?"

He bobbed his head. "Of course."

"Don't count on me to solve all your problems anytime soon, then. Why can't you marry a wealthy woman and support me?"

"Because I already have my eye on someone, and I'm sure she wouldn't have more than a few cows to her name."

Steele quirked an eyebrow at him. "Oh? Tell me about her."

He twitched his lips to the side and frowned. "I've only met her once, but her eyes dazzle like stars in the night sky, and her smile takes your breath away...," he trailed off wistfully, his eyes taking on a dreamy look.

"Aw, look at you. A romantic at heart."

Dal grinned as he spooned more of the stew into his mouth, and Steele felt a twinge of *something* as she watched him eat. Something akin to jealousy or sadness or longing. Not jealousy in the way most would think, though. She liked Dal, but considered him a brother. It had just been a very long time since she had allowed herself to like someone. Or had the time to. Her lifestyle kept her busy enough that she rarely thought about the future in terms of having a family, but she was sure Tazmeen would say something next time she went home. Tazmeen wanted almost nothing more than to see Steele settled and happy.

But she *was* happy, in her own way. She was free to do as she liked and had people like Dal, Twitch, and Spar to talk to and laugh with. And she had the horses. She was never happier than when she was on the back of a horse.

"If it doesn't work out between you two, I'm dragging you home with me, and Tazmeen can fatten you up with her cooking. You're so skinny."

He wrapped his fingers around his bicep, and Steele assumed he was flexing. "Skinny?" He snorted. "Look at this muscle!" There was a challenge in his eyes, so she reached across and squeezed his arm, nodding at him when she felt hard muscle under her fingers. He *had* filled out some since she's last seen him.

"Word on the street is girls love a man with muscles, so you may win your girl over with just that," she said. "If she's lucky, you won't even have to talk to her."

21

"Hey." He scowled. "I'm good with words. I can woo anyone I set eyes on." He glanced around the room and grinned. "Even Mistress Kai."

Steele snorted. The mistress of the inn was notorious for her fiery tongue and lack of tolerance for anything except ale. "Next time I'm here I'll let you prove yourself."

"Deal." He focused his attention back on the stew, and Steele tipped her bowl to the side to scoop the remaining broth onto her spoon. They sat in silence for a few moments, and she sat back into her seat, staring at the other people gathering around the tables.

"Steele," he started, cutting into her thoughts, his tone a bit stretched. "Have you noticed anything…strange going on in the towns?"

She narrowed her eyes. "No, but I've been mostly in the woods lately. Camping and training."

"Right. Of course." He paused, scratching his chin. "I don't have any facts. Just a feeling... People seem like they're on edge, I guess, is the best way to describe it, and I don't see some of the folk I used to. It's like they've vanished, and I can't shake this nagging feeling that I should keep looking over my shoulder."

She tipped her head to the side, pondering his words. True, it didn't seem like much, but usually small, seemingly trivial things held tremendous importance. A town or city, no matter how big or small, always had an energy to it. Some places pulsed with vitality and excitement; others drifted by in a lazy, peaceful way. This particular town usually had a calm atmosphere intermixed with winds of change. Many people used this town as a temporary home, a middle ground between a sprawling city and a small village, so it was common to see new faces on each visit. Yet, if Dal sensed that something was off, she would not discard it.

"Anyone you knew personally?"

"No. Some thieves, sure, but a couple were some people who held a little higher standing in the town."

"Has anyone said anything?"

Dal laughed once. "I'm not going to. I don't care enough about them to offer myself up."

Steele gave him a flat look. "Surely people in their circle of friends have said something."

Dal shrugged. "I wouldn't know. The soldiers here don't seem too bothered by it, so I'm sure it's nothing, but like I said, it just feels wrong."

She tapped her fingernails on the table and raised her eyebrows at him. "If you're right, you must be even more careful than before. This is your town, but don't let that make you careless."

She expected him to roll his eyes at her. He did that so often she was surprised his eyeballs hadn't rolled right out of their sockets yet, so his solemn nod surprised her. She reached across the table and grasped his hand. "Look, I mean it, if anything happens to you I wouldn't know what to do."

He squeezed her hand and laughed. "Sure you do. You would track down whoever hurt me and show them just how fierce you can be."

"And then I would strangle you for taking up so much of my precious time." She clicked her tongue at him, and he grinned.

She tipped her head, thinking about Tazmeen and Ali while Dal scraped his spoon against the bottom of the bowl. Surely if anything was actually going on, it was just an isolated event. It had to be. The thought of random people going missing everywhere made her want to leave Snap with Dal and go directly to Rhia to check on her family.

But Dal didn't have anything solid to go off of. It was probably just people who decided to move in a town that had a high turn around as it was. If the soldiers weren't worked, surely nothing could be seriously wrong.

She sat back and rubbed her eyes, already dreading setting up her tent. She would have loved to sleep in an actual bed, but she couldn't leave Snap alone in the woods for too long. It would cost too much to stable him, and she was afraid someone would recognize the striking gray color of his coat. They were still too close to where she had taken him to risk leaving him anywhere in Asha.

After securing her scarf back around her face and over her hair, she stood. "Do you want to help me get settled in?"
He nodded and dropped a few bronze coins on the table. "Of course."

They left the inn, and Steele led the way down a couple of winding side streets, keeping an eye out for any unwanted followers.

She studied the few people they passed, looking for anything odd. A man in a gray coat lit his pipe, face illuminated by an orange glow, and he walked off, shaking his head as he exhaled a puff of smoke. A girl in a ratty dress tripped over a box, and the noise earned her several startled stares. Two women wearing dresses that may have once been considered very fine, exited a shop, linked arms, and glanced around before continuing on their way. Nothing extraordinary.

It was dusk and the buildings cast long shadows over the streets, the darkness creeping toward the walkers, reaching. An alleyway yawned open on the right, and people seemed to skirt around it, though there was nothing obviously unusual about it as Steele and Dal passed by.

They walked in silence, appearing to mind their own business, but anyone looking closely would be able to see the almost animalistic sway of their bodies. They were ready for an attack, muscles taut and poised, prepared to spring into action. Dal's hand rested on his hip, just over a pair of knives Steele knew were tucked into his pants. You didn't live to be very old in the thieving world without learning how to defend yourself. Though he had been on the streets longer than she had, it made her sad, knowing he had to live like this. Instead of learning how to trust or to love, he had learned the art of manipulation.

His life reflected something all too familiar, and she scowled.

Finally, they reached some thick foliage at the end of the town, and she exhaled hard, as if she'd been holding her breath. She ducked under a tree branch and continued forward, Dal following silently behind her. They pushed their way through branches and brambles, eventually arriving at the small clearing where Steele had left her belongings and Snap.

The horse looked well. His light gray coat took on a muted glow in the waning sunlight, and his dark legs blended in with the undergrowth. It almost appeared as if he were floating. Nostrils quivering, Snap stretched his nose out to her, and she stroked it while pointing toward her pack.

"That's a nice-looking horse," Dal said as he shook the canvas tent out of her bag.

"I know. I call him Snap." She pulled a handful of grass from the ground and offered it to the gray, which he took gladly. While he munched on it, she settled on the ground and pulled part of the tent into her lap.

She and Dal worked silently until part of a sapling she had been trying to fit into position snapped. The broken end flipped back, smacking her fingers, and she uttered a muffled swear and shoved her fingers into her mouth. Dal laughed, earning a glare from his companion.

"You need to get a simpler tent. This one is much too complicated to put together. Mine only takes a minute to set up, and I can do it on my own."

She sighed, peering at her fingers in the faint light. "I know, but I can't afford to buy a new one."

Dal pulled his eyebrows together and gave her an exasperated look. "That excuse never makes sense to me. You're a thief. Steal one. You've done it before."

She remained silent. *Thief.* She hated that label. The list of all the items she had stolen over the years ran through her head. Little things, really, but they clung to her conscience. She looked at her tent again, this time more closely, and tried to imagine stealing a new one. She frowned.

It was not a necessary steal. Her current tent may be complicated, but it served its' purpose. She could sell it, though, she mused.

Dal rolled his eyes. "You're an odd thief."

She chuckled and rummaged through some sticks on the ground, pulling out one that could function as a rod. "You're only now realizing this? *That's* odd."

They rose, and with a few more tugs and pulls, the tent also stood. "Tell you what," Dal said, brushing his hands on his pants, "I'll steal you one, and then you won't have to feel bad about it. It'll be a gift."

She stared at him, unamused, and shook her head.

He grinned, giving his own head a shake, and helped her move her pack and other supplies into the tent. As he turned to leave, he hesitated, then said, "Take care of yourself, Steele."

She elbowed him. "You too. Stay out of trouble." He grabbed her in a rough hug. She wrapped her arms around his middle. "I mean it, Dal. Be safe."

Pulling away, he scratched the back of his neck. "I will. You'll let me know next time you're passing through?"

"Of course. See you when I see you."

Dal grinned and turned, disappearing soundlessly into the surrounding forest.

CHAPTER 3

Steele awoke with a start, inhaling deeply through her nose. Silence surrounded her, but something had caused her to wake. She forced her breathing to even out as if she were still asleep and listened. A faint *snap* cracked in her ears. Next came footfalls. They sounded like they were right outside her tent. The shadow of the intruder played across the canvas, a fuzzy silhouette outlined by the moonlight.

Steele quietly inched toward the back of the tent. She had left it open, and had tied Snap at the end, giving her more immediate access to him should she need to make a quick exit. She eyed the man's shadow as he approached Snap's ties, tensed and ready to move as soon as he had passed her. Snap snorted, clearly agitated and sensing the danger. The man paused, the shadow of his legs even with her head.

She needed to time her attack just right.

She carefully slipped her knife from underneath her pillow and waited. Branches rattled against her tent, sending her heart into her throat, and she took the opportunity to roll onto her belly. She pushed herself into a crouch and peered out of the tent, her eyes focused on the intruder, who was on the move, as well. He stood next to Snap, who pulled away from the man and sat down on his haunches, likely attempting to break his ties and flee.

Now that the intruder had passed her, she crept toward him. This was it. She pounced onto the man's back, using her arm to squeeze the flat side of her knife to his throat. He sputtered, clawing at her arms, but she ignored him, pressing the blade against his throat until he staggered forward to his knees and his frantic pawing slowed. A few moments more and he slumped forward, unconscious. He was lucky; many thieves would have just killed him. She looked at the knife in her hand and shuddered.

She pulled her pack toward her, fished out some rope and bound the man's hands behind his back.

She quickly gathered up the rest of her belongings and approached Snap. He breathed heavily but reached his nose out to her, more curious than afraid now. She secured her pack over her shoulders and rubbed Snap's neck before bridling him. She turned to fold up her tent, halting when a pair of alert eyes stared back at her. The man was awake and already wriggling out of her knots. She would have to leave the tent.

She used a stump to boost herself on the horse and guided him toward a road that snaked around the backside of town. It was obvious why the man desired to take Snap from her. The stallion's long legs and delicate ankles indicated that he'd been bred for speed and could be a winner in racing. His whole demeanor pulsed with pent up energy.

Once they were back on the road, she loosened the reins and heeled him in the ribs. He pricked his ears and bucked, clearly happy to be moving. Steele grinned, appreciating his excitement, but pressed her heels into his sides more firmly to encourage him to increase his speed. Finally, he settled into a smooth canter. A fence ran alongside the road for as far as Steele could see, so she pointed Snap toward it, figuring they would save time cutting through the field as opposed to going around it.

Snap arched his neck as they approached the fence and extended his stride. A few paces before they collided with the fence, he pushed off his hindquarters, launching them up into the air. For a few blessed moments they were airborne. Steele beamed, glancing at the ground beneath her before returning her attention to their destination across the field. He landed neatly on his front hooves and effortlessly cantered on.

She laughed and leaned forward again, as he raced along the grass. His previous owner had seriously misused him. Snap was meant to fly.

They cleared the fence on the other side of the field, too, and Snap carried her farther from Asha. A quick look over her shoulder told her no one was around, and she whooped loudly. Snap pressed forward even faster, feeding off her enthusiasm. She should save his energy, she thought as she grinned at the back of his head, but she couldn't bear to rein him in when he had just had his first real taste of freedom in who knew how long.

She would slow their pace soon enough, and she would tell Snap all about his new family and the eldest daughter who would treat him like a king.

The girl and her family had caught Steele's eye the last time she was in Falu. Steele had overheard her asking about the horses at the market one day, but her father had only been looking for one to pull the plow. The girl had looked happily at the horse they'd purchased, but Steele knew Snap would be a wonderful gift for her. The family had the means—and the heart—to care for him, as well. Of the things that she doubted in her life, her judgment of character was not one of them.

She planned to tell them that her family was leaving town and could not take her horse. That story usually worked, and if the people insisted on paying her, she always replied that she loved the horse too much to accept money for him. She just wanted him to have a good home.

Pulling back slightly on the reins slowed Snap to a walk, and he snorted, breathing heavily. He was probably glad for the break. She looked up at the stars and referenced their position in the sky to direct her. She was headed for a canyon that she had come across years ago completely by mistake.

It had been a cold, windy night, and she had been desperate for any semblance of a shelter. Frustrated with her lack thereof, Steele had given her horse a free rein, and the animal had brought them to the canyon. She had been surprised to see packs and tents scattered across the ground. A portly man with a friendly grin had appeared out of nowhere, grabbed the horse's bridle, and welcomed them to the Valley of the Thieves. The name was misleading, though, since it was not a valley, but a canyon.

She smiled at the memory, recalling her surprise at finding a thieving community in the wild and her mistrust of those encamped there. She had tried to stay awake all that night, ready to defend herself against another thief, but no attack had come. Eventually her eyes had fallen closed, and by morning, half the tents had been packed up and most of the people had left.

She had returned to the canyon many times since then. Some days it was empty and other days full, but every time, the other thieves gave her the privacy she desired. She had shared the location with Dal, Twitch, and Spar, and they now used it as a meeting place.

When they reached the edge of the canyon, Steele pulled Snap to a stop so she could listen. She watched his ears twisting, also listening for any indication that something curious or possibly scary lay up ahead, and she sniffed the wind, trying to pick up the smell of smoke. She could smell nothing but wet earth, and Snap's ears drooped to the side. They were alone.

She nudged the horse forward, and the walls of the canyon sprouted up on both sides of them. The jagged rocks intrigued her, climbing high into the sky as if they had reached for the clouds and frozen there.

A shallow river cut its way through the base of the canyon, and Steele followed it toward a cave she knew was nearby. Snap pulled his head toward the water, and Steele loosened the reins so he could take a drink. He did so noisily, and his slender ears twitched rhythmically as he swallowed. After drinking his fill, he blew ripples into the water and began splashing with his right front leg.

"Oh no you don't," Steele said with a chuckle, pulling his head to the side and nudging him back along the path. He was a playful horse, but experience had taught her that when a horse splashed in the water, it was usually a prelude to a bath. She prodded his ribs, and he broke into an easy trot, quickly covering the ground to the cave.

CHAPTER 4

Steele unbridled Snap and laughed when he ambled to the water's edge
and dropped to the ground. His dark legs kicked the air as he rolled,
flinging droplets of muddy water every which way. He was going to be a
mess. Snap then heaved himself to his feet and shook his entire body
with a snort. Swinging his head left and right, he seemed to take in his
surroundings. Steele did the same. The short sandbar where Snap stood
transitioned into grass and shrubs as it stretched away from him,
colliding with the canyon walls surrounding them. Above, the night sky
expanded as far as the eye could see, an inky blackness inlaid with
diamonds.

Snap trotted into the grass, and after sniffing around, dropped his
head to eat. Steele was confident he wouldn't run away, so she turned her
attention to readying the cave for their stay. A look inside revealed the
ashy remnants of a fire but nothing else. After rearranging the rocks that
had once surrounded the fire, she went back outside to find kindling. It
didn't take her long to collect some dry branches, bark, and leaves, and
she tossed them next to the rocks in the cave.

Even though it was still the middle of the night, she was hungry
from the journey, and she studied the river. While she was awake, she
may as well try to catch a fish. Her stomach grumbled in agreement, and
she kicked through the shrubs and brush until she found a narrow branch
she could use as a fishing pole. She fastened a long string to the
makeshift pole and hooked an insect to the end. Her hook was seeing its
last days, and she'd lost the spare she usually kept in a small pouch with
other knick-knacks to an incredibly stealthy pickpocket. She'd realized
what had happened moments later, but the thief had already disappeared.
While in Falu, she would need to find the metal to make or possibly buy
a new hook, otherwise she would be overcharged in Azubah.

She sat cross-legged on a smooth rock that jutted out over the water,
watched the insect and string disappear beneath the surface of the water,
and lazily gripped the end of the pole.

With a satisfied smile, she arched her neck to look at the stars. The
night sky always brought her comfort, and shooting stars never failed to
delight her. Some of her favorite memories of her father involved them
doing just this, staring into the unknown and making pictures with the

stars. He would point out different constellations and tell the stories for which they were named. She had been young, but the memory was etched in her.

The pole twitched in her hand, and she tightened her grip, waiting for another jerk. When it came—this one more pronounced—she yanked the string out of the water, her wrists tensing as the fish flopped aggressively on the end. She pulled the fish toward her and quickly killed it. It was a big river fish with enough meat on its bones to fill her belly, so she set the pole aside and carried her catch back to the cave.

After arranging the kindling, she struck a couple of rocks together until the dry leaves and brush caught a few of the sparks, and spread to the wood. The fire snapped to life, flames licking upward, and Steele cupped her hands toward it, absorbing the heat into her palms.

When she was sure the fire wasn't going to burn itself out, she turned to the fish. Skinning it and chopping the meat did not take very long, and her stomach growled gratefully as she shoved the pieces onto a long skinny branch and held it over the flames, rotating it periodically. Her stomach growled again, and she pulled a small cube off the stick and popped it in her mouth. The fish was hotter than expected and burned its way down her throat. Eyes watering, she wheezed and coughed. Snap looked up from where he was grazing and watched her while he chewed.

"What?" she rasped. He twitched his tail and resumed eating. She cautiously removed another piece of meat and blew on it before setting it on her tongue. It was warm and delicious.

When she finished the fish, she lay back on the sand, feeling full for the first time in a long while. She crossed her arms behind her head and studied the stony ceiling above her, finding designs in the twisted and protruding rocks.

Sand suddenly sprayed over her, and she jolted to a sitting position, one hand gripping her knife, the other protecting the fire. Two faces stared down at her, twin grins stretched across their mouths.

"You're getting easy to sneak up on, Steele," Twitch said, setting his pack on the ground. "Or I'm getting better at sneaking." He raked a hand through his dark hair, his blue eyes twinkling.

Spar snorted as she flung her pack down. "Don't be ridiculous, brother."

Steele frowned, annoyed they really had managed to surprise her, but, she reasoned, they had been thieving much longer than she had. They had come by the trade much like Steele had. Their parents had died from a disease many years ago, but unlike Steele, they had been forced to fend for themselves since then. They were quite successful at scamming snobby rich people out of jewelry and then selling the gems in other cities and on various underground markets.

Then she looked from Spar to Twitch, and her frown dissolved, happiness taking its place. "You got my message!"

Twitch flipped their magi stone in the air and caught it, grinning. "We did! Luckily, we were already headed this way."

Spar nodded at Snap. "He's pretty! And he looks fast...people would probably bet a lot of money on him at the races."

"Don't get any ideas," Steele replied, raising an eyebrow.

Spar chuckled, shaking her golden hair out of its braid. "You're far better at stealing horses, Steele. You'd take him back before I'd even realized it. I'll stick with things that are not alive."

"I'm glad you two are here." Steele smiled, adding, "It's been too long since we've seen one another. I was starting to think maybe you'd been arrested."

Twitch settled beside her. "We've had a couple close calls, but nothing out of the ordinary. Right, little sis?"

Spar rolled her eyes and sat on Steele's other side. "Twitch seems to think that nearly getting caught makes life more adventurous."

"That's not very wise," Steele said, elbowing Twitch. "And I'm sorry I don't have any fish left. I would have caught a second, but I didn't know if or when you'd show. You can use my pole if you want."

"That's all right." Twitch pulled his pack toward him and upended it. Bread, fruits, and cold meats tumbled out. "We stopped at a market on our way here."

Steele whistled. "That's impressive."

"The people were easy to distract," Spar said. "A wink or smile from yours truly at just the right moment, and Twitch could take an apple right from a merchant's hand." She batted her eyelashes.

"You're such a flirt," Steele replied with a laugh.

Spar reached across Steele to grab a piece of meat. "All in a day's work."

"Which we've been doing nonstop these days," Twitch grumbled. He bit into an apple and spoke with his mouth full. "Jewels have been in high demand recently." He swallowed and then nodded at Snap. "What about this horse? Are you finally keeping one or dropping him?"

"Dropping him and then stopping by Azubah before finally heading home."

"Be sure to give Gemma trouble for us," Twitch said, tossing the apple core aside.

Steele chuckled. Gemma ran their favorite inn in Azubah. As far as Steele knew, the woman still liked her, so she wasn't going to risk that by being a pest on account of these two.

Spar looked back to Snap, a thoughtful frown on her face. "I see more and more horses being manhandled and abused. It's just awful that so many people see horses only as tools rather than living, breathing animals."

Twitch pulled his red scarf loose. "Yes, but people need the animals to work."

Spar threw a pebble at him. "You're going to set her off."

"Most people think caring about the wellbeing of horses is stupid or a waste of time because," Steele grimaced, "horses are nothing but big, dumb animals. It makes me sick."

"I agree with you, even if Twitch doesn't see the importance. They're a lot like us if you look at it the right way, and we wouldn't turn the other way if a child was being hurt." Spar nudged her, yawning. "We've been traveling most of the night, so I hope you don't mind if I try to catch some sleep."

Spar curled on her side, presenting her back to Steele, who swallowed a yawn of her own. "Fine by me. I was about to go back to sleep before you two rudely interrupted me." The repressed yawn pushed itself between her teeth, and she nudged Twitch. "Will you halter him? I call him Snap, and he's sweet. Won't bite you or anything."

Twitch sighed dramatically as he stood, and soon returned, leading Snap along behind him. Steele smiled as the stallion lowered himself to his knees, rolling sideways so he was lying down. A long sigh quivered his nostrils, and Steele chuckled, feeling the same exhaustion.

"Will he run away?" Twitch asked, rubbing the lead rope between his fingers.

"No, I think he's too tired to run off."

A stiff breeze whistled through the canyon, and Steele lay on her side, facing Spar's back. Twitch dropped on her other side, and she was warmly sandwiched between the siblings. The fire would help, but body heat was always welcome in the crisp air of the cave.

Spar's words about protecting children lingered in Steele's mind. There were so many others who looked the other way, their memories short, their feelings, though maybe genuine in their concern, too shallow for them to change their current path. She furrowed her brow, recalling Dal's message about people vanishing. She wondered if anyone else, like King Ax, had noticed, or if any of the royal family would even care about commoners disappearing. Did people like her even matter to the royals?

She sighed. If she continued down this line of thought, she would never get any rest. Forcing her eyes shut, she hummed softly to calm her mind, and it didn't take long for the crackling fire and cadenced sound of the others breathing to lull her to sleep.

CHAPTER 5

Steele slept until the sun burned against her eyelids. She groaned, glaring at where the sunlight peeked through a hole in the ceiling of the cave. She never slept this late and was thankful the town of Falu was less than half a day's ride.

She grinned as she sat up, seeing Snap still lying flat out, lost in whatever dream world he visited. Their night ride had worn him out as much as it had her.

Snap stirred and lifted his head off the sand to watch her as she packed her meager supplies. He gathered his legs underneath him and stood, scattering the sand below him.

Steele peered out of the cave. Twitch and Spar were at the edge of the river twisting dirty water out of various items of clothing.

"Good morning, Sleepy!" Spar called as Steele approached.

"Are you heading off soon?" Twitch asked, a giant yawn overtaking his speech.

Spar gave the shirt she was holding a particularly violent twist. "Do you need any help training Snap before we go? We always learn so much when you let us help."

"We?" Twitch snapped his shirt at his sister. "I'm fine with not helping, thank you."

Steele laughed, bending to wash her face. "I actually don't think there's anything he needs more work with. He's been a quick and willing learner." She cupped some water in her hands and sucked it into her mouth, swished it around, and spat it onto the sand. "The owner almost caught me this time, though."

"The owner saw you?" Spar asked, incredulous, as she stretched her wet shirt on a rock so the sun could dry it.

"Yeah, it was a close call for sure." Steele shrugged, then stretched her arms above her head. "Where are you two headed next?"

"Either Asha or Rhia," Twitch said, ambling up the riverbank to pat Snap's neck.

Steele gave him a sharp look. "Rhia?"

"We know. Closer to the palace means more security," Spar admitted, testing the shirt for dryness. "But we'll make more in a larger town."

Steele chewed on her bottom lip. "Well, here." She crouched down and scratched a rough outline of the town in the sand. "If you insist on going to Rhia, Tazmeen lives there. Ask around for her if you get lost. Tell her you know me, and she can give you a place to sleep and a good meal."

Twitch and Spar bent, studying the map. "Are we really at the meet-the-family stage? It's only been three years." Spar grinned.

Steele smirked. "It'll make Tazmeen happy to know I have friends."

Twitch laughed, straightening. "We can tell her you're the most popular thief in the land. The guards hate you, and the people love you."

Steele chuckled, eyeing the sun. "I should get going if I want to make it to Azubah before the day is finished. Finding Snap's new owner in Falu may be a task." She wiggled her eyebrows cheekily. "If you want to finally meet Dal you could always stop through Asha."

"Ha, ha," Spar said dryly as she picked her shirt off the rock and folded it over her arm. "When will we see you again?"

"I can let you know the next time I'm headed to Azubah. After today, of course," Steele said.

Twitch exchanged a glance with his sister. "We should be there for the Wolfkiel Festival in two months."

"How can you plan that far ahead?"

"We follow the festivities. Business is good, and the nobles get very drunk on wine."

"I should have known. Following the festivals may get you caught someday, you know," Steele half smiled.

The three of them made their way back to the cave. Spar and Twitch packed up their supplies while Steele readied Snap for the last leg of their journey.

Once everything was settled, Twitch draped his arms around Steele and Spar, pulling them into a hug. Steele arched her neck back to look at him. "I still think Rhia could be a bad idea, so if you go that way, stay out of trouble."

"Says the girl who calls Rhia home," he replied with a smirk. Steele had to smile. "I know it isn't exactly smart to go back, but Tazmeen and Ali are there and they've become my family. I have to see them."

Spar elbowed her brother away and hugged Steele again. "We'll tell Tazmeen you're fine if we see her."

"Thank you," Steele said, ignoring the pang of jealousy. She would see Tazmeen and Ali soon. *No need to be envious.* "And if for some reason you decide to stick around Rhia, I'll see you then." She hesitated.

"And if you see Tazmeen, tell her I'm coming back soon and to be careful. Please."

Twitch and Spar nodded, and with a final grin and a wave, they scampered from the cave, and disappeared around a bend.

Snap pawed the ground as Steele double checked that she had her belongings, and she patted his rump. She could tell the horse was eager to get moving, but he stood still as she swung onto his back, stepping out only when she asked him to. Their weeks together had been useful, indeed. She was confident Snap was now ready for the family in Falu.

CHAPTER 6

By late afternoon, the sounds of the Falu market were alive and pulsing with the snapping of flags on poles, the rise and fall of conversation, and vendors calling back and forth to one another. Snap tensed beneath Steele, and his ears swiveled around, preparing for any danger. She gently pressed her legs against his sides and murmured soothing words, encouraging him forward. After a few jerky steps, he seemed to understand that the noisy people weren't going to hurt him, and he relaxed considerably.

They turned down a side street, and Steele pulled him to a stop to look around the market before she searched for his new owners' farm. They'd been around this area, so she dismounted and removed her satchel to stash in the alley.

Steele felt a twinge of sadness as she scratched Snap's cheek. She would miss him.

The stallion followed her readily down the alley, and the rhythmic clopping of his hooves on the cobbled street beat out a familiar pattern. A few people spared them a glance but most kept about their business, focused on the day at hand.

She led Snap around a corner and into a small courtyard that smelled of livestock. A few vendors were scattered around the edges, and holding pens were occupied by pigs, goats, and sheep. With a sigh of relief, Steele spotted the older girl and her siblings next to a pen that was filled with chickens. Nodding to herself, she put on her friendliest smile as she walked up to the girl and tapped her on her shoulder. "Excuse me, do you have minute?"

The girl looked over her shoulder at Steele. Her green eyes fell on Snap, and she nodded. "Just a minute, though, Mama will throttle us if we aren't home soon."

"You're from Willowbridge Farms, right?" Steele combed her fingers through Snap's mane and didn't wait for a response. "My name is Emelia," she said, giving the girl her mother's name. "My family lives on the outskirts of town, but we're moving to Oakenjara. Pa says we can't keep two horses in the city where we'll live. Anyway, this is going to sound absurd, but I would like to give my horse to you."

The girl eyed her skeptically. "You want to *give* me your horse? But we don't even know each other."

Steele sighed and put on her best distressed face. "Yes, I do. Word on the street is you were looking for a horse and are an accomplished rider. And the money...Well, I wouldn't dream of accepting money for my friend. It just doesn't seem right. I only want him to have a good home where he will be loved."

The girl straightened at the praise, but she pursed her lips rather than smiling.

Not discouraged, Steele continued, "He's a wonderful animal, well behaved, and a joy to ride. He's no stranger to hard work, either. I have no doubt he would quickly learn his way around a farm if you wish. My father thinks he had some abuse when he was younger, and he can be a bit skittish around harnesses, but I think time and patience will easily fix that," Steele paused, rubbing behind Snap's ear. "I know I haven't given you much notice, but I have a good feeling about your family. Will you take him?"

The girl licked her lips and looked around before reaching out for the reins. "It feels wrong to take him without giving you anything in return."

"Knowing that he is in a good home where he is loved is all I need from you." Steele dropped a kiss to Snap's forehead.
Snap reached his nose out and bumped the girl on the arm. "What's his name?"

"I call him Snap."

The girl led Snap in a circle, watching how he moved. "He *looks* fit and sound. Can I see him trot?"

Steele swung onto Snap and asked him to trot a large circle around the girl. "It's as smooth as fresh cream!" She watched the girl eyeing Snap, the desire in her eyes sparkling.

"He *would* make a good friend to Felipe, our old plow horse, and Daddy *did* say I could get a new horse soon. He couldn't possibly get upset about one who cost me nothing," the girl murmured, more to herself than to Steele.

She hopped off Snap and offered the girl the reins. "May I?" the girl asked.

"Have at it."

The girl mounted Snap and breathed, rolling her shoulders back.

"I'm sorry I don't have a saddle to give you. The one we have is so old it's falling apart, so I mostly ride him bareback."

The girl waved a hand in Steele's direction. "We have a spare that I'm sure would fit him fine."

Steele crossed her arms, observing the girl as she rode Snap around in circles, testing his transitions. Snap looked to Steele, a bit confused by the change in rider, but he listened to the girl well. When he hesitated at a turn, the girl gently worked with him, biting her lip in concentration. He eased into the turn and flexed his neck. A proud grin on her face, she guided him back to Steele.

"You said he was abused?" she asked Steele after dismounting.

"We think so, but he's been incredibly willing and smart whenever I work with him," Steele responded.

After a few moments of silence, the girl nodded to herself. "I'd be happy to take care of him for you."

"Thank you," Steele said with a smile and nodded in agreement. "I best be on my way, then."

She turned to walk away, but the girl grabbed her arm. "At least let us feed you something. It would make me feel better about taking him." Steele hesitated. She could count on one hand the amount of times she had let strangers feed her. "I really should be heading home."

The girl brushed a hand through her long, light-brown hair. "Please, Papa would faint to see me walking home with a horse. He wouldn't believe someone just gave him to me," she pleaded. "Mama will think I stole him!" She laughed at that ridiculous notion.

Steele rubbed her nose, hiding a grimace. "Food would be lovely, but I really must go home and help my mama."

The girl smiled, her green eyes understanding. "I'm Jayn, by the way. You said your name was...?"

"Emelia," Steele replied.

Jayn called her siblings over to show them Snap, and Steele stepped to the side so they could meet the newest addition to their family. Her chest swelled with pride as she watched Snap calmly take in the chattering voices and patting hands of the younger children. He would have a good life with this family.

"Tannan!" Jayn's frantic call broke through her thoughts. "Tannan, where are you?"

A young boy with sandy hair came running around the corner, and relief washed over Jayn's face. "There you are! You scared me, Tannan! You know you aren't supposed to run off like that!"

The boy scuffed the ground with his shoe. "I know, Jayn, I'm sorry. I just wanted to look at the lizards! The lizard man won't come again this year!"

Jayn ruffled his hair. "I know. I just worry with all the disappearances."

Tannan shrugged. "Mama said you were telling tales just to scare me."

Steele blinked. "Disappearances?"

Jayn glanced at her. "Mama and Papa won't talk to me about it. Have *you* seen anything?"

"No, but I live outside of town. We aren't around people enough to hear the news." Her skin prickled uncomfortably. So whatever was going on wasn't isolated to Asha. It was good she would be heading home the next morning.

"It's just so scary. People I've known my entire life just vanish overnight, and no one knows why. Or if they do, they're too frightened to say anything. It's not normal."

"Why are they afraid to speak up?" It made sense for Dal to avoid the authority in Asha, but ordinary townsfolk shouldn't feel silenced.

"I've heard it's useless. The concerns are brushed aside, and you can only be ignored or made fun of for so long before you stop trying."

Steele shook her head in agreement. She decided to ask Gemma about it when she got to the Azubah later that night.

"Papa said the town is thinking about setting up a curfew. But I don't see how it will help."

"Mama's going to wash your mouth out for lyin', Jayn," Tannan mumbled.

Jayn frowned at her brother.

Steele shrugged, absentmindedly patting Snap on the rump. She tried to smile. "Thank you again for taking care of him. He's going to love you."

Jayn nodded. "Thank you, Emelia. Take care." She gathered her siblings and waved at Steele as they headed out of the courtyard.

Steele watched them go, her mind reeling.

She meandered through the alleys until she ended up back where she'd stashed her bag. She fished through it and quickly uncovered a few crude bracelets she had woven. Though they were nothing fancy, she had sold some in this market in the past, and a couple of coins would buy a decent meal at Gemma's.

She turned down the street and paused a moment to take it in. The street was awash in color. Scarves fluttered in the breeze, heavy carpets hung from balconies, flower vendors lined the street, gemstones flashed in the sun, and Steele saw the so-called lizard man standing with cages full of vibrant reptiles.

A few carefree children scampered around while their parents watched them closely, but Steele noticed that most of the parents kept their children under a tight rein. A finely dressed woman with three young daughters stood off to the side, and Steele nodded to herself. She may be open to buying bracelets for her wide-eyed girls.

"Excuse me?" Steele smiled at the girls. "I was wondering if you would like to buy some bracelets."

The youngest, a girl with shining blond hair, gave a delighted gasp, "Oh, Mama, please? I would love a bracelet!"

One daughter with strawberry hair grinned, but the other, who seemed to be the eldest, folded her arms and looked Steele in the eye. "How much?"

Steele and their mother laughed.

"Darling, you must be polite." The woman looked at Steele apologetically. "This is their first trip to the market, and they're a little overwhelmed by it all."

Steele smiled at the girls. "I was the same way."

"May we *please* see your bracelets?"

"Of course!" Steele held three out for the girls to see. They gasped and grabbed for them, admiring and exchanging them. They were her three best, made with twisted, colorful yarn, but she wanted these girls to have them. While they admired the bracelets, comparing the colors, their mother handed Steele three silver coins.

Steele gasped. "This is too much! I was only going to ask for one." She tried to push the coins back into the woman's hands.

"I insist. Ever since," She paused, sadness drawing her eyebrows together. "They lost someone recently. It does my heart well to see them so thrilled."

Steele's arms fell limply to her sides. "I'm sorry," she offered weakly.

The woman placed a hand on Steele's shoulder. "Thank you. Girls, what do you say to…?" She drifted off and looked at Steele.

"Emelia."

"What a lovely name."

Steele grinned as the three girls turned to face her with beaming smiles.

"Thank you!" They chimed in unison before ambling off after their mother.

Steele pocketed the coins and adjusted the straps on her pack. Three silver coins was more than she had ever made at one time and plenty enough for a meal at the White Horse Inn in Azubah. She decided to end on a good note and make her way out of town.

She walked through the market, and even with all the people around her, a pang of loneliness struck her. Everyone passed by or bumped into her, most without acknowledging her presence. A few smiled, but they were soon off chasing a child or a spouse.

What must it be like to live in one place all the time?

A part of her yearned for that sort of stability, to build a house, have a family, and create a life. On the other hand, her nomadic life allowed her to see parts of the world she would only dream of seeing if she were stuck in one place for the rest of her life. That thought made her wince. With all the traveling she had done, she knew that remaining forever in the same town might make her feel trapped.

A group of girls who looked to be around her age passed by, giggling over their shoulders at a boy. One girl whistled boldly at him, and her friends collapsed on one another in horrified laughter as they walked away. Steele sighed wistfully. As she adjusted the straps to her pack, she tried to picture Spar and herself being bold enough to whistle at a boy. The thought made her smile, and she shook her head as she made her way down the path that led to the woods.

Light peeked in through the yellow-green leaves of the trees as Steele twisted her phoenix feather between her fingers. It gleamed gold and red and orange as the stem spun, almost as if the feather had burst into flame in her hand, paying homage to the phoenix it had parted from. The feather was the last tangible object she had from her parents, and she was forever grateful that a phoenix, feathers and all, was basically indestructible. Her father never had the chance to tell her where he had claimed this quill, and she had yet to hear others speak of the rare bird except in fairy-tales.

Steele sat on a rock, nestled between the roots of a grandfather tree, and set the phoenix feather next to her. She leaned against the roots and wiped a cloth over her sticky skin. She was ready for this journey to be over already, but she would not rest for long until she reached Azubah.

For now, she needed to mend the hole in her boot. She pulled out the sewing kit from her pack to replace the seams that were breaking open. She made the hole more visible with her awl, then attached the thread to the boar bristle. A vision of her mother's hand guiding her own consumed her thoughts. She had not wanted to learn to sew, preferring to be in her father's blacksmith shop, but the lessons her mother had taught her had paid off. Sewing was a useful skill to have as a thief. Steele smiled. Most days, she found it had been so long since her parents had died that their physical details were hazy, but she could still remember her mother's hands, her father's beard, and his smoky scent. She closed her eyes and breathed in disappointingly clear air.

She rested against the trunk of the tree after tying up the last knot and worked on her braid. Several dark strands had escaped and clung to her skin, so she braided her hair again from the top, careful to secure her feather in the locks as she did so. Everything seemed to cling in this dry heat, and Steele peeled her shirt away from her skin to cool off.

A man's deep laughter resounded, echoing off the trees and into her skull. She slammed her foot into her boot, collected her pack, and pulled herself onto the tree limb above her. Her resting place was off the path, but she'd been surprised before and had nearly been killed by bandits who had wanted her horse. Though she was horseless now, she wouldn't put it past a bandit to find some reason to use her or her things for his own gain.

The deep laughter sounded again, along with the squeaking wheels of an overloaded cart.

"If we're lucky, we'll make it to the palace in four days, Riff. Your donkey looks ready to collapse," said a softer male voice.

"Rock has never faltered before, my friend," the deep voice responded. "I told you he could easily take our produce to the palace market, and we will get the best prices there."

The two men came around the tree with a cart full of baskets holding colorful assortments of food. The larger man walked beside the donkey who was pulling the cart, holding onto a rope connected to the donkey's halter.

"Yeah, yeah, you dream big, Riff. I still don't see why we can't sell our things in Azubah, seeing as it's much closer." The man sounded worn down.

"I told you, the man from Rhia was insistent we bring our produce to the palace market. He even sent me a contract guaranteeing he would buy a good portion of the crop. Looks like he has need for the military or something," Riff explained. He rubbed his belly with his open hand and rolled his shoulder back. "We are almost to Azubah, my friend. We'll stop there for the night. It looks to me like a storm may be coming. If we could be so lucky."

"Did your palace friend say anythin' about Prince Hadrian's sudden death? Still seems a bit shady if you ask me, even for an illness."

Steele narrowed her eyes as the men turned down the bend in the path. The Prince Heir's death earlier that year had shaken the kingdom of Solarrhia. His younger brother, Prince Aldair, had a colorful reputation regarding royal conduct. From what Steele knew, the general public consensus was that the younger brother would be the ruin of the

Zhanbolat reign if he did not shape up. She had only seen him the one time six years prior, and the most prominent visual she had of him was a cocky grin and swooning ladies.

The voices continued down the path, but Steele remained where she was, waiting to make sure the men weren't being followed by bandits or thieves. When she was satisfied she was alone, she dropped carefully from the tree, remaining in a squat until she could no longer see the farmers' cart. Steele carefully reorganized her sewing kit into the satchel and buttoned up the bag. She stood up, stretching her toes in her mended boot, and threw her bag over her head and onto her opposite shoulder. She'd have to hurry now to make it to Azubah before dark.

CHAPTER 7

Azubah was not the largest town Steele had seen. The buildings were not the most spectacular, either, not when compared to Solarrhia. Still, Azubah had a particular charm about it that kept Steele passing through. The town thrived on the market in the center square, and Steele enjoyed how loud and vibrant the town could be even after the day vendors closed and the families had turned in for the night. A few night vendors lined the road, booths lit with lanterns and candles that cast a myriad of colors on the street. One merchant was selling what appeared to be sticks to a small gathering of people. Steele paused, wondering why sticks would gather a crowd. Then the merchant lit the stick on fire, and it burst into a shower of sparks, causing everyone to gasp in wonder. Some teenagers turned away, smiling, and Steele found herself grinning along with them. She enjoyed how easily she could get lost in Azubah's rambunctious crowd.

She made her way through the town quickly. A call here and there was made out to the crowd of people passing by, but the evening seemed to be coming to a close. A man in a gray tunic sat on a stool and laughed at his long-haired companion, who could not shut his overflowing wooden chest. The long-haired man glared at his friend, and attempted to jump on top of the chest. Unfortunately, whatever he had in there proved to be more resilient and rebounded him into the air.

Steele looked ahead and was grateful that she did not have to walk for much longer before the logo of the White Horse Inn appeared. The stallion on the sign stood tall and proud, his left leg lifted and bent as if he were about to paw at the ground aggressively. She rubbed the side of the doorframe affectionately. Steele had not been here in ages, and while she tried to not frequent the same sites, this was a place she would always return to. She hoped she would never be forced to abandon it. Steele had an understanding with Gemma, the innkeeper's wife and business partner, and had since the early days.

If Gemma had not taken her in the night Steele had stumbled into the village, weeks after taking a horse to its new home, Steele may not have ever survived on her own. She had been too skinny to start with and had lost considerable weight from the drastic change in diet from blander foods to berries and plants from the forests. Steele had been wandering around Azubah, looking for some forgotten bread on the ground when a woman with calloused hands had grabbed her arm. Steele had squinted up, blinded by the sun, at the silhouette of a woman with bushy hair piled high on her head. After a moment, Steele's vision had cleared and she could see the graying of the woman's hair and a frown on her surprisingly striking face. Gemma had taken pity on her and had given her a place to stay for the night and a hot meal.

At first glance, the inn did not seem memorable, and dusk cast a rather gray setting over the place. The bar was on the wall directly in front of her, and there was a large group of men sitting at the tables to her right.

Gemma's husband, Net, was behind the bar and nodded at her without pausing as he poured a drink. He slid the glass down the bar toward a man who looked like he had seen better days. His shoulders were hunched over the counter, his secret burdens threatening to crush him. Steele tore her gaze away from the sad man and turned left, away from the ruckus the men in the corner were creating.

Steele sat with her back against the wall near the rear of the inn. From there she could see everything. The man at the bar drowning his sorrows glanced at her, then returned his stare to the wooden countertop. Nearby, another group sat playing with dice. One man wearing a wide-brimmed hat whistled a bit before throwing the die onto the table. A chorus of groans rang out from around him, and his grin widened.

One of the men she had passed when she'd entered the inn stood up and turned toward the rest of the crowd. He had shoulder-length curly hair and a few days' worth of scruff on his chin. "Listen up, all Azubah…ians, my friends! My friend here, Ardeth," he said and pulled one of his mates up. He squeezed his shoulders. "He's not danced with a lady in far too many seasons. Let us play some music and be merry this night!"

Ardeth did not look amused with his friend. The ladies in the room clapped and giggled. A brave woman in a burnt orange dress stood and presented herself before Ardeth, and when she turned toward the middle of the room, Steele observed a pretty and youthful face.

Ardeth looked back at his friends, who cheered him on. "Shall I be the only one dancing, then? This is not right! We should all be celebrating, for we are returning home!"

Next to her, the manic man with the wide-brimmed hat chuckled to himself. "What I would do to dance with a pretty lady. No, pretty ladies get you into trouble."

Steele took off her coat and set it on the satchel, which she had placed on the chair beside her. She looked toward the kitchen when she heard a familiar laugh echoing from within the walls. Gemma appeared, wiping her hands on her apron. The older woman glanced at the dancing that had now grown from one couple to four, but her gaze settled on one couple in particular. She raised an eyebrow at Ardeth, who did not seem to be very good at feeling the rhythm.

Steele did not chance leaving her things at the table in order to catch Gemma's attention, so she waited until Gemma's eyes scanned the rest of the crowd. They brightened when she saw Steele.

Gemma ambled over to her, pausing to say a word to guests here and there. "Steele! I didn't think I would see you again this year."

She sat down, tucking a strand of gray hair behind her ear, and turned her attention back to the dancing and whooping couples. She did not look at Steele when she whispered, "Soldiers have been roaming about more frequently these days, so you should sleep in a spare room tonight. Wouldn't want anyone to accidentally stumble upon you in the woods."

Steele licked her lips, relief flooding her limbs. "Thank you. Is there a new festival approaching?"

"No. Weeks back a drunk guard told Net that their commander was concentrating on cleaning up the streets more carefully than they had in the past." Gemma smiled at Net from across the room. He strode up to his wife, who stood to greet him with a kiss.

Steele grinned at the sight. Gemma was wiry and inches taller than her husband, while Net looked as if he spent too much time taste testing the meals in the kitchen. For being as round as he was, however, Steele would think twice before challenging him to a fight. He was stout in more than one sense of the word.

"Gemma, have you noticed anything strange happening in town recently? Other than more guards around." Steele pursed her lips, thinking of Asha and Falu.

Gemma and Net exchanged a look. Net squeezed his wife's shoulder and left them to catch up. Steele arched a brow at her, and Gemma sighed, easing herself back onto the chair. "I wasn't going to worry you with speculation." She glanced around discreetly before continuing, "Things *have* been off. People don't seem to be traveling as much. Business isn't as good, merchants aren't selling as much, and it wouldn't be an issue except most of our income comes from thieves like you."

Steele laughed at the irony. Gemma swiveled around as yells erupted from the bar, and the smile fell from Steele's mouth. Gemma had said nothing about people vanishing, only that business was bad. So perhaps business was bad because of the people missing from other towns? Really, there wasn't much Steele could do to change what was going on if anything was out of order. She could help a person or two, but she was no one. That was the Zhanbolat's job.

Gemma twisted back to face Steele, and her smile slid back into place.

"Now I don't want you worrying over what I told you. Net and I don't need you stealing any money or anything for us. Business isn't so bad that we're desperate." She gave Steele a pointed look, and Steele raised her hands in defense.

"You know I only take horses, Gemma. Twitch and Spar are the ones you'd have to worry about."

Gemma laughed. "I suppose that's true. Now you sit tight, I'm going to have your dinner brought to you."

Steele pulled a silver coin from her pouch. "I know you'll refuse it, but please, it makes me feel better to pay for my meals."

Gemma sighed, but took the coin. "With this coin, I'll bring you a nice drink, as well," she said cheerfully as she stood.

Steele smiled her thanks and resumed watching the room. A man grunted in annoyance as he pushed away from the dicing table, and the man with the hat saluted him as he strode away. Steele fingered another silver coin, debating buying into the game, but as she was rising to join the men, a pint of cider appeared before her. She pocketed the coin and wrapped her hands around the mug. Rhythmic clapping started up near the bar, and Steele watched the couples spinning and twirling around the dance floor. She tapped her foot to the beat and took a sip of the cider, savoring its bittersweet fruity flavor. A bowl of savory stew was placed in front of her next, and she hungrily spooned the soup into her mouth, pausing only to swallow her cider.

"Excuse me?"

Steele stiffened and looked up from her drink and into dark eyes. It was Ardeth, but she could not see his face properly because of the backlighting. Her hand tensed around her spoon. "Yes?"

"May I sit here for a while?" He gestured to the seat across from her. "Some of my company have stepped out, and I was," he paused, "I was hoping to disappear for a bit. You seem to have picked the best spot for that."

She glanced at the table where his companions had been. It was empty save one man and the woman in the burnt orange dress. It appeared that Ardeth had been passed over. She looked back at the intruder of her peace to find he had already taken the liberty of sitting down and was already settling in.

She had been wrong before about his eyes being dark. The torch beside their table reflected in his eyes. They were an intense blue. An image of a stained-glass window she had once seen in a cathedral briefly flashed through her brain. She stared into these eyes just as she had inspected that window, feeling as if she had seen everything and not enough at exactly the same moment. It was not a sensation she was used to, and she could not explain it. She had never expected to see such beauty in a window, and now found she was at a loss with how such beauty could be captured in a pair of eyes.

Unnerved by the direction of her thoughts, she blinked and took in the rest of him. He may have been around her age, maybe a little older. He wore a simple brown traveling jacket over broad shoulders, and while he was clearly well muscled, there was a comfortable ease to the way he carried himself. His angular jaw was covered in the start of a beard, there was a faint scar crossed over the left side of his lips, and his dark hair was cut close on the sides, leaving the top a little longer.

His stained-glass eyes crinkled at the sides. "You aren't much of a conversationalist, are you?"

Steele raised an eyebrow, banishing those thoughts of memories and unexplainable beauty. She scraped the bottom of her bowl, torn between the disappointment of finishing her meal already and relief that she could go to her room soon.

Ardeth chuckled and drank from his cup.

She looked at him curiously. He was still grinning as if the cup had said something incredibly funny. Confused, she asked, "What?"

He set his cup down. "Yes?"

"What was the laugh about?" Steele set her spoon down and sat back in her chair.

He glanced up at the ceiling. "The eyebrow."

"My eyebrows amuse you?" Steele grazed a finger across the hair on her brow. "I don't understand."

"My mother raises her eyebrow in exactly the same manner. I am leagues away from her, and yet she still manages to follow me around." He waved a waitress over, leaned in toward Steele, and smiled again. "Care for a pint?"

Steele smirked. "You will not get me drunk, sir."

"Not my intention. A pint on a night like this settles well in the stomach and helps weary travelers like ourselves to sleep while we are far from home." He held two fingers up to the girl. "Two pints of your finest beer, please."

"What is your aim—" She noticed a horseshoe tattoo on his wrist when he lowered his arm. "Are you a blacksmith?"

He followed her eyes to his tattoo and shook his head. "No, although I have plenty of respect for that profession. I got this while on my first trip abroad. Well, first trip as an adult abroad. My father was none too pleased when he saw it, but he is a bit old fashioned."

"Horseshoes usually indicate blacksmiths," Steele explained. "My father used to sign his letters with that symbol beside his name."

He grinned. "It's almost as if we were destined to be friends."

She narrowed her eyes at him. "I don't believe in destiny."

"What? Why not? You are not a believer that we have a destiny greater than what is in front of us, then?"

A lengthy conversation about destiny was the last thing she felt like having, and yet something about this Ardeth intrigued her. "What do you believe?" she challenged him.

He did not answer straight-away. Instead, he folded his hands over his stomach as he settled deeper in his chair. The waitress returned and set their drinks on the table. Steele hesitated, eyeing the dark liquid before taking a sip. She had never had a beer before. It felt smooth and heavy against her tongue, but she didn't hate it.

"I cannot say whether I believe in destiny or not," Ardeth admitted. "But I will say that many people have more potential than they give themselves credit for." He paused and dipped his head toward his shoulder. "Then again, some think too highly of themselves. No matter. I have traveled too many places and have seen too many people wasting their lives when they could be making something of themselves."

"I have a friend who thinks similarly to you, sir." Steele sipped some more beer, thinking of the conversations she'd had with Dal on this very subject.

He waved his hand in the air. "Please, call me Ardeth."

"Ardeth," she repeated. He looked at her expectantly, but she pretended not to notice. "I can't afford to think of grand things like that."

"What do you mean?" he stared at her quizzically.

"In my world, you can only look at what's in front of you and prepare yourself the best you can for whatever outcome. You don't think of grander things because those things will never come, and then you will only be unsatisfied with what you do have. I've known so many who have mistreated their friends, their animals, or people they think are beneath them. Like they deserve more."

"I hear you. Those people are wrong, but to believe in something greater is not the same as a false sense of entitlement." He leaned forward and clasped his hands together on the table.

She assessed his comment and nodded. "All right. I see your point."

"I'm sorry. I don't mean to sound condescending. My friend, Em, says I need to watch how I speak to people if I want them to actually open up to me."

"He sounds like a good friend." She leaned closer to the table, too. "I'm not offended, though. I was thinking of the people I've met on my own travels, the self-righteous ones who think they have the right to do whatever they please no matter how offensive their behavior."

Steele fumed as the face of the first man she rescued a horse from swam before her eyes, and she took a deep breath before diving into the memory. "There are some men who have absolutely no respect for anyone but themselves. I remember one who couldn't even treat his horse properly. Thankfully, I was able to assist in rescuing the horse." Her eyes widened as the words left her mouth, while her brain frantically questioned how wise it was to speak even this vaguely about her lifestyle. Hopefully Ardeth did not realize her form of rescuing was not done lawfully.

He nodded solemnly. "I'm sorry to hear that. You should think of creating an organization for rescued horses. If you haven't already, I mean. Have you?"

She shook her head, and her shoulders slumped slightly. He was ever the dreamer. If only an organization like that could come to be, but she did not see much hope for it when people could not even care for their neighbors suitably.

"You know, I just saw a leaflet in another town about people who have taken it upon themselves to steal horses." He finished his beer off and carefully set the cup down. "Have you heard of them? I do wonder how they get themselves in that deep."

Though she was sitting down, Steele's heart jolted. "I have heard of them, yes." She was aware of more than one poster with her face on it. Her palms began to sweat, but she tried to keep her voice light. "Were there sketches on these leaflets? It'd be good to know who to keep an eye out for."

He shook his head. "Not this one, although I'm sure there are plenty around town."

She knew Gemma did her best to take down any posters with her face on it here, while Dal did the same in Asha. Still, her nerves burned.

She considered bringing up the fact the maybe the horses had been abused, but she doubted this man would see her point and showing sympathy toward horse thieves might not be in her best interest. Even knowing that, the desire to defend her actions was strong.

"I've always admired horses," she said, thinking for a moment on the giant draft horses in her father's shop. "If a horse was being abused I think it would be hard to do nothing."

Ardeth smiled. "Is that what these thieves are doing you think?"

"Of course not," she said with a laugh. Anxious to change the subject she gestured at him. "I do have a question for you." He raised his eyebrows, and she set her palms on the table. "What are you doing here? You look like you could afford to stay at a proper inn, not a low-key one like this. You're not clean, but you don't look like someone who is used to life on the streets." She pulled her hands to her lap.

Ardeth's eyes followed the motion of her hands, and he cocked an eyebrow at her. "I seem to have you on edge. Are you often like a cat trapped in a tree?"

She stared at him. A cat in a tree? "You couldn't trap me in a tree if you tried. Just answer the question."

Ardeth laughed.

"What is so funny?" she asked frostily.

"Just imagining trapping you in a tree."

She shifted in her seat and was captivated once again by her companion's eyes. They were even more striking when laughter colored them. She licked her lips. "You were about to tell me what brings you and your friends to Azubah."

"Was I?" Ardeth scratched the scruff on his cheek. "I'm traveling through town and on my way home with the rest of the soldiers."

Steele blinked. He was a soldier, too.

"Oh, is that it? Well, I hope you find the inn accommodating," she replied, ready to end the conversation. He was a soldier, she repeated to herself, and she needed to keep her distance. "I must be going."

It was Ardeth's turn to blink. "You're leaving? So late?"

"I know. It really is late, and I need to get some good rest." She stood, and Ardeth caught her wrist.

"You didn't give me your name."

Steele smirked, "You're right, I didn't. Thank you for the pint."

Ardeth's surprised laugh followed her as she wound around tables to the stairs that would take her up to the bedrooms. She shot Gemma a grateful smile when the woman passed her a key, relieved she would not have to spend another night outside.

CHAPTER 8

The next morning, Steele woke to a commotion outside her window. The sun shone bright and warm when it fell across her face, and she rubbed her eyes wearily. Though she had slept soundly, exhaustion was heavy in her bones. Curiosity won out, however, and she rolled out of bed to peer out the window, briefly wondering if she was about to discover what was behind the strange behavior of people throughout the kingdom, when she saw a tall, yellow-haired girl picking up a trash bin and mumbling the whole while. It seemed the girl had driven a wagon into the bin, knocking over all its contents.

Steele searched for anyone else, anyone who could be a possible assailant, but there was no one lurking anywhere.

With as much speed as she could muster in her sleepy state, she pulled on her trousers, short-sleeved shirt, and vest, smiling at the thought of seeing Tazmeen and Ali. The journey would take her three days if she hurried, and she still wanted to take a look around the market before she left. It was early for merchants to be selling anything, but if she could catch one or two before the streets became too crowded, someone might be willing to buy her craft. She pulled her coat on and shouldered her bag.

She jogged down the steps, almost running into the yellow-haired girl from the alley. With a nod to the girl, Steele pushed open the door to the dining room.

Ardeth stood in the doorway, mouth forming an *O* as he narrowly avoided receiving a blow to his nose by the edge of the door. He clearly had not accounted for the door to swing back and it hit his head with a deep *thunk*.

Steele grimaced, grabbing his shoulder. "I'm so sorry!" She pulled his head down to examine where he had been hit, eyes widening as if her hands were acting on their own accord. Quickly, she pulled away, releasing her hold. "There's no blood, just a small bump, maybe."

Ardeth rubbed the back of his head. "Thanks. I've had worse."

They stood there, looking at each other. Still embarrassed by her actions, she fidgeted with the bottom of her shirt.

A cough sounded behind her. "Excuse me, supplies coming through!"

Steele and Ardeth stepped to the side, allowing the blonde from the alley to pass.

"Net, your wagon won't unload itself, and I can't carry your crates and whiskey all on my own!"

Net appeared from behind the bar and winked at Steele. "You'd never know I own the place with the way these women speak to me."

The girl blushed, but didn't retract her statement.

Steele shared a smile with Ardeth. "Do you need any help, Net?" she asked. She was anxious to be going, but could make up the time by traveling through the night if she needed to.

The robust man turned in the small hallway, giving Steele and Ardeth a once-over. "You, boy, you look fit. I know the girl can pull her weight. Follow me."

"I'm sorry again. I only meant to volunteer myself," Steele whispered as they headed to the back of the inn.

Ardeth's eyes crinkled with delight as he held the door for her. "It's my pleasure."

There were more crates and casks in the wagon than Steele had expected, but with the four of them working together, it didn't take long to finish the task. Net quickly put Steele and Ardeth in the cellar, unloading the boxes and organizing the drinks, and by the time they opened the last box, she was sticky with sweat and thoroughly hungry.

Ardeth wiped his brow with a cloth and handed her a fresh one. She smiled gratefully. "Thank you."

She passed him a bottle of wine. "I hope you didn't need to be anywhere this morning."

He shook his head. "I had planned on seeing the market this morning, but there was nothing set. I haven't been here since I was a child."

"Really?" she asked. "Azubah's a wonderful place. I try to come here whenever I'm free."

"You do?" He smiled.

She nodded. "The market is the best, people bring the most interesting trinkets from all over the different kingdoms, and the events hosted here are the kind you don't want to miss."

"What kind?"

"Some are annual, like the Wolfkiel Festival where people bring their family's meals and compete for the best. There was a barn raising one year. My favorite has to be when more than half the town woke up to watch a star shower. That was spontaneous, started by a group of blacksmiths, and word traveled fast. I was lucky to experience that one."

"That sounds," he paused, "perfect." He sighed, observing the empty boxes, a faraway look in his blue eyes.

Gemma peered into the cellar, then. "Have you eaten?"

"No," Steele replied as Ardeth said, "Yes."

"Right then. You've both earned a meal on me." With that, the silver- haired innkeeper disappeared into the kitchens.

"Now a free meal?" Ardeth grinned. "I think I should stick around you, nameless girl."

She stacked the boxes in front of her. "Nothing is ever free."

"If you will not give me your name, I will need to come up with something to call you," he said, moving to stand beside her. He was very tall, and she had to tilt her head to really look at him.

She debated giving him her name; he had been pleasant enough company, very nice and helpful to give up his morning to Net's needs, but...Her gaze shifted away from his face and settled on the wall just beyond him. She smiled, though it was with great effort, and she knew she looked strained rather than content.

He took a deep breath, sounding resigned at her silence. "I suppose you have your reasons, and I shouldn't pry."

Surprised by his concession, her eyes drew back to him, and she watched him, his casual stance and the hint of a smile constantly resting on his lips.

"I've set your plates on the table you two used last night," Gemma called to them. She caught Steele's eye as they headed out of the cellar and into the kitchen. The woman's lips were pursed and her brows raised. Steele shrugged and headed for the table.

Their plates were filled with an assortment of food she would never have been able to afford. "Gemma, this is too much!"

"Nonsense. You just saved me hours' worth of complaining from Net and Katerina." Gemma waved a hand before wiping it clean with her apron. "Eat up before we get busy."

"Will do!" Ardeth laughed and promptly dug into his food.

She did the same. The eggs were tasty, and Steele savored each salty bite.

"So, Ardeth," she said, breaking the contented silence, "what made you decide to become a soldier?"

He set his fork down and scratched his chin. "My parents suggested it, actually. Said I needed to learn how to be a better leader. I think they also thought I needed to be ordered around a bit for character building." He laughed. "They never expected I'd actually take to it."

She smiled. "And how is it?"

"What?"

"Getting ordered around?"

"For the first few years, it was rough. I needed the adjustment in attitude, however, so I'm grateful that Emdubae, the soldier assigned to supervise me at first, didn't send me home."

"The first few *years*? How long have you been serving?" Her stomach clenched. She'd asked the questions, picked the topic, but she almost wished she'd left things alone. Knowing more about his history as a soldier did nothing to help her.

"I began training at a young age, traveled some with the King's Guard when I was fifteen, but I didn't join officially until I was seventeen. So, it's been," he paused, surprise evident in his face, "nine years. Well, then."

Steele exhaled slowly. "The King's Guard?" Not only was he a soldier, but he was one of the elite. "Their job is to protect the royal family, right?"

"That's one of our duties, yes, but not all."

"Ardeth," the man with a strong jaw and shoulder-length curly hair from the night before interrupted. His dark eyes settled on Steele for a moment too long, and she sucked in air, wishing she had a scarf to cover her face.

"Yes, Edin?"

"Our friend has returned to his table in the market. Do you wish to speak with him now?"

She didn't hear Ardeth's response as she was focused on the two soldiers entering the inn and heading their direction. The dining room was beginning to feel a little too confined. Normally her heart would be pounding with the need to flee the scene, but today she didn't think it was beating at all. She quietly set her fork down, stuffed a piece of bread in her bag, and stood.

"You're leaving?" Ardeth asked.

Avoiding his eyes, she nodded. "Yes, I've got a long journey ahead of me. Thank you for helping Net earlier."

"You'll have to show me around Azubah the next time we're both here." He winked at her.

Not likely, Steele replied silently, noting another soldier entering the inn. "I wish you well."

"And you."

Steele strode purposefully over to Gemma, who was pouring Net and herself a drink. "It's coffee," she explained, "Even I can't start the bottle this early."

"I only wanted to say a quick thank you for everything. I wish I could stay longer," Steele jerked her head toward the soldiers who were now exiting the inn, Ardeth at the lead.

"Never thought you were in the habit of keeping company with the military, Steele," Net said gruffly.

"That was *your* doing," she retorted.

"Was it?" he asked, a knowing look in his eye.

Gemma threw her husband a distasteful look. "Net likes to play matchmaker."

"*That* would be a match," Steele laughed. "A soldier and a thief!"

"Ah, but you could start a new life then, start a family," he said, wrapping an arm around her shoulders. "I'd love to see little Steeles running around here."

"Net, my dear, you need to mind your own business," Gemma scolded. "Steele's far too young for all that! She might be living a dangerous life, but a husband is not always the answer."

They quickly fell into bickering. Not seeing an end to the argument and feeling incredibly uncomfortable about the subject, Steele backed away slowly, calling out, "Thank you! Hopefully the next time I see you, I will be able to pay you with a gold coin."

Gemma paused mid-sentence. "Don't get yourself caught in the meantime."

Steele rolled her eyes. "I won't let that happen."

The couple smiled at her, but the moment Steele's fingers touched the wooden doors, she heard their debate about Steele's lifestyle erupt again.

The street was crowded with vendors setting up their carts. The commotion didn't surprise Steele, but the lack of interested customers did. It seemed Gemma hadn't been exaggerating the lack of business. Steele pulled some bracelets out of her pack and eyed the vendors. She didn't need more money for the trip home for herself, but extra change was always a blessing for Tazmeen.

She spotted a woman carefully setting up her cart, arranging necklaces and earrings so they were displayed perfectly. Steele fingered her crudely made bracelets and redirected her movements. A scrawny man a couple of carts down didn't have much to sell, but he smiled at those who passed by. He might make something from her craft.

The man welcomed her graciously, and she nervously returned the gesture with a smile. She had found that acting shy and nervous usually made people feel compassion toward her.

Hoping it would be so with this man, she cautiously held out her bracelets. "Would you buy these from me, sir?"

He considered the bracelets and chuckled. "Child, you do realize that I am the one selling merchandise?"

Steele managed to blush. "Oh, sir, I am so sorry! I didn't realize. I haven't been to many markets, and I am almost desperate to sell my first bracelets. Mama says it's pointless, and Papa agrees with her. I would like to prove them wrong."

She pulled her bracelets back, and started to turn away when the man grasped her shoulder. She smiled at the ground before turning back to him. "Sir?"

He handed her three bronze coins. "Show these to your folks, eh?"

She took the money and beamed at the man. "Oh thank you, sir!"

He set the bracelets out for people to see, and Steele flashed him another smile before continuing on her way.

"I see what you did there." A deep voice at her ear caused her to jump, and she reached reflexively for her hood. She turned to find Ardeth grinning at her, blue eyes twinkling. He had changed into his soldier's uniform.

"I don't know what you're talking about," she murmured, trying to push past him. Her shoulder caught briefly on the maroon-and-black sash that crossed his uniform, and she jerked away.

He laughed and stepped in beside her. "Don't play coy with me. That poor man stood no chance."

She speared him with a glare. "What do you mean?"

His lips twitched. "You only had to flutter your pretty eyes at him, and he would have given you all his money and more."

She stumbled to a halt. *Pretty eyes?*

"I did no such thing," she maintained, trying to shake off the compliment. "I needed to sell some bracelets, so I did."

She hopped onto a low brick wall that lined the edge of the street.

Ardeth chuckled. "Okay." He cast a sideways glance at her, then went on. "If you won't tell me your name, at least tell me where you are from?"

Steele considered telling him when a guard in the distance distracted her. She hopped off the wall and quickly changed directions to one of the alleys between the shops. Ardeth followed her movements, his only protest being a raised eyebrow. She sighed. Anonymity was difficult to maintain with other people in the picture, especially with people who lived within the law.

"Nowhere," she replied. He looked at her, unamused, and she continued, "Far away. I haven't been there in a long time."

Ardeth studied her face and sighed. "You have many secrets don't you." It was a statement, not a question, so Steele only raised an eyebrow in response, earning a smirk from him.

They reached a crossroad between the alleyways, and Steele turned to head out of the city. To her surprise and slight annoyance, the soldier followed her.

"Are you lost, Ardeth?"

He chuckled. "No, my men and horses are actually waiting for me at the edge of town."

A trap?

Steele slowed, though her heart was racing, and Ardeth turned to glance at her. "My journey is taking me in another direction I'm afraid," she said, turning away from him.

He eyed her skeptically. "Somehow I don't believe you."

"Believe what you want. It was interesting meeting you."

Steele crossed the alley, and Ardeth called, "You as well, Nameless Girl!" as she disappeared down another side street.

How many goodbyes was she to have with this man?

Once out of sight, Steele crouched and waited until she heard Ardeth's retreating footsteps. He was, unfortunately, walking in the same direction she needed to go, but she was not going to willingly walk up to a group soldiers. Especially a group that had horses. She was fast, but she had yet to outrun a horse.

Risking a look around the corner, she smiled to herself as she watched him walk away. She slunk in the shadows behind him, pausing when he paused, and scurrying along when he picked up his pace. At the end of the alley, a small group of men and horses stood. Ardeth approached the group, who greeted him jovially, and he swung easily into the saddle of a brown gelding. Steele had time to appreciate the fine lines and sturdy legs of the animal before Ardeth and his friends rode off. She watched them until they turned sharply to the left, and she sighed in relief. She would not have to worry about staying out of their way, for her journey would take her to the right.

The forest welcomed her with the sound of birds, trees creaking in the wind, and the slight hum of insects. Steele closed her eyes and inhaled the pine-and-earth scent of the woods. As much as she loved Azubah, it wasn't until she was in the woods that she felt she could breathe again. The towns…They were not her world. Maybe they had been once, when she'd lived in the city of Solarrhia with Tazmeen, but she had not truly felt at home there since she had made herself an outcast by stealing that first horse. Tazmeen, however, she could always call home.

Some days her heart hurt and longed for a sense of belonging, but then she remembered taking Snap to another town, the look on Jayn's face when she revealed him, and how Jayn had calmly reached for Snap's nose and waited patiently for the curiosity of the horse to kick in. Steele smiled at the memory and checked the sun's placement in the sky. The thought of seeing Tazmeen and Ali had quickened her pace unknowingly. There was even time enough to stop at the lake and wash herself.

It didn't take her long to reach the faint trail that veered off the main path, and with a quick glance over her shoulder, Steele stepped onto the path. She never would have found the lake on her own; Twitch and Spar had shown it to her ages ago. Small thorny branches tugged at her clothes as she walked, and she grinned when she ducked under a limb and finally saw the lake sparkling at her.

She had not washed for over a week, and her skin looked like she'd been baked in the sun. Gemma might not have minded Steele bathing at the inn, but the task of drawing up water and hauling it to a tub hadn't seemed very appealing to her, and Net was busy enough.

After a look around to ensure she was alone, she shed her clothes and stepped into the lake, wading out to her neck. The water was refreshing in the heat of the day, and she scrubbed at her arms, grimacing at how much dirt swirled away into the water.

Breathing in, she lifted her feet and then sank below the surface. Silence surrounded her. No birds. No trees. She hadn't realized that even with the sound she had moments ago described as beautiful, nothing compared to this rare peace. When had silence become so soothing to her?

Perhaps the constant paranoia that accompanied her lifestyle was wearing on her more than she realized. Her lungs burned, reminding her that she needed air, and she kicked her way to the surface.
She swam to the shallow part of the lake, and sat, hugging her knees to her chest.

She thought of Jayn and Snap again. She knew she couldn't stop doing what she did and ignore a mistreated horse, especially knowing there were so many others she had yet to see. But, how would she ever become anything more than an outlaw if she continued? She didn't want to spend her entire life running from town to town, did she? Destiny and potential and an empty future weighed on her.

She felt a tickle in her nose, and her eyes suddenly felt pounds heavier and burned with unshed tears. With a sharp exhale, she shook her head and pulled herself together as best she could. The tears vanished, but the heaviness did not quite leave her heart.

She skimmed her fingertips on the surface of the water. The sun cast long shadows against the water, and she exhaled as goosebumps pebbled her skin. It was time to get dressed.

CHAPTER 9

A smile played across Steele's lips, as she walked down the streets of Rhia. She was almost home and the thought of surprising Tazmeen and Ali made her giddy. But first, she wanted to check one particular place out, and she followed the road as if a hook had a hold on her heart, pulling her down the path.

Near the furthest corner of the street sat a house Steele had lived in with her parents. She walked up a slight hill before coming to a stop in front of a small, sturdy house. A blacksmith's forge was connected to the left side of the home, and her eyes slid over that building before settling back on the main house. Garrick and Emelia had not lived in the grandest house on the street, but they had been incredibly proud of the view. A view that was better appreciated from higher up.

Steele knocked on the door to see if Master Lorne or his wife, Mistress Purtha were home. Master Lorne ran the smithy now, and never minded when Steele stopped by to visit her old home. No one answered the door, so she climbed the shabby fence and pulled herself onto the roof.

The view dazzled her, just as it had so many times before. The royal palace dominated the skyline, yet somehow the craggy Farest'Del Mountains that jutted up in the distance made the palace seem small. She had never been close enough to see if the palace was made of white marble or some other stone, but she loved how the sun splashed the towers and turrets in color depending on where it was in the sky.

The watchtowers situated at the corners of the palace were her favorite parts of the view. Legend had it that a rogue wind blew walls of sand from the Nasshari Desert toward the palace, and four magi stood to protect it. As the sand slammed into the palace, their magic prevented it from doing any damage. Instead, the sand swirled up to the heavens, forming the towers she looked upon today. Steele smiled, remembering how she used to sit up here imagining all that took place behind those walls.

She leaned back, crossing her arms behind her head. The brilliant blue sky was deepening, and if she waited long enough, the first stars of the night would peek through the growing darkness. So many nights

Steele had sat on this roof, squeezed between her parents as they watched the day turn to night.

Part of her yearned to stay on the rooftop all night, but with a sad smile, she climbed down from the roof, glancing at the smithy when she landed. She hadn't been inside since the accident. Her heart gave a painful squeeze as she turned away and retraced her steps to the main road.

As she neared the curve in the road that would lead her to Tazmeen's house, she heard a commotion. A couple of people on the street turned toward the noise and, aside from exchanging a tense look with each other, went about their business. Steele spared the people a concerned glance before picking up her pace. Guards may be around to settle whatever was going on.

She rounded the corner and let out a deep breath. Firelight flickered from behind the one window at the front of Tazmeen's mud and rock house. Someone was home. She quietly tested the doorknob and pushed the door open a smidge. Inside, she heard Ali shout something to his ma. He was outside around the back of the house. With a grin, Steele quietly stepped inside, shut the door, and tip-toed through the front room. Tazmeen stood on the opposite side of the room, facing the table in front of an open window on the back wall. Her long dark hair hung loosely down her back.

"Yes, we need more wood. This fire needs more life!" She replied to her son through the window. She resumed cutting the stems of a flower bouquet and hummed to herself.

Steele covered Tazmeen's eyes and quickly said, "Guess who?"

Tazmeen stiffened and grabbed Steele's hands. When she turned around, her hazel eyes were teary and her smile stretched across her face. She pulled Steele into a hug and squeezed her tightly. Steele breathed her in, the scent of fresh linen, and bent to press her face into the woman's shoulders.

"My girl." Tazmeen pulled back and cupped Steele's cheek. They embraced again.

Steele stepped away and her bag down next to the table.

"Sit! I'll make tea while you tell me about your travels," Tazmeen grabbed a pitcher off the table and poured water into a pot.

"I don't want to interrupt what you were doing."

"Oh, that?" Tazmeen gestured to the bouquet. "That's for Lena. Her husband was arrested last week, and she's in need of a little emotional support."

"Rohon was arrested?" Steele said, obeying Tazmeen's command to sit. She pulled a chair from the wooden table in the center of the room and shrugged out of her coat. Rohon and Lena were decent people who followed the laws carefully from what she remembered.

Tazmeen nodded and hung the pot in a small fireplace. She adjusted a burning block of wood and the flame breathed, creeping a little higher toward the pot. "I was going to take them to her before dinner."

"Steele?"

Steele looked to the back door to see Ali standing there, his eyes wide and arms full of firewood. He strode over to the fire and emptied the load in a basket. She jumped from her seat and they crashed into a hug.

"You're huge!" She tipped her chin up to study him. He had a bit of stubble on his chin, and his brown eyes were sparkling.

"I never realized how small you are," he returned with a wink.

"I'm hardly short. Maybe I can't reach the top shelf in the cabinet, but I'm tall enough to see you desperately need to clean out your ears." She ducked out from between his arms and spun around just out of reach as he grabbed at her. They froze as Tazmeen grabbed both of them by their hair.

"Do I need to throw you outside before you break something? Honestly, not even five minutes home, and the two of you can't be civil."

Steele and Ali grinned at each other.

"I promise to behave, ma," Ali patted his mom's shoulder. Steele agreed, and the older woman released her grip.

Someone knocked on the door, and the three of them hushed. Steele wondered which neighbor would be stopping by, someone she liked or someone who would use the knowledge of her whereabouts for his or her own gain.

Ali glanced outside the front window and frowned. Out of the corner of his mouth, he whispered, "Room."

Without hesitation or a word, she moved down the short hallway to Tazmeen's bedroom, passing her old one. She was there before Tazmeen could reach the door.

Tazmeen opened the door slowly. Before she could speak, two men stepped inside the house. Guards. Steele whipped her head back around the doorframe to get out of sight and very slowly let out her breath. Had they seen her?

"You're Tazmeen, the seamstress, and her son, Ali?" He asked monotonously, as if he was reading aloud from a parchment.

"Yes, that's me."

"We need the two of you to step outside."

"Any reason, sir?" Tazmeen sounded nervous.

"It looks like you're overdue on your taxes. You were given a week to make up the difference, and the collectors informed us you've missed your date."

"I have a client who needed a few more days to pay me. I'll have the money—"

"A deadline is a deadline, miss. You can give me the name of your client on the way."

Steele narrowed her brow.

"On the way where?" Ali asked.

"Your mother is being arrested, and you being a minor cannot be left here unattended."

Steele's heart dropped to her stomach. She heard the door open and people exit the house. She peeked around the corner. The main room was empty, so she headed for the back door and exited the house. As quietly as she could, she used the back window as a step and hauled herself onto the roof. She crawled up the slope and peered over the top.

A group of five men stood in front of the house. They were definitely Solarrhian Guards, dressed in the white tunic decorated with a maroon sash, brown trousers, and tall brown boots. They all looked similar, dark brown hair and olive-brown skin. One pulled Tazmeen's arms behind her back and began binding her wrists with rope. Ali protested, and two others held him back.

Steele's heart pounded. *What do I do?*

There were a group of horses tied up near the house. They could escape on those. Knowing she didn't have much time, she descended down the other side of the roof and leapt off, landing on one of the men holding Ali. As she and the guard fell, Ali pulled himself free. The man softened the impact for her, and he hit the ground with a shout. Dust clouded around the two of them.

Steele hopped up. "Ali, get your ma!"

The man she'd knocked over grabbed at her legs. She yanked her ankles free, and Ali threw a punch at the guard who'd bound Tazmeen. The guard just moved out of the way and yanked Tazmeen with him. Drawing a knife, he held it to her throat. Steele and Ali froze in unison.

"What are you doing?" Steele pleaded with the guard. "She said she could pay you. I have money. Please."

"The law's the law. And you just assaulted a guard," he pressed the knife closer to Tazmeen's throat. Ali grimaced, but his mother stood there calmly. She looked to Steele and ever so slightly, shook her head. Steele clenched her jaw and looked away from her. A tall guard grabbed Ali's arm and twisted it behind his back. He cried out.

A round-figured guard pulled a piece of parchment out from his satchel. "Winlen, look at this."

Oh, no. Steele hadn't covered her face in the rush of things.

Winlen glanced at the page and fixed his eyes on her face. He grabbed the parchment and held it next to her face. "Perfect match. Looks like we caught a thief today, too! She's not a part of our original orders, but think about the reward!"

"And won't it be nice to be known as the guards who finally caught the thief of Solarrhia," the other guard said casting a smug glance at Steele.

She scoffed. "One of the fifty? Remarkable."

"The first one is always the one they make an example of." He grunted, then turned to the other guards. "You take these two to the drop-off site. We'll meet you after we deliver this one to the palace."

Steele glanced at Tazmeen, who jerked her head. "You can help us," she whispered.

"She can't if she's dead," the man said, and he latched onto Steele's arm before she could step away.

She felt a bubble of panic rise in her throat. Jumping away, she twisted her body in an attempt to break free. The grip on her arm loosened, so she leaned sideways and planted a well-aimed kick on the man's hip. It was enough of a shock to him that he let go. She turned on her heel to run, but Winlen lunged at her, knocking her to the ground.

Her elbows burned against the gritty sand, and she turned her face just in time to avoid splitting her chin on the ground. Winlen lay across her legs, so she struggled to crawl forward, pulling herself along while trying to kick free of the man. Ali yelled out as a shadow fell across the ground in front of her, and Steele bit back a cry of frustration. The guard who had recognized her loomed overhead, laughing down on her, and white-hot fury burst from her heart.

Not like this.

She was not going to allow Tazmeen and Ali to be taken away, and she surely wasn't going to let them see her being taken off to certain death.

She reached for the short knife that was hidden on her belt. Her fingers closed around the hilt, and she pulled it forward, swiftly plunging it into the side of the round man's calf muscle. She pulled the blade out, and he shrieked in pain, stumbling back. Winlen jumped up from her legs, and for a blessed moment, she thought she was free. She struggled to rise and was quickly forced back to the ground by a foot between her shoulders. From his stance above her, Winlen brushed the sand off his pants, and she ducked her head into her shoulder to keep the grit out of her eyes, though she could feel it raining on her head.

The man she'd stabbed roughly kicked the knife out of her hand and crouched down next to her. "You're lucky we need you alive to collect this reward." He limped over to the other men, and they closed into a tight circle, rattling off at one another.

The pressure of the boot on her back remained steady, so she lay quietly, cheek in the dirt, staring at Tazmeen and Ali. The guard towered over Tazmeen. Tears traced their way down her vaguely lined cheeks, and Ali looked like he was doing his best to be brave.

Steele tried to give them an encouraging smile, but she could feel her lips trembling. "Don't worry about me. I'll get out of this somehow. I always do. I'll see you soon, okay?"

Ali nodded. "Deal."

Steele managed a smile just before the men pulled her to her feet, the shallow scratch on her cheek burning as grit and sand stuck to it.

"You're a good liar," Winlen said, pulling her around the house to where a group of horses were tied and away from Tazmeen and Ali.

CHAPTER 10

Tazmeen. Ali. Tazmeen. Ali. Their names beat in time with the horse's steps, and Steele bit back a sob, staring at her bound wrists. She would not appear weak to these men. The horse stopped, and Winlen grabbed her shoulder and roughly pulled her from the saddle. Startled, Steele glanced up and gasped. They were at the palace.

It really was beautiful up close. The high arches were so marvelously designed; beautiful hand-chiseled flowers wrapped up and around the columns, the stone glittering in the light like stars peeking from behind the petals. She sucked in a deep breath as her eyes took in the cloisters.

A bird chirped behind her, singing a beautiful melody. She wished she'd taken a better look at everything. The woods, the rivers, the inns. Stealing was punishable by death, let alone stealing something as valuable as a horse, and if she did not come up with a plan soon, the palace would be the last thing she ever saw. That guard she'd stabbed had been right. How on earth was she to get out of this predicament? She doubted she'd find sympathy among the privileged.

One question repeated in her mind: where were they taking Tazmeen and Ali? That "summons" had looked more like an arrest.

One foot in front of the other. Right, left, right, trip. Steele's foot caught on one of the stones in the path. The guard holding her right arm yanked her upright. She grimaced at the burning in her foot and her shoulder, but the pain was good. It kept her thoughts focused.

The guards on each side of her pulled on her arms, forcing her to a halt.

A woman with hair as dark as a raven's wing and piercing gray eyes stepped from the shadows, and Steele fought the urge to pull back. Thin black lines scrawled up her neck and across her cheeks.

"A thief?" she questioned.

Steele's guards nodded quickly, and Winlen held up the poster he'd used earlier to identify her.

The woman nodded once. "Search her."

Steele grunted as Winlen used a sharp knife to cut away her vest. Rough hands ran along her arms and sides, and she shut her eyes as the

69

guards searched her. Hands paused along her trousers before plunging in her pockets.

"What's this?" a guard asked, holding her communication stone in front of her face.

Keeping her face impassive, Steele shrugged. "Just a rock." She prayed the guard wouldn't recognize it for what it truly was. "A present for my younger brother."

"A rock?" Winlen chuckled, and Steele watched as he tossed the stone on her discarded vest. "Throw that out. We have no use for it."

The woman gathered Steele's things and when her fingers brushed the communication stone, her gaze flicked to Steele for a moment. "I'll take these for you. The king will see you now," she said before turning on her heel and heading down the hall.

Steele was marched along until she was jerked to a stop. She looked up and stared at the tall double doors that lead into the Royal Court. Her fate lay just on the other side. Suddenly, as if her mind and body were finally in agreement about the present situation, the giant walls did not seem so large. In fact, they were closing in on her, and she could not breathe. The doors opened from the inside, and the guards stepped forward.

Pushing her heels against the stone floor, Steele threw her weight back, writhing and straining against the hands gripping her arms. The two guards who held her were burly men, but Steele put up a good fight. Her dark hair whipped across her face as she struggled, and her clothing ripped as one of the guards fumbled with her sleeve to regain his grasp on her arm. Another set of strong hands shoved her from behind with such force that she stumbled forward. She continued to struggle against the guards until they were in the middle of the room.

The lively court hushed the moment the guards dragged her in. She caught a glimpse of a woman with her mouth frozen open, a curious expression in her eyes. She casually held an ornate goblet in her hand as if appearing at the Royal Court was nothing but a regular occurrence for her, a duty she had to put up with. Steele tore her eyes away from the woman and barely had the chance to look at the rest of the now-silent crowd before a guard kicked her in the back of the legs. When her knees hit the ground, she hissed and gritted her teeth, briefly wondering if her skin would even have a chance to bruise before blood stopped flowing in her veins. How quickly did they perform executions?

Angry tears stung her eyes as a female guard Steele had not seen before shoved her shoulders down. Since her hands were bound together it was hard to catch herself, and she nearly hit her nose on the ground. She looked at the floor, concentrating on the swirls of white and gray marble, refusing to look directly at anyone until the tears were at bay. Every now and then, the gray would twinkle in the sunlight, and it strangely calmed her frenzied nerves. A shudder ran the length of her body, but no tears fell from her eyes.

She heard a cough and a snicker come from nearby, but no one spoke. Then, footsteps clicked behind her until a heavy robe grazed her side.

"Your Royal Highness," an unfamiliar voice said. Steele glanced to her side to see a man bowing before the king. She only caught his profile, a bird-like nose and a face made even longer with a stylishly pointed beard.

"General Fijar." The king's voice sent shivers down Steele's spine as if he had already passed judgment on her life. The sound of his voice spoke of his many years in war securing the kingdom's boundaries. King Ax was as unyielding as a mountain just as her father had described him.

"Your Majesty, I have brought before you a thorn in our government. She undermines all that we have accomplished in your glorious kingdom. Your Highness, she has stolen, and she has been thwarting the guards for years, laughing at the laws your grandfathers so rightly enacted in a lawless land. She refuses to bow down to authority, and in doing so, she has made others scoff at you as king." General Fijar paused, letting his accusations settle into the minds of the king and court. His absurd claims sent fire through Steele's veins. She did not laugh in the face of the king! He knew nothing about her!

"I wish to make an example of her so the rest of the offenders in this kingdom know that we will not take their thievery lightly," the general proposed.

"How do you recommend we do that, General Fijar?" The king sounded firm, but Steele detected a hint of weariness. She supposed he did not like to hear about his citizens defying his laws.

"The only way we could get the word out in the proper way is by public execution."

General Fijar's tone infuriated her. She was in the wrong according to the law, yes, but this man knew this ordeal would end in her death, and he sounded almost pleased. Who could be so callous as to not care for human life? Her blood went from fire to ice in a split second. There it was. Her death sentence. Now it was up to the king to either have mercy upon her or to send her to the scaffold to be executed in public.

"I would like to look upon her face, General Fijar."

"Of course, Your Highness," he replied.

Steele grunted as General Fijar grabbed her hair and jerked her head up. A muscle burned down the left side of her neck, and she tried to hide her wince. The woman holding her down now pulled Steele up by her shoulder. She remained on her knees, and her head spun with the rush of movement. She breathed in slowly, her neck throbbing, and she looked up at the king.

Her shoulders slumped as his brown eyes bored into hers. Upon his peppered black hair sat a simple golden crown. Faint lines fanned out from his eyes, but even with visible signs of age and a graying beard, he did not appear to have weakened. In fact, he looked as much a part of that stone throne as his sculpture in the square.

The longer he studied her, the more her nerves calmed, catching her by surprise as she realized that the intensity of his stare did not frighten her. Instead, though he was to name the end of her days, she felt almost legitimized by the man underneath the crown through those eyes, as if he could see her entire life set out before him and had determined she was an individual who did indeed have value. She knew this was likely untrue, but she supposed that was why he had lasted so long as king. Having the ability to make people believe he cared for them while he simultaneously used them as pawns must have been an incredibly useful skill. And that face…A memory scratched at the back of her mind along with a sense of familiarity, but she could not place it.

A person in the crowd muttered that they couldn't see her clearly enough.

Steele narrowed her eyes at the comments, though she did not take her gaze off the face of the king, as he was the ruler of her fate.

"What is your name?" King Ax gestured to her with one hand. His other rested calmly on the armrest of his throne.

Steele stared at him, but she did not respond. Tazmeen and Ali had already been taken in, so revealing her name would not result in their arrests anymore. Yet, even here, her habit of not revealing her name created a barrier between her and exposure.

General Fijar knocked the back of her head with his elbow. "Answer the king when he asks you a question."

Steele hissed, throwing a threatening glare to the general.

"General Fijar, you do not need to abuse the girl." King Ax frowned. The general grimaced at being chastised, and slowly clasped his hands in front of his hips.

"My name is Steele." She winced at how weak and small her voice sounded in comparison to the king's. She had meant to come off as resolute and strong.

"Is this your face, Steele?" the king asked, motioning to Winlen, who still held the scroll.

Parchment rustled next to her, and the wanted poster uncurled before her eyes. "Yes, Your Majesty," she answered, eyes sliding from the poster to the king.

"What exactly have you stolen, Steele?" King Ax asked. He peered into her eyes, and for a moment, she felt the conviction she'd suppressed for years breathe in her heart. It was a very brief moment, however, because her next thought was of Ali's muted cries as he tried to be brave through his own unjustified arrest. Her heart exhaled, the conviction fading.

General Fijar looked like he was about to speak for her, so Steele spoke quickly. "Horses, Your Highness."

A few people shouted out their opinions to her confession, voices bouncing off the marbled walls. The female guard squeezed Steele's shoulder hard enough that she felt fingernails biting through her shirt. Steele ripped her shoulder out from under the guard's hands, teetering a moment on her knees while she caught her balance. The woman grunted and reached to take hold of her again, but the king held up his hand.

The guard dropped her arms, and Steele found enough mirth inside her to smirk. If she was going to die, she was going to go out with dignity. She had made her choice long ago to steal those horses, and she refused to regret saving their lives just because she was now facing her own death. Her mind grasped the image of Jayn beaming as Snap began to trust her, approaching her and resting his nose in her hand.

With this newfound resolve, she took her eyes off the king and studied those around him. Other than a guard on his right, a man stood just slightly behind the king on his left side. A golden circlet sat upon this dark haired man's head, matching the king's. This must be Prince Aldair, she thought, pausing to study him. His arms were clasped behind his back from what she could see, and his eyes appeared unsettled when she made eye contact. He stared at her with a pale and grim expression, jaw clenched, and her attention was drawn to his tightened lips. A familiar scar crossed the edge of his mouth.

Steele stiffened, and her mouth fell open. The man from the inn! Ardeth was the prince! She snapped her mouth shut and immediately dropped her gaze to the swirls on the floor again. She wondered idly if maybe he had a twin brother who had been banished from the kingdom, but of course she knew this was a ridiculous notion. How could she have been so blind?

"They were suffering, and there was no other way—," she started to explain, but was silenced by the king.

"Our laws are clear as to the punishment for stealing a horse, correct?" The king fingered his beard as he addressed Steele.

She nodded. "The punishment is death, Your Highness."

"Yet you still chose to break the law knowing this." He paused and glanced at his son. Steele followed his gaze. Whatever recognition Prince Aldair had shown before was now quickly hidden behind a composed mask, void of any emotion. It didn't appear that he would say anything to help her. Her heart throbbed within her chest. As far as she knew, there had never been an exception for executions before now, so she doubted the prince having compassion for her would change anything. Her fate was set.

The king stood up from his throne and stepped down from the platform. "Thieving is inexcusable, no matter the reason. I do not need to explain myself to you, but I will tell you that even if it was a good reason, I will not rescind the punishment. My job is to protect my citizens, and you have disregarded my authority by taking from them. General Fijar is right that you have disrespected me and those you stole from by blatantly ignoring the laws that have kept this kingdom from chaos."

She glared at General Fijar's pompous smile.

The king continued. "The people know the punishments and that we will discipline criminals according to their deeds. You have sealed your own fate. You will be executed, but we will do so privately."

The grin slowly faded from General Fijar's face, but Steele did not dwell much on his disappointment. A seed of dread planted itself firmly in the pit of her stomach. Her heart, her precious heart, thrummed in her chest. The court had sprung to life at her sentencing, but all she could hear was a soft humming.

Guards pulled her to her feet by her elbows, and she swayed before regaining her balance.

There's always a way out, she reminded herself. She could see the tip of General Fijar's saber out of the corner of her eye. If she pulled the saber hard enough and fast enough, perhaps he would lose *his* balance, fall, and she would have some sort of leverage. She could still hold a saber with her hands tied. But before she could move, the guards gripped her arms so fiercely that she could not move them. What little hope she'd had withered and disappeared.

Steele looked up into the king's eyes, and though she found no mercy there, his mouth had settled into a displeased frown.

The guards forced her to turn toward a door to the side of the room. General Fijar led the group out, but before she left the court, she risked a glance over her shoulder at the prince. His head hung, and his stained-glass eyes were closed. He must have felt her staring at him because he looked up at her not a second later.

Steele swallowed, and didn't take her eyes from his until the guards yanked her through the door. Once in the hall, she inhaled, savoring every breath and every movement her body made. She counted the beats of her heart. The beats and her breaths were clearly numbered, after all.

CHAPTER 11

With one wall open to an expansive courtyard, the hallway of the palace would have given Steele many opportunities to escape had she been able to break away from the guards. The gray atmosphere of dusk made it difficult for her eyes to focus, and were she free, she could easily have faded into the background.

Unfortunately, her wrists were bound and she had five guards surrounding her, excluding General Fijar who was leading them. Winlen and the female guard held her arms and forced her to walk quickly, paying no mind as she stumbled to keep up. Never had she felt so demoralized. The adrenaline that had rushed through her body earlier in the court had evaporated, and everything around her seemed to tick at a slower pace. She felt drunk and heavy.

General Fijar glided down the hallway. As he walked, he unbelted his long brown robe and shed it from his shoulders to reveal a smart-looking soldier's uniform. It was only different from Ardeth's—Prince Aldair's, she corrected instantly—by a solid maroon sash around his shoulders. A servant appeared within seconds and, with his head bowed, took the robe from the general.

Steele cursed to herself, frustrated that she'd failed to realize that Ardeth's sash had signified how highly he was ranked. She'd assumed it was common, considering his companions had worn similar colors, but she should have made the connection. She knew better.

About five paces in front of her, General Fijar came upon a staircase. He turned slightly to check on his guards' progress. He paused to grin at her, and she shrank back, fear pooling in her belly. That grin looked more like a grimace, but it was his dark eyes that made her want to cower—black and lifeless. She had a feeling they mirrored his soul.

The guards finally allowed her walk more slowly as they descended down the winding stairs and into the darkness of what she could only presume was the dungeon. She breathed deeply to keep from panicking and reminded herself that her eyes would adjust after this moment of blindness. Just because a way out was not immediately clear, did not mean one would not present itself eventually.

A flash of light illuminated the hallway and revealed General Fijar holding a torch. They continued down the hall, leaving the stairs and fresh air behind, and Steele's body began to tingle, a queasiness settling deep within her; there was no way to escape down here. Sucking in another deep breath, she pushed the panic down and fought a gag. The hall reeked of decay and mold, and she held her breath to keep from vomiting.

The walk was silent, save for an occasional mundane comment from the guards, and the sound of men breathing. They passed numerous barred cells, but from what Steele could see, they were empty. Strange, since she knew for a fact that people were arrested regularly for crimes less damning than her own, and held in the palace dungeons for questioning. She looked for Tazmeen and Ali, hoping to find them in one of the cells, but as she continued to pass empty cells, her anticipation dwindled into fear.

Where could they be if not in the palace?

The men who had taken them had mentioned a drop off point, but she hadn't thought that meant they would be taken someplace other than the palace. She had assumed they were taking a different route to the palace to keep them separated.

"This one will do," General Fijar said, stopping at the end of the hall. He gave Steele that hollow grin once more before facing a barred door on the right and unlocking the padlock. Winlen pushed her through the now-open entry and forced her toward the wall. He pulled his knife from its sheath and cut the binding around her wrists. As he twisted her hands up to her shoulders, the sharp pressure on her joints caused her to flinch.

Another guard fingered the chains on the wall, smoothing his hands over the iron until he reached the cuffs. The flickering torchlight distorted his features, and Steele found herself pushing back against the dungeon walls to put space between them. He sneered at her and licked his lips. In an instant, the drunken heaviness fled, and fury boiled in her veins. She spat at his feet and kicked out at him, but the guard holding her arms yanked them upward. Her shoulders wrenched, and she fell to her knees with a hiss. The guard holding the cuffs promptly snapped the iron around her wrists and kicked her in the hip. In her kneeling position, she could not lower her arms to shield her body from further abuse, so she buried her face in her shoulder to keep from crying out from the pain.

The bars clanked as the guards shut the door.

"Sir?" The guard who had cuffed her faced the general.

"What is it, Lac?"

"Was her public execution not promised to the Lothar House?"

"We'll find some other high profile criminal to pacify the Council Houses. You would think they could use some of their own guard to help clean up the streets rather than relying solely on the Crown. However, since the king prefers a private execution, there's no reason we cannot use this to our advantage," General Fijar replied.

Steele frowned slightly. Lothar House was one of seven High Houses in Rhia, and she knew they liked to use prisoner executions to make a statement.

"Yes, sir." Lac said, clasping his hands behind his back.

General Fijar turned to Steele, his stare calculating. Without a word, he motioned for Lac to follow and strode down the hall.

"See you in the morning," Lac winked at her and waggled his eyebrows. "Enjoy your last night."

Steele's stomach lurched at his words, but she would not give him the fear response he was trying to provoke. A retort nearly jumped from her lips, but she decided against fueling the fire. She would not waste her remaining breath on this man.

Lac walked away from her cell, whistling. Occasionally she heard the tune stopped, but instead of silence, a chuckle would echo against the stone walls.

Now that she was alone, she let out a groan and resituated herself, as best she could when chained to a wall, so that she was sitting on her backside, her knees aching. A thought came to mind, and a short laugh burst out of her. Since it seemed she was to be executed in the morning, her body would have time to bruise after all.

She rested her head against the wall and sighed. Any attempt to move her arms resulted in the iron cuffs biting into her wrists, and she kicked at the ground. Grunting with annoyance, she pulled her now throbbing heel back toward her body. She looked around the cell and gasped, quickly pushing herself closer to the wall. Now she understood the smell.

Not a body's length away from her sat another human being. Or rather, what was left of one. The skeleton was partially illuminated by the small window near the ceiling of the cell, but was mostly covered in shadow. Steele squinted and could barely make out a set of chains just above where the skeleton sat. The skull hung over its ribcage, and one of the arms had already disconnected from the rest of the body.

Steele wasn't sure how many times her stomach could lurch without her last meal coming up. Her insides bubbled, ready to be relieved, and she groaned.

In less than a day she would be dead. She had to find a way out, and the faster she acted, the better. Tazmeen and Ali needed her, and she needed to find out where and why they had been taken. The only way to do that would be to pick the locks on her cuffs and somehow climb out through the window, but she had no tools. Those were in her saddlebag.

She looked at her cellmate. He'd, or she assumed it was a male, had only been wearing pants, his clothing was ratty and torn. Pale bone could be seen through the holes. Rodents must have feasted on this person, and she clenched her jaws to keep the bile at bay.

Then an idea danced in her mind, but she quickly dismissed it with a shudder. The idea bounced back, and she begrudgingly considered it more closely. This person was no longer in need of their bones, and if she could somehow detach one, she could whittle it down to a point to create a lock pick. It was far-fetched, but if it didn't work, Tazmeen and Ali would be lost to her. She would be lost to *them*.

She hesitantly reached out with her foot and managed to reach his pelvic bone. Ignoring the cuffs cutting into her skin, she hooked her toes underneath the bone and slowly pulled the body toward her. The bones scraped across the ground, and her foot jerked as the skull detached from the body and rolled down to her leg. She screeched and quickly pulled the rest of the body to her. The skull rolled across her legs and clattered against the bars of her cell. She waited a moment to see if anyone had heard, but no one came. The other exits must be far enough off for her to be securely alone.

Steele rolled her eyes. *Idiots.*

"What bone would even work?" she whispered, looking at the pile before her. She had no idea. Frustrated, she lifted her leg and slammed her foot down on the bones. They were still strong, but a few ribs broke off from the spine, and one in particular broke in half at a point. Steele laughed quietly and grabbed the bone with her feet. Carefully, she bent her knees as close to her hands as she could. Her hands could not reach the bone. Undeterred, she straightened her legs and scooted onto her lower back so that she could lift her feet closer to her hands. She hit her head against the wall as she rolled backward, a yelp slipping through her clenched teeth. It worked though, and while her head throbbed, she grabbed the bone from her feet.

Standing up proved to be harder than she had expected. She clumsily swiveled around so that she was facing the wall, and grabbed the chains to pull herself up. Her arms were twisted now, but at least the chains had more give. Gripping the bone with her left hand, she carefully began to chisel the bone against the other cuff to sharpen the point. She looked behind her and saw only darkness punctured by splotches of torchlight down the hall. Hopefully she would have enough time before the guards patrolled.

✶ ☽ ✶

Blood trickled down her forearm, but she refused to stop the rhythm of sharpening the rib against the cuff. It was a much slower process than she could afford because of the tension in the chains and her crossed forearms, but she was lucky enough to get some friction between the bone and iron.

"There," she panted with a satisfied grin.

Sweat rolled down her face in spite of the dungeon chill. Her wrists were scraped raw from the hours spent whittling, but she somehow ignored the burning. She examined the point of the rib. The piece was only the length of her palm now, yet it was amazing how such a small thing could stir up a familiar feeling of excitement and adrenaline. Heart pounding, she shoved the pointed end toward the hole in the cuff on the outside of her wrist. Even though it was a perfect placement for the keyhole, her crossed arms prevented her wrists from rotating enough to pick the lock. She grunted and hit her head against the wall again.

"Ow!" She growled and yanked on the chains. Pain seared through her arms as she struggled against the iron, and she kicked the wall as her frustration mounted. She could almost feel the panic sliding through her veins as well, lodging itself in her mind, tugging at her rational thoughts. What if Tazmeen and Ali could see her now? She could *not* panic.

Dropping her forehead against her arms, she began to sort out her thoughts, compartmentalizing her frustration. Her wrists were raw and bloodied, and she was still chained to the wall. She pressed her face harder against her arms, and took a couple of shaky breaths. Tazmeen would be devastated to see Steele break down like this. She chuckled as she pictured Tazmeen's face. She would be devastated to see Steele in chains to begin with, and Ali...Steele shook her head with a grunt. She didn't even want to think about him.

"I am going to die here if I do nothing," she whispered.

A gruesome idea fixated in her mind accompanied quickly with a metallic taste in the back of her throat. She groaned and grabbed the end of the bone with her teeth. It tasted of salt, dirt, and rust, and she gagged. Whimpering, she gritted her teeth against the bone and wedged the point into the lock. She twisted. She tried to pull on the cuff with her other hand, but her fingers kept slipping off the iron.

A man's laughter sounded in the distance, triggering a sense of desperation in Steele that she had rarely felt before. The cuff still wouldn't budge. She growled and almost choked against the bone. She grabbed it before she could drop it, and leaned her forehead on the wall. The coolness against her skin helped soothe her nerves.

She pulled her undershirt out and dropped the bone down her front. Hopefully the guards would not think to frisk her again. She untwisted herself so that her back was against the wall and slid down to the ground. She spat, ridding herself of the nasty taste the bone had left in her mouth. She studied the mess she had made of the skeleton, crushed and scattered. Skully here would definitely catch the guards' attention no matter how dense they were. She pushed the bones she could reach back toward the wall where the body had been sitting before.

Footsteps echoed down the hall, accompanied by a rattling of some kind. The sound paused briefly before starting up again, setting her teeth on edge. By the time the sound reached her cell, she saw its source. A guard was dragging his saber against the bars of each cell while holding a torch in his other hand. His features were difficult to make out through the flickering shadows of the firelight.

Steele wondered if he had been trying to scare her. What more could he think to do to her with her death already planned? Torture? She swallowed and decided to take the offensive.

"Oh, hello," she called out when he stood there and said nothing. "Hey, I know it's late, but do you have any food on you?"

The guard's head jerked, as if he were startled she was talking to him. He said nothing in return, so she chuckled.

"I could really use an apple or some bread. Or maybe some leftover stew from the palace kitchen?"

"You, thief, are not a guest here," he retorted. Sheathing his blade, he secured the torch in a mount on the wall.

"Has anyone ever compared you to a swan before?" Steele said sweetly. She scratched her head as if in deep thought and peered at his incredibly long neck. In fact, he was long everywhere and reminded her of a noodle.

"A what?" He leaned his shoulder against the bars.

"Oh, you need to get out more," she declared. She stretched her legs out in front of her before bringing her knees up to her chest. "There aren't many around here, but believe me, they are worth the stress of the travel."

"It is good to hear you in such high spirits, pretty," came a rumbling voice behind the long-necked guard, who stood up straight and jutted his chin out upon hearing the voice. Steele squinted into the shadows and saw the brawny man called Lac. "You do not have much time left to smile."

"Couldn't get enough of me? I'm flattered," she replied flatly, her teasing mood fading away.

"Cassim, pick up that torch and stop ogling her." Lac unlocked the cell door and stepped inside. He turned to Steele and smiled. "You're a sight, even covered in dirt and smelling like the rodent you are."

His approach felt almost predatory to her, and she recoiled against the wall. His grin widened, and he crouched down on his knees just in front of her. "You're lucky I have no taste for skinny rats."

Steele spat in his face. Fury glinted in his dark eyes, and he backhanded her. He reached for her, and she braced herself for another attack. Instead, Lac unlocked both the cuffs and yanked her on her feet before deftly tying her wrists behind her back.

It was only after he took his eyes off her that she licked the cut on her lip that she'd received from the blow.

Lac grabbed a piece of Steele's tunic from between her shoulder blades and tugged until her strides matched his pace, guiding her through a different door than the one she'd entered. Lac dragged her up a flight of stairs and through a hallway that was just wide enough for the two of them to walk side by side. Even though her eyes had adjusted to the dark long before and Cassim's torch lit their path, she could not make out where she was.

The trio paused for a short moment at an outer wall to the palace. There was a small wooden door that a man was guarding. He saluted Lac. "Purpose?"

"Just taking care of a little thief, soldier," Lac said.
The guard nodded and tapped on the door twice before opening it. They stepped through the door and turned left down a pathway. Two more men joined in their march, and Steele snickered.

Lac shoved her head down and grasped the back of her neck. "This is an ill-time for you to be laughing. What is it?"

Steele stumbled on an old building foundation. Her toe throbbed from yet another stumble. This was turning out to be a painful couple of days.

"I'm just surprised by the maximum security for a little girl like me," Steele finally answered, mustering up as much sweetness as she could. She smiled and batted her eyes.

"Hmm," Lac murmured and squeezed his fingers around her neck. "From someone who has evaded the King's Guard for years, I am surprised to hear you degrade yourself."

She scowled as her frustration spiked, and she turned her attention back to the uneven ground and kicked a rock, which was strangely relaxing. The sharpened bone was in her undershirt, but was still useless until she had a plan. The guards must be taking her outside the palace grounds to a place designated for executions, and the farther they went into open land, the harder it would be for her to escape and disappear. To fight off four guards would be something only a trained fighter could pull off, and while Steele considered herself strong and spry, she was in a weakened state. The last time she'd had any good food or water was two mornings prior, and her muscles continued to remind her of this fact. Her brain told her all she needed to do was get free of Lac and disappear in the shadows, but her body debated whether even this would be possible. She couldn't even climb until she'd untied herself, so she'd be stuck on the ground.

Where would she even go?

CHAPTER 12

The first glimpse of light peeked above the horizon. Normally Steele would have thought the way the sun made the desert shimmer in the distance beautiful, but even the beauty of the land could not bring peace to her heart today.

After a glance at the changing light, Lac quickened their pace. Confused, Steele speculated as to why he would be in a hurry. Maybe his shift was finished once he rid the world of her. That sick feeling returned, crawling from her stomach to her throat. If Lac was in a hurry, at least death would come quick. His sword clanked against her side.

Would she die on her knees with a sword to her throat? She shuddered as she visualized the cold metal pressing against her neck, slicing her open.

Lac pulled her shoulders up, and she found herself standing in front of something she had never seen before. A chain of large wooden crates, each five or so horses wide, stretched out across the horizon. There were at least eight of these crates, and Steele was stumped. What were these for? Transportation to the execution site? She hoped this was not where her body would be stashed once she was executed. She imagined rotting corpses already in the crates, and her stomach threatened to void herself of anything she had left in her system. She eyed the contraption warily.

"Alec. Rashim. Load this one into the last compartment of the train. The general said to keep her isolated," Lac ordered.

Steele had been so busy staring at the crates that she hadn't noticed that at least ten other guards, besides her own entourage, were hustling to lock up the boxes. She watched, puzzled, as some jumped inside them and did not exit.

To her right stood six shirtless men with gold shackles binding their wrists to collars around their necks. Thick gold chains also linked the men to one another. Each man had the most fascinating different colored markings covering their skin, as if designs had been painted onto them. She'd seen similar markings on the woman in the palace hallway who'd taken her things. She wondered briefly what they had been charged with.

One of the men's markings began to glow purple, and she squinted to get a better look. She shook her head just in case she was seeing things, but the purple glow remained. A guard took a whip and popped him, causing the glow to fade into a haze before disappearing. Hunching his shoulders, the man gripped his arm where the whip had cracked across his skin.

Alec and Rashim took her by the arms, and pushed her toward what Lac had called "the train." Alec pried a door open and hopped inside. He grabbed her by the armpits and pulled her through the door.

There was another shackled shirtless man inside, whose skin had the same interesting markings on his upper body, including his head. The only difference that she could see was that his markings were a dark blue instead of purple.

"Magi, get to your station. Captain says we're about to embark," Alec commanded, as Rashim joined them in the train.

A magi?

The magi stood almost a foot taller than the guards, but even if he had not dwarfed them, his stare would have set anyone on edge. Steele could read nothing in his eyes, and that scared her.

The magi winced then, as if he had been struck, and he moved to the wall to the right of the room, where another door opened. Steele blinked and shook her head when the blue markings began to glow, and he stepped from the room.

"I hate magi," Alec said with a whistle as the door closed. "I wish they weren't used for transportation. You never know when they will find a way to rebel."

"You know they can't, Alec. He has them under contract." Rashim grabbed a set of chains from the ground and secured them to a thick staple on the wall. He gestured for Alec to bring Steele closer.

"With those rings?" Alec scoffed. "Why don't we all get a magi anyway? Lac shouldn't be the only one granted with magis to do his bidding."

"You speak too much," Rashim scolded as he secured Steele to the wall. Her chains were long enough that she could sit down, so she slid to the ground to rest her legs.

A horn blared from somewhere, and Alec jogged over to the entrance and pulled the door shut, entombing them in darkness. Steele shuddered, wondering if this was what death would feel like. One moment the world was filled with vibrant light and activity, and the next, nothing.

She did not have to dwell on these thoughts long, thankfully, when four torches on the walls sparked and ignited. The torches must have been lit with magic, and she eyed the flames warily. She had never encountered a magi before, but she had not expected to be so frightened by one. She paused, recalling the woman who had taken her things.

She'd had strange markings along her skin. Could she have been a magi? If she was, what would she think about her people being ordered around as slaves?

The box they were in shook, knocking Alec into Rashim before both men fell to the floor. Steele would have toppled over, too, had she not been chained and already seated, but she was more concerned with the quake. She had felt the earth shake before in one of the outlying lands closer to a fire mountain, but she had never experienced one near the palace.

"What was that?" she asked Rashim, who was double-checking her chains. He ignored her and turned to his fellow guard.

"If I had a magi, I would wish for an infinite number of wishes," Alec said with a grin as he dusted off the seat of his pants. He leaned against the wall and crossed his arms.

Steele held back a snort, but Rashim did not. "Do you know nothing of magi? Their ability to grant wishes is a legend. A story told to amuse children."

Alec rolled his eyes, and studied Steele's chains with skepticism. "Is she secured?"

Rashim nodded and gestured at her. "She won't be able to get out of these. Even if she succeeded, we'd be too far away from any civilization for her to survive long in the desert."

After giving her chains a final shake, Alec nodded. He and Rashim turned and followed the magi's footsteps into the connected room. The door shut soundly behind them, and she could no longer hear them talking.

Her shoulders sank, and she relaxed against the wall, propping her arms on her knees. She had no idea where they were taking her—other than through the desert—but that did not keep relief from settling in her bones. She would take all the time she could get.

Rotating her wrists, she studied the new locks. They didn't look too different from the ones that previously held her, so she untucked her shirt, snatched the bone just before it fell out of reach, and began to fiddle with the cuffs. The iron was tricky, and she bit her lip as she wiggled the bone shiv into the hole. Blowing her hair out of her eyes, she looked around for something strong enough to stick down into the narrower part of the lock. As she studied the room, her eyes were drawn to the nails that held the floorboards down. All the nails had been expertly hammered in, but some protruded a little more than others. She studied the end of the bone before wedging it between the metal and wood, determined to try everything.

★ ☽ ★

It was getting hotter in the box. Steele wiped her brow with the sleeve on her forearm. She had managed to pry one nail about a finger's width up from the ground, but the sharp edging along the sides of the nail kept it from coming out of the floorboard. She tried jamming the bone pick against the edging and with a *crack*, the bone splintered in her hands. Frustrated tears built in her eyes, but she blinked them away and tossed the bone fragments aside. She flexed her hands before working the nail with her fingers, pushing back and forth on it until it began to wiggle.

Every muscle in her back tensed as a floorboard creaked on the other side of the connecting door. She placed her foot on top of the half uprooted nail, and she relaxed against the wall just before the door opened. Alec walked in, scratching the scruff on his face. He glanced over at her, nodded, and walked back into the other room. She heard another door open and the laughter of other guards before the door to her compartment slammed shut, muffling the sounds of merriment.

She counted to sixty before attacking the nail with even more fervor. She'd lost track of how long she had been on this train, and the dimness of the compartment was disorienting. Was it midday yet?

She jumped as the door opened again and someone stepped silently into the room. In her surprise, she had mustered up enough adrenaline to pull the nail up, but she inwardly groaned at the timing of the success.

"You do not need to be afraid," a voice drawled. Steele turned and shrank back. It was the tall magi with the blue markings. From this close up, it was clearer that the designs were a part of his skin, like a tattoo.

"You do realize it sets a person on edge when people say that," Steele countered. She tucked the nail into her palm, hoping he had not seen what she'd been doing.

The magi bowed his head and moved toward her. His walk resembled an eagle gliding over a meadow, perfectly at ease yet capable of the quickest movement to either catch its prey or retreat into the air. Was he to be her executioner?

To her surprise, he knelt before her and looked into her eyes. The coldness she had seen before was replaced with a look she could only compare to one her father used to give her. This magi meant to help her.

"Hold out your wrists," he commanded. Though she didn't think he meant her any harm, she cautiously held out her hands, unsure that his help would come without some sort of price.

His blue markings shimmered, casting a faint glow on her hands, and the iron cuffs snapped open and fell to the floor with a clang.

"Thank you," she whispered, gratitude and hope swelling in her heart. She was free.

"I need to go before they notice I am gone. Do not hesitate. Just leave," he said firmly.

"Wait! You can't come with me?" she asked as he made his way to the door.

He turned and smiled sadly before giving his head a shake. "Lac has my pridestone, and I will not abandon my brothers here."

"We can get them out, too!"

Steele faltered when he turned around and closed his eyes.

"We have our masters, and we cannot go against them." His shoulders did not slump like a defeated man, but she heard the sorrow in his tone.

"You helped me," Steele argued.

"There are...loopholes to being a magi. We cannot directly disobey whoever possesses the jewel we are bonded to, but you were not a part of my original orders." He smiled as if it hurt him to do so. "I have been gone too long." He opened the door and peeked his head in before entering the other room.

"What is your name?" she asked before he closed the door.

"Bero. And you are Steele."

She didn't have time to reply before the door shut, leaving her alone once more. Alone but free. She smiled to herself and examined the compartment. How was she to get out of here?

She tried to pry open the door through which she had entered, but it appeared to be magically sealed. There were no boarded-up windows, and she doubted leaving through the same door the magi had used would prove to be helpful. She paced and studied the room, looking for a weakness, but the room was apparently without a single flaw. She fiddled with the nail that was still firmly clutched in the palm of her hand, debating whether she would be able to create a hole in the floor to escape, when she tripped on a warped board.

"Yes!" she whispered.

The board was loose on one end, and it came up easily. Golden sand passed below and she frowned in confusion. Maybe they were on the outer edge of the city? She stuck her face through the opening and inhaled sharply. The sand was everywhere she looked. Why was the train heading into the Nasshari Desert? She glanced around a final time and was surprised to see that the train floated above the ground. She didn't see any wheels at all, and when she looked toward the end of the train, all she could see were dark marks etched into the sand, as if it were running on invisible blades. She sat up, thinking of Bero. He and the other magi she had seen earlier must be used to make the train float.

The view through the gap also revealed that there would be quite a drop to the sand below, but freedom was worth a bruise or two. She would not be able to fit through the hole with just one board gone, of course, but it was a start.

She ran her palms over the next board, feeling for any give.

It proved more difficult, but she eventually managed to get it partially dislocated from the floor by sheer determination. She held onto the edge of the board and pulled until it lurched loose. She grunted as she fell on her backside. The board flopped back into place, and she grabbed the first board to move it out of the way when she heard a door open. A glance behind her showed that the compartment was still empty, so someone must be on their way to check on her. She dropped the board back into its original position and leaped to where her chains were, quickly snapping the iron cuffs around her wrists so that they appeared to be locked.

She held her breath, praying that the guards had not heard anything suspicious. To her dismay, the door creaked open, and Lac strode in. She froze as he surveyed the room. His eyes slid over where the loose boards lay, but he didn't seem to notice anything amiss.

He walked toward her.

"What was that sound?"

Steele stretched her eyes wide, feigning innocence. "I heard nothing."

His dark eyes roamed over her body and landed on her chains where they narrowed in suspicion. Before she had time to react, his hands were around her throat. "Don't lie to me," he growled. "I've heard stories of your cunning."

She gasped for air and tried to remain still. He had not realized her hands were free, and if she didn't oppose him, maybe he would leave.

"How is it that an uneducated, sick-looking rat like you could make me look like an imbecile? I searched for you for years, ever since your first theft, but it was as if you were a shadow to the world." He pressed harder into her throat and leaned in so close that their noses were almost touching. Less than a hand's width away, he paused and murmured, "To think, I am almost free of you. When we arrive at Camp Two, I will personally see to it that you are the first one on stage. Although..." he flexed his fingers against her neck. "I could be free of you right now. If no one remembered you then, no one shall remember you now, and I doubt your presence will be missed when we arrive."

Camp Two? What's Camp Two?

Alcohol-tinged breath wafted over her face as he exhaled slowly. "I really would kill you now, but the compensation for you will be too high."

Even with that comment, however, the pressure around her windpipe increased. A bubble of panic burst in her middle, and she threw her arms forward, cuffs sliding off her wrists, and shoved her thumbs into Lac's eyes. He staggered back with a yell, releasing the grip he'd had on her neck.

While Lac clutched his face, Steele sucked air into her lungs and crouched, ready for a fight. She glanced around and grabbed one of the torches off the wall. Once she removed it from its wall mount, however, the fire died out, leaving her with a makeshift club. She held it between her and Lac, who continued to moan as he leaned against the opposite wall and held his hands over his eyes. He would recover at any moment, and his angry groaning needed to be silenced quickly.

Placing her hands on both sides of the torch, she lunged across the compartment and forcibly shoved it against Lac's throat. His hands flew from his eyes to his neck as he hit the back wall, and he tried to yell but could only emit a hoarse grunt. He reached for her, furious, but she dodged him easily and cracked the club across the back of his neck. He swayed but then regained his balance and pulled out his saber. Steele gripped her weapon and shifted her weight to the balls of her feet. A sharp saber made things more difficult, but she was confident his lumbering size would slow him down enough to give her agility an advantage. Plus, his vision was bound to be a little compromised.

An ugly sneer twisted Lac's lips, and he lunged, swinging his saber downward in her direction. She threw herself forward, but the saber still caught her on the left shoulder. Biting back a cry, she rolled expertly into a crouch. Lac staggered a few steps toward her, carried by the momentum of his swing, and he stumbled when he tried to turn around. She took advantage of his dizziness and once again crushed the club against the back of his head. This time he sank to floor with a satisfying thud.

Steele froze, her ears straining for any indication that her fight with Lac had been overheard. Nothing happened, and she hurried over to her escape route. She ripped the two boards up and peered through the sizeable gap in the floor. Soft sand flew by below her. Lac still lay unconscious, she observed, as she pushed up against the loose side of the board until she had enough space to fit through. She swallowed her fear and lowered herself through the hole.

Thinking of Bero, she frowned at the door, wishing she did not have to leave him.

"Stay safe, friend," she whispered.

She supported her weight on her elbows as she kicked her feet around, searching for a foothold. It wasn't long before she found one, and she lowered herself the rest of the way down. She grasped the beams that ran along the bottom of the train and studied the ground below her. She would much rather try to land in a sand dune, so she held on to the beams as tightly as she could, while she searched for one. She needed to find one soon, or she might find herself confronting Lac again. A dune approached, and while it was not as large as she had hoped, it would have to do. For a brief moment, she considered staying on the train, but where could she hide?

She took one last look at the ground and gulped before letting her body drop. Her arms flailed, but she tucked into a roll as soon as she landed on the sand dune. She tumbled down the hill, crying out as the grit from the ground dug into the fresh wound on her shoulder, and she landed with her face deep in the sand. She pushed herself onto her knees and spat out as much sand as she could. It clung to her lips, and she desperately wanted water.

Leaning forward on her hands, she breathed in deeply and coughed. Her throat burned from Lac's attack against her windpipe. She probed her neck with her fingertips and winced. She was going to have yet another bruise.

Steele remained on her knees until she could no longer see or hear the train. Even then, she remained where she was, letting the sun press down on her back. Finally, motivation to move returned to her, and she shaded her eyes with her hand to survey her surroundings. So this was the Nasshari Desert. "Lovely."

She ripped the bottom of her tunic and tied it around her shoulder. The cut wasn't as deep as it could have been, but it was bleeding quite a bit. Her arm already felt sticky with warm blood, and the sand clung to her. She used her right hand and her teeth to awkwardly secure the cloth.

The sun baked down on her now, and she raked her eyes over the land, hoping to spot some shade. She sighed when all she could see in every direction was sand, sand, and more sand. She almost regretted jumping from the train. Almost.

Lac had said something about stopping at a camp, and there was a possibility they could have taken Tazmeen and Ali to the same one, if they were being judged as criminals. Why else would they be taken by a group of soldiers?

Steele no longer thought Lac and his men were taking her to a place to be executed. It was too much work to transport a prisoner who was just going to be killed the moment she arrived, so the guards must be taking her elsewhere for another purpose. Either way, she needed to find Tazmeen and Ali quickly. Maybe she should have hitched a ride on the bottom of the train or found a way to climb on top until they came to an inner desert village.

She pushed herself onto her feet and slowly stood up. She hated it, but she had no idea where to go, and the only direction that she knew would end up *somewhere* was wherever the train was heading. Tracking it just might lead her to her family.

CHAPTER 13

Steele's boots protected her feet some, but the scorching sand burned through the soles as she trudged along, the sun pulsing on her back and regret shadowing her every step. Yet, if she hadn't jumped off the train, the guards would have surely found her and she would have been chained up again. Or dead. Even though Lac had said she was being taken to a camp, he'd already tried to strangle her. He had also mentioned something about compensation, but this part confused her.

Why had they bothered sentencing her if they weren't going to follow through with the punishment?

And how was Ardeth, the intriguing man at the inn, actually Prince Aldair? Life was always surprising her, but this was the biggest shock yet. He had been so kind and fascinated with everyone. Definitely not how she expected a prince to behave like. She should have been able to clearly spot a prince in the room, but he had not stuck out in the crowd, other than when his friends had spotlighted him.

So that's why his friends poked so much fun at him, she thought with a laugh. Who wouldn't take the chance to make fun of a prince if they knew they wouldn't get in trouble for it? He had blended in fairly well as a soldier, and he had been respectful to her, a commoner. Despite her initial annoyance, she had enjoyed talking with him, and he seemed to enjoy her company, as well.

And hadn't she admired his eyes as if she was a little girl looking upon her first crush? She looked up to the sky with a sheepish grin and rolled her eyes. Of course he was handsome. Women probably fawned over him frequently.

And now you're one of them.

Steele groaned and gingerly rubbed the side of her neck. She studied the sky through squinted eyes. The blue that stretched overhead was not as brilliant as those stained-glass blue eyes had been.

With a shake of her head, she dropped her gaze to the sand. She had not seen the train in hours, but while it floated above ground, the magic's impression in the sand remained deep enough for her to follow. She hoped that she could keep up with the tracks before they began to disappear.

The slight breeze picked up, swirling sand around her feet, and all thoughts of the prince and the train vacated her mind. Relishing the moment, she pulled her sweat-slicked hair off her neck using her right hand and sighed as the wind cooled her skin.

She forced her legs to jog along the tracks to make up time. Her muscles were too tired to protest, and she demanded her brain to forget exhaustion. Tazmeen and Ali, like the regret she had felt before, danced in the shadows around her, reminding her that she could not give in to the pain and fatigue now.

She alternated between jogging and walking for the next hour or so, driven and overtaken by the determination not to fail her family. Every so often, her legs would falter, and she would wonder if this was when her body would decide she was done and would collapse. Each time, however, she would muster up enough strength to continue.

The wind picked up during this state of numbness. She might have noticed it earlier had she been more alert, but even then, it would not have mattered. As the sand swirled about, stinging her arms and whipping her hair, she turned around to see a looming cloud chasing after her. Her heart sank to her toes, and her resolve broke.

"Please, no. Not now," she prayed, knowing it was futile. A sandstorm was coming regardless of her pleas. It happened quickly. The sand whirled around her, disorienting her until all she could see and breathe was sand.

With her eyes squeezed shut, she fumbled with the collar of her shirt and pulled it up over her mouth and nose. Sand whipped at her skin, and it stung. She opened one eye, attempting to focus on the now only slightly visible tracks in front of her, but she couldn't keep her eye open long. Sand clung to her, and it gritted against her eyes any time she dared to open them. Groaning in defeat, she dropped to the ground and pressed her face to her knees as the sandstorm raged around her.

She remained curled in dejection until the wind died down and the sand settled. The air felt eerily still, as if it had been hours since her entire world had been turned upside down by the tempest. She slowly sat up and looked around. The trail was completely gone.

She stood and pivoted, looking for anything that would point her in the direction of the train. She knew where the tracks had been, but what if the train turned west or east at some point while she continued south? Or what if she had been so disoriented during the storm that walked in the complete opposite direction? Either way, the desert south of the palace was massive and a place she rarely entered since her childhood. It could be days before she saw another human being.

Why did I jump from that stupid train?

She took a few deep breaths. If she panicked, she would die. Her thoughts snapped together, pushing the fear down. With the monster locked away for now, she was able to concentrate on her next step: follow where she knew the tracks had been and hope for the best. She had survived a life of hardship before now, and she could do it again.

Her resolve regained, she brushed as much sand off her clothing as she could. She carefully grazed her fingers over her sensitive shoulder and trekked south.

Cold. It was cold. Steele tried to move and groaned, opening her eyes. Blackness greeted her. When had the sun set? She wished for the sun to return, even though the mere thought of its scorching rays made her cringe. She licked her lips, recalling her thirst. Her limbs protested she pushed herself into a sitting position and tried to get her bearings. The sickle moon gave her enough light to see that the desert stretched out on all sides of her before vanishing into the darkness.

Something gritty moved against her teeth as she licked her lips again. Sand. There was sand in her mouth! She spat and then used a finger to scrape the grains out. She blinked and looked for her tracks, groaning against the dull ache in her neck. The sand was covered with footprint-shaped dimples all around her, and the feeble moonlight warped the shadows. She was definitely lost.

A frustrated sob built in her chest, scraping the walls of her throat as it burst from her mouth. Why did she ever think escaping the train was a good idea? She had no provisions, no direction, and this desert seemed endless. And, she flinched, her shoulder was extremely sore.

Her jaw ached for water, and she pressed her palms into her eyes, trying to recall the last drink she'd had. She'd been served cider and a beer at Gemma's. The prince had bought it for her. She giggled. The prince had bought her beer! Was it just beer? Her mind fuzzed, blurring out specifics.

Another stiff breeze easily cut through her thin trousers and loose short-sleeved shirt, and she desperately wished she had her coat. She had used it as a blanket in the past, and it would have provided her with some protection from the wind. Was there anything else she could use? Her heart sank as flat sand stretched in all directions and her shoulders slumped. Part of her yearned to continue searching for the train, but with no tracks to follow, she'd only do more harm than good. So if she was stuck here, she may as well try to sleep while it was cool and dark. She would need her rest for the next day.

She pushed the sand around, creating an indent large enough for her body. It didn't take her long, and when she curled into the depression, the wind was partially blocked. Bits of sand sprayed down on her, and as she shut her eyes, she prayed that no more sandstorms would come in the night.

CHAPTER 14

Steele awoke with a gasp, but remained curled on her side. She'd been having a nightmare, and while she was glad to be free from it, she found no joy in waking. She grunted and rubbed her neck, wincing at the soreness. The nightmare had started with her execution, which considering everything, wasn't surprising, but then her parents had been there, watching the scene unfold. The dream had shifted then, and she became the one watching them die. She hadn't been with them when their wagon had collided with another and overturned, but she had seen the results when their bodies were returned to Rhia, and she could imagine what it had been like. Her nightmares were born from those thoughts.

She thought of all the times Tazmeen had comforted her after a bad dream and squeezed her eyes shut. She pushed herself into a seated position, bits of sand tumbling from her clothing. She opened her eyes and groaned, her head spinning, but she needed to get up. She couldn't find Tazmeen or Ali if she remained curled up in the desert.

Why did the sand look so much like water? The grains rose and fell and rippled across her vision. She rubbed her eyes, and the motion stopped. She was seeing things. Her stomach tightened as anxiety blossomed in her mind, but she pushed it away. If she kept going, she was bound to find water somewhere.

She struggled to stand and held her arms out, wobbling on unsteady legs. She forced her legs forward, shoving down the urge to worry over how wobbly her limbs were. As she trudged through the sand, she had to admit that one positive thing to being this deep in the desert was the open sky. It was incredibly blue, giving her freedom to breathe, and while the sun could be torturously overbearing, occasionally there were moments when it felt like the light was simply smiling down on her. If she ever found another horse, she would gallop through these lands with strange appreciation and respect.

She moaned as the muscles in her legs cramped. Born from where the desert meets the mountains, she prided herself on being tough, but now she was being challenged in a way she had never dreamed.

As she walked, she thought of a plan to keep herself from focusing on her present situation. First thing, get out of the desert. Her best bet would be finding one of the groups of nomads roaming the Nasshari. They were rumored to be dangerous, but she had nothing to lose by trying. At the very least, she could work for food and water and regain her strength, and maybe they would help her get out of the desert. Then she could track down those guards who took Tazmeen and Ali. She didn't know how to extract the information of her family's whereabouts from the men, but she *would* find them.

Once she did, they could go home and put this whole mess behind them. She frowned and stumbled, coming to a halt. She was still a convicted thief, and once word got back to the palace that she'd escaped, she might have an even more difficult time evading the guards.

She whimpered and moved forward again, head bowed from the heat of the sun. What had her life become? What could she do? She couldn't ask Tazmeen to leave Solarrhia for her. Tazmeen had a life for herself there with Ali and her sewing business, and Steele only had a date with an executioner waiting for her. What a mess.

She walked for what felt like hours, until her stomach twisted and her throat ached for water in a way that was impossible to ignore. She glanced behind herself to see how far she'd come, and her tracks shimmered and undulated against the sand. She watched the tracks swing from side to side and she squeezed her eyes shut, head swaying.

A part of her knew that her mind was playing tricks on her. Fear tickled at her nerves, but she was so very tired. She needed to find water soon. If she squinted at the horizon line, the air sparkled like water. The sun pulsed down on her, and she peered up at it and then back at the skyline. Maybe the sun was actually trying to encourage her. She'd heard that the sun could make watery mirages in the desert, but maybe this time it was guiding her. The sun really was a nice thing. She swayed.

If I lie down and soak in your light will you tell me if I'm going the right way?

She sat down and flopped onto her back, her shoulder barely throbbing now. She stared at the sky and grinned at the sun, waiting to feel led by it. Light filled her eyes, and when the brightness became unbearable, she turned her gaze away. The sun was not as kind as she had once thought. It didn't want to help her; it wanted to blind her. She sat up and rubbed her calves, scolding herself for being so silly.

Something copper flickered at the edge of her vision, and she froze. She slowly turned to the left, and squinted. A blurry figure standing on a dune. She shaded her eyes with her hand, and her jaw dropped when the scene slid into focus. There before her stood one of the rarest creatures in the world—a unicorn.

The unicorn stood tall on the dune, as if observing her down below. He stood like the king of his species, regal and wise. When he stamped the ground, sand jumped up and danced around his caramel body, which easily blended in with the desert. His red mane and tail stood out like the flame-colored stripes on his legs.

Steele had never seen a unicorn before, and she openly gaped at him. Barely believing her luck, her eyes traveled to the horn on his head. Red swirled in with the caramel until the colors fused with white at the base, melting into his forehead. He looked like he had been born of sand and fire.

She struggled to her feet, and then cautiously stepped forward, her hand outstretched low, in front of her hips. A part of her wondered if she was making the right choice, but she also thought she might be seeing things. She had already mistaken the sand for water, after all.

Another step and the animal bowed his head and pawed at the ground again. Steele staggered to a stop, her arm frozen in front of her. He might think she meant to harm him. The tip of his horn shimmered in the sunlight, and she wrinkled her nose, imagining how easily he could kill her with that horn. The unicorn snorted. Instinct told her to crouch, so she did, resting her forearms on her knees.

"I wish I knew if this was real or not," she muttered.

Red-tipped ears flicked toward her, and she blinked. Would a mirage react like that? She lowered her eyes to the sand and dragged her fingers through the grains.

When I look up, he'll be gone.

It made sense that her mind would conjure up one of the rare creatures, but she was disappointed by the idea, nonetheless. Maybe when she looked up, the unicorn would be joined by a phoenix and a firecat. If she was losing her mind, she could try to make it entertaining at least.

Hot air puffed against her hairline, and she stopped breathing. That felt real enough. She stared at her doodles in the sand, afraid that looking up would startle the creature. The unicorn moved his head down toward her shoulder, pressing his jowl against her left cheekbone. She slowly lifted her hand toward the horse and rested her palm against his cheek, her heart fluttering.

He pulled his head out of her grasp, but he did not step away. Steele looked up and moved her hand to the bridge of his nose.

"I'm Steele," she croaked, her voice anything but inviting or relaxing. Her throat yearned for moisture.

She almost expected the unicorn to talk back, but he behaved like a normal horse, giving her a blank stare.

"I don't have anything for you, I'm sorry." She bowed her head and slowly stood. She tentatively reached out and rubbed his nose. He nodded his head in her hand, using her as a scratching post. She giggled and gently patted his neck. "I think I'm lost. Will you help me?"

The unicorn snorted again, and she gasped as he lowered himself to the sand. He grunted, twisting his head around to look at her, as if beckoning her onto his back. She hesitated, then stepped forward and slid her leg over him.

She gripped the creature's fiery mane and settled awkwardly on his back. The unicorn waited a moment before lurching to his feet, and Steele gripped his sides with weak legs. Her head spun, and she squeezed her eyes shut, willing the dizziness to subside. She released his mane, placing her hands on his shoulders, and breathed evenly through her nose.

"Okay," she said through gritted teeth, "please take me out of this place."

The unicorn swung his head from side to side, ears twisting, before turning to the left. Steele wobbled on his back and splayed her palms over his shoulders to steady herself. The sun was relentless as they walked through the desert, and sweat rolled down Steele's body. A bead dropped from her nose to the unicorn's back, and she glared at the traitorous liquid.

Stop sweating, she commanded herself. Didn't her body know it needed that moisture?

She rolled up the sleeves of her shirt so that her shoulders were bare but for the bandage. Without warning, the unicorn broke into a canter, and Steele scrambled, grasping for his mane as she slid backward. She hissed air in through her teeth as the movement stung her cut.

"Thanks," she mumbled.

The unicorn flicked an ear at her, but continued loping across the sand. She knew she should be committing this ride to memory, but all she could focus on—now that she wasn't about to fall off—was the breeze. While they walked, the air had been still, but at a canter, a wind blew against her face and arms. She sighed in relief.

When the unicorn slowed, Steele wasn't sure if they'd been moving for hours or minutes. The animal wasn't breathing hard, but his sandy coat shimmered with sweat. Again, the unicorn swung his head from side to side, as if he was searching for something. The horse flung his head back, piercing the air with a melodic whinny, and she nearly toppled from his back in surprise. The horse trumpeted a second time and then stood still on all fours, ears pricked forward.

Silence greeted them, and the unicorn snorted, sounding frustrated. Steele giggled. "What're you looking for?" she asked, patting his neck. The unicorn rolled an eye back to look at her and shook his nose up and down. Steele tilted her head, perplexed by his behavior. Having been around horses most of her life, she should know what he was trying to communicate, shouldn't she? But her mind was fuzzy, and she rubbed her eyes. When she lowered her hands, they were shaking.

She swayed as the unicorn started walking again, and she used his withers for balance. Her shoulders pumped up and down, keeping in time with his steps, and her head dropped forward. As long as the unicorn decided to stay at a walk, she could probably fall asleep.

"No," she muttered, pulling her head up. "No, I shouldn't fall asleep."

On and on they walked, until the sun didn't seem as hot or as bright. Steele risked a glance at it and frowned. It still hung in the sky, but the light didn't hurt her eyes like it had before. Panic filled her heart. Was she going blind? Dal had mentioned something about sun-blindness before, hadn't he? Her head slumped forward again, and she moaned.

The unicorn paused to look at her, nickering quietly. She returned his gaze, and he pawed the ground before turning his head forward again. Unsure of what he meant to communicate, she gripped his mane and pressed her legs against his ribs. The animal lurched forward into a gallop, and she struggled to maintain her grip. Her hands felt so weak, and her legs were quivering.

They flew across the sand until her hands slipped. The unicorn slowed and snorted, this time sounding worried.

"I'm sorry," she whispered. "I can't hold on."

The unicorn continued to walk, and she grunted. He seemed to be walking faster than earlier in the day, and it made for a much bumpier ride.

Hunger was gnawing at her insides, and she welcomed the distraction. The gritty dryness was still in her mouth, and she still ached for water, but hunger pangs were something she was used to. The growling in her stomach brought a sense of normalcy to the situation. If she could ignore her thirst, she could pretend she was riding a stolen horse to another village. She'd done this dozens of times. She was fine. They were almost to the village, weren't they?

Sand stretched in every direction, the vastness of it destroying Steele's imagination as sense of hopelessness settled over her. She scooted back and dropped her forehead against the side of the unicorn's neck. Closing her eyes, she breathed in, smiling at how a unicorn smelled like a regular horse. Spar would probably have found that funny.

Suddenly, Steele was falling. She sat up and clung to the unicorn to keep from tumbling to the ground. It was then that she realized she hadn't been falling, but that unicorn had lain down. She sat on his back, unsure of what to do. The horse jerked, rocking his body, and she slid off and into the sand. Before she could turn around, the unicorn was back on his feet and stepping away from her.

Desperation clawed at her insides, and she scrambled through the sand. "No, please, please don't leave," she begged, fear trembling in her voice.

The unicorn trotted toward her, briefly touching his nose to her shoulder before spinning away and vanishing in a spray of sand.

CHAPTER 15

A tear slid down Steele's cheek and onto her dried lips. Why had the unicorn abandoned her now? Why had he come to her in the first place? She dipped her fingers into the sand, closed her fist, and relished the feeling of the silky sand slipping through her grasp. As it fell from between her fingers, it had a fluid look about it, and she raised her hand to her mouth. The moment the sand touched her cracking lips, she spat and coughed, appalled by what she had done. Her knees had sunken deeper into the soft sand as if she was rooted there. Is this what became of people who wandered too far in the desert? Did the lands take them, claiming them as its prize?

I'm going to die out here.

The slice on her shoulder was stiff and burned as she moved, and she pulled the collar of her shirt down to look at the cut. It had stopped bleeding after she had changed the bandage, but without treatment, it wouldn't heal right.

What's the point in worrying about this?

She shut her eyes against the wave of dejection spreading through her.

"No," she whispered. "You're still alive. One thing at a time," she croaked, shaking her head. "One thing at a time."

A white light flashed in the corner of her eye. She rubbed her eyes and squinted. Yes, the gleam she saw was in fact a cloud of water coming toward her.

That's strange.

She grinned anyway. Water! The cloud grew larger and even snorted like a horse at times. Oh, in the midst of the cloud was the form of a horse. A horse cloud.

"I thought I was hallucinating for a moment!" The horse cloud said.

She knew horses didn't talk, but she shrugged. The unicorn must have brought her to this water-cloud thing for a reason. Had to be magic.

The cloud separated, and a man formed from the mist and knelt beside her. She slowly turned to look at him, but it was hard to focus. His eyes were the color of water reflecting the bluest of skies, and right now they were the most beautiful color she had ever seen.

"Here." The man with the water-colored eyes extended a pouch toward her, but no matter how hard she tried, her arms remained by her sides. Her body no longer wanted to respond.

Her eyes drifted back to his face where a jagged scar ran down his right cheek, cutting into his full beard. He pursed his lips and lifted the pouch to her mouth so that the gloriously cool liquid dribbled onto her chapped lips. They burned, but this burn was different than the pain in her shoulder. This pain brought hope, and suddenly her shaking hands were cupping the pouch, tilting it higher.

"How long has she been in the desert do you think?" part of the horse cloud asked.

Steele blinked and shook her head. There was no cloud in front of her. In fact, what she had imagined to be a cloud was actually a group of three men on horses—a long buckskin, a palomino, and a gray. She squinted. No, the buckskin wasn't long; it was two horses standing close together. She shook her head, and the one long horse separated into a buckskin and a paint. Four horses. Three men. Why only three? She looked for a fourth man or woman, but found no one.

"I'm not sure, but there isn't a village for hours. She must have been caught out in that sandstorm," one of the three men stated.

Steele searched for the man with clear-blue eyes, but he had retreated back to the buckskin and was digging through a saddlebag.

Another dark haired man appeared next to her and extended a hand. He smiled crookedly. The inviting expression transformed into concern as he studied her more closely. "You are injured."

She looked up at him and hesitated before placing her hand in his, pushing down to steady herself in an attempt to stand. She stumbled in the process, and he placed his free hand on her elbow to help. Legs trembling, she tried again, but they wouldn't support her. The man's face slid in and out of focus, but she did notice a nicely shaped nose and a scar. His was finer than the other man's, and it cut down from the side of his nose to the edge of his upper lip.

She tried to speak, to thank them, but all she could do was cough. Her throat ached. Why did her throat ache? Since her voice failed her, she nodded and did her best to smile. He seemed to understand, his eyes—an intense, brilliant blue—studying her every breath. Those eyes seemed strangely familiar, as did that crooked smile. She knew this man.

The third man had yet to appear by her side. Instead, he sat upon his golden horse, scouting the area. "Aldair, would you like to set up camp here? It will be dark soon."

Aldair? The wheels in Steele's head wrenched, but her mind felt as if a fog had settled in.

"Yes, Kaleel, thank you. Em, we need to get her out of the sun," said the familiar man with brilliant eyes.

The water-colored eye man called Em crouched beside her. "Is it okay if we move you? We need to take a look at your shoulder and get you out of the heat."

"You're an angel, really," Steele's throat caught, and she coughed again. A triumphant smile tickled her lips. She'd managed one sentence, so she tried for another. "Did the unicorn send you?"

The two men looked at each other before Em nodded and moved out of Steele's line of vision.

"Did you say you saw a unicorn?" The man named Aldair asked.

Steele nodded, waving her hand around. "I know you from somewhere." She tried once again to stand, but her stomach swayed and her vision swam. She stilled, holding out her arms for balance.

The familiar blue eyes examined her face more closely. A hand hovered over her face, and he hesitated briefly before gently pushing her hair behind her ears. His eyes widened, and he nodded.

He leaned forward, fingers lightly running across her cheeks, and exclaimed, "You're supposed to be dead! I thought you looked familiar, but I was sure it was just my guilt." Steele suddenly found herself crushed to his chest, and he released a joyous laugh. "How are you here?"

She twitched an eyebrow at him when he released her, and his joy faded slightly as he regarded her. "Are you dead and haunting me because I didn't save you from execution?" His voice was sober now. "I tried. I spoke with my father and told him I knew you and wanted to get more information, but he would not hear of it. I was told you had already been executed."

She heard what he'd said, but her eyes glazed as he continued to speak. The cadence in his speech, that face with that scar, those eyes. She knew him from a tableside, but the prominent memory featured him sitting next to the king. "You're the prince!" she rasped. Then she added weakly, "You're not an angel sent from the unicorn, then."

He shook his head.

"You tried to speak for me?" She rubbed her temple, convinced she had to be dreaming. First a unicorn, and now the prince? Impossible.

He nodded. "I can't say stealing was right, but I pride myself on having good instincts and those said not to give up on you." He stepped forward and helped her stand. She wobbled a bit, but her legs held. "Now, we need to look at that shoulder, and you need more water. Steele, correct?"

She nodded, still rubbing her temple and processing. Did he not know she'd been on a train? She moved to take a step forward and stumbled, the prince catching her elbow for a second time. Her legs simply were not functioning. She could stand, but she would rather lie down and take a nap. The prince must have felt her weight buckle as his grip shifted from her elbow to her shoulders while his other arm scooped under her legs, and then she was in his arms.

"I can do it," she breathed. His chest vibrated against her ear as he chuckled.

"I believe you," he replied, his tone sprinkled with suppressed mirth. "This is faster, and we want to get the horses out of the sun as well."

"Oh." She nodded, her eyes closing, "Yes. The horses must get a break." Her head slumped against his shoulder, and she closed her eyes.

Her throat felt like fire when she swallowed, and coughing hurt, despite her needing to. She tried to wheeze to keep from coughing. Still, the burn returned, and tears leaked from her closed eyelids. She opened her eyes at the wetness on her cheeks, and vaguely wondered how she had any moisture left in her body to produce tears.

The prince sped up his pace. His blurry face peered down at her. "Em, can you get my water pouch?"

The light of the sun dimmed as they stepped underneath a covering the men had set up. The swaying stopped, and she was lowered onto a soft blanket. Something cool and wet pressed against her lips, and water dribbled into her mouth and down her chin. She'd never tasted anything so wonderful. She reached up for the pouch but Prince Aldair's companion, Em, held it just out of reach.

"You must take it easy, lady," he insisted. "I know it seems absurd, but too much water at once will make you ill."

Steele licked her lips and struggled to sit up. A hand pushed down on her shoulder, and she remained propped on her elbows.

"My name is Emdubae," the man added. "But please call me Em."

She looked up at Emdubae and found herself wanting to trust him. He reminded her of her father in the way he smiled, his lips curving up mostly on the right.

The prince stood behind Emdubae but she didn't see the other man.

"Thank you," she breathed. For the water, for finding her, for helping her—all this she wanted to say, but couldn't get out. She hoped they understood how deep her gratitude went.

"I will need to take a look at your shoulder," Emdubae said. "But I think you need to lie down before we work on it. It's going to hurt and it will be better for you if you've rested some first." Turning to the prince, he lowered his voice a fraction. "To help her fully recover, we should remain here until tomorrow at least. That short of a delay should not hinder our plans."

Steele thought she saw the prince nod, but her vision blurred. While she was sure he was speaking, he sounded muted as if she were listening to him from underwater.

Water.

Licking her dry, cracked lips, she closed her eyes and tried to rest, but her mind buzzed, refusing to shut off. Her thoughts jumped from the palace, to the prince, to the magi, before stopping on Tazmeen and Ali. Her heart hurt as she thought of them. She had to find them before it was too late, but how could she now that she had lost the train?

She peeked at Prince Aldair who was talking to the scout. He was lanky in comparison to the prince, with longer, curling dark hair. He had an unassuming air about him. It was likely he could easily fade into a crowd.

Kal something is his name, she thought. *Kaleel.*

She wanted to sleep, but they were strangers. They had saved her, yes, but that didn't mean she trusted them enough to relax. They were from the palace, and she was a thief. She doubted they would let an escaped prisoner get very far from them. She had spent her entire thieving life doing all she could to avoid men like these. Her head throbbed and she moaned, pressing the heels of her palms to her eyes.

"Unable to sleep?" Emdubae asked, kneeling beside her.

"I can't relax," she whispered, lowering her palms to glance at him.

Emdubae pursed his lips, frowning slightly. "You are safe now. I promise no harm will come to you."

"Maybe not today," she said heavily.

His frown deepened, and then he sighed. "Tell me, how did you escape the palace?"

She did her best to smirk. "I have many talents." She cringed. That sounded much better in her head.

Prince Aldair's eyes flicked over to her, then back to the map Kaleel had just pulled from a bag.

Emdubae's water-blue eyes squinted as he smiled. "It *is* good to see you alive."

"Thank you," she whispered. "It's good to be alive."

Prince Aldair returned to them, holding a freshly wetted cloth. He passed it along to Emdubae who sniffed it. "Where did you get lavender? Your mother's washroom?"

The prince's eyes twinkled. "Actually, Kaleel can't seem to part with the salts. He made sure there was room."

"You should be thanking me," Kaleel called out from outside the covering.

Emdubae snickered but grew more serious as he motioned to her neck. "I can't help but notice your bruises. They look new."

"A small price to pay." Steele fingered her neck gently. "I don't think those herbs will help me sleep."

"They have a solid reputation," Emdubae said. "Or you might try telling her one of your stories, Aldair. That could put her to sleep faster than this." He chuckled, easily dodging the half-hearted punch Prince Aldair threw his way.

The prince turned to her. "Would you like to hear something?"

"I don't remember the last time someone told me a story." Her lips pulled into a smile, and she closed her eyes. "I would like it to be real though. I've had enough imagination for the day."

He laughed. "All right."

Steele briefly cracked an eye open to look at him. His nose wrinkled as he thought, and she could almost hear him mulling over something to talk about. Finally he laughed once.

"Did you know that the royal family is permitted to speak to dragons?" he asked.

She furrowed her brow, but kept her eyes closed. "No?" She questioned in a whisper.

"Try not to speak. Just nod or shake your head. Did you even know dragons existed?"

She nodded.

"Really?" The prince sounded surprised. "Most people consider dragons to be nothing but a pixie-tale."

She opened her mouth to talk, to tell him that her parents had taught her all about dragons and phoenixes and unicorns, but the prince placed a finger across her lips, silencing her.

"I told you not to speak." Steele thought she heard a smile in his voice. "Just relax, and I will tell you about the dragons while we rest here."

She nodded, content to lie back and listen. She enjoyed listening to stories and had always been curious about dragons. The prince was right: most people thought them fictional beasts of folk lore. Considering all the inconsistencies in people's stories, she was curious to hear the truth.

"Once upon a time—"

"I said a real story!" Steele protested, her voice cracking at the wrong moment making her sound petty and childish. She gave him her best glare, and he replied with a perturbed look.

"Let me finish." He ignored her frown and continued. "Once there was a prince, who lived in one of the best kingdoms in the world. He was a younger brother, second in line to the throne, but all he really wanted to do was ride on his stallion and fly with the dragons. His older brother and best friend—though sometimes his greatest enemy depending on the day—tried to make the younger prince a more serious boy, but *nothing* ever took his mind off the dragons." His voice had a wistful tone to it, and Steele wanted to open her eyes to look at him, to see the expression on his face. But her eyelids felt like they weighed a thousand pounds each, so she lay there, content to just listen.

"You see," he continued, "for hundreds of years, the royal families have had a covenant with the dragons. As a coming-of-age ceremony, when a member of the royal family turns thirteen, he or she is taken on a journey into the Farest'Del Mountains to speak with the dragons. Every young prince and princess dreams of the day they will meet the magnificent flying beasts. Their tutors drill them with proper dragon etiquette like what to say and how to move your body when you are around them. Dragons are extremely dignified. They understand people, but sometimes the way we move or phrase sentences can greatly insult them and it would never do for a possible king or queen to insult the dragons.

"Dragons communicate with people through the mind, and this prince was extremely curious about how that was possible. They were obviously magical creatures, like magi, but could he learn to speak with others in the same way? That would be a very important skill to have as a member of the royal family. Think of all the tricks he could play on his brother!" He gave a soft chuckle, and she could feel her mouth curve into an easy smile.

"The day finally came when the younger prince looked into the trees he had to pass before reaching the cliff where the dragons would be, he swallowed nervously. His brother observed the boy's restrained terror and squeezed his shoulder. The younger brother smiled gratefully at the encouragement, and he set off up the hill and through the trees...." The prince trailed off. Steele wondered if he was thinking of his brother, Hadrian.

"Anyway," he cleared his throat and continued, "the boy reflected on the four days it took to get to this point as he headed up the rocky terrain. The days had passed so quickly. He did not feel very tired at all, although he knew this to be a mix of nerves and excitement. He exited the forested area and stepped onto a rocky outcropping on the edge of a cliff. It was so high up, he felt a bit light-headed and extremely vulnerable as he walked along the ridge. Warily, he sat down near the point, clinging to the rock. The winds were much stronger than he had anticipated, making it difficult for him to find any security in his resting spot, but he must stay here and watch for the dragon.

"He waited, wondering if maybe the dragons had found him unworthy, his heart sinking into the pit of his stomach. Tears filled his eyes as he debated returning to his family with a shame as enormous as this or disappearing in the mountains, living off the land and seeking to find honor again. He was just about to promise the Creator that he would not use mind-speak against his brother or anyone else when he heard it: a great, rhythmic thumping sound unlike anything he had ever heard. The thrumming was so deep it rattled his bones, and he eagerly searched the skies for the beast, surprisingly unable to place where it was coming from. One moment, he sat there listening to the thunderous thumping, and the next, a great white dragon rose up before him. The dragon perched lightly on the rock in front of the boy, folding his wings neatly behind his back. His long, reptile tail curled up to rest on the rock behind the boy's back."

Steele opened her eyes when he paused. He rubbed the stubble on his chin and grabbed a water pouch. He tipped it toward her, but she declined. With a shrug, he took a long drink.

A small smile played on the prince's lips once he was done with the water. "That dragon was one of the most beautiful creatures this prince had ever seen. Tears, not from shame this time, fell down his cheeks, though he quickly wiped them away. The dragon waited a moment before speaking, and even with all his training, the boy flinched as the voice resounded in his skull. The boy had thought he had felt vulnerable before as he walked along the cliff, but now he felt transparent before this magnificent creature, unable to hide any darkness inside." He paused a beat. "Unfortunately, the story has to end there. The young prince swore never to speak the contents of that conversation to anyone outside the family, and even if he could, he would assure you that you would probably be very bored."

"You need to work on the ending a bit," she said, the corners of her lips turning slightly upward. "Are the royals the only people who can ever see and speak to the dragons?"

It was something she had always wondered about. One rumor said that if you ever saw a dragon, it would be the last thing you ever saw.

"The dragons keep to themselves in the mountains without bothering us because we made a pact with them many years ago. If a dragon comes down to our town, we have permission to kill it. Any dragon coming that low is probably sick or has intentions to kill. On the other hand, if any human goes into the Farest'Del Mountains, the dragons have permission to kill the human. Breaches in this agreement are rare, but they have happened. Usually on the human end. As a peaceful race, dragons are very respectful of the arrangement."

Steele pursed her lips. So at least some of the stories the townsfolk told about dragons were real...to a point. The village children were told that if they wandered off too far, the terrifying dragons would snatch them up and take them back to their caves to eat them. Steele herself had been nervous wandering too far from her parents' watchful eyes, even though they had never participated in such story-telling. They had believed in brutal honesty rather than making up a story about faraway beasts wreaking havoc on troublemakers.

Still, her neighbors did not hold the same convictions, and she found herself cowering at shadows in the skies whenever she was alone in the streets. As she grew older, she realized that the stories were told to scare the children into not running away and that the adults really didn't believe in the tales. Even so, there were enough stories about people wandering into the mountains or deserts and vanishing, to make a person wary of venturing out too far anyway.

Emdubae approached where Steele was curled on the bedroll and squatted down so he could look her in the eyes. "How are you feeling? Would you like to try using the herbs to relax?"

Steele flashed him a grateful smile. "My throat hurts, but it's feeling better than before. The air in the desert was so hot I felt as though every breath was blistering my insides." Her neck was also sore where she had been choked, but to complain about that would be pointless. Besides, she was afraid that if she began, a dam would burst, and she'd never stop finding something to be negative about. "Some water would be nice, if there is a little more to spare." She sat up, ignoring how her arms wobbled, and stretched her neck from side to side. She was still woozy, but her thoughts seemed to be coming together well enough.

Kaleel sauntered into view then. "Drink this," he said, holding a pouch out to her. He waggled his eyebrows. "It will make you feel like you're soaring higher than an eagle!"

Seeing him up close, he had a wild look in his dark eyes, and she eyed him warily as she took the pouch.

Prince Aldair rolled his eyes at Kaleel. "What he means is that it will energize you. Make you feel better."

She took a tentative sip of the drink and a tingling coolness spread through her limbs. Emdubae chuckled as he wrapped the rag around her forehead and she felt him tugging the ends, knotting it into place. It smelled faintly of something unfamiliar but also relaxing. As she reached to push the rag higher above her eyebrows, the sight of her arms alarmed her. The parts of her skin that had been exposed to the sun were an angry red and covered in blisters.

With a feather light touch to her cheeks, she determined that her face must be in a similar state. "Augh! What happened to me?"

"You've never had a sunburn before?" Kaleel asked.

"A minor one, yes." She looked back down at her arm. "These blisters, though..."

Emdubae smiled at her. "I can't say I am surprised. The sun is brutal in the Nasshari and you must have been out there for hours."

Was it hours or days? Steele thought she had slept at least a night, but it was impossible to know for sure.

She offered Emdubae a weak smile. "Will my skin heal?"

"We have a salve for such occasions. With your permission?"

Emdubae held out a small bowl, revealing green gunk inside. She eyed it before nodding and was quickly rewarded with a cooling sensation that calmed the stinging as he slathered it on her skin.

"Thank you," she sighed in relief. Emdubae gave her a smile and she started, a memory surfacing. "I've seen you before."

"From court?"

"No, from years ago. I passed you in the streets once." She pointed to the deep scar on his cheek. "Your wound was fresh then."

Emdubae looked up at her. "That was a long time ago. I'm surprised you remember."

"It was a memorable gash, and not many people have eyes as light-blue as yours," she replied with a shrug.

A knife flashed in front of her eyes, and Steele flinched back as Kaleel crouched beside her. "You must be hungry?" She shook her head, but her stomach betrayed her with a loud growl, and Kaleel chuckled. "I can cook us some dinner if you like?" he asked, looking to the prince.

"That sounds wonderful, Kaleel, thank you," Prince Aldair said, offering her another water pouch.

While she sipped from the pouch, she studied the men and the gear they had packed into the small tent. So far they had contradicted everything she'd believed about soldiers and royalty with their kindness and she wanted to believe it was genuine, but still she was wary. "So what's a prince doing out here in the desert. Don't you have a kingdom to help run?"

The prince laughed once. "My father can run things just fine without me. He's probably missing these two more." Kaleel nodded from where he knelt and the prince gave his head a shake before continuing. "Emdubae is a captain in the Kings Guard, and Kaleel is a lieutenant."

Kaleel snorted. "I prefer to be called the Reaper."

"No one but you calls you that," Emdubae said with a laugh.

"Anyway," Prince Aldair said, looking from the men to Steele. "We are following a lead. Where were you headed when we found you? And how did you get this far into the desert without a horse?"

"Following a lead," she repeated with a small smirk.

"Oh?" He smiled. "A lead? What sort of lead."

Her lips twitched, but she said nothing.

"You will not tell me?"

A part of her wanted to tell him everything she had heard on the train, but the soldiers responsible for her presence in the desert were also employed by the palace. If Lac was involved with the camp, then who was Steele to say that the king was not supportive of the entire situation?

The prince tilted his head, "I guess you are used to keeping secrets in your line of work." Her eyes shot up to meet his, and he laughed. "It was such a shock to see you that day. It took everything to not let on that I knew you."

Steele huffed. "You were shocked? I thought you were just some man I would never see again, and then you turned out to be the prince! And I was being tried for such a serious crime..." She trailed off, dropping her gaze.

"I wish I could have done something to save you. I didn't want for you to be executed," the prince said softly.

"Well in case you didn't notice, I don't really need anyone to save me. I can take care of myself." She tried to sound confident, but his unexpected support gave her a pause. For a moment they were no longer in the desert, but in Azubah, connecting over drink and conversation. This...pull she felt toward him confused her.

He arched an eyebrow. "And in the desert? You were on the edge of roasting to death."

"I've been in tricky situations before. I would have figured it out." She avoided his eyes and wondered if he felt a similar connection to her. A part of her, a small part, hoped he did. She shifted uncomfortably as she realized that. She didn't know this man. What did it matter what he thought of her?

Prince Aldair eyed the bruises on her neck, and his eyes traveled to her left shoulder. "We should clean that cut now."

She shrugged, testing the soreness in her shoulder. Her skin tightened as the dried blood cracked open around the gash, and she ducked her head to hide her wince. A smoky smell drifted in through the tent as the fire snapped and cracked outside, and Kaleel hummed to himself as he cooked the meal.

Emdubae appeared with a cloth and a basin of warm water. He reached for the grimy bandage wrapped around her shoulder, and she shied back from him.

"I'd like to unwrap it, if that's okay." It was a statement, not a question, so the men let her do as she wished. The blood had dried to the cloth and it was almost impossible to pull the cloth away without groaning in pain. By the time the last bit of cloth was removed, the wound had reopened, sending fresh blood trickling down her arm. She wrinkled her nose. "I'm surprised it's bleeding so much; the cut itself is not very deep."

Emdubae hesitantly reached for her shoulder again, and this time she leaned toward him. He tried to gently scrub away the sand, dirt and blood, but even the gentlest of swipes seemed to grind sand into the wound.

"Does it hurt?" the prince questioned.

She turned to him with raised brows. "Of course it hurts."

He used an extra cloth to mop up the blood that had run down her arm. "You must have a higher pain tolerance that I do. It looks extremely painful, but you wouldn't know it looking at your face. How did you receive such a gash?"

She gritted her teeth and ignored his question. "I've learned to control my emotions. If you show pain, you show weakness. People can take advantage of weaknesses."

She noticed the men exchange a glance out of the corner of her eye, but she ignored them, having accepted long ago that this was the truth. At least, it was in her field of work. Once, she had thought differently, waltzing up to an owner of a mare who was probably beyond saving at that point. Even so, even an hour of relief from the man's so-called-care would have been enough. Steele recalled the man's face when she had requested to take the mare off his hands. He had scoffed, and she had snapped, yelling at him for his cruelty. To her horror, he had taken the mare—his possession as he called her—and beat her right there, relishing in Steele's pain.

It had been a valuable lesson to learn, to keep her emotions under control so that no one could hurt her or those she cared for. That mare had passed during the night, and Steele blamed herself, knowing she could have done more.

She sighed deeply, caught up in thought, and both men looked up at her.

"Are you all right, my lady?" Emdubae asked.

"Yes. It really doesn't hurt anymore." She jerked her head toward her shoulder.

The prince wrung out his cloth. "That wasn't a painful-sounding sigh. You sounded sad."

"Oh. I was just thinking about a horse." The men stopped cleaning her shoulder, probably hoping for her to open up, but she wasn't willing to give them that. "She was a beautiful mare, and I couldn't save her."

"What made you think of her?" Prince Aldair asked.

Steele clamped her jaw shut and dropped her eyes to her shoulder. "I guess that cut was deeper than I thought."

He frowned. "All right, keep your secrets."

Kaleel reappeared then and held a plate under her nose. A steaming hunk of meat sat on the plate, and Steele's mouth watered.

"How about a meal before they sew you up?" He set the plate on her knees, and she pulled the meat apart with her fingers, too hungry to care about proper etiquette.

"Thank you," she mumbled between bites.

Kaleel leaned over Emdubae's shoulder and pointed to her shoulder. "If Batya had come with us, we would be able to heal it quicker so there wouldn't be much of a scar."

Emdubae smiled at her as he held up a needle and thread. "Now this is going to hurt. I am sorry to have to do this to you, but there really is no other way."

"Wait one moment, Em," the prince motioned to Kaleel, and the man disappeared to the other side of the tent. When he returned, he was holding a copper flask.

She took it and sniffed the opening. It was alcohol.

Prince Aldair laughed. "It's better to finish it all at once."

Steele tipped her head back, swallowed the contents of the flask, and her throat burst into flames. She coughed, sputtered, and glared at the prince.

He nodded, a small grin on his mouth. "It will help to take the edge off, and I bet you'll sleep through the night."

The effect was almost instant. Her limbs sagged in relaxation, and her skin tingled, growing numb. "Let's just get this over with," she murmured.

The needle pierced her skin, and she couldn't help jumping away from the jab. "If that drink takes the edge off, I don't want to know what this would feel like without it," she said.

The prince held out his hand toward her. "You can squeeze as hard as you want."

She hesitated before taking a deep breath and gently placing her hand in his. His skin was rough, calloused in a way you wouldn't expect of a member of the royal family. These were the hands of a working man, possibly from wielding a blade.

He squeezed her fingers, and she looked up at his face. Those eyes still reminded her of stained-glass. They were brighter here than they had been in the inn, though. He smiled sympathetically, and a sharp pain exploded in her shoulder, surging up through her spine to her head. Her instincts told her to run, but she bit down on her lower lip hard and grunted into her closed mouth.

She tilted her head to look at the man stabbing her, but the prince deftly grabbed her chin and held her gaze.

"You have to keep still," he commanded.

Steele grunted again, distracted by the burning jabs and uncomfortable tugging on her skin. She wanted to watch Emdubae sew her skin back together. She had stitched up many a gash on the horses she'd rescued, but either they had a higher pain tolerance than she did, or she was a better doctor than this man.

As he worked on her shoulder, drowsiness settled over her like a heavy blanket. The pain slowly lessened, and she was able to fully relax. When it was over, he used a small blade to cut the thread and sat back to observe his work. "Twelve stitches. Like Kaleel said, you will have a scar, but it should not be too noticeable."

Steele's eyelids begin to droop. "Thank you for taking care of that." She blinked, the difficulty of opening her eyes again too great to manage. "I think that drink finally made me tired."

Someone chuckled, and a voice said, "Yes, it has been known to do that." She swayed to her right, and the last thing she was aware of before sleep overtook her were hands of the prince laying her back down.

CHAPTER 16

For a moment Steele had no idea where she was when she awoke. She rolled over, wincing as the motion sent spasms of pain through her body. Her throat was scratchy, and she coughed and sat up on her bedroll, massaging her neck. Even something as small as coughing felt uncomfortable. Her arms and legs felt unusually heavy, too, and though she'd slept the entire night, exhaustion clung to her. She rolled her shoulders, testing out the stiffness of the one that was injured. It hurt less than the day before, but it was still painful enough to cause her to inhale sharply.

"Is your shoulder bothering you?" Emdubae asked, fastening the buckles on his saddle pack.

Steele glanced at him and shrugged, more preoccupied with how her burns had healed. Whatever they had used yesterday had reduced them to faint brown marks. "What was in that salve?"

"I am not entirely sure. You'd have to ask Kaleel," he replied.

"Good, you're awake," Prince Aldair said, knocking the flap of the tent open and ducking into the enclosure. "We should try to move on as soon as possible."

Steele blinked. "We?"

The prince bent to rifle through a bag. "Yes, we."

Emdubae glanced at Prince Aldair before turning to Steele. "We know that you are out here for your own reasons, as we are here for our own. Our journey will not take us back to the palace, but probably farther into the Nasshari. If what you seek is in the desert, you are welcome to join us, as we have enjoyed your company, but we will not force you to come."

She nodded as Emdubae stood to speak with Prince Aldair. It would be easier if she just had herself to worry about, and she wasn't anxious to spend time among a captain, lieutenant, and a prince. But it couldn't hurt to stay with them while she regained her strength and see where they may lead her. If things became too complicated she could always take one of their horses and leave in the night. Her nose wrinkled at the thought. She didn't want to steal, but she didn't want to end up back behind bars more.

The prince and Emdubae were deep in conversation, muttering over a couple pieces of paper. Their exchange paused and Emdubae turned and made his way over to her. She pulled her knees to her chest and eyed him.

"No need to look so wary," he said kindly, sitting beside her. "I would only like to ask you a question."

Her eyes darted from Emdubae to Prince Aldair before she dipped her head.

"I am assuming you are well traveled?"

The question caught her off guard and she blinked. "Yes," she said slowly. "I've been to several cities in Solarrhia."

Emdubae smiled. "While in these cities, did you hear of anything odd?"

"Like people going missing." The prince added, coming to sit on her other side. He pulled a saddle bag over and started to roll up the blanket Steele had used.

Her lips parted in surprise. "Why would you ask that?"

"We are in the Nasshari because we're tracking a crime ring," Emdubae explained. "We've gotten word that people are going missing in the kingdom, and we are trying to figure out why and how to put an end to it. We think the disappearances might be connected to the crime ring."

"We haven't been out here long," the prince continued. "Only a couple of days before we found you, so we haven't had a chance to visit many towns. I thought that perhaps you might know something we don't."

Steele could hardly breathe for the tightness in her chest. They were trying to find missing people! If what they sought was connected to what happened with Tazmeen and Ali, the prince could lead her to her family.

"I did hear about strange things happening in Asha and Falu," she said. "In both towns I heard that people seemed to be vanishing, and I hear that business in Azubah isn't as good as it used to be."

Prince Aldair tilted his head to look at her. "The inn seemed plenty busy when we were there."

She laughed once. "Gemma's is always busy."

Emdubae pulled a folded piece of paper from his pocket and smoothed out the creases. It looked like a map, but a much more detailed one than Steele had ever seen. He pointed to Asha and Falu and tapped the paper. "Those two for sure." His finger slid to another city. "And Tuliu, Borun, and Wrey." He chewed on his lip and looked at the prince. "Then what we heard about in Rhia itself."

Steele's gaze flew to Emdubae and she winced as the motion sent a spasm of pain through her neck. "What about Rhia?"

Emdubae looked from her to the prince before answering. "The day before we left we got a report on people being taken."

"Around six people if I remember the list correctly," Prince Aldair continued.

"You have a list?" Steele asked, turning to look at the prince. He glanced down at the papers in his hand and she peered over his arm. "Can you read me the names? Maybe I know someone."

Prince Aldair shrugged one shoulder. "There's a girl named Zada. Says here she was taken outside the butcher shop and that she has light brown hair, but doesn't give her age. Next is a man named Nyle. Says he has dark hair and green eyes, but doesn't list his age or job. Then there's a seamstress listed. It says her name is Tazmeen and that her son was taken with her…"

If the prince continued to read, Steele didn't hear him. Blood roared in her ears, drowning out any other sound and for a moment she forgot how to breathe. Tazmeen and Ali. They were listed as missing. She had a much better chance at finding them if she stayed with the men.

Someone shook her shoulder, and she blinked.

"Do you need to lie down," Emdubae was asking her. "You've gone very pale all of a sudden."

She sucked in a deep breath. "I'm okay. I just, I did know a couple of those names." Her voice caught and she cleared her throat. "I think I will travel with you. At least for now. As long as you're sure you don't mind."

Prince Aldair smiled at her before squeezing her knee as he stood. "If we minded, we would not offer."

"It's our pleasure," said Emdubae. "It will be good to have you with us so we can monitor your shoulder." The men exchanged a glance, and the prince frowned slightly before carrying a few bags out of the tent.

Steele did what she could to help the men pack up the small tent, but her body felt weak and slow. Outside, she was surprised to see four horses tethered together, and she went over to stroke their noses. She vaguely remembered hallucinating about a horse-shaped cloud the day before, and she laughed. She'd been really out of it.

She wasn't sure how long she had stood there before Prince Aldair came up behind her. He motioned to one of the horses, the paint. "This is who you'll ride. His name is Kesif. We've been using him as a pack horse, so I imagine he will welcome a rider very much."

Kesif was beautiful. Steele had always loved paints because of how unique their coloring was, and he was no exception. He was more white than brown, like someone had poured white paint over his neck and body and as it had dripped down, it diverted around brown splotches on his chest and sides. The sun glinted off his forelock and ears, turning them a brilliant copper, and a bold white blaze cut down the middle of his face.

As Steele patted his shoulder, he rolled an eye back to look at her, and she noticed his liquid brown eyes were ringed with white, giving more expression to his face.

Steele stepped away and looked at the prince. "Thank you. You didn't have to give up your pack horse for me, but I would much rather ride than walk in the sand again. Where did you find him?"

Prince Aldair grinned, and Kaleel laughed once. "The prince is always trying to find the most unique horses he can. He found Kesif in the Barrowlands. Notice the mare he rides for himself." He motioned to a horse at the end of the picket line. "You will not see another mare like his Cahya in our kingdom."

Steele moved down the line to look at the horse, and her eyes widened. The mare was beautiful.

She stood proud and shook her inky mane out of her alert eyes. In her travels, Steele had seen snow before, but only once. Yet she knew that Cahya's coat resembled snowflakes resting on a wet stone. She smiled, running her hand over the mare's rump where the dappling was concentrated, half-expecting a snowflake to brush off on her palm.

Steele leaned against the mare to rest. Would her legs always feel this weak? "You just collect horses, then? As a hobby?"

Prince Aldair ran a hand along his mare's mane and chuckled. "Kaleel left out the fact that I actually do enjoy them. Cahya is one of my closest friends—one of my oldest at that."

Emdubae snorted and threw a brush at the prince. "She's one of your *only* friends."

Once the horses were saddled and loaded up with their supplies, Steele bridled Kesif and pulled herself into the saddle, grateful she was strong enough to do that, at least. She sighed. It felt wonderful to be astride a horse once again. She gathered the reins and ran her hand down Kesif's neck. He bobbed his head and started forward, eager to go, but she pulled him up. "Not so fast, Kesif. I'm not sure which way we're going."

"Kesif is a wonderful horse, but he does not like to stand still." Kaleel chuckled as he pulled his palomino up next to her. "We will head north for the time being. The desert is flatter there, and the horses would enjoy a nice canter to stretch their legs."

Steele grinned. "I understand that feeling all too well. What's your mare's name? She's a beauty."

Kaleel ran his hand down the mare's golden neck, pride shining in his eyes. "Her name is Rhub. She's been my traveling companion for many years." He gestured to the buckskin standing quietly with Emdubae on his back. "That's Ortak."

Prince Aldair surveyed the campsite a final time before turning Cahya away. Emdubae motioned for Kaleel and Steele to follow, and they fell in line.

The group began their trek to the north with Prince Aldair leading the way. He rode confidently, she noticed, and Cahya appeared to be enjoying her place up front, attacking the ground with fervor. Steele pressed her left leg into Kesif's side, and the horse shifted his path toward the right. Amused, she pressed her right leg into his side, and he shifted back toward the left. Emdubae laughed from behind her.

"They are trained to respond to leg yields so that if you are in a battle and cannot use your reins to steer, you still have control of the animal."

Steele turned in her saddle. "That's smart." Emdubae also rode with an air of confidence, one hand loosely holding the reins, the other hanging at his side.

After they had been walking for a bit, Prince Aldair slowed Cahya to ride alongside Steele. "There should be a small oasis in a league or so. I figure we can stop there for a bit, and the horses can have some water and a rest. There is also a place where you can rinse off, if you wish."

Steele glanced down at her dirt-smeared arms. "That would be very, very welcomed, Prince Aldair."

The prince chuckled. "You are pretty filthy. I can hardly tell what's skin and what's dirt. And please, call me Aldair."

She shook her head at him. "If I were a normal girl I would take offense at that comment. You're lucky I agree with you."

He smiled. "You are in no way a normal girl."

She stared at him, trying to read that smile and those words, but they were lost to her "You're not looking so polished yourself, Prin—um, Aldair."

He laughed, and Steele thought she heard Kaleel snort. "We will all benefit from taking a dip in the water."

They rode in comfortable silence until they reached the small oasis the prince had mentioned. It was not much to look at, but the sparse palm trees provided shade from the heat of the sun, and the watering hole looked refreshing as it sparkled at them. They untacked the horses and led them to the water, where the animals drank deeply before retreating to the shade of the palm trees.

Emdubae motioned at the pool. "My lady, we will finish with this. You go ahead and rinse off. You will have privacy."

Steele thanked him and turned just as Aldair threw a bundle at her. "Here, you can wear these when you are finished if you want. They're not very clean, but it is better than what you have on now." Steele opened the bundle and had to laugh. The prince had thrown her clothes, but they obviously belonged to one of the three men because they were much too big for her. "I know they are too big but—"

"I'll manage," she smiled, cutting him off. "Thank you."

The men turned away to give her privacy, and she made her way down the sloping sand to the pool. She removed all her clothing, save for her undergarments, and sank into the surprisingly cold water. The coolness felt so good against her sun beaten skin that a sigh escaped her lips. She lowered herself in the water until her entire head was submerged and her feet hit the silky sand at the bottom of the shallow pool. She floated at the bottom for a moment before kicking back up to the surface. When her head broke, she rotated to her back and floated for a while, eyes closed, savoring the weightless feeling and the coolness of the water that enveloped her.

A snort from one of the horses broke through her daydreams, and she paddled over to where the water was shallow enough for her to stand. As she unbraided her hair, clumps of wet sand dropped into the water, and she massaged the rest of it away with her fingertips. Her phoenix feather floated at the surface, and she swirled it through the water to remove any bits of sand that clung to it. When she was satisfied her hair was as clean as she could get it, she braided it and tossed it over her shoulder. She took her time with her injured shoulder, carefully rubbing the skin along the wound, trying to loosen up the remaining dried blood and crusted dirt. The skin around the stitching was puckered and red, redder than the rest of her skin, and it was very tender.

"If this is infected…" she muttered, silently cursing Lac. "He probably dipped the blade in poison before starting on our trip."

Satisfied she was as clean as she could get, she focused on washing her clothes. Swirls of brown bled out from where she scrubbed at them and when they too were clean, she reluctantly made her way up the beach. Despite only being in the water for a short time, Steele felt refreshed, and she quickly shrugged into the clothes Aldair had given to her. The shirt was more like a short dress on her, but it would have to do. The baggy trousers were so long she had to roll the bottoms up several times, and she used a leather cord as a belt to keep them from falling down. She adjusted the clothing one final time before moving away from the water, so the men could have time to enjoy the pool.

☽

122

Steele made her way to the base of a palm tree where the men had left all the bags strewn on the ground, and she sat with her back against the trunk. She tipped her head up and stared at the sky, light blue winking through the green palm leaves. Her eyelids slid shut, and she pushed all thoughts from her mind. It felt good to be this relaxed. It also felt strange. She wasn't used to feeling like she could let her guard down around strangers. Maybe it was this place, a small bit of relief in an endless desert that told her she could trust these men. She also wondered if she was just too tired to trust her judgment.

A loud splash by the pool brought her head down, and she looked to see what had caused it. Aldair was stripped to the waist and was trying to coax his mare into the water. Cahya clearly did not feel like going for a swim; she shook her head and pawed at the water, snorting anxiously. Aldair looked like he was talking to the mare, but at this distance, only mumbled sounds drifted to Steele's ears. Her gaze moved from the horse to Aldair and then abruptly down to the sand.

She gave herself a mental shake. Now was not the time to be distracted by the prince, but thin lines across his chest and back caught her eye. She glanced back up at him. They must be scars, either from battle or training.

She tilted her head and watched him work with Cahya. The mare dropped her head to drink and noisily blew out her nostrils, causing the water to ripple. She jerked her head up with a snort, backing up a few steps, and Aldair's amused laughter carried across the sand. He ran a hand along her dappled neck until she relaxed, and he patiently coaxed her back to the edge. Cahya tentatively placed a hoof in the water and was rewarded with a pat on the shoulder. Once Aldair was convinced she was content, he waded forward, gently pulling on the rope.

A strong breeze knocked over one of the bags at Steele's feet, and as she straightened it, she noticed a wooden figure sticking out of one of the bags. Curious, she pulled the object from the bag and found it to be a carving of a dog. She rotated it in her hands. It was the most realistic carving she had ever seen. The wavy fur appeared soft to touch, and the tongue that hung out of the dog's mouth looked like it was ready to lick the first face it came across.

"I'm carving that for my daughter." The deep voice startled her, and she dropped the dog back into the bag.

Emdubae sat down next to her and picked the dog up. He ran his fingers over the dog's back and down its tail. "Every time Aldair and I go on a journey, I carve a different animal for my Maeya."

Steele studied the dog. "Is it just you and your daughter?"

Emdubae smiled wistfully for a moment. "No, I have a wonderful wife, Sarai, and she is due to have our second child any day now. I hope for a strapping son, but my Sarai would love another girl…" He trailed off and turned the dog over in his hands. "I hate to be gone, but she'd shove me out the door if I tried civilian life."

Steele smirked. "Did she prove that to you once?"

"No, though she's adamant it won't agree with me. Ever the traveler, I am." He hesitated, then glanced at Steele out of the corner of his eye. "How does your family feel about your travels?"

"My parents are dead. They died when I was young. My mother's friend took me in and raised me." She spoke in clipped tones and leaned her head back against the palm tree.

Emdubae clicked once and said, "I am so sorry. I'm sure they would be proud of you if they were still alive."

She sat up and looked at him. "I doubt they would be proud of a horse thief, Emdubae."

He placed the dog back in his bag. "No, not the profession, but they'd be proud that you fight for what you believe is right. If Maeya grows up into someone who will fight for what she thinks is right, I will be proud of her."

Steele offered a small grin. "I hope she never chooses this life. It's not an easy one."

"I hope she never thinks she has to," Emdubae replied. Then he chuckled. "However, if that ever happens, Aldair owes me for getting him out of more than a few skirmishes."

A laugh from above startled them both, and they glanced up to see Aldair leaning against the tree, smiling at them. "Oh, Em, I don't know if what you've done for me is enough to cover that." His hair was wet, and some water droplets landed on Steele's arm.

Emdubae snorted. "You say that as if there was only one thing I have done for you when in fact I can think of many times I have saved your neck."

Aldair pulled his eyebrows up and grinned, feigning surprise. "Oh can you now?"

Steele glanced between the two men. "I would love to hear these stories, Emdubae."

Emdubae chuckled, and Aldair shoved off from the tree with a grunt. "We should be heading out. We've got a ways to go before we camp for the night, and Kaleel has the horses almost ready."

As he pushed himself to his feet, Emdubae offered his hand to Steele. "Remind me tonight, and I will gladly tell you some stories."

She grabbed his hand with her good arm and was pulled easily to her feet. "I won't forget."

After, she adjusted her saddle, she carefully pulled the bridle back over Kesif's ears. As she ran her fingers along the throat latch, she noticed Kesif had a brown splotch behind his jaw that looked like an upside-down heart. She traced the uneven heart, then patted his neck and swung easily into the saddle. Like last time, Kesif fidgeted beneath her, but she easily pulled him to a stop while balancing herself. Once settled, she looked around for her companions. Kaleel and Emdubae were mounted and looking to Aldair for instructions.

Aldair caught her eye and grinned at her. "Ready to run?"

"Always."

He pulled up next to her and reached out to rub Kesif's ear.

From her perch on Kesif's back, Steele was able to look down on the prince and his little mare. "Your mare looks strong."

Aldair twisted a piece of Cahya's mane between his fingers and looked up at her. "She is a very hardy animal. She's small, but don't let her size fool you. She's incredibly quick." He looked over at Emdubae and Kaleel and nodded. "Good to go?"

Steele nudged Kesif to follow after Aldair. She rode several paces behind the others, left alone with her thoughts. She could feel herself growing attached to these men, and that scared her.

"I can't let myself like them," she muttered, and Kesif twisted a brown ear back to her. "Not you, Kesif. You don't care what I've done. These men are just a means to an end to find Tazmeen and Ali. And I barely know them." Kesif continued to swivel his ears back to her, a perfect listener. "If…*when* I find them, there's no way these men could be my friends. Even if they like me, that doesn't change the law."

Her thoughts drifted back to her trial. There had been too many people around when she'd been sentenced to death for her to go back to Solarrhia not expecting punishment.

"I may just have to disappear. Make sure Tazmeen and Ali are safe and then leave. Move to another town or even another kingdom and not get caught this time. Maybe Dal and I could actually go to the beach!" She laughed, observing all the sand around her.

A spray of it jolted her from her thoughts. Aldair circled Cahya next to her and, with a sly grin, took off at a gallop across the sand. Steele felt Kesif jump out from beneath her, upset at being left behind, so she crouched forward and loosened her grip on the reins. The gelding exploded into a gallop, and Steele laughed with glee. She could feel Kesif's powerful muscles bunching and releasing to propel them forward across the ground. The wind roared in her ears, and bits of sand stung her face, but she loved every second of it.

Her eyes flicked toward Aldair, and she had a sudden urge to try to catch him—catch him and then pass him. She crouched lower over Kesif's shoulder and kneaded her hands along his neck. "Come on, boy, let's get them! I know you can do it!"

The horse responded, and Steele marveled at how powerfully he shifted into a faster pace. His stride lengthened and his powerful hindquarters powered them with more force than before. Steele pumped her arms along with the rocking motion of the gallop, and she gauged the distance between Kesif and Cahya. They were gaining. Slowly, but the gap was closing. They crept up on Cahya's flank, and Aldair glanced over his shoulder, surprise registering across his face when he realized they were closing in on him. He jerked his chin at her, encouraging her to keep coming, and Steele narrowed her eyes in determination.

We've almost got them.

Now they were even with Cahya's belly and still gaining ground. Kesif's long legs pulled them forward, and Steele felt extremely confident that they would pull even in a couple of strides. Suddenly Aldair's head snapped up, and he sat back with his hand up, signaling her to slow down. Steele applied pressure to Kesif's mouth, and the horse reluctantly began to slow. Aldair turned Cahya in a circle and headed back to Emdubae and Kaleel.

With a frown, Steele turned Kesif after them and cantered over to Aldair. "Why did you stop?"

Aldair glanced back over his shoulder. "The sand gets deep and hilly, so it's dangerous for the horses to run through it."

Steele rolled her eyes. "I know that would be dangerous for a horse."

"Yes," Aldair replied, "I'm sure you do, but I also saw what looked like a caravan, and I don't want us to be seen."

Steele eased Kesif to a ground-eating trot, and glanced over her shoulder as she followed Aldair, but she didn't see anything that looked like a caravan.

CHAPTER 17

A sigh escaped Steele's lips as she stretched out over the sand. It felt wonderful to lie down after a full day in the saddle. She pointed her toes and reached behind her head, wincing as her tired muscles tightened with the movement. She traced her fingertips lightly over the sand, and her thoughts drifted to the mysterious caravan.

Aldair was confident he had seen something, and since they hadn't gotten a good look at the caravan itself, they had followed what he believed to be traces of it until it had grown too dark to safely continue. If they had not been normal desert nomads, who were they and why were they in the desert? Could it have been Lac? An involuntary shudder passed over her as she recalled the sinister look in his eyes.

The light smell of smoke reached her nose, and she sat up to find Kaleel tending to a small fire. She gestured to the flame and asked lightly, "Is it wise to do that with the possibility of another camp nearby?"

Kaleel pushed a dark curl out of his eyes. "The wind's in our favor tonight. They won't smell the smoke. And if they do, and they decide to investigate, well, then we'll learn who they are." He shrugged and returned to the fire.

Steele hid a smile. He was right, but she wasn't sure they'd have the upper hand in that situation. If the people were friendly, or their numbers small, that could help. She rolled onto her belly, and rested her chin on her crossed arms. The flames produced enough heat to warm her face, and she stared at the dancing reds, oranges, and yellows.

Aldair and Emdubae appeared on either side of her, and Emdubae knocked her shoulder with his foot. "Would you like some water?"

Steele turned to smile at him. "No, thank you. But I would like to hear how you've gotten Aldair out of trouble."

Emdubae laughed and crouched down. "Ah, yes, and I will take great pleasure in telling you."

Aldair grunted as Emdubae relaxed into the sand, an intensely amused expression on his face as he thought of stories. With the three men distracted, Steele took advantage of this time to watch them. Aldair shifted uncomfortably as he stared at Emdubae, awaiting the inevitable embarrassment. Emdubae didn't seem like the type to be a jokester, but he appeared to enjoy making the prince squirm. Behaving as if this was an everyday occurrence, Kaleel went about his business, reading over a piece of parchment and occasionally stoking the fire.

Emdubae's face broke into a wide smile. "Aha! I thought of one."

Aldair snorted. "Took you awhile."

"Only because I have so many to choose from."

Steele chuckled at Aldair's wrinkled nose. She liked this Emdubae. He was happy to badger the prince and was unafraid of the consequences.

"Many years ago," Emdubae began dramatically, "when Aldair here was quite young, his parents permitted him to go on his first solo mission."

Aldair dropped to the ground beside Steele and drew shapes in the sand with his index finger. "I should have known he would pick this story," he muttered.

"When the princes were younger, they would sometimes accompany the soldiers on tours and missions, typically to see the villages and cities in the kingdom and to gain exposure. Hadrian was the first to travel being the older brother, but Aldair quickly convinced his parents to allow him to come at the young age of fourteen. He has always been able to talk his way into anything."

Emdubae threw Aldair a knowing look, but the prince only chuckled, staring into the flames.

"She doesn't need a history lesson, Em."

"I don't mind," Steele said, smiling at Aldair who shook his head at her.

Emdubae cleared his throat and continued, "For some reason on this particular tour, Hadrian could not accompany us—"

"I remember *this* one." Kaleel interrupted with a laugh. He looked up from his paper. "Hadrian was confined to the palace. He had, in a rare moment of genius, played the most fantastic prank on the maids. He'd taken all the linens from the washrooms and dressed the sculptures in togas. Harmless, really, but it didn't help that Queen Evelind and Princess Reagyn happened to be guests at the time."

"He couldn't have done that all by himself," Steele mused.

"He didn't."

"Remember the prank Aldair pulled on his parents during a feast with all the High Houses and courtiers?" Emdubae asked with a sly grin, "The food dyed everyone's teeth purple for days."

Steele's eyes widened, and she burst out in laughter. "How?" She asked, peering at the prince.

Aldair grumbled, but laughed. "A secret I'll take to the pyre, I believe. One never knows when it will be useful again."

"All right, all right," Emdubae cut in. "Now, let us return to the original story, for Aldair's sake."

"Yes," Aldair grimaced, "I'm sure it's for my sake, indeed."

"I'll spare you the details of our particular reasons for being in this town as I'm sure you are not interested in economics, corrupt town leaders, and diseased pigs. I *will* say that our Aldair was very excited to be without his brother for once—"

"*Especially* since his older brother was the one in trouble for once," Aldair interjected.

"*Aldair*, unfortunately, having little experience with certain beverages, especially these local ones that had a bit more kick than the diluted ones he had been given in Rhia, enjoyed the drinks a little too much that night. Before long, the young prince felt the need to challenge anyone and everyone to a duel." Emdubae paused for effect and added, "He agitated one tall man with reddish hair, I recall, but thankfully the man had sense to realize Aldair was not quite himself. As the night drew on and Aldair grew brasher, I decided it was past time to escort the prince to bed, by force if I had to. Aldair staggered after me, speaking nonsense and slurring words—he was particularly fascinated with the most mundane things like people's moles and hairstyles—when he smiled a little too long at the mistress of the inn. A pretty girl for sure, but very much married. Her husband was none too pleased, and as Aldair had been creating a scene the entire night, it was time to put an end to it."

Steele giggled, and Aldair stabbed at the sand ferociously with his finger. "I think, Em, that it would be wise to mention that this man was also not completely sober."

"You always were quite the flirt," Kaleel piped up. "I kind of miss that side of you, come to think of it. It always served to be incredibly entertaining."

"I didn't flirt!" Aldair protested. "Not that time, at least. I was just being friendly."

Emdubae laughed. "It was more like a leer than a smile. Anyway," he continued over Aldair's mutterings, "the man was insistent on killing Aldair, but I managed to talk him out of it by offering to fight in the prince's place. So I tucked the prince into bed and met the man outside, and I fought him, who as Aldair mentioned before, was inebriated himself. I bested him fairly easily, and he begrudgingly accepted defeat."

Steele rocked to her side and propped her head on her hand. "Well, Prince Aldair, I'd say that yes, you do owe Em a favor if his child decided to break the law occasionally."

Emdubae laughed, and Aldair leaned toward her. "Maybe I was faking it to see Em get into a fight."

Steele snorted. "I will never believe that."

"Would you say the view was great from underneath the covers, then?" Kaleel sniggered and promptly received a punch in the shoulder from Aldair.

A lizard scampered into sight opposite them, and Steele threw her short knife at it, gritting her teeth as the knife sailed over the reptile who quickly skittered off and disappeared into the sand. It had been large enough that they could have had some meat with their dinner.

"I'm betting you never won a knife throwing contest?" Aldair guessed.

Ignoring him, Steele stood to retrieve her knife. The men watched her, amused as she sat, rolled to her stomach, and stabbed the sand with the blade. "I can fight hand to hand better than throwing blades, yes." she replied finally.

A knife suddenly sliced into the sand inches from her nose, and Steele flinched so violently that she knocked into Emdubae. "I could give you some pointers," Kaleel said, chuckling.

"*Now?*" Steele exhaled in a huff. He could have killed her, and he was laughing about it.

Kaleel shrugged. "Why not?"

"It's pretty dark out."

"It's light enough."

"Kaleel doesn't believe in limits," Aldair explained.

Steele raised her eyebrow and nodded. She was starting to see that.

Kaleel stood to find a target, and Steele nervously thumbed the end of her blade. She wished Emdubae and Aldair would leave so her poor knife-throwing skills would be visible to Kaleel only. Moments later, he returned and threw a branch down some feet behind her. She turned to face him as he used his foot to push the branch into the sand.

"It's so small." Steele considered it uncertainly. It was roughly the size of her thigh, but tiny in comparison to everything else she could hit by accident. She considered feigning exhaustion but her pride wouldn't allow it.

"With my instruction, you'll be able to hit it just fine." He offered her a knife. "You can keep this one. We have plenty of knives and sabers as it is. Now. Show me how you throw, so I know what I am dealing with."

She gripped the handle of the knife, eyed the branch, and let it fly. It sunk into the sand blade first a few paces from the branch.

Kaleel whistled. "Better than I expected. Throw another."

She took another knife and threw it, uttering a surprised grunt when it landed next to the first knife. "I'm aiming for the branch, I promise."

Kaleel clucked his tongue. "You're angling your wrist too far down when you release the blade. That's why it's falling short."

Steele mimicked throwing a knife, and Kaleel grasped her wrist, holding it in place. He rotated it up a fraction. "Not a huge change, but it will make a difference." He handed her another knife and stepped away.

Steele practiced throwing it a couple of times before actually letting it go, and when she did, the knife overshot the branch. She groaned. "I overthought it. Let me try again."

This time she took a deep breath and focused on clearing her mind. She studied her target and threw. The knife landed in the branch with a satisfying *thunk*. "Oh! I did it!" she exclaimed, grinning excitedly at the men, and Emdubae clapped.

"Yes," Kaleel grinned widely. "Now, do it again."

She wondered if Aldair was impressed with her skill, if he truly thought she was doing well. Her cheeks warmed at that sudden thought, and she was grateful the dark hid her blush. She pulled the knives from the branch and moved to where Kaleel was standing.

Confident in her abilities, she wasted no time in throwing the knife and swiftly felt the sting of embarrassment as the knife landed past the branch.

Well, at least you didn't vocalize your confidence, she thought as she accepted a second knife from Kaleel.

The next knife stuck in the branch, but the next soared over. "I can see I'll need to practice a lot more before I'm any good."

Kaleel chuckled. "You are better than you think, Steele. Your determination makes you a quick learner."

She shrugged. "What else can I learn? I feel grossly under accomplished around you three."

Emdubae patted the sand next to him. "Maybe with a blade, but you have skills we don't possess. I can teach you some swordplay sometime if you would like?"

Steele nodded eagerly, sitting beside him. "Thank you." Emdubae gave her a leather sheath for her new knife, and she attached it to the belt on her trousers.

Kaleel sat on the other side of Aldair. "Everyone does poorly initially. It's good to learn your limitations and to battle through them early on. That determination I spoke of will take you far." He winked at her. "You may learn even faster than the prince did."

Aldair grunted. "I'm sure you're just saying that because she is prettier than I am."

Steele blushed as Kaleel snorted. "Think what you wish."

There wasn't a cloud in the sky that night, and Steele lay back against the sand, watching the stars twinkle. Beside her, the dying fire popped. Her legs still ached from her days trekking the desert, and it felt good to rest.

She wondered what Tazmeen and Ali were doing and if they were safe. They weren't criminals, like her, but the guard, Winlen, had mentioned taking them to some drop-off point. That meant they had to be taken somewhere. Was it possible they were being transported on a train like she had been? Her stomach knotted. Had they been on the train with her the whole time, while she'd only thought of her own escape? Her eyes filled with hot tears.

She sat up, pushing the emotion down. She needed to think, not cry. "I'm going to groom Kesif. Can I use a brush?"

"There are some in my bag." Emdubae pointed to the horses.

She stood and swallowed her surprise as Aldair stood with her. "I'll go with you," he announced. She gave him a small smile in return.

They walked in silence until they reached the horses. Kesif eyed Steele as she bent to retrieve a brush from Emdubae's saddlebag. She walked over to him, and he stretched out his nose to sniff the bristles. As she flicked the brush across his back, she watched Aldair run his hands down Cahya's legs.

"Have you always liked horses?" she asked.

"For as long as I can remember. I think I rode more than I walked when I was a boy."

"Hmm." She studied him. "And what sort of man lists a horse as his longest-standing friend?"

Aldair paused, hands cupped around the top of Cahya's hoof. "When you're in the military or confined to the needs of the palace, you aren't granted the luxury of having friends who stick around for a long time." He patted the side of the mare's leg before rising. "Or maybe I just prefer the company of horses to people. Surely you can understand that."

"I'm actually not sure," she admitted, flicking bits of clumped sand from Kesif's coat with a fingernail. "I haven't had a horse long enough to know what I prefer." When she looked up, Aldair was studying her with those intense blue eyes, and she quickly dropped her gaze. "Haven't Emdubae and Kaleel been in the military with you? You must count them as close friends."

"I do, but since Hadrian passed, Cahya has been with me the longest."

"Oh." Steele felt the sadness of his words and watched him run his hands down Cahya's other leg. It was strange that the prince was being so transparent with her. Even with the other two men for that matter. Wasn't he worried that someone would exploit that somewhere down the line? "People spoke highly of your brother. Were the two of you were close?"

Aldair stood and faced her, a small smile on his mouth. "Hadrian was my best friend. Were he still living, he would have Cahya beat. Does it make you feel better to know that?"

Steele smiled in spite of herself. "I never said there was anything wrong with having a horse for a best friend."

"No, you didn't. You only implied there was something not right about it." The edge of his mouth tugged upward, and he leaned against Kesif, forearms resting on the animal's back.

"Not wrong, just different." She shifted to her left so Aldair wasn't directly across from her. "I'm sorry if bringing up Hadrian is painful for you. I didn't mean to bring up something sad."

Aldair studied her before smiling. "Talking about him, *thinking* about him, does make me sad, but I don't want to not talk about him. The pain of his absence surrounds me. My heart's still broken, I think." He swallowed, kicking at the ground with his toe. "I don't think a person ever fully heals from that kind of loss, but every day it gets a little easier to get up in the morning even though I know he's not there." He glanced up and gave her a rueful grin. "Sorry, I didn't mean to ramble on like that."

"It's okay," she said quickly. "As someone who has known loss, I can promise you that even though it's hard now, your heart will heal."

They fell silent. Steele looked into his eyes, giving him a half smile.

Aldair opened his mouth, and then shut it before patting Kesif. "I do count Em and Kaleel as close friends though." He used his shoulder to scratch the side of his face. "Kaleel served with my brother, and after Hadrian died, he joined with me. Since Em is ten years older than I am, he's been a mentor and a friend. I respect him a great deal, but the bond with a sibling is different. Do you...Is that something you understand?"

"A little. The woman who took me in has a son. We're not blood, but I've always thought of him as a brother."

Aldair shrugged. "I don't think blood automatically makes a bond stronger. I've known plenty of siblings who despise each other."

"You have more experience being around people than I do, so I guess I'll have to take your word on that."

Aldair tipped his head. "That I do. I've been told I am a people expert."

She laughed. "You aren't what I pictured a prince to be like, you know."

He arched his eyebrows. "What were you expecting?"

"I don't know," Steele mumbled, embarrassed by her own transparency now. "You're not that different from Ardeth from Azubah."

"Well I don't know if you know this, but we're actually the same person." There was laughter in his voice, and he winked at her.

Steele pursed her lips, fighting a grin. "What I mean is that the Ardeth I met in Azubah seemed like a regular man. He was funny and normal and a little annoying. Aldair the prince is much the same. He has a more regal air about him, but he's not the uppity, condescending man I thought he might be."

"So you're saying I'm nothing but an ordinary man?"

"It's a compliment."

Adair's lips twitched. "I believe you." He patted Kesif's shoulder. "How is it that a horse thief wouldn't know if she preferred the company of horses to people?"

"I didn't steal horses to keep for myself. I only had them with me when I moved them from one place to another."

"Oh." He narrowed his eyes at her. "You're the most unusual thief I've ever heard of. Most steal for their own gain."

She shrugged. "Removing a horse from a bad place and giving it a new home makes me feel good, so you could say it *is* for my own gain."

He chuckled. "I suppose that's true. Were there any horses you wanted to keep for yourself?"

"All of them," she said simply. "I would keep them all if I could. If you aren't careful, I might slip away with Kesif," she teased.

"Is that so?" Aldair raised a brow at her. "I don't blame you though. He's a solid horse."

Steele only nodded, running her fingers along Kesif's spine, feeling for any response in his muscles. If they quivered, he could be sore, and he *had* been carrying a pack before she came along.

"Have you always liked them? I remember you saying your father was a blacksmith."

Steele outlined the brown splotch that covered part of Kesif's rump, feeling strangely touched that he had remembered. "You remember right. With certain clients, I was allowed to ride the horses around after they were shod. It was one of my favorite things to do. My father taught me the basics of riding like how to stop, turn and not to fall off. My mother taught me how to train the horses…" She drifted, thinking of when her mother used to sit on the fence barking orders at her.

"Tell me about your parents." Aldair leaned against Cahya. "You said they died. How old were you?"

Steele ducked under Kesif's neck to brush his other side. "Twelve."

"Ah. And you are how old now?" Aldair stepped to his left, giving her room, and patted Kesif's rump, sending little puffs of dust into the air.

"Twenty-two," she replied.

"What did you do when they died? You mentioned a woman with a son took you in."

"I—" She frowned. Prince Aldair was too easy to talk with. If she wasn't careful, he would learn all there was to know about her. "I, I can't tell you that."

Surprise flitted across Aldair's features. "And why not?"

"I can't be too open with you, Prince."

"Why would you say that?" He nudged her shoulder.

She stepped away from him. "Because I can't trust you. If I stay with you and your men until we return to Rhia, I'll be back behind bars before I can blink, so why volunteer private information about myself?"

"My men," Aldair repeated. He breathed in slowly and added, "I'm not going to turn you in, Steele."

She rolled her eyes. "Of course you are. You're the prince. I broke the law. Everyone saw me sentenced."

He sighed. "I know it sounds crazy, but I promise I won't turn you in."

"Why wouldn't you?" Steele folded her arms across her chest. Aldair didn't respond, so she continued. "Do you think that if you went to your father about my case that he would listen to you and let me go just because you're the prince and his son? That's not the Iron King I know."

Aldair stiffened at her comment. "That nickname was pinned on my father during a time of war. My father may be strict and expects his citizens to respect the law, but he is a reasonable man."

"I'm sorry," she said, facing him. "That came out harsher than I meant. But it doesn't make what I said any less true."

Aldair turned to stroke Cahya's neck, and his shoulders visibly relaxed before Steele's eyes. "I've thought about this some. A few people might recognize you, and some posters may still be up, but most people will think you're dead. You may have to worry about a person here or there, but our soldiers won't be after you."

"Maybe not your soldiers, but my face is on posters in more places than just Rhia."

"That's a bridge we'll have to cross when we get there. In the meantime you'll have to trust my promise. Either way, I may just turn my back one day and discover you gone."

"Even liars make promises," she protested, unable to believe he would simply allow her to walk free. "For example, I promise I won't hit you in the arm."

Aldair huffed a laugh as her knuckles hit his arm with a *smack*. "Not everyone makes empty promises though," he replied, rubbing his arm.

"Many do."

"Like?" He nudged her shoulder.

"Well." She paused. "Okay, this may make you angry, but it's an honest opinion."

Aldair turned from Cahya to lean against Kesif's rump, facing her. "Go ahead."

"Well it's like when the king promises the people that this year we'll have more food, and this year the taxes will be lowered, and this year things won't be so hard." she braided strands of Kesif's mane together as she spoke. "But things don't change for us. We're still hungry. We still have to pay for things we can't afford. And you just, I don't know, stop believing in promises when so many fall through." She looked at Aldair, trying to read his face. "I'm not trying to offend you."

"I'm not mad, I promise," he said with a wink. "You're just being honest, and you've given me valuable information to ponder."

She smiled in spite of herself. She crossed her arms over Kesif's back and studied Aldair's face, searching for anything to indicate he was lying. He met her gaze openly.

"Search all you want, Steele. You won't find anything to condemn me with." He smiled widely at her suddenly wrinkled nose.

"Even if you weren't the prince, I'd be skeptical." She put the brush back into Emdubae's bag. "You can't blame a girl for being careful."

"No, I suppose I can't." Aldair scratched Kesif behind the ear. "You can head on back to camp if you want. I'll get them some water."

"Thank you," she said. She turned away from him quickly to hide her smile. He didn't seem so bad. For a prince.

CHAPTER 18

The sound of Kaleel's light snore filled the tent and Steele groaned to herself. She was already having trouble sleeping, and the grating noise was not going to help. She stared up at the canvas above her. She should have been asleep hours ago, but every sound had her on edge. The men had been kind to her, but her thieving instincts screamed at her to stay alert.

One of the horses snorted from outside the tent and an idea formed in her mind. She always felt more settled on the back of a horse, so a quick ride should help to put her mind at ease. She sighed deeply and rolled to her side so she could observe the men. The moonlight was weak, but from what she could tell they appeared to all be sleeping soundly. She smiled.

Breathing lightly, she crept from her bedroll, pausing near the entrance to make sure everything was quiet. Satisfied the men still slept, she peeled back the flap and noiselessly slipped outside.

As she edged away from the tent and toward the picket line, she studied the stars, committing her location to memory. Vlaar shined at her in the north and she smiled up at the star. It was named for a legendary hunter, and many people used it for navigation.

She murmured to Kesif as she approached him and slipped the bridle over his head. The paint obediently followed her away from the picket line, and she glanced back at the tent a final time before jumping onto the horse's back. Kesif snorted, and she flinched against the sound, pressing her calves against his side to put distance between themselves and the camp. A part of her wanted to take Kesif for herself and leave, but there was no way that she was leaving now that she knew Aldair was tracking missing people, and that Tazmeen and Ali were listed as two of the missing.

Fear of being seen danced along her nerves, but the farther they got from camp, the more she relaxed. The shuffling of Kesif's hooves in the sand and the occasional snort were soothing to her. Letting the reins dangle loosely, she arched her neck back to look at the sky. The motion hurt, but the pain was worth the view. The moon was a sliver, and the thousands of stars glittering down at her felt like old friends. Her eyes danced from star to star, and the sudden longing she felt for her parents brought tears to her eyes. They would have loved to see a sky like this.

Her thoughts turned to Tazmeen and Ali and Aldair's list. All her life, she'd never been one to share much about herself, and when she became a thief, she'd learned to keep a tight seal on what she said about her personal life. She'd never been very good at small talk on top of that, so keeping quiet seemed the natural thing to do. She wanted to protect herself and keep what she knew private, but if her knowledge could help her find her family, she needed to tell the men what she knew. She doubted they would care about who she had lost. Tazmeen and Ali meant nothing to them, so she didn't feel like they needed to know those details. She stroked Kesif's neck as they walked and nodded to herself.

In the morning. You'll tell them about Winlen and Lac in the morning.

Something curled darkly against the sand, and she pulled Kesif to a stop, afraid for a moment that they had stumbled upon a desert serpent. She had no desire to see the supposedly huge reptiles in person so she watched the dark spot closely. The shape didn't move, and Kesif didn't act like a dangerous reptile was near. She nudged the horse forward.

Her heart jumped when she realized what it was. Deep gashes cut through the sand looking exactly like the imprints her magi train had left behind. Loose sand had filled some of the marks, but by the way the sand had been pushed, she could tell the train had been moving south. Maybe what Aldair had thought was a caravan was actually a magi train. Could it be the one she'd been on?

She checked Vlaar's position, torn between going back to camp and following the tracks. She patted Kesif's shoulder. "We won't ride for long," she promised. "Just a few minutes more before we'll go back. I just have to see if this is my train, or if Tazmeen and Ali are there."

She nudged the gelding, and he broke into a trot and they followed the tracks, pausing every so often to listen for voices. Just as she was considering turning around and going to bed, the sweet scent of burning pine met her nose, and Kesif pricked his ears forward.

"Finally," she murmured, rubbing Kesif on the neck.

Faint voices drifted toward her on the wind. She glanced around, looking for a place to tie Kesif, and spotted the gnarled remains of a long dead tree. She left the paint tied to a weathered branch, afraid to bring him closer in case there happened to be guards patrolling the area. She rubbed his nose, and he barely twitched an ear as she crept off to investigate the train.

The gouges in the sand snaked around the base of a sand dune, and she paused before continuing forward more cautiously. She hadn't gone very far when she heard the low murmuring of people talking. She froze. She wasn't close enough to hear what was being said, but she assumed they were unpacking their supplies for the night. The firelight threw long shadows against the sand, and the dark forms didn't seem to be moving closer to her. Sucking in a breath, she crept back until she was behind the dune once again.

She needed to climb the hill and get a look at the camp. The risk of being seen up there was high, but she trusted her stealth. Squaring her shoulders, she stepped toward the mound, when strong arms grabbed her from behind and a hand clamped down over her mouth.

She grunted, refusing to scream despite her terror and thrashed against the arms, but with her own arms pinned to her sides, there wasn't much she could do. Frustrated, she threw her head back and winced as the back of her head smacked against something hard. The grip on her mouth tightened, and her heart galloped off as panic raced down her limbs. Growling, she wiggled and squirmed, fighting to free herself.

Not again! Tears stung in her eyes, but before they could fall, she realized whoever was holding her was speaking to her.

"If you would stop thrashing around, I can let you go," a familiar voice whispered urgently. "And don't scream. I can't uncover your mouth until I know you will not give us away."

Aldair? Steele went still, not entirely convinced it truly was the prince who held her.

"Promise not to scream?" That voice did sound like it belonged to Aldair, so she nodded slowly.

The grip on her mouth loosened, and Steele whirled around, shoving a very smiling Prince Aldair solidly in the chest. Since he still gripped her with one arm, she fell with him as he stumbled back and collided with his chest.

"Ugh," she spat, pushing herself away, adrenaline crashing down on her. "Don't ever sneak up on me again!" She sucked in a breath to calm her nerves. "You scared me."

Releasing his hold on her arm, he scrubbed a hand over his mouth, hiding a grin. "I'm sorry," he whispered, beckoning to her as he backed away. "I needed to let you know I was here in some way."

She hesitantly followed him away from the dune, casting a backward glance at it as she moved. "What are you doing here?"

He grabbed her wrist and pulled her away faster, his eyes darting around. "I'll tell you when we can talk without being heard."

"I was doing just fine until you showed up and ruined everything!" she hissed after he led them a safe distance from the dune.

This time, Aldair did not try to hide his grin, and Steele found the way he ruffled his hair and regarded her with that grin to be more than a little disarming.

"I'm not sorry I followed you," he said, crossing his arms. "I am sorry that I scared you, but you *were* stealing my horse."

"I wasn't stealing him!" She protested. She considered explaining more, but hesitated when he cracked a grin. She shook her head, but she couldn't help smiling back. "Apology accepted. Now can I get back to what I was doing?"

"Which was what, exactly? Flirting with disaster?"

She opened and closed her mouth. "Of course not. I was going to spy on that train to see if I could learn anything about it."

Aldair furrowed his brow. "Train?"

She nodded. "Yes, Prince, a train. From what I could see of the tracks, the caravan you saw could be similar to the type of train I was on."

"Hmm. Well, I suppose since we're here, we might as well investigate," he mused. "So you got out here by a train?"

"We?" she asked, ignoring his comment about her transportation. "I'm not sure I trust that you won't get us caught," she teased.

"I snuck up on you, didn't I?"

She nearly laughed at the wicked grin he gave her. "Only because I let you."

"What was your plan?" he whispered, peering down at her.

"I was going to get a layout of the campsite from the top of the dune, and then see if I could sneak closer." She folded her arms across her chest, determined not to look away.

"Fair enough."

"Try not to get us caught, please," she said with a smile before turning back toward the dune.

He chuckled quietly from behind her as they crept forward. Snatches of conversation were caught by the wind, and Steele paused, head cocked. Aldair came to a halt beside her, and they both listened. A few men and women at the campsite were conversing about how to fix a broken door on the train, which could be useful later should she need to get inside it.

Steele used the opportunity to scramble to the top of the dune and glance over the edge. A dying fire smoked in the middle of the campsite, the embers burning a deep red. The train curved around the back edge of the camp, and she squinted, trying to see if it was Lac's train. It certainly looked similar from what she could see.

Seven people sat around the flickering fire, all facing away from the dune. Didn't they know to have someone watch their backs? She quickly surveyed her surroundings, just to double check they'd not been fooled. There was no one nearby except for the prince.

Since the train's occupants were still awake, though, Steele was content to lie on the dune and wait. Digging her fingers through the soft sand, she rested her chin on her hands. A glance to her right showed Aldair mimicking her movements. She shivered as cool air blew over her, caressing her legs and arms, and pulling itself through her hair. She should have thought to bring an extra tunic.

As the people chattered, she quickly determined these were not the people who had been with her train. Their accents were different. Closing her eyes, she tried to picture where she had been when she had heard similar voices. It had been a long time, but memory told her she had been near the mountains and King Ferdinand's land when she'd last heard that cadence. What were people from Hamonsfell doing in the desert, though?

Looking to Aldair, she studied his profile. His jaw was clenched, brows drawn in concentration. Concentration or confusion, that was. It was hard to read his face in the dark, but he would know the northern accent well if she was correct. King Ferdinand was his grandfather.

"...should be at the camp by...prisoners will need...that's what he said..."

Steele's head shot up. She had been grateful to the wind for hiding them, but now she wished it would be still so she could hear the conversation more clearly. They were talking about a camp and prisoners. Did that mean there were prisoners on the train, as well?

"...rest tomorrow and move...meet with the boss...days from now...sleep."

Steele wanted to scream in frustration. It was almost better not knowing anything than almost knowing something. She risked another glance over the dune. The men and women had settled around the fire, which was burning more brightly now, and they appeared to be done talking for the night.

Aldair scooted next to her and studied the campsite.

She jerked her chin toward the train, and conflict danced across his face before he shook his head. Her heart sank. Didn't he realize that there might be people in that train who needed their help? She couldn't just leave them.

Aldair pushed himself down the hill, grabbing her ankle when she didn't follow right away. Her fingers left lines in the sand as he gently pulled her down, regret and guilt weighing on her. When they reached the bottom, Aldair led her away a few steps before his mouth found her ear.

"We'll talk about this. Just not right here," he breathed, pulling her away.

She allowed him to guide her away, and when they were far enough away that they could speak freely, he pulled them to a stop and faced her with weary eyes.

"I know you want to see if there are prisoners on that train."

She grunted. "Of course I do. I can't believe that you don't."

He rubbed his eyes. "Steele, we heard them mention prisoners and a camp. So they're either transporting prisoners to the camp, or they're bringing supplies to a camp that already has prisoners. In this moment, I am not willing to risk our lives to investigate which of those it is. What we will do, though, is continue to track this particular train and see where it ends up. I will not abandon innocent people, if that's what you were thinking I was doing in leaving just now."

She clenched her jaw, knowing his plan was a good one. Even she could begrudgingly see that. But it didn't rid her of guilt. "I want to help," she whispered. "That train looks similar to the one I escaped from."

"Yes, you mentioned that. I…" He paused, frowning. "I suppose my theory was correct then. Self-exile never did seem to fit your personality." He walked to where the horses were tethered, but instead of untying Cahya, he sat on the sand, propping his elbows on his knees.

"You had a theory?"

He nodded. "Since finding you out here, I've been wondering just how you ended up half dead in the Nasshari. It doesn't makes sense that General Fijar or the palace guards would drop you in the desert to die, especially after they informed us that your execution had been carried out."

"You could have just asked."

"And you would have told me?" Aldair gave her a knowing look.

She shrugged and patted Kesif's neck, glad that Cahya had been able to keep him company, and then hesitantly sat next to the prince.

He glanced at her. "What really bothers me is that I didn't know you were being taken from the palace. I don't know if that was a singular event or if prisoners have been taken like that for a long time. I don't know where you were being taken or why you were not executed as my father decreed. I'm sorry," he placed a hand on her shoulder. "I am extremely happy that you were not executed. I'm just trying to process this."

Her hand was twitching to reach out to him, but she rubbed her eyes instead, suddenly very sleepy. "I have some information I think you need to know. A man named Lac put me on the train. He mentioned taking me to a camp and I assumed he meant where I was to be executed, but that obviously wasn't the case." She looked that the prince and he was frowning.

"You're certain his name was Lac?"

She nodded slowly. "And I know a man named Winlen was involved in the incident in Rhia. I saw him."

Aldair grunted. "And then he brought you to the palace."

"Yes," she said quietly. "I heard him mention taking people to a drop-off point before he brought me in."

The prince gave a heavy sigh. "We'll have to tell Em and Kaleel about this in the morning."

Steele nodded again. "That train back there may be a completely different thing than what happened with me, but I just have a feeling that it's all connected somehow."

He gave her a tired smile. "I have a feeling you are right."

"I was also thinking that those men didn't seem like they were from this area," she said carefully. She didn't want him to think she was implying anything negative about his family. "They sounded like people I've been around who are from the mountains."

Aldair nodded. "Their clothing was that of the mountain people as well, but what would they be doing out here?" He dropped his head in his hands, and when he looked up at her, his dark hair was disheveled.

"We could march in there right now and demand to know?" Steele suggested with a wry smile.

He grinned back, and it made her strangely happy to know she was responsible for putting it there. "I don't know how much the two of us could do against seven people," he said, pushing himself off the ground and offering his hand to her. "Especially with you so tired."

Taking it, she shrugged as he helped her up. "Unfortunately you're probably right, but if I was my normal self, I think we could hold our own."

Together they packed up the grain bags, and when she pulled herself onto Kesif's back, she found Aldair watching her. "Yes?"

Giving his head a shake, he half smiled. "Nothing. Kaleel and Em are going to be angry at us for sneaking out."

"How did you know to follow me? Did you hear me leave?" She hoped that wasn't the case. She knew she was good at sneaking around, and when she replayed her exit in her mind, she could think of nothing she did that would have woken him. Less than a week in the desert and she was already losing her touch?

"I don't know actually," he said. "I'm a light sleeper, but there was nothing specific that woke me. I *was* disturbed, however, to find you gone. I got up, saw some tracks, and followed them."

She grunted. It bothered her that he had managed all that with her none the wiser. That never should have happened.

Aldair edged Cahya closer to Kesif as they walked. "So if I hadn't followed you, what would you have done? Get information, and then leave?"

Steele glanced up at the hint of sadness in his voice. "No, I was coming back. As much as I like Kesif, I couldn't take him from you."

Aldair reached forward and ruffled Kesif's forelock fondly. "I'm glad." He straightened, and Steele noticed he was riding bareback, as well. "I don't know about you, but I am so tired I may fall asleep before we return. How about we canter them out until we get closer to camp?"

She nodded, fighting a yawn. "Are you going to cheat again?" Before he could answer, she heeled Kesif in the ribs, and left Aldair and the campsite behind in a spray of sand.

CHAPTER 19

When Steele awoke the next day, sunlight was streaming in through the open tent flap, and she threw an arm across her face, groaning. Though it was clearly past the morning time, she wanted nothing more than to roll over and go back to sleep. Raising her arm a fraction, she cracked an eye at the bedroll across from her and was relieved to find Aldair was still asleep. At least she wasn't the last to rise.

Emdubae ducked under the flap and smiled at her. He had a steaming plate of food in his hands and, with a glance at the sleeping prince, offered it to Steele. She struggled to sit, wincing against her stiff muscles.

"Thank you, Em," she whispered, taking the plate.

"Kaleel found some lizards this morning, and when mixed with some spices, it does not taste too bad." Emdubae didn't bother to whisper, and Aldair stirred on his bedroll. "Any particular reason the two of you slept so late this morning?"

"We'll discuss it in a moment," came Aldair's sleep-heavy voice. "You don't have to speak so loudly, Em."

Emdubae chuckled, jostling the prince's shoulder with his foot. "It would seem Kesif and Cahya have been ridden recently. I'm sure that has nothing to do with you sleeping late either?"

"Em." Now Aldair's voice was a growl. "Please go away."

Steele laughed, taking a bite of the lizard meat. "I take it Prince Aldair is not a morning person." Her voice was rough with fatigue, and she coughed, clearing her throat.

Kaleel swept under the flap then, carrying in another plate of food, a manic grin on his face. "Aldair and mornings go together about as well as thunderbirds and phoenixes."

Another growl emanated from Aldair's bedroll, and he rolled to his stomach, rubbing his face in his hands. "You would sleep late, too, if you were up half the night." His voice was muffled by his hands.

"You have no one to blame for that but yourself," Kaleel chirped, settling on the edge of Aldair's bedroll, legs crossed. "So why don't you tell Em and me what the two of you were up to."

He looked pointedly at Steele, and she dropped her gaze to her food, cheeks red. "I couldn't sleep, so I took Kesif for a ride...and I came across a campsite. *He* followed me."

Aldair grunted, finally moving to sit. Shadows ringed his eyes, and his dark hair dropped across his forehead. He accepted the plate offered by Kaleel and rotated his neck, earning a few cracks. "We need to discuss what we found."

Emdubae sat on the floor beside Steele. "You did not think to wake either of us when you left?"

"Obviously," Aldair spoke around a piece of meat in his mouth.

"That was foolish," Emdubae chided.

"I agree," Steele muttered, scraping the last bits of food into her mouth.

"It was foolish of you as well, Little Thief," Emdubae glanced at her, blue eyes growing thoughtful. "Unless you meant not to return to us?"

She set her plate in her lap and sighed. "I wasn't planning *anything*, but you don't live long in the thieving world without knowing how to sneak and spy."

"I'm assuming there's more to this campsite than people getting together for some late-night song and dance, or you'd not felt the need to tell us," Emdubae said, looking to Aldair. "Was it the caravan from the other day?"

"A train, actually." Aldair leaned forward, setting his plate on the ground. "Thank you for the food, by the way."

"A train?" Kaleel glanced from Steele to Aldair.

"Perhaps Steele would like to explain," Aldair answered, leaning back on his elbows. "She has some information that might help us out."

"Oh? What sort of information?" Kaleel asked, running a hand through his dark curls.

Steele wet her lips. "I was placed on a train the morning after my trial. The train seemed to be powered by magi, and it floated above the ground. The marks it left in the sand looked the same as the marks this train leaves."

Aldair sat up again, eyes narrowed. "Magi?"

She nodded, thinking of Bero. "This train looked similar to the one I was on, and Aldair and I overheard the men and women with this one talking about prisoners and a camp."

Emdubae scratched his beard, blue eyes narrowing. "What sort of train transports prisoners?"

Aldair threw his arms in the air. "I have no idea. If Father is aware of it, he said nothing to me."

Emdubae spared the prince a glance before continuing. "Were these men and women people from Solarrhia? Or anyone you recognized?"

"They weren't the ones transporting me." She shuddered as Lac's leering face floated in her mind.

She glanced at Aldair and he nodded. "The man who put me on the train mentioned a camp as well. His name was Lac, and he was working with men named Rashim and Alec, I think."

"Lac?" Kaleel and Emdubae turned to look at her, surprise and doubt etched on both of their faces.

She nodded hesitantly. The disbelief in their expressions was enough to make her question her own information.

"Could be worth mentioning to General Fijar, or your father," Kaleel suggested, and Emdubae nodded his agreement.

"There was also a man named Winlen," she said softly. "I know he was involved in taking people from Rhia to a drop-off point."

"What sort of drop-off point?" asked Emdubae.

"I don't know that. Just his name. He mentioned the drop-off point right before he brought me to the palace."

"Lac, Rashim, Alec, Winlen..."Emdubae muttered the names quietly. "Thank you for giving us this information," he said to Steele. "It does help."

"We think this group is from the mountain region," Aldair said, resting his elbows on his knees and dropping his face in his hands. "But why would guards from Grandfather's land be transporting prisoners or supplies to a camp through the desert without my knowledge? What could we be missing?"

The tent fell silent, and Steele lay back on her bedroll, her mind weary and confused.

"How did you manage to escape your train, Steele?" Kaleel asked.

"I had help," she replied slowly, not wanting to betray the Bero's identity.

"I've learned, my friends, that she will not give us any more than that," Aldair noted, sounding amused.

A smile crept its way up her face. "You are correct."

"What if telling us would help solve this mystery?" Aldair pressed.

"If that were the case, I'd tell you, but I don't think it would help much at all."

"So what are we going to do?" Emdubae said. "I, for one, do not feel it would be right to leave the train be. We should keep an eye on it."

"That's the plan for now," Aldair said, blankets rustling as he reclined and rolled to his stomach. "Track the train and see if we can determine who the prisoners are and if they are innocent. If so, we try to rescue them."

Steele glanced sideways to find him smiling at her, and she smiled tiredly in return.

"Should one of us set out to scout the train now?" Kaleel asked, standing and stretching his arms above his head.

"I don't believe so," Aldair said. "They were resting today and then heading out."

"That's how it sounded to me," Steele agreed.

The prince nodded. "We'll decide tonight who goes."

"And for now?" Kaleel asked.

"For now." Aldair yawned. "I don't know about Steele, but I could use a little more sleep. So for now, your only job is to wake me in two hours, unless you need me before then. I'll send a message to Father after I wake."

Emdubae chuckled, and Steele felt him pull her blanket over her. When had she closed her eyes?

"Thank you, Em," she said drowsily. "I'll only sleep a little while longer."

She didn't even hear when Emdubae and Kaleel left the tent.

A scraping sound pulled Steele from unconsciousness, and she lay still as her mind worked to remember where she was. She turned her head to the right, feeling the muscles stretch. In the excitement of the previous night, she had almost forgotten how bruised her neck was. That dull ache brought everything back. Too-tired muscles tried to support her weight as she sat, but her arms wobbled and she slumped back to the bedroll with a groan.

Aldair looked up from where he was sharpening his knife against a stone and grinned at her. "You're awake. Are you hungry?"

Steele started to say no, but her stomach growled. "I guess I am. I feel like a bottomless pit these days." She paused. "I thought Em was supposed to wake us?"

"He tried, but we decided to let you sleep. Your body took a beating while you were on your own in the sun, and you needed the extra rest." A small frown furrowed his brow, and he studied her face. "It makes sense that you would be hungry. When was the last time you ate before we found you?"

"I'm not sure." She closed her eyes, trying to think. "Actually, I think the last full meal I had was in Azubah with you, and they put me on the train the day after I was sentenced, so count back from there?"

"Azubah?" Aldair moved to sit beside her. Steele curled her legs toward her chest to give him room. "You must be joking."

"I'd only been in Rhia a little over an hour before I was caught."

"We met in Azubah seven days ago, and you were in the desert for two days without water or food?" He shook his head. "I can't believe you have any strength left."

A wry grin tugged at her mouth. "Maybe I'm tougher than you give me credit for."

"I think you're tough, but seven days without food in normal circumstances is taxing on *any* body. Were you not given some rations in the palace though?"

Steele laughed once and attempted to sit up once again, this time ignoring the aches and exhaustion that had seemed to settle in her bones. "If you think a person who is sentenced to death would be given food, you are sorely mistaken, Prince."

"Even prisoners condemned to death are provided the most basic of needs," Aldair argued. He focused on the edge of his knife again, his brow furrowed. "My father commands it."

"Then I think you have a breakdown in communication somewhere. I certainly saw no food." She rubbed her eyes, trying to ignore the stiffness of her injured shoulder. "But it makes sense, doesn't it? Why should food be wasted on people who are only going to be dead in a couple days' time?"

"Because you never know when they might show up in the desert," he replied, eyes moving from her face to her neck before settling on her wrists. "I meant to ask you about those." He gestured to her wrists which still bore angry red marks from her handcuffs. "Did you get those cuts from the palace as well?"

She flexed her wrist, wincing as a scab cracked. "Yes. There and the train."

Aldair scratched the scruff on his cheek. "Since you were not cuffed when we found you, I'm assuming you were able to pick the locks."

She wrung her left hand around her right wrist, staring at where the iron cuffs had bit into her skin when she was trying to pick the lock. She guessed she would carry those marks with her the rest of her life.

"Like I said, I had help." she said softly. "But he didn't leave the train."

149

Her brown eyes searched his blue, and she almost smiled. That Aldair wanted to know more was obvious. His mouth opened and closed before settling into a small frown, and he sighed, resigned.

"I suppose I am indebted to him," he said finally.

"Oh?"

"If he had not helped you, I wouldn't have had the pleasure of seeing you again." This was said without a smile, and Steele's cheeks warmed under the intensity of his gaze.

Searching for a distraction, she reached for a knife one of the men had left out on his bedroll, but she didn't see another stone to sharpen the blade with. Aldair offered his stone to her. She smiled and took it, incredibly aware of when their fingers brushed against each other. That little contact sent tingles from her fingertips straight to her heart. She ducked her head and concentrated on moving the blade against the rock.

"Did you really try to talk your father into not having me executed?" she asked, lightly pressing her thumb against the end of the knife to test its sharpness.

Aldair cleared his throat. "Ah, yes. I did."

"Why?" She peeked at him while he focused on refitting his boot. He glanced at her then, his lips turning up into a small smile.

"I like you," he admitted.

Her cheeks warmed, but before she could respond, he added, "I enjoyed spending the morning with you at the White Horse. I thought you were intelligent and honest—well, except for not telling me you were one of the thieves we were talking about. But that's beside the point. Regarding the sentencing, you didn't seem like an unreasonable person who wouldn't amend her ways if given the chance." He paused and sighed, picking at a fray in his shirt. "It's not really how we do things though, so I had no idea how to properly approach Father about it. I failed, obviously, and like I told you last night, we were told the execution had been carried out."

She let his words settle, thinking on them and their time at Gemma's. Finally, she nudged his shoulder with hers. "Thank you for trying."

She thought on her conversation with Gemma. Their talk about the increased amount of soldiers in the area, and Dal's and Jayn's thoughts on people going missing seemed like so long ago. She'd never dreamed that Tazmeen or Ali might also be in danger.

Tazmeen's frightened face swam before her, and she suddenly found her eyes heavy and her chest warm. Sucking in a breath, she willed the tears to subside. Even the veins in her wrists were pulsing, and her arms tingled as the sensation spread up her arms. Aldair rested his hand on her shoulder as she wiped clammy hands on her trousers. Instead of shying away from him, she found comfort in the gesture and leaned into him.

"Are you all right? I'm sorry if I said something to upset you," he said earnestly, and when Steele looked at him, she saw concern reflected in his eyes.

She rubbed her eyes, forcing the tears back. "No, what you said didn't upset me. I got arrested because…well, because I was trying to protect some people I know. They were taken away right in front of me. I thought maybe they were being arrested at first because the men who took them were working with Winlen. But they weren't criminals at all, and even though life could be hard, they always kept up with their payments."

Aldair pinched his bottom lip between his fingers. "I'm sorry you had to see that. It seems as though we're right on the brink of discovering something huge, but I almost don't want to find out what." He exhaled through his nose. "Does that make me a coward?"

She considered him before shaking her head. "No."

"I know you are anxious to be rid of us once we return to Rhia, but would you stay to help us? If not, that's fine," Aldair continued quickly. "I have never really been capable of separating myself out or asking others to get dirty for me."

"What does that mean?" she asked suspiciously.

A muscle twitched in his jaw. "I may have phrased that wrong. I mean, do you help people if you owe them nothing? One minute I think I have you figured out, but you continue to remain a mystery." He smiled, and she relaxed a fraction.

"I'm not someone who will withhold help when it's needed, but I've learned to be cautious. If you help the wrong person, you may very well end up dead."

He nodded once. "I suppose I should have known that."

She smirked. "I'm actually glad that you're confused. I would be a poor thief indeed if you could easily figure me out—now my friend, Dal…he will only extend help to someone he trusts, and they usually do owe him something. He calls me a confused thief, unsure of what side I'm on."

Aldair raised an eyebrow, and he leaned in so close that even with the afternoon shadows the tent cast across his face, she could make out freckles speckled below his eyes. Old instincts screamed at her to back away, that he was too close, but she didn't move, keeping her eyes on his.

"I would have to agree with this Dal," he said. "I do find you fascinating, but I did even before I found out you were a confused thief."

She was unsure of how to respond. Prince Aldair continued to surprise her, too. She had never interacted with anyone like him. He was honest, but not weak in his honesty. He was a leader, but one who led with an easy confidence and a grin. Her concentration traveled down his nose to the scar above his lip.

She dropped her eyes. "Where are Em and Kaleel? It's much too quiet out there."

Aldair chuckled. "They're checking on the train. I told them we would start to pack up the camp."

Steele groaned, but stretched out her legs. "I assume that will take awhile?" As she spoke, she took in the interior of the tent. Various bags, filled with supplies sat around the edge, weapons leaned against the canvas, and then there was the bedding.

It was then that she noticed that there were only three bedrolls. "Has someone been sleeping without padding?" she asked, concerned that one of them had given up his bed for her.

"Kaleel," Aldair replied, grinning at her panicked expression. "But don't feel bad! He doesn't sleep much anyway, and it's not the first time he's slept on the ground." He stood, offering her his hand. "I promise."

"If you say so…" She cleared her throat. "Now where do we start?"

CHAPTER 20

The camp was nearly packed up when Emdubae and Kaleel could be seen in the distance, and *of course* this was when Steele's stitches chose to rip. It wasn't like she had been doing anything strenuous. Just hoisting tent poles from the ground onto Kesif's back, but an uncomfortable tugging sensation followed by a sharp stab of pain pulsed from her saber cut. Gritting her teeth against the sting, she shoved the poles behind her saddle before pulling the edge of her shirt down to look at her wound. Blood oozed from where five of the twelve stitches had popped open, and she scowled. The cut looked better overall, but that didn't mean the peeling back of the skin hurt any less. Yanking her shirt back in place, she turned as Emdubae and Kaleel came to a halt, sand spraying out from their horses' hooves.

Aldair was instantly in front of them, arms crossed. "Well?"

"You were right," Emdubae said, swinging down from his horse. "They're planning on moving out in a couple hours' time. If the wind stays as it is, we will have no trouble tracking them."

"But we all know how unpredictable the desert winds can be," Kaleel added with a grunt as he jumped from his horse's back.

"How long until we need to head out?" Aldair asked, squinting up at the sun.

"Oh, I would think we have time to eat something before we need to leave. They were only just beginning to discuss what to pack when we left, and I do not believe they have any human prisoners with them. If they do, they have hidden them extremely well." Emdubae tossed his water flask at Steele, and she caught it awkwardly. He narrowed his eyes at her. "Is something the matter, Little Thief?"

She shrugged and sipped the water. "I'm fine," she replied, screwing the cap back onto the flask. Her shoulder stung, but she didn't want to bother them with fixing the stitches before she had the chance to try herself.

"Why then, is your shirt red?" Kaleel asked. He didn't seem too concerned, though, since he passed by her to stalk some lizards.

She twisted her shoulder away, a small smile on her lips as she watched Kaleel creep toward the unsuspecting reptile. When she turned back, Aldair and Emdubae were both directing very pointed looks at her.

"If your shoulder is indeed fine, you won't mind if I take a look at it?" Aldair reached for her, and she flinched, frowning at his satisfied grin.

"It's only a few stitches. I was going to take care of it myself." There was stubbornness in her voice, and she didn't try to hide it. After all, she was certainly not helpless.

"You're not serious," Aldair exclaimed while Emdubae replied, "That is all very well, but at least allow us to oversee your work."

She put a hand on her hip. "Why?"

Emdubae and Aldair exchanged a look.

"No need to get defensive," the prince said, a smile softening his words. "I do not doubt you can stitch up your own shoulder. We only want be there in case you need help or the wound is infected."

"I don't think it's infected," she mumbled, gently probing her shirt around the wound.

"Em, I need your help," Kaleel whispered urgently.

"Whatever for?"

"There is a huge serpent in this log, and I think we can eat him if we catch him, but I need you to help me corner him." Kaleel spoke quickly, arms gesturing frantically.

"Sounds dangerous." Emdubae chuckled as he unsheathed his saber and jogged toward Kaleel. "And don't worry, Steele, Aldair is more than capable with a needle and thread!"

She turned to the prince, eyebrow raised. "Oh, you are?"

Aldair glared at Emdubae's back, but when he looked at Steele, his blue eyes turned teasing. "Oh yes, instead of weaponry with Father, I spent my afternoons learning embroidery from Mother." He shook his head. "In all seriousness, we mend our own clothes in the military, and we're required to learn basic doctoring skills before we set out on missions."

Steele smiled but was more concerned with his proximity as he approached her. He gently pulled down the corner of her shirt and assessed her wound.

"What's the verdict?" She asked after watching him for several moments.

"I think you will survive." He gestured to one of the logs by the ashy remains of the fire. "Take a seat, and I'll bring you the supplies." She sat and studied her shoulder. It would be awkward to repair the stitches herself, but she was fairly certain she could do it. The wound itself was an angry red—it had already stopped bleeding—and she used a fingernail to scratch some of the drying blood away. When Aldair returned, he handed her a damp rag, and held the edge of her shirt down so she could clean the area. Whatever the rag had been soaked in made the cut sting, and she hissed through clenched teeth.

"Do you want any of the drink to dull the pain?" he asked, gaze rising from her shoulder to study her face.

She shook her head. "I don't want to be drowsy so close to leaving."

Handing him the rag, she took a deep breath. Sewing her skin back together was going to hurt, there was no denying it. "Tell me again why you don't have a magi traveling with you?"

Aldair chuckled as he handed her a threaded needle. "Let me know if there is anything you want me to help you with."

"I will." Biting her bottom lip, she used three fingers to try to pinch the skin together. Her finger and thumb guided the end of the needle to the edge of the cut, and before she could change her mind, she poked the needle through the skin.

The pain made her gasp, but she kept the needle moving so it punctured through the opposite side of the cut. The thought of doubling back nearly made her give in and ask for that drink, but she clenched her jaw and forced the needle through again. She awkwardly tied off the first stitch with her teeth, then slumped forward, resting her head in her free hand.

Aldair rubbed her forearm. "You're doing a great job. I'm actually impressed you were able to do that."

"You don't have to sound so surprised." She glanced at him and then back to her shoulder. "One down, four to go."

"I know you don't need help, but I can hold your skin together if you want. Might make it easier, though with the edges of the cut so irritated, it will be painful no matter what."

She shrugged her uninjured shoulder. "That's fine. Thank you."

Her hand shook slightly as she brought the needle back to the wound, but she managed to tie two more stitches before tears escaped her eyes and her lower lip started trembling. After the third stitch, she looked at Aldair, swallowed her pride, and handed him the needle. He gave her arm a squeeze before taking it, and she dropped her head in her hands, wincing against the flaring pain.

"If I end up with an ugly scar, I'm blaming you," she muttered through gritted teeth.

"Yes, that's fair since I'll only have done two." He inhaled and held up the needle. "Do you trust me?"

She opened and closed her mouth. That was a loaded question. "I trust you to sew up my shoulder," she replied carefully.

He grunted as he bent over her arm. "That was very specific."

"Were you implying something else? I—Agh!"

Aldair had pierced her skin, and she flinched away from him.

"Don't move," he ordered, expertly following the movement of her shoulder. "I suppose I was implying an overall trust. You are more open with me, but your eyes are still guarded." He chuckled. "You're like a horse who has never before seen an apple. Ears ridged, eyes wide, muscles taut, ready to flee at a moment's notice. But once the horse decides to trust that the apple won't attack her, she relaxes and trust is built."

"So you're saying you're an apple?" she asked, gasping against the next jab of the needle.

He laughed. "Maybe I'm the person holding the apple. When our skittish horse realizes the apple holder is a friend, she learns to trust him." He tied the stitch off and sat back, giving her a moment to relax.

"That's an interesting comparison," she snorted. "What exactly is this apple you're holding out?"

He shrugged. "Now this stitch is going to hurt most I think. Your skin is more irritated along this spot, but I'll be as quick as I can." He sat forward, studying the cut.

"Just do it," she said, balling her hands tightly into fists. Her fingernails bit into her palms, but she kept squeezing. Aldair was right. It was agony. He was fast, though, and the stitch was soon tied off.

She released her breath slowly. "Thank you," she said, wiping her palms on her trousers.

"Anytime you find yourself with a stab wound, I'll be there to sew you back up." He smiled almost slyly before quickly going on. "Do you want me to wrap it for you? It may help with any rubbing."

She nodded. "Sure. If you think it will help."

He stood, picking up the needle and rag, and when he returned he had some gauzy white bandages with him. He eyed her shoulder and frowned. "Um, is there any way you can pull your arm through the top of your shirt? The bandage may hold better if it wraps under your arm." He ducked his head, looking through the supplies, and Steele had to grin. He was very pointedly not looking at her.

By loosening the buttons at the top of her shirt, she was able to pull her arm up and through the opening while easily keeping herself covered. She glanced at him and grinned to find his back still turned toward her. "The shoulder is all yours."

Aldair glanced at her then and tossed the gauze wrap at her. "Hold this until I need it."

"I was thinking," Steele said, rubbing the bandage between her fingers, "even if your skittish horse learned to trust the apple holder, what's the point? It's not like the skittish horse and the apple holder can remain friends for the rest of their lives."

He held a piece of material against her stitches and looked at her. Dark hair fell messily across his forehead, and the glint of the sun turned his eyes to blue ice. "Why not?"

She studied him, sadness and frustration mounting in her chest. "Because it would be impossible. Even if you do as you promise and don't turn me into your father, I won't be able to remain in Solarrhia. There are too many people there who know me."

Aldair wiped his forehead with his arm before motioning for her to hand him the bandage. When she did, he sighed as he unraveled it. "I suppose I can see where you are coming from. I just want to be able to give you the luxury of not having to feel that paranoia when you're around someone new."

"Why? Why do you care so much?"

"I don't know."

"I'm not saying I think you, Em, and Kaleel are bad men. I don't, actually. You three are some of the most genuine people I have met outside my friends in the thieving circuit. I also think there are varying degrees of trust. Like I said, I trust that you did a decent job with my shoulder. I trust that Kaleel will catch that serpent so we'll be full when we follow the train. And I trust that Em is a loving husband and father."

"So you trust me as a doctor?" he challenged, teeth flashing white against his tan skin as he grinned at her.

"Yes," she replied with a laugh. "And..." She paused, surprised to feel her cheeks warm. "And I trust that one day, you will make a good and fair king."

He looked up at her and raised his eyebrows. "Thank you. I hope you are right." He finished wrapping the bandage around her shoulder and tied the ends off.

He turned away, so she could maneuver her arm back through the hole. The wrapping covered her shoulder and part of her upper arm, though, so she was not as flexible as she had been before. With a grunt, she maneuvered her arm back in her shirt and buttoned it. She tested out the mobility of her shoulder by wiggling it around and then throwing a clod of sand away from her. "Well, Prince, Em was right. You are handy with a needle and thread."

Aldair gave her a grin when he turned to look at her again, extending his hand to help her stand. "You'll have to let him know."

* ☽ *

When Emdubae and Kaleel returned from their serpent hunt, they walked side by side with a giant snake stretched limply between them. Steele shied away from them, earning a chuckle from Kaleel.

"You do not like snakes, Steele?" He used his saber to cut the skin away from the reptile.

Shuddering, she shook her head. "I prefer them to scorpions, but not when they're the same size as me!"

Emdubae knelt by the ash and struck two rocks together to create a fresh fire. "Desert snakes are a delicacy."

When Kaleel had cut the snake into pieces, Aldair skewered the meat on sticks and held them over the now-cracking fire. Steele settled next to him, holding a few sticks of her own. The meat did not take long to cook, and before long, all that remained of the snake were the bones and skin. Kaleel broke a small rib away from the backbone and used it to pick his teeth.

Emdubae arched an eyebrow at his friend before kicking sand over the fire and getting ready to leave. "How would you like to follow the train, Aldair?"

The prince broke the stick he was holding in half and tossed it into the fire. "Here are my thoughts. We ride together during the day, following the train's path. One person will go ahead to scout out any changes, with the rest not far behind. At night, I think it'd be best to keep an eye on the train's camp. We'll rotate in pairs at night for rest. I'm curious to see who this boss is that they mentioned."

Kaleel nodded, poking at his gums with the edge of the rib. "I would also like to know what they are doing so far from the mountain region."

"Steele, would you like to scout the train first?" Aldair asked, pinning her to the ground with a very deliberate look.

"Sure," she answered, avoiding his eyes, and rose to her feet. "I see what you're doing, by the way. But you know it's always easier for the apple holder to offer trust to the skittish horse," she muttered when she passed him.

Kaleel snorted. "And what does that mean?"

"Nothing," Aldair said with a laugh, climbing into his saddle.

Emdubae looked from Aldair to Steele before shrugging. "Kaleel, it appears we are not meant to know this joke." He fastened a bag behind his horse's saddle and surveyed the campsite, looking for anything they may have forgotten. Satisfied that they had everything, he swung into the saddle.

Steele could feel eyes on her, so she turned her back and mounted Kesif. "How long do you want us to ride ahead?"

Aldair squinted from the sun to the horizon line. "It'd be good to see if they're going in a general direction or if they're inconsistent. If they stop for a break, come back, but otherwise it's your judgment. We will ride up to relieve you should you be gone too long. If you're seen or you notice anything strange, return straight away."

Nodding, she gathered her reins, circling Kesif. As usual, the paint was anxious to be moving.

"Try not to get lost," she called over her shoulder, sharing a smile with Aldair. As Kesif jumped into a ground eating canter, the laughter of the men resounded from behind her, and a small grin twitched across her lips.

CHAPTER 21

After a day of following the train, Steele discovered she found the process extremely dull. During her breaks, she'd taken to making bracelets out of leather and cloth scraps from broken equipment and torn clothing. The project killed time, but it wasn't very productive. Even the stars emerging from the dusty-purple sky could not distract her from her boredom. The thrill of scouting ahead, gauging just how close she could get to the train without being discovered, had worn out. On top of that, she found herself missing the almost constant banter between the men when she was alone. Which was a very interesting thing to be missing, she mused. When had solitude become a distant friend?

She pulled Kesif to a halt at the bottom of a large dune and dismounted. She was careful as she peered around the wall of sand. She could be closer than she thought.

While the train wasn't directly behind the dune, it wasn't too far off, either. It was a dark silhouette against the sky, and Steele jumped back, knocking into Kesif. She waited a few moments before edging around the sand dune again to check the train's progress and swallowed an annoyed growl.

This must be the slowest moving train ever built.

She was a little surprised no one had caught onto their trail by now. It seemed the train's crew didn't care if they were caught. Either they were used to their daily routine and had slackened their security, or they thought they were completely within their rights to travel throughout Solarrhian lands.

She turned at Kesif's breathy nicker. Emdubae was trotting toward her, the beige coloring of Ortak's coat blending so well with the sand in the twilight that Emdubae looked as if he were floating.

"Are they stopping for the night?" he asked, slowing his horse to a stop.

Steele rubbed the tiny star on the horse's forehead. "They must be. They're still moving, but at a snail's pace."

Emdubae chuckled. "Perhaps you will find restocking supplies to be more interesting."

She gave him a quizzical look. "What?"

"Kaleel rode off to give Rhub a chance to stretch her legs and found a nomadic tribe. Since we are running low on basic supplies, Aldair wants to see if they are willing to trade, but they may listen to the wishes of a lady over the likes of Aldair and Kaleel."

"I'm not a lady," she said with a grunt.

Emdubae pursed his lips and shrugged. "Depends on who you ask. Have you encountered a nomad camp before?"

She shook her head. "I've never been this far into the desert. I tried to travel to Oakenjara once, but the desert is too vast and dangerous, and the mountains are no place to wander alone. I learned that quickly. Glad I didn't know for sure about the dragons then." She glanced at him. "How many tribes have you visited?"

"Not too many," he admitted. "But the folks I have met seem friendly enough."

"I've heard they can be dangerous. It's been said that if you wander into the desert, you may be taken captive by the nomads and never released."

He chuckled. "I have heard that, as well, but if people are never released, who then do you think tells the stories?"

"You know, I have wondered that myself," Steele said with a laugh. "Maybe the nomads start the stories so people will leave them alone."

"Now that is an interesting theory," Emdubae agreed. "You should head back. You'll need to meet with the nomads before it gets too dark."

★ ☽ ★

"We have to make sure no one will recognize you," Kaleel said as he chucked clothing at the prince. "These men and women are known for their solid memories, and they may be the sort who would rather rob than help us." He turned back to the bag in front of him, sorting out materials and tools they could trade.

Steele hid a grin. Both Kaleel and Aldair had dirt-streaked faces, and though their clothing may once have been fine, weeks in the desert had worn it down.

"I don't think either of you need to worry about that." She pulled a long swathe of cloth out of the bag and tied it around her hips like a skirt.

Kaleel folded a maroon shirt and set it aside. "Are you implying, dear sister, that we look like ruffians?"

"Sister?" Steele wrinkled her nose.

"You and Kaleel will be pretending to be brother and sister. You look the most alike out of the three of us," Aldair explained, adding a pair of mostly intact trousers to the pile beside Kaleel.

161

"And who are you supposed to be?" she asked.

"I'm your childhood friend. We are traveling with your father, and he sent us out to trade for supplies." Aldair wiggled a ring off his finger and pocketed it.

"Weapons?" Kaleel looked to Aldair.

The prince took his saber and looked at it for a moment. "Best to leave them, but take your knives." He took Kaleel's saber and his own and set them inside the tent. He exited, tucking a knife into his boot.

Steele rubbed her eyes. "Tell me, why does *Pa* always send us out to do his work?"

"He's trimming the horses' hooves, of course," Kaleel countered.

Her heart warmed at the answer. Her own father had done that plenty of times. A yawn threatened to pull her jaws apart, but she swallowed it. Exhaustion was a part of life she was used to, but that didn't mean she didn't feel the effects. Somehow sitting on the back of a horse all day had made her wearier than sneaking a horse from one town to another.

As Aldair tied the clothing bag, she scooped up the other items they would try to trade, and by the time she rose, Kaleel had the horses ready.

"I'm assuming you know how to get back here?" she asked as they rode toward the moon, and the exasperated look Aldair gave her made her grin.

"It might be difficult seeing as Kaleel and I have no experience in navigating the desert at night," he said dryly.

Kaleel chuckled. "Learning to navigate by the stars was something I struggled to grasp the most. Nothing Instructor Dov tried stuck until he threw me in the desert with Hadrian, who had strict instructions not to assist me."

"I have never heard this story." Aldair said with a laugh. "Did he help you?"

"You know Hadrian. He offered no blatant help whatsoever, but would slip suggestions into our conversations when he saw fit. He had a different way of looking at the night sky, and for whatever reason, when he showed me the way he saw the stars, things clicked. I'll never forget Instructor Dov's face when we returned. I think he half believed I would get us more lost, and then he would be responsible for a missing prince."

Steele laughed. "If you were as bad as you claim, I can see why he would be nervous."

"I can't believe he sent just the two of you out," Aldair said. "I would be more worried that you would leave on a grand adventure than wind up lost."

"Well," Kaleel drawled, "whenever I suggested heading east, Hadrian would nod and occasionally say something like, 'While the palace is in that general direction, I have heard rumors of a creature the supposedly resides south of here, and we would be wise to investigate that.'"

Aldair chuckled. "That sounds more like it."

"Did you find anything?" Steele asked, twisting in the saddle to look at her companions.

"Nothing terribly exciting. A large firecat or what may have been a phoenix. But I will say that I am better at throwing knives than navigating the wilderness." Kaleel ran his hand down the pale mane of his golden horse. "How did you learn to navigate, Steele?"

She drummed her fingers on her saddle and thought of nights spent on her roof. "I've always had a good sense of direction, and I love the night sky. I love the stars. I've watched them travel the sky so many times they've become familiar to me, and with that familiarity I suppose I just developed a knowledge of how to use them to guide me from town to town."

Aldair held up a hand, and they came to a halt. The sound of laughter and clanging pots carried over the air, and he exchanged a glance with Kaleel before dismounting.

"What are you doing?" Steele asked, staying put on Kesif's back.

"If all of us ride in on horses, we may come across as intimidating or hostile. We'll walk alongside them for now," Aldair explained. "You can stay on Kesif if you want. They wouldn't expect us to make our female companion walk."

Steele wiggled her feet in the stirrups, nodding. "Okay, but you better mount up quickly if something happens. If I can only save one of you, I can't promise it will be you."

Kaleel clamped a hand over his mouth to stifle a laugh, and Aldair blinked before a startled grin tugged on his lips. "Good to know you have my back," he replied with a wink.

He turned from her, securing another blade underneath his tunic. "Weapons hidden?"

Kaleel nodded, and she saw a muted flash of metal as several knives disappeared up his sleeves.

"Put this somewhere you can easily hide it," Aldair said, offering her a knife.

"Thank you," she said, tucking it into the band on her trousers. The folds of cloth hid the blade well enough.

"Good," Aldair said, patting Kesif's neck. "Let's go."

CHAPTER 22

The nomad camp was not what Steele had been expecting. The colorful tents were far from glamorous, but they were well cared for. And there were so many! It looked like a little village instead of a temporary camp. Small fires dotted the area, and groups of people sat around them, the flames catching the light of jewelry and smiling faces.

A larger fire lit one edge of the camp, and Kaleel strolled forward with an easy confidence. "Excuse me, good people. My sister, friend, and I have been sent by our father to see if you would be open to trading supplies with us?"

The chatter around the fire fell away as he spoke, and a large man stood, crossing his arms over his chest. "What brings your family this deep in the desert?"

The nomad only sounded suspicious to Steele's ears, but she knew they were walking a very thin line. Aldair, who was leading Rhub and Cahya, shifted next to her. She ran her hand along Kesif's neck. The horse snorted loudly as the smoke drifted toward them.

Steele let out a ridiculous-sounding giggle.

"Bless you, Kesif! Silly horse must not like the smell of smoke!"

Her overly bright voice was annoying even to her, but she saw a certain tightness leave the large man's shoulders.

"You're probably right," Kaleel said, somehow managing to sound annoyed yet fond of her. It was a tone she had often used with Ali, and she wondered if Kaleel had siblings to practice on. "We're moving from our village," he continued, looking back to the man. "My mother died of disease, and my father wants to see the ocean."

A woman rose and stood next to the large man. "Please come closer," she said warmly.

Aldair dropped the horses' leads, and they stayed where he left them as he moved forward. Steele saw the large man give his wife a tired smile. "Nava would invite everyone in the country to sit at our fire if she could."

"And Dex would invite no one," the woman—Nava—said, gesturing for Kaleel to sit by the fire.

"That sounds like Ma," Steele said in that chirpy voice. "Well, sounded like her," she corrected, layering her words with sadness. "Pa always told her to be friendlier because you never know who might need help."

Nava chuckled, rubbing Kesif's nose. "It sounds like your father is a reasonable man, dear." A smug look was directed at Dex, who rolled his eyes. "We can tie your animals on our picket line." She motioned to where a few horses were tied.

"Oh!" Steele exclaimed, earning startled looks from Aldair and Kaleel. "I left Kesif's water with Pa, and he didn't get a chance to drink anything before we left!"

Aldair covered a laugh with a cough, and Steele looked at Nava. "Could he please have some water? In return I can give you a bracelet I made."

"Of course he can, dear. The others, too. And you don't have to give me anything. Now slide on down and join your brother at the fire."

Aldair offered her his hand, and Steele frowned. Her knife would show if she dismounted normally, and as nice as Nava and Dex seemed, she doubted the sudden appearance of a weapon would keep them at ease.

"Just a moment, Mistress Nava," she said, willing Aldair to realize her problem. "My dress seems to be stuck on the saddle."

Aldair furrowed his brow, eyes traveling from her skirt to the saddle and then up to her face. "Just jump," he whispered. "I'll catch you."

"I have to get off on the right," she muttered under her breath, adjusting the skirt and pulling down on her shirt so the blade was better covered. "If I jab you, it's not my fault."

"Do you need help?" Nava asked. "I know skirts can be difficult."

"Oh no, I've got it." She kicked her left foot free of the stirrup as Aldair moved to her other side. "Catch me, Ardie!" she exclaimed, before pushing herself sideways.

He grunted when he caught her, and she shrieked as they both tumbled to the ground. "Are you all right?" she whispered.

Aldair laughed. "I am."

"You know, attention-grabbing stunts like that won't make Ardeth like you, little sister," Kaleel chided, earning laughter from those seated around him.

Cheeks flaming, she untangled herself from Aldair's arms, stalked over to Kaleel, and socked him in the shoulder. Picked-on little sisters were always receiving sympathy, and one good thing about her bright and cheerful voice was that it made people believe she was much younger than her twenty-two years.

As one of the nomads led the horses away, Aldair sat on the other side of where she stood, and she moved to the opposite side of the fire, next to Dex.

The large man chuckled softly. "You remind me of my daughter."

Steele swirled patterns into the sand with her index finger. "I do?"

"Yes, but that could be because she too has an older brother who teases her constantly. They are a couple fires over if you want some space from them." He nodded toward Aldair and Kaleel.

She pretended to mull the idea over before shaking her head. "No, I shouldn't. Pa said not to leave their sides."

"Ah, so what is it you want to trade for?" he called across the fire as Nava settled next to him.

"Basic supplies, really," Aldair said. "We just left an oasis earlier in the week and have enough water for our journey. We're aware it's difficult to come by here." He looked to Kaleel for confirmation, and he nodded.

Steele chewed the corner of her cheek. It was interesting to see Aldair defer to Kaleel, and for Kaleel to take the lead so effortlessly. She wondered if they did this often as a way to cover up the prince's identity. Whatever the case, it was working. Most of the people seated at the fire had eyes for Kaleel and only briefly regarded his blue-eyed friend.

"What about food?" she asked brightly. "Pa said we were set with meat, but I miss the taste of fruit!" A little dramatic perhaps, but Nava laughed.

"We could give you some fruit, I think," she said, looking to her husband.

Dex nodded. "Absolutely. I'm afraid we can't let it go for free…" He looked to Kaleel who was nodding.

"We brought clothing for you to look through. Since we are leaving the desert region, Pa wants us to get rid of some shirts and pants."

"Apparently he thinks we won't need them where we're going," Steele said, words laced with annoyance. "Have you been to the sea, Dex? Will we regret trading you our clothes?"

"I haven't," Dex answered with a tiny sigh. "But I would love to go. I hear it's beautiful."

"Oh. With all the people we've seen in the desert, I hoped someone would have been to where we're going." She glanced at Aldair and Kaleel and almost laughed. Lips parted, they regarded her with shocked disapproval at the risk she took with her words. She smirked.

"Hmm," Dex mused, the corners of his mouth turning down in a small frown. "Now that you mention it, there have been more people in the desert recently."

"Is that not normal?" she asked, stretching her eyes wide. "Should we be scared?" She glanced to Kaleel and back to Dex and wrung her hands.

Nava reached across Dex and patted Steele's knee. "I don't think you're in any danger, dear. It just could be that more people are crossing the desert now because it's not as hot as it was earlier this season."

"So this much desert traffic is normal?" Aldair asked, sounding very politely interested.

A blonde woman with very blue eyes shrugged. "The desert is unpredictable. Some years many cross it; some years we see no travelers. There appear to be many foreign travelers though. We saw—" She stopped talking abruptly at a sharp look from her husband.

"It's all right, Ruben," Dex said. "Calla can speak."

"How do we know they aren't trying to make us feel comfortable so they can rob us later on?" Ruben asked gruffly.

"Are there robbers around this part of the desert?" Steele asked in a small voice. She curled into Dex's side, acting frightened even though she agreed with this Ruben.

Dex patted her shoulder. "No, no, you're quite safe around these parts." He leveled a glare at Ruben.

"What I was going to say," Calla went on, flashing a smug grin at Ruben, "was that we saw what looked like a long caravan heading east and from the looks of it, we thought it had come from the sea." She smiled at Steele. "Perhaps if you find them, you will learn about your new home."

"Maybe," Steele said uncertainly, looking to her "brother" for reassurance. Kaleel and Aldair were both looking at her with something, admiration perhaps, in their eyes. Naive little sister was becoming a very useful character.

"Your pa has assured you many times that you'll be safe," Aldair said kindly. "You don't have to worry."

"You don't have to be nice to her," Kaleel muttered. "She'll figure it out eventually."

Nava chuckled but gave Kaleel a knowing look. "Being the oldest is quite a chore sometimes."

"You mentioned clothing to trade?" Dex prodded, standing and dusting off his hands on his pants. "Let's see what you've got."

Aldair pulled the clothing out and passed it to Dex. A couple of people stood and gathered around the clothing, exchanging shirts and trousers and discussing the items in whispers. Steele unwound a couple of bracelets from her wrist and tossed them at Aldair. He deftly caught them and, after inspection, added them to the pile of clothes.

Before long, the clothing had been dispersed, and those who had taken something, excused themselves to fetch items they would trade in return. Steele was happy to see water skins and some fruit among the items, along with other leafy foods and even what appeared to be a fishing pole.

An elderly man with silver hair offered her the pole. "Since you're going to the sea, you might find this comes in very handy for catching fish." He smiled widely, revealing three gold capped teeth.

She took the pole, her heart softening at his generosity and thoughtfulness. She almost didn't want to take it, knowing that, in reality, they would have no use for it. A vision of Dal rolling his eyes popped into her head, and she laughed once as she thanked the man.

"My father thanks you for your kindness," Kaleel said, grasping Dex's hand once the supplies had been distributed. "We must return to him, or he may think something happened to us."

Calla appeared, leading Cahya and Rhub, and handed the leads to Aldair. Ruben followed, leading Kesif, and helped Steele into the saddle. "This is a fine animal you have. Take good care of him."

"Oh, I will! He belonged to my ma, and I promised her I would keep him forever!" She kissed the top of Kesif's mane for emphasis and dropped a couple of melons to the ground. While Ruben bent to retrieve the fruit, she checked to make sure her knife was still hidden.

"Oh thank you," she exclaimed as Ruben handed her the bundle. "My brother claims I have oil on my fingers because I drop things so often."

Ruben chuckled as he took the melons back, deposited them in a sack, and tied it behind the saddle. "There. You won't have to worry about dropping it now."

Steele smiled her thanks and turned Kesif so they were standing between Aldair and Kaleel. Now that her group was standing, she was anxious to be away and check in with Emdubae.

She waved to Dex and Nava as Aldair led the horses away. Even though she was ready to leave, she had enjoyed her time at the nomad camp. Perhaps after Tazmeen and Ali were found, she could make her way back to them.

They were silent as they moved away from the nomads, the sound of laughter and even the strumming of a fiddle fading away. Steele pulled out a melon and used her knife to cut a slice. She bit into it, savoring the tangy juice. Kaleel glanced at her and held out his hand. She passed a piece to him.

Kaleel handed Steele what remained of the fruit before untying the animals. She finished the melon before handing the pit to Aldair.

"What am I supposed to do with this?" He asked, eyebrow cocked.

"See if Kesif wants it, please."

He shook his head and offered it to the horse, who lipped at the pit before turning his head away, uninterested. Throwing it aside, Aldair patted Kesif's neck before looking up at her. "I have to say that I'm impressed with you," he commented, offering Rhub's lead to Kaleel, and swinging into the saddle.

"Ah, thank you." she half bowed over the saddle.

"It's no wonder our guards could never catch you," Kaleel added, nudging Rhub with his heels. "How many people have you pretended to be?"

"I've lost count," she admitted. "I've found silly young girls gain the most sympathy. Or rather, they make people more trusting."

"It was brilliant," Aldair said, riding alongside her. "That voice though…"

She laughed. "It's awful, but it works."

Kaleel slowed so the three of them rode side by side. "Aldair, I'm really thinking we should just keep her around when we get home—have a magi alter her appearance or something. She's proving to be quite useful."

Steele swallowed, hands tightening on the reins. Since people thought she was dead, she might be able to stay in the kingdom, just not in Rhia. There were still too many guards who might recognize her, and the king had sentenced her to death. If for some reason he pardoned her, people might doubt his decision-making, and really, he had made the right choice. Rubbing a palm around her neck, she glanced up to find Aldair watching her.

It was hard to read his expression since the moon was at their backs, but he appeared to smile after a moment.

"I'm sure Kismet could turn her hair white and give her new clothes," he said, "but I don't think Steele has a face that is easily forgotten."

She wet her lips, unsure of what to say.

Luckily Kaleel laughed. "I suppose that's true. It's most unfortunate that you were cursed with that face." He elbowed her in the arm.

"I hope you mean that as a compliment," she remarked, glancing between the two of them.

"He does," Aldair said quickly.

Kaleel agreed, head bobbing. "Do you remember how to get back to where Em is, Steele?" he asked, looking around

She rotated her neck, her eyes following the stars. "I believe so."

They followed her as she made her way toward the train. It took longer than expected to find Emdubae because he had moved to what appeared to be a sandy valley. A tiny pinprick of light floated above the sand where he waited, and as they rode down the slope, Steele could see he had lit a torch and stuck it in the sand. He stood as they drew closer, and Kaleel chucked an apple at him.

Emdubae caught the fruit and instead of eating it, tossed it back and forth between his hands while he waited for them to ride closer.

Aldair dismounted and faced Emdubae. "What is it? What did you learn?"

"There appears to be an important meeting in a couple of days. They never mentioned the name of this ringleader though, but I wasn't close enough to catch everything they said. I tried getting closer, but they seemed more on edge tonight. More of the crew was roaming about." He scratched his beard and sighed. "I believe they mean to leave early, so we may as well sleep here. We're far enough away that I do not believe they will see us, even if they decide to patrol the area for any reason."

Aldair grasped Emdubae's shoulder. "I've been meaning to tell you that you clump around when you walk, so be extra careful." He grinned at his friend.

"Don't let Em think his mission was the only important one," Kaleel commented, rolling his eyes at Steele.

"And what did you discover?" Emdubae asked, finally biting into the fruit.

"The nomads say there has been an increase in desert travelers this season," Aldair said, loosening the cinch around Cahya's belly. "They thought one looked like it could have come from the Barrowlands."

Emdubae frowned. "Why would Queen Evelind be doing business out here? Can you be sure they did not just say that to get you out of their camp?"

"Normally I would consider that, but no. We owe that certainty to Steele."

"Oh? Somehow that does not surprise me," Emdubae said with a smile.

Kaleel snorted as he dug in around one sack of supplies. "I am trying to convince Aldair that we should just keep her around when we get home."

"Yes, that's not a bad idea," Emdubae said.

Steele looked at him, and while he smiled, there was a knowing sadness to his eyes. He knew why she could not remain in Rhia, and that small understanding caused her smile to slip. She should feel relieved that one of these men seemed to understand her, shouldn't she?

The thought left quickly as exhaustion overcame her. It seemed they were all tired, actually, for it wasn't long before they'd settled into their blankets for the night. Steele shivered, missing how the tent blocked the cold night air. Remembering the last night she had spent in the desert without shelter, she left the covers and dug into the sand, leaving a small crater for her body to rest in so the wind would blow over her. She settled back into her blanket and closed her eyes. It must have worked because suddenly she was much warmer, and she drifted off to sleep.

CHAPTER 23

Steele rolled over, and her eyes snapped open at the pinching pain in her shoulder. She'd forgotten about those stitches. As she pushed herself up, she realized three sand-sprinkled blankets covered her, and she looked at the men, sore shoulder forgotten. Perhaps digging a hole to sleep in hadn't been what kept her warm after all.

Not too far from her, Kaleel broke a piece of charcoal off a torch and leaned in front of Emdubae to study a parchment. Aldair acknowledged her being awake with a half-smile before he turned back to the men. They spoke in low tones, and eventually, Steele grew tired of straining to hear them.

"Care to share what you're discussing?"

Emdubae beckoned to her. "We're comparing locations. Would you like to see?"

Gathering the blankets in her arms, she moved to stand at Aldair's side. This map was more a crude drawing of the land than the official map Emdubae had, and she cocked her head as she looked at it, trying to determine where they stood.

A dark mark appeared on ride side of the parchment as Kaleel poked it with the charcoal. "We figure we're around here." He tapped the papers again, sending black flecks scattering across the page.

Steele took in the pursed lips and drawn eyebrows of the three men. "And that's bad because...?"

"My father has various lookouts stationed along our borders, and he sends groups of palace guards to patrol the desert regularly, so it's strange that they have seen nothing suspicious. Not one of those stationed in the outposts have made reports about increased activity in the desert. I should know if there are Meadowlanders and Hamonsfellans traveling through our lands."

"Were any of these scouting parties led by Lac?" Steele asked.

Emdubae scratched his cheek. "He would have been on one, yes. Which, with what we now know, makes sense why we didn't hear anything."

Aldair rubbed the back of his head. "I'll send word to Father and let him decide how much he wants to share with others. We already have people who shouldn't be here maneuvering through our lands."

Kaleel walked to where Rhub was tied and led the mare forward. "They looked about ready to leave when I checked earlier. I'll head now to make sure they haven't begun their journey."

"I'll be with you shortly," Emdubae said to him. "Please don't get caught before then."

Kaleel saluted his friend, and with a quick glance at Aldair, he turned Rhub and rode away from the camp.

"Do we need to get the rest of our things from camp?" Steele asked, suddenly remembering they'd left their weapons in the tents the day before.

"Aldair and I collected everything before dawn," Emdubae explained, taking the blankets from her. He shoved them in a sack before tying them behind Ortak's saddle. "Here," he said, taking a sheathed saber from one of his packs. "You'll need this."

She accepted it with a small smile. "Thank you." She fastened it to her belt, and pulled the blade from its casing to examine it. It was curved and just shorter than the length of her arm.

"You're welcome, Little Thief." Emdubae tipped his head. "My wife forged it."

Steele looked at him. "Are you sure you want me to use it?"

"Of course. She'd love for it to be in a woman's hands again." He turned from her then and began picking up the remainder of his things.

Beside her, Aldair was still silent. He looked deep in thought, so she tentatively touched his arm. "Are you all right?"

He faced her, and though his eyes were troubled, he smiled. "I think I will be once we get to the bottom of this. If Lac is not only a disrespectful palace guard, but also part of something illegal, there must be corruption within the palace. That worries me."

Emdubae approached them and stood beside Steele. He crossed his arms, a pensive look on his face. "If there is corruption, would that make it deeply rooted?"

"I don't know." Aldair's shoulders slumped.

"At least you know we're on the right track," Steele said, trying to sound helpful. The dejection in Aldair's posture made her heart twist. "You've been giving information to your father so he is aware of what's happening, and who knows, maybe we'll finally see the boss when we scout later tonight."

Emdubae smiled at her, clear blue eyes crinkling at the sides. "She's right, Aldair. If there is corruption, we know about it now, and it will be dealt with."

Aldair sighed. "You're both right. Dwelling on the problem won't answer any questions at the moment, so…." He folded the piece of parchment with a snap and put it away.

✶ ☽ ✶

The train didn't stop for two days. In fact, it seemed to pick up speed, and the four had to maintain a canter to keep up until it stopped in the early evening.

"We'll use the train for cover," Aldair said, leading Kesif to where Steele stood. "And the dunes should give us some cover, too."

She nodded, taking the reins. Aldair was growing impatient, so the plan was for him and Steele to try and sneak farther into the campsite where they would hopefully uncover more information.

Emdubae ran a hand through his dark hair as he came to stand beside them. "I know you do not anticipate anything happening to you, but please be careful. And you," he looped an arm around Steele's shoulders. With his other arm, he tapped his spyglass that was attached to his hip. "You keep an eye on Aldair. If you don't, we'll know."

Aldair laughed as Steele nodded. "I'll do my best."

"You don't have to worry about me, Em," Aldair said. "She's the one who has been prone to sneaking out in the middle of the night."

"*You* followed me," Steele protested, sticking her foot in the stirrup and pulling herself into her saddle. "Besides, if I hadn't gone on that ride, we wouldn't be where we are today, so it ended up being a good thing."

Emdubae squeezed her shoulder and stepped away as Kaleel strolled toward them. "She does have a point, Aldair."

"Of course she does," the prince replied with a teasing grin as he untied Cahya.

Kaleel patted Cahya on the rump and the mare snorted, flicking her tail at him.

Aldair swung into his saddle. "Try not to blow our cover," he called, turning Cahya away from Emdubae and Kaleel so they stood next to Steele and Kesif. "Ready?" He asked, looping a scarf around his face.

"Yes. Where did you get that scarf?" Steele patted her head, wishing she had something to keep her hair from her face.

"Here," Emdubae offered, handing her a dark brown scarf. "I meant to give this to you earlier."

"Thank you," Steele said, accepting the cloth and looping it around her face like the hood of a cloak. "Now I'm ready."

Aldair smiled turning Cahya away from the men, and Steele followed him. As they rode away from Emdubae and Kaleel, Steele's

174

thoughts turned to Tazmeen and Ali. She knew they were not on this particular train, and the only thing that kept her from howling in frustration was that hopefully, whenever they figured out who this leader was, they would inadvertently tell her how or where to find her family.

If she learned where they were, then what? Leave Aldair and his men to find them on her own? She shook her head as soon as that thought crossed her mind. Even if she wanted to do that, she knew she would not be searching alone. There was always the chance that Tazmeen and Ali's arrest or whatever it was had nothing to do with criminals being transported on trains. But that thought was almost too much to consider because if that was the case, she would have absolutely nothing to go on besides the information Aldair had on the crime ring, which was frustratingly little.

"You seem preoccupied." Aldair cut into her thoughts.

"Hmm," Steele grunted in reply, scratching her thumbnail over the hilt of her saber.

"Well, thank you for clearing that up," he said dryly.

"I was just thinking about the people on the trains. What if not all of them were criminals?"

"Okay," he said slowly, nose wrinkling in confusion. "I'll bite. So what?"

"It wouldn't make sense."

"No, it would not."

"So then why would people who aren't criminals be taken?"

Aldair cocked his head at her, puzzled. "I'm not sure I follow."

"The people I knew who were taken were just ordinary people. Sure, they were poor and had to live with some fear of being robbed, abused, or used in some way, but they weren't criminals. The only way I can justify their arrest is because they had some connection to me. That makes sense, but they would have been tried with me or something." Guilt stabbed at her heart, and she exhaled in a rush.

"That sounds like a stressful way to live." Aldair sounded mystified. Whether by the conversation or the lifestyle, Steele wasn't sure.

"Not all of us were privileged to grow up with bodyguards," she replied flatly.

Aldair pulled Cahya to a halt. "What do you mean by that?"

Steele sighed, stopping Kesif. This was not a conversation she had been expecting. "You grew up very differently than I did. When you were a boy you had people to do things for you. You had people to watch out for you. I didn't. Tazmeen, she's who raised me, taught me to care for myself since she couldn't be with me all day every day."

"You think I've been coddled my whole life." Aldair pulled his head scarf down and ran a hand through his brown hair, causing it to stick up.

Steele pushed her scarf back from her forehead so it dropped to her shoulders. "All I'm saying is that you never had to wonder if you were going to get a meal. You never had to wonder if someone was going to try and pick your pocket on the way home from the market. You never had to worry for your safety because you're not a woman traveling alone. That's what I grew up with, but I don't even think about it anymore." She looked up from where she had been stroking Kesif's neck and blinked at the expression on Aldair's face. "I'm sorry if I offended you. I was just trying to explain myself. I—"

"Don't apologize," he said, cutting her off. "I didn't mean to frown at you like that. It's just that I've never considered that. I do seem to have been coddled." He wrinkled his nose and scowled. "You are right. We have led very different lives." He stared intently in the direction of their destination. "Though you may not see it, my upbringing came with a price."

"A price?"

"Freedom," he sighed, looking much older than his twenty-six years.

Steele opened her mouth to reply, but he held up his hand. She narrowed her eyes at the silent command, yet she obeyed.

"You had burdens, yes, and I am so sorry that I spent so much time ignoring my duty as a leader in the kingdom," Aldair looked at her then, his troubled eyes a stormy blue. He swallowed and continued, "Some days, I thought I was free; others, I felt chained to that throne, unable to choose my own path because of the family I was born into. At times, the thought of wearing that crown felt like the weight of a thousand horses. Yet, instead of being a petulant child crying out that the world was against me, I could have walked outside and actually done some good. I could have done so much."

Unsure of how to respond, Steele kept silent.

"Maybe then you wouldn't have starved or felt the need to steal for a living."

"You give yourself too much credit if you think I wouldn't have stolen anything had you been born with a completely different mindset. No one can be perfect, Prince. I was hungry before I became a thief, but I had never stolen until that horse. It wasn't about stealing at all, and even if that wasn't the right choice, I'm glad the horse was able to live out her days in peace. However, if we can go back in time, could you maybe establish a law to protect animals from abuse, or at least prevent idiotic people from owning them?" With a click of her tongue, she added, "Or maybe I could have a wiser brain and could come up with a better plan than stealing to save the horse."

Aldair's lips twitched, but he did not smile.

Sighing, she placed a hand on his forearm. "Maybe you will understand people's pain more because you have some of your own now. Everyone has a journey, and from what I've seen of yours, you're doing well."

He looked at her hand on his arm and hesitated before covering her hand with his own. Steele's heart jumped at the contact, and she blinked. When he shifted his eyes to hers, she immediately looked anywhere except his face.

He released her hand with a quick squeeze and nodded. "Thank you. My brother said something similar in one of his letters."

"Your brother was a smart man." She smiled softly, trying not to concentrate on the phantom feeling of his hand on hers. She clenched her hand into a fist and then stretched her fingers out.

Aldair coughed and spurred Cahya into a walk. Steele followed suit, trotting to catch up to the mare's side. "You seem to be making up for all that coddling here in this awful desert."

He smiled and rubbed his scruffy cheek. The half beard and the odd way his hair stuck out made him look a bit wild. She laughed.

"What?" His smile grew.

"Has Kaleel been styling your hair recently?"

He quickly ran his hand through his hair and shrugged. "I wouldn't put it past him."

They both were silent a moment, Steele focusing on the back of Kesif's head where his mane faded from red to white. She thought again of the train and those people and whether they were innocent or not. And Bero. He had helped her, and she had just left him there.

"It was a magi," she blurted, unsure of why she wanted to share this information with Aldair all of a sudden.

"What was?"

"A magi named Bero. He's how I escaped the train. He undid the locks on my cuffs so I could move about and find a loose floorboard." She glanced at Aldair and almost smiled at the look on his face. "Bero is a good man, Aldair. I wanted him to leave with me, but he would not leave the other magi behind. I want to free them, too, because I don't think they were happily on the train."

Aldair laughed once. "I don't know why I am continually surprised by you and your experiences." He spoke dryly, but when Steele looked at him, he was smiling. "Let me guess, the phoenix who gave you that

177

feather actually flew down from the heavens, plucked the feather from its wing, and gifted it to you."

Steele laughed at the ridiculous scene she was imagining. "My father gave me the feather," she said. "And he told me that the phoenix strutted across the ground to offer it to him." Aldair's jaw dropped, and Steele grinned widely. "I'm joking. Though the feather *was* a gift from my father."

Aldair chuckled, shaking his head. "I would not be surprised to find your story true."

Her own smile faded, and she looked ahead. The topic of their conversation did nothing to ease her heart, but she felt pleased that she had managed to make Aldair smile again. She would not forget those sad eyes and burdened shoulders for a long while. She had seen the same look in Tazmeen, and her surrogate mother was only trying to feed two children, not a kingdom.

Her heart constricted. Tazmeen.

Aldair nudged Cahya closer to Steele. Studying her face, he asked, "Are you all right?"

"Tazmeen, the woman who brought me up, was the person taken. She and her son, Ali. It's her name I recognized on your list," Steele replied, her voice sounding dull to her own ears. Squaring her shoulders, she looked up at him, grim determination settling across her mouth. The wind pulled her dark hair across her face, and she brushed it roughly behind her ear. "I promised Tazmeen and Ali I would find them, and when I heard her name on your list I believed I had a chance to do that, but I'm so afraid this train and this boss will tell us nothing about where they might be." Her throat caught, and she broke off, tears brimming in her eyes. A hot tear escaped, and she wiped it off her cheek with her shoulder.

Aldair raised a hand to her face and hesitated. With a sigh he reached out and gripped her shoulder. "Why didn't you tell me this before?"

"Because it didn't seem like something you needed to know."

He studied her face and clenched his jaw. "I promise you, we won't return to Rhia until we know something about where your family might be."

Steele peered into his face; there was an earnestness in his eyes that she hadn't seen before, and the fact that he referred to Tazmeen and Ali as her family stirred something within her. "Thank you."

Releasing a shuddering breath, she closed her eyes and counted to three. When she opened her eyes, the tears were gone and the doubt was safely compartmentalized away. Emotion could not lead her here.

Aldair nodded, seeming to understand her thoughts. "How about a canter?"

Nodding, Steele adjusted her hold on the reins. She touched her heels to Kesif's side and the horse shot out from under her. He had grown restless while she and Aldair had spoken and was clearly happy to be moving again.

Despite the suggestion, she didn't try to keep Kesif at a canter. She wanted to run, to clear her head and racing over the sand was perfect for that. A glance at Aldair showed her that he did not mind the increase in pace. Although...Steele narrowed her eyes, it was hard to tell, but he seemed to be holding Cahya back. That seemed odd. Unless he was purposefully giving her space.

She grunted as Kesif galloped over the sand. Why had she felt disappointed when Aldair had only squeezed her shoulder instead of touching her face? And when he promised her they would get information she believed him without a doubt. Exactly when had she decided to trust him so much? These thoughts danced in her mind, keeping in time with the rhythmic thudding of Kesif's hooves in the sand.

CHAPTER 24

Steele lay in the sand next to Aldair and shuddered, wishing they had decided to wait with the horses until darkness fell. At least they had found some shrubs and small trees to block the stiff northern breeze that was currently biting through her clothing. The space was a slight dip in the sand right at the base of a smaller sand dune, and as they hid in it, any hope she had of that small dune shielding them from the wind was quickly dashed. Instead the wind pulled thick, gray clouds over the setting sun, and time crawled in the cold. An involuntary shiver trembled down her spine, and she shifted so she was lying on her arms, hands pulled up under her chin so she could breathe on them for warmth. Would it ever get dark enough to move?

Suddenly she was very aware of Aldair's body pressing against her left side, and his grip on her shoulder prevented her from jerking away. "You're cold. I'm cold," he whispered. "We can keep each other warm until it's time to move."

She couldn't have protested if she wanted to; he was much warmer than the sand, and the added heat made her realize just how cold she was. He linked his arm with hers, and she snuggled against him, beyond caring that she probably shouldn't be using the prince to keep warm.

"Better?" he asked.

"Much," she answered, even as another tremor ran the length of her body.

He laughed quietly. "You're like a block of ice."

"I've been worse, but I really can't remember when," she said, willing her teeth to stop chattering. "It wouldn't be so bad if it weren't for the wind."

Aldair nodded in agreement, and they fell silent. It was hard to hear anything over the whistling of the wind, but occasionally they could hear voices. Steele assumed they belonged to either guards or lookouts.

The wind refused to die down as they lay there, and it kicked up sand as it blustered across the desert. Sand that stung cheeks and arms and any other exposed skin. She sighed and let her head drop onto the ground, facing away from the gusts.

"What is it that draws someone to steal horses?"

Steele raised her eyes to Aldair's and bit the inside of her cheek as she considered the question.

"I was always drawn to them I guess. To their beauty and power and grace. I used to ride around on the giant draft horses that would come for new shoes and they made me feel fearless." She paused, and Aldair moved his face nearer. She assumed it was so he could hear her better, but she was very aware of how close his face was to hers.

"I don't like saying I stole them, though," she continued. "I understand why you said it, and why I'm considered a thief. I took things that didn't belong to me without paying for them, but it never felt wrong because I was removing an animal from an abusive situation. When I took a horse, it always felt more like a rescue mission than something bad."

He studied her before smiling slightly. "It's frustrating when people put a label on you, isn't it?"

"What label have you had besides prince?" she smiled so he wouldn't think she was being rude in her question, but she was curious.

"You never heard of the Spare Heir Aldair?" he asked, eyebrow raised.

"No. At least it rhymes?" she offered with a soft laugh.

His lips twitched. "Probably because it was coined when I was young by my peers who were also young."

She noticed the way his eyes tightened and she gently nudged his shoulder with hers. "That was painful for you?"

"It certainly didn't make me feel very good about myself. As I can imagine being called a thief wasn't amazing for your self-esteem."

"No. But sometimes being called a thief was the kinder of the names. We're seen as bad or dangerous because we break the law, so I can't fault people for looking down on us, but I do fault them for being cruel about it." She frowned slightly. "I bet your friends were jealous of you. I think a lot of times meanness is born from jealousy."

"You are wise for a horse rescuer," he said with a wink.

Her cheeks warmed. "Thank you."

"I still can't believe you never heard Spare Heir," he said with a laugh. "I was convinced everyone did."

"I wasn't in Rhia that often. I did, however, hear more about your reputation."

"Oh?" he sounded wary, like he knew what she was referring to. "And what was that?"

"I heard that you were more of a wild prince."

He grunted. "Unfortunately that's true. I let being called a spare get under my skin, and I figured since the kingdom was in good hands with

Hadrian, I didn't need to be so polished. I don't think I would consider myself wild, but I have years I wish I had spent differently."

Voices sounded from the direction of the campsite, and they fell silent, trying to listen for anything to indicate someone from the camp was heading in their direction. Aldair raised his head from the sand to look around, and Steele shut her eyes, straining to hear anything over the sound of the wind. After a few moments she opened her eyes, and Aldair laid his head back down. They were still undiscovered. She considered what Aldair had been saying before they'd been interrupted.

"I think a lot of people could say that," she offered. "Saying that they had years they wished they could redo. I wondered about your past though when you said Cahya was your oldest friend. I assumed a wild prince would have a lot of friends."

"I had a lot of friends, but it was more quantity than quality. Not to sound like I'm speaking down on you, but when you're royal, people tend to want to be close to you for something other than friendship."

"That sounds lonely."

He nudged her. "I could say that about someone who is a thief."

She smiled. "You could. What was it that changed your outlook?"

"Hadrian. He sat me down and said that just because I was labeled as a spare didn't mean I couldn't stand for something. He said that in some ways it gave me more freedom than he had, and he was disappointed I was choosing to spend my freedom the way I was. He stressed that the names people give us don't hold any power unless we allow them to, and I'd let the label of spare heir become my identity." He fell silent and then laughed once. "It was a verbal beating that I desperately needed. He was a good brother."

"It sounds like one I could have used as well," she admitted. "Sometimes it just feels easier to accept what people place on you."

He tipped his head to better look at her and smiled. "I know I don't know you *that* well, but I can assure you, you're much more than just a thief. You are compassionate and strong."

Her heart tripped in her chest. "I…thank you. That's very kind."

"I mean it," he said, nudging her again.

She was quiet for a moment, trying to get up the nerve to speak boldly. "You're a good man, Aldair," she said finally. "Your brother was right in what he said to you, and I think you've risen above being just a spare heir and turned into someone worthy of being king someday. If Hadrian was still alive, I think he'd be honored and proud to call you his brother." Her breath caught when she noticed the way Aldair was watching her. "Who would have thought we'd have something in common," she said quickly, uncomfortable by how much she enjoyed the prince looking at her that way.

He gave her an easy grin. "Overcoming labels that people or society places on you is no easy thing. I'll help you remember you're more than a thief, and you can help me remember I'm not an unfortunate spare."

She laughed quietly. "All right."

They fell silent again, and drowsiness crept through her body, slowly replacing the cold. Her heavy eyelids drifted shut, and she heard Aldair chuckle. Then his mouth was at her ear. "You're not bored, are you? I thought we were having a good conversation."

She shook her head. "We were. Just very tired all of a sudden." She pried her eyes open, and Aldair's face filled her vision. "I can stay awake."

He touched his forehead to hers so briefly, she wondered if it had actually happened. "Sleep if you can," he said, looking away from her. "I'll wake you if I need to."

Steele jerked as something—or someone—prodded her in the ribs. She must have slept more soundly than usual because she was curled up tight against Aldair and she had no memory of moving. She groaned, not quite ready to peel herself from him, but it was clearly dark enough to start their scouting of the camp.

"You're not too tired to do this are you?" he whispered with a smirk.

She arched an eyebrow at him and tried to suppress a yawn. "Not at all. I'm ready when you are."

They sat up, and she hugged her arms to her chest. "Why didn't we think to bring extra clothes?"

Aldair rubbed his arms. "An unfortunate oversight, I suppose. Maybe this will not take long, and we can be back in front of a fire sooner than we think."

After shaking loose sand from her clothing and rewrapping the scarf around her face, Steele crouched, trying to stretch her stiff muscles. A quick glance over the top of the dune revealed nothing but bumpy, swirling sand, so she stood, cringing at the ache in her back.

Aldair studied the land and frowned. "This is less like a dune and more like a very wide hill. We'll have to just go straight up and hope no one sees us."

"That makes me incredibly nervous," she admitted, biting her lip.

"It doesn't appear as though many people have walked back here," he whispered, squinting at dimples in the sand. "Do these look like footprints to you?"

"Not really, but it's hard to tell." She looked over her shoulder in the direction of the horses. It was a long way to run if they were caught.

"One of us should go up first while the other keeps watch down here. Just because we haven't seen anyone doesn't mean they aren't out here somewhere."

He nodded. "I'll keep watch until you give a signal."

"Okay." She reached up and pulled the front of his scarf over his eyes before quickly turning and climbing the dune.

What in the name of Vlaar are you doing, Steele? She felt her cheeks flame. *The man can ready himself.*

The climb was slow, but the wind was now on her side, the whistling of the air helping to mask the sound of the sliding sand beneath her feet. She hated climbing with her back so exposed, but knowing Aldair was behind her brought her comfort. He may be a prince, but she figured he cared enough about her not to let a guard sneak up and take her. She paused just under the peak, listening for any sound coming from the other side. People were speaking, but they sounded far away, and the smell of smoke from a campfire was very faint.

Heart slamming against her ribs, she risked a glance over the lip of the dune and almost wept in relief.

The train sat along the base of the other side of the dune, curving away from her, the glow from a fire flickered through the gaps in the rail carts, and each end of the train was lit by a smaller fire. The dune wasn't tall enough for her to see over the train, but since it was between them and the travelers, she figured she and Aldair could slide down the dune without being seen. She motioned for him to join her and wordlessly they pulled themselves over the edge.

The trip down was much quicker than the climb up, and Steele stumbled to her knees when she hit the bottom of the slope. Aldair slid down after her, the shushing sound of the sand making her grimace. It sounded incredibly loud to her ears. She remained crouched on her knees as he settled beside her, and they peered around, searching for their next move.

"The trains?" she mouthed, jerking her head at the large carts.

He nodded, and they crept toward the train, pausing when they reached the wooden structure. Steele ran her fingers along the edge, frowning when she looked at the bottom of the cart. The train she'd been on had floated, but this one sat on blocks. There were no wheels, though, so it seemed likely that the blocks were used to support the train while the magi were not powering it. Aldair was also studying the train, but his headscarf cloaked his features.

A shuffling and creaking sound from inside one of the crates made Steele freeze, eyes flying to the prince. He tipped his head to the side, listening. The muffled shuffling sound continued, but he stepped back, grabbing her arm.

There *were* people in the trains!

She raked her eyes over the crate, searching for a lock or door when the grip on her arm tightened, and Aldair started pulling her away from the train. She shook her head, prying at his fingers, but he would not release her. Only when they were back at the base of the dune did he loosen his grip on her arm.

"There are people in there!" she hissed. "We can't just leave them, not when we're this close!"

"I know, I know. We were wrong," he muttered. "But we can't let them out."

"Why? They need our help!"

"Do they? You can't know that for sure."

She opened her mouth, but no words came. Innocent people like Tazmeen and Ali could be on there!

"Steele." Aldair captured her face in his hands, and looked into her eyes. "I mean no offense, but you were on the train as a convicted thief. We cannot know for sure that the people on this train are innocent. They could be rightfully convicted as you were."

Though he spoke the truth, his words stung, and she tried to look away as shame burned at her cheeks.

"There could be murderers or bandits on that train, and we would be doing a terrible thing if we were to free them."
Steele finally raised her eyes to meet his.

"And what if they're innocent?"

"Where would we keep them if we were to free them? How would we feed them? Where would they go? How would we free them without risking exposure? I want to help them as much as you do, but only if they are truly innocent and only if freeing them would be beneficial to them. Right now, we would hurt them more than help them."

She glared at him, hating his logic yet knowing he was right. The thought that the prisoners could be murderers or thugs or bandits had not even crossed her mind. Her only thought had been of Tazmeen and Ali

"How could we have missed this?" she asked, pressing her palms against her eyes.

Aldair released her face, and squeezed her shoulder before stepping back. "The crew could have the magi put a sound barrier around the train. Something like that would block sounds and even smells." He glanced back at the train. "If we hide under it, we should be able to get an idea for how the camp is set. Then we can move forward if it seems safe."

She nodded, and he gave her a sad smile before leading them back to the train. The thumping from within seemed louder and more accusatory this time, and she gritted her teeth as they crawled under the structure.

They settled side by side in the sand, and Steele had a thought. "What if it's magi prisoners on the train? My train had magi prisoners, and helping them would work in our favor."

"I thought about that, too, but again, we wouldn't be helping much."

"Why not?"

"If we were to let them out, they would not be able to go far if their gems are kept by a person in the camp. A magi is tied to their pridestone, and without it, they can only do so much."

"Right. Pridestone." Steele exhaled, remember Bero telling her about that. "What if we found the gems, freed the magi, then convinced them to help the other people on the trains? If there are any." She paused. "They could take everyone to the palace dungeon to be questioned."

"If you see any jewels, let me know," he said, his lips a thin line.

She racked her brain for ideas, pondering the loophole Bero had mentioned. He'd not gone directly against his orders by uncuffing her. Maybe these magi would help in a similar way by providing a little help for the prisoners to escape. Unfortunately, that did nothing to help the magis themselves.

The sound of voices approached, and she stiffened, pressing herself as flat as she could into the sand. A man and a woman stepped into view, stopping far enough back that Steele could see both of them too clearly for her liking.

"See what the magi can do about the stench," the woman said, her voice rough from either yelling or smoking. "He doesn't want to smell any of this while he is here, and he will be here at any moment." She gestured to the train as the man next to her nodded quickly.

"I'll get right on it." The man turned, and jogged to the left of the train.

The woman studied the train, hands on her hips. The longer the woman stared, the more convinced Steele became that the woman knew they were there and was just waiting for them to acknowledge her. A wave of yellow light covered the train, and Steele shielded her eyes.

Heart racing, Steele edged herself back from the train when Aldair stopped her with a leg across her ankle.

"What're you doing?" he hissed.

"Uh, leaving. Or at least looking for a way to escape before they catch us." She glanced forward. The woman was gone. "Where did she go?"

"She left," he said, his hand finding her wrist. "This isn't a trap. It's magic."

Steele blinked, waiting for him to explain further.

"Like I was saying, I'm assuming they're using a block; a way to keep things like sounds and smells contained. Father uses something similar when he has important meetings."

"Oh." She relaxed a fraction. "Now what? We go closer?"

"We go closer." He moved his leg from hers and pulled himself out from under the train.

She followed more slowly, eyes darting around, looking for guards. The fires at each end of the train gave them enough light to make out what appeared to be a three tents ahead of them.

They crouched in the sand, watching the tents closely. Shadows passed over the canvas, but they were too long and disjointed to be outlines of people inside the tents. It seemed the tents themselves were empty, and as she and the prince crept closer, they found that to be true.

They were almost to the tents when voices sounded from across the campsite and Steele dropped to her stomach, anxiety dancing along her nerves. Aldair was beside her, ear cocked to the noise.

"He wants everyone here, so hurry up," a man was saying loudly. *He?*

Steele's heart jumped. Maybe the boss was finally here! A meeting with him was the only reason she could think of that everyone would need to be in one place.

A couple people scurried forward, but Steele couldn't see where they went because the tents were blocking her view. The tents were set up in a line, and it looked like the middle one had a flap at the back, most likely to give someone easy access to the trains.

More voices flared, sounding excited, and Steele used their distraction to pull her saber free. She used the blade to ease the tent flap open a fraction. The interior was empty, and relief flooded her limbs. It seemed that luck was with them so far.

She mouthed to Aldair, "*Should we go in?*" Tents would provide much more cover than trying to eavesdrop another way.

He nodded, pulling his saber out as well, and he ducked as he pushed through the tent flap. Steele followed him, leg muscles burning as she crouched. There were four bedrolls inside, and she paused to make absolutely certain that they were empty. The front of the tent was tied halfway open, and Aldair was lying down at the entrance, saber gripped tightly in his right hand. She got down beside him, resting her chin on the side of his shoulder so she could see out.

A large fire burned about twenty paces from the front of the tent, and a small group of people gathered around it, dishes discarded haphazardly at their feet. Steele spotted the rough-voiced woman and man among them, and some of her previous paranoia retreated. The people were facing one man, who stood by the fire. He must've been the leader. The shadows from the flames obscured parts of his face, but Steele could still make out a long nose and beard.

"You have nearly reached your destination," the man said. His voice was quiet, but commanding, and Steele narrowed her eyes. She knew that voice.

"What is your name?" he asked one of the men dressed in uniform.

"Tarbel," the guard answered quickly.

"Bring one of the prisoners over to clean this mess, Tarbel."

"How much farther, sir?"

"Only a couple of weeks at most," the leader replied, and Steele felt Aldair turn to stone beside her. Apparently he recognized the voice as well, and she twisted her neck to look at him for confirmation. But he did not look at her. He was looking intently at the man, eyes wide, mouth open in what looked like disbelief.

"Will we get more money for the extra time we have spent out here?" the rough-voiced woman asked.

"Of course," the man droned, turning to look at the woman. His face caught the light of the fire, and Steele's heart fell.

It was General Fijar. The head of the entire Solarrhian army was in charge of these caravans heading to the camps.

Really, she shouldn't have been too surprised considering she'd been on a train destined for a camp just after she'd been sentenced to be executed. However, seeing him there was a shock.

She recalled his comment on taking advantage of her private execution. And there'd been something about a Council house wanting an example made out of her. She didn't know how the two comments were connected, but she was sure they had to be. She paused, refocusing on the scene in front of her. If General Fijar was involved, this meant that there was deeply rooted corruption in the palace. What was he up to?

"The people on your train are classified as what exactly?" Fijar asked, dark eyes glittering in the firelight.

The rough-voiced woman stepped forward. "Thieves, sir."

Fijar nodded. "Men or women?"

"Both, sir. We were planning on separating them before we got to the camp."

"See that you do. We want them to either begin training as soon as they arrive or be prepped for a sale."

"Training for what?" a younger man asked, shrinking back a step as Fijar walked toward him.

Steele hoped Fijar would answer the man. She was just as confused as he was by the mention of training and a sale.

Fijar's lips thinned as he circled the man, his hands loosely clasped behind his back. "Enlighten me, what gives you the right to ask me questions?"

The young man raised his hands, backing up a step. "We were told everything would be explained to us when we dropped the loads off."

"You are being paid for your services, and your families are sleeping well at home. What more do you need to know?"

"Don't mind him, sir. We don't want to know anything," the woman stated, throwing her colleague a dangerous look.

"Smart woman," Fijar mused, stroking his chin. "The less you know, the more innocent you appear if the wrong people question you. I suggest you remember who you take orders from in the future and just do as you're told."

The group of people shifted, clearly uncomfortable. Steele tipped her head to look at Aldair. He hadn't moved other than to set his mouth in a hard line and his gaze remained forward. She wondered what he was thinking. It must be taking an incredible amount of self-control to not confront the general right now.

Fijar clasped his hands behind his back. "There's no need to fret, my friends. You will receive your pay like I said. I will tell our benefactor of your good progress through the desert, and perhaps he will see fit to reward you for that should you keep it up."

He smiled, but it did not look pleasant. "You are nearing the end of your journey. Once you arrive at Camp Two, my men shall examine all the stock. I expect everything to be in order and no questions about what goes on there. If you find yourself getting curious, I suggest you do not scratch that itch or you may not find that camp to be as gracious as I have been tonight."

"Are you not traveling with us?" a tall, heavyset woman asked.

"I have other assets to attend to," the general replied, adding, "There is a nomad camp not too far away. If you leave in the afternoon, you should avoid them, as they tend to move in the early mornings."

The guard called Tarbel returned with an older man with graying hair. He looked like he might once have been strong and in good health, but could not manage a few steps without stumbling. Tarbel kicked at the older man's heels, sending him to his knees. "Clean this up," the guard commanded.

With narrowed eyes, the man obeyed, albeit his movements were slow and disjointed. Fijar's attention turned to the man as the dishes clanged together.

"This will not do."

"Water, please," the man whispered. Steele had to strain to hear him.

Fijar leaned in. "Of course, of course, but first you must complete this task."

"Please, sir." The man frowned as he spoke, "We've been crammed in that box for weeks, and I haven't had a drop in days."

Fijar scoffed, effectively cutting off the man's pleas. The general looked at the people surrounding the fire and clicked his tongue. "Not even an hour's taste of freedom, and he's already demanding things."

He grabbed the collar of the prisoner's shirt and pulled him closer. They were the same size, but in this light, with the shadows cast around the general's body, he seemed to tower over the other man's kneeling frame. "You are not a guest. You are hardly a servant. You are *lucky* we picked you up off the streets at all, giving you some use in this life, swine. If you cannot complete even this *little* task we ask of you, how exactly am I supposed to make a fortune off you? We may as well leave you here for one of the giant snakes to feast upon."

He released the man's collar and beckoned the rough-voiced woman over. "Bring me that basin." He pointed to a nearby bowl.

She obeyed, holding the bowl before Fijar, who dipped his hands inside, cupping water in his palms. The prisoner eyed Fijar's hands.

Fijar let the water fall, some dribbling out onto the sand, and rubbed his hands together. "It wouldn't do to catch some disease."

He laughed, and the woman joined him, though she did not sound particularly mirthful. Anger spiked in Steele's heart and it took everything in her to not help the older man who stood there looking dejected.

When one of the men pulled out a couple of bottles of alcohol and began serving the group, Steele saw their exit. She scooted back from the opening, expecting Aldair to follow her, but the prince remained frozen to the ground. Hooking her hands around his arm, she pulled.

"We need to leave while they are preoccupied."

He slowly turned his head to look at her, blue eyes dazed, and she noticed the white-knuckled grip he had on his saber.

"Please, Aldair, please, we need to go." Her eyes danced from him to the fire and back, expecting the group to see them at any moment.

He shook his head slightly and blinked. "Yes. Yes, let's go."

They backed out of the tent and hurried back to the trains, ducking to crawl under a train cart. Steele glanced over her shoulder once they were out from under it, checking to see if they had been spotted. Convinced that they remained undetected, she looked at Aldair, and her heart sank.

Shoulders slumped, he knelt in the sand with his head in his hands. She reached out to touch his shoulder, and when he looked at her, she recoiled. The moonlight glinted off his eyes and highlighted his cheekbones and nose. His jaw was clenched tight, and those eyes...Those were dangerous eyes. Gone was the dazed looked, replaced instead with a coldness she had not seen before. He pulled up his headscarf, hood shadowing everything but his jaw, and turned to climb up the dune.

She paused before following him, considering the change in him. His reaction was appropriate, she decided, and she found herself thinking Fijar was lucky to still be walking free. Remarkably, she had not known that level of betrayal, but she doubted she could have kept silent if it were Dal at that fire instead of Fijar.

When she landed on the other side of the dune, she was startled to see a hand extended to her. She took it, eyes traveling up Aldair's arm and to his face. His scarf was shoved back, and a small smile was on his mouth.

"That was certainly a surprise," he said as they walked toward the horses.

"I'm sorry," she said softly, glancing up at him.

Aldair shrugged. "We got information. It's not what I wanted, but at least I know the truth."

The sorrow that clung to his voice made her want to comfort him. He pulled his hood back over his eyes, and she slowed, giving him space to walk alone.

CHAPTER 25

It was only after they had ridden a good distance from the camp that the silence started to worry Steele. She didn't know Aldair well, but from what she did know, this silence was not like him. Pressing her heels to Kesif's side, she moved alongside him, and when he looked at her, the smile he gave did not quite reach his eyes.

"What will you tell Em and Kaleel?" she asked, almost desperate for conversation.

Aldair lowered his headscarf and rubbed his eyes. "The truth. But you knew that."

She nodded. "I know. I'm sorry. I used to like the silence, you know. I blame you three for my change of heart."

He laughed once. "I apologize for being so quiet."

"Don't apologize." She shook her head. "You have every right to mull things over. I shouldn't be so pushy." She pulled on a leather strap that hung from her saddle. "I was thinking that if you three want to make plans, you know I'm sticking with you from here on out, so I could stay at the train listen for more information on that end and—"

"No." That one word rang with such authority that her mouth closed with a snap.

"I was just trying to make a suggestion, Prince."

He grunted. "I know. I know you want to help, but…." He paused before continuing with a sigh, "Fijar's presence changes things. I would not want anything to happen to you while I wasn't around to protect you."

Steele blinked. "Oh."

"I know that you can take care of yourself. That's not it. I never thought Fijar could be so cruel to another human, but I do know that if he saw you alive and free, you'd not be so for long." He lightly grasped her elbow. "We've all grown quite fond of you."

She closed her eyes as her heart quirked. "It's different knowing people care about you outside the thieving world," she admitted, opening her eyes to look at him. "Thank you. I suppose Kaleel and Em can scout out the train."

Aldair chuckled. "They'll be glad to know they have your permission."

★ ☽ ★

When Steele and Aldair arrived back at camp, they found Emdubae and Kaleel seated around a small fire. Kaleel was cooking something over the flames, and Emdubae turned around, surprised when they rode up to them.

"You're back soon." He eyed Aldair's face and frowned. "You have bad news to tell us."

Aldair nodded, dismounting. "I'll tell you when the horses are put away."

Steele dismounted and led Kesif down to the picket line. The gelding tried to eat some leaves off a small bush as they moved. She allowed him one bite before hooking him to the line, where she began undoing the buckles on her saddle.

When she finished, she approached Aldair, palm outstretched. "I can take care of Cahya for you," she offered.

He glanced up, considering her offer for a moment before shaking his head. "Thank you, but I'd like to do it."

Steele wilted, a little chagrined that she had been turned down.

He gently gripped her arm before she turned away. "Surely you understand the enjoyment of taking care of your own animal."

"I do, yes." She knelt to stoke the dying fire and threw him a small smile. "A prince who takes care of his own horse? Perhaps not as coddled as I thought."

Aldair laughed as he led Cahya away, and Steele was pleased. That laugh sounded almost genuine.

She sat beside Emdubae and held her palms out, absorbing as much heat as she could. Spying on the train had been enough to push the cold away, but now that the mission was over, the chilly air bit through to the bones.

Emdubae glanced at her. "I have an extra pair of gloves if you want to wear them. I'm sorry that they'll be too big." He held out a pair of brown, fur lined, leather gloves.

She met his gaze, touched by his thoughtfulness. "Thank you, Em. I think I nearly froze to death out there."

She slipped the gloves on. Her exposed fingers still felt numb, but it was better than nothing.

When Aldair returned from the picket line, he settled beside Kaleel and poked at the kindling with a branch before sighing and looking up.

"Fijar is the leader," he said, voice calm.

"What?" Emdubae said softly as Kaleel shook his head, incredulous.

"And there are people on the train," Steele added.

Kaleel frowned. "How did we not know that?"

Steele poked at the sand with a stick. "A magical barrier. The magi are doing more than just transporting the train."

Emdubae shook his head, eyes wide with disbelief. "First Captain Lac, now General Fijar. Who else I wonder?"

Aldair propped his elbows on his knees and dropped his face in his hands. "There's no way of knowing that until we get home, but if Fijar is in charge, he has plenty of men who would follow him without a thought. He's their general."

"So what should we do? Go after him?" Kaleel asked, spinning a small knife between his fingers.

"No, I think we need to continue to follow this train. Fijar said he would meet them at a camp somewhere, so if we keep following them, we will find him again. In the meantime, we can communicate with the palace and request reinforcements."

Emdubae reached around to a bag and pulled a fist-sized green stone from it.

Steele inhaled when she realized what it was. "Oh! A communication stone. I had one of those."

Emdubae handed it to her, and she turned it over in her hands, squinting at the surface.

"They're called somenstones," Aldair said, holding out his hand. "The magi make them, though my father gave this one to me."

"He also asked that you keep him updated on our travels," Emdubae said, tying the bag closed. "Something tells me you have not been checking in as you should."

Aldair clicked his tongue. "He doesn't need weather updates. *And* I am not so anxious to inform him that the thief he sentenced to death is alive and traveling with us."

"Have you used it at all?" Steele asked. She'd not seen him with it before now.

The prince nodded. "He knows we are well."

"What are you going to say?" Kaleel asked, scooting forward. "We don't know anything except that Fijar and Lac are involved. We don't know where the camp is, how big this organization is, or what they mean by taking people and making a profit off them."

"What did Fijar have to say?" Emdubae asked.

Steele glanced at Aldair. The prince was staring into the flames, mouth set in a grim line, so she cleared her throat. "He didn't say much; something about training the prisoners or preparing them for a sale."

Kaleel paused in twirling his knives to exchange a glance with Emdubae. "What sort of sale?"

"He didn't say," Steele answered, looking to Aldair again. "He just said some would be trained and some would be sold."

"He also said the camp was about a week or two's ride away," Aldair said, blinking and looking up from the fire. "So we won't have to track them too much longer."

"It didn't seem like the people running the train knew anything about the camp. It sounds like they're just doing a job to get paid." Steele pursed her lips, thinking for anything else to add.

Aldair scratched the back of his neck and pressed the side of the stone. Steele watched, mesmerized, as a small depression appeared on it, deepening until it looked as though Aldair held a small bowl in his hand. Inside, the stone's surface seemed to ripple as his fingers shifted.

"Mine didn't do that," she said, leaning closer to look at it.

"They can be made to do different things, though I only know what Batya, my magi friend, taught me, which is how to send a message to my father's stone." He tapped the stone, looking between Emdubae and Kaleel. "He needs to know people in his military are doing business behind his back. As for the camp, the moment we know the location, we'll send a second word so he can order soldiers to set out. The desert is too vast to send them out with no direction now."

Aldair turned the stone over in his hands before bringing it to his lips to speak.

His words were surprisingly muffled by the small stone, and when he was finished, the sides of the bowl fused together. A bead of light illuminated the inside of the stone for a moment before winking out, and Aldair tossed the stone back to Emdubae. "We need to keep an eye on that."

"Does King Ferdinand normally transport prisoners through Solarrhia?" Emdubae asked, sliding the stone into his pocket.

"Perhaps General Fijar is acting on your father's orders, and you've not been told?" Doubt was heavy in Kaleel's voice. He ran a hand through his hair and grimaced.

Aldair drug his hands down his face. "He'd have told me, especially since he knew we were following a lead through the Nasshari. As king, he has the authority to do this."

Steele frowned. "No one has the authority to sell a human being."

"I agree with you, but I meant he wouldn't have to hide it." Aldair looked back into the fire. "I wish Hadrian were here. He would know what to do."

Kaleel snorted loudly. "Your brother was good at pretending he knew all the answers. He felt the pressure to be perfect at everything, and he refused to admit he didn't know how to handle something. You've always been the one to ask questions, and along the way, you learned the value of seeking counsel. There's nothing wrong with that. I believe he'd be handling the situation just about the same. Investigate, gather facts, and alert the palace if something truly is amiss. You're doing a fine job."

Some of the tension lifted from the prince's shoulders, and he sighed. "Thank you, Kaleel."

"You know I mean it. Your ego's never needed boosting before." Kaleel easily dodged a stick that Aldair threw at him, and he chuckled. The amused smile on his face faded slightly. "I miss him like hell though."

A silence fell over the group. Steele shifted and watched Kaleel fiddle with his knife. He tucked it in his boot and quickly stood. "Anyone care for some fruit?"

He didn't wait for a response before heading away from the fire.

Emdubae rose from his spot and swiped sand off his trousers.

"Are you going after him?" Aldair looked in the direction Kaleel had gone.

Emdubae shook his head. "He'll be fine, but he has a point about some food."

He strolled off, and Steele sighed, mesmerized by the flickering light of the fire.

"Are you finally warming up?" Aldair asked, turning to Steele.

"Yes." She held out her hands so the leather gloves caught the firelight. "Em lent me these."

He rubbed a finger over the top of the glove. "That was kind of him."

She nodded, hugging her knees to her chest. "I was thinking about what you said earlier about your father being involved." He looked at her, and she smiled slightly. "Your father is a good man, Aldair. He makes good decisions."

"He sentenced you to die."

"I was a thief."

"Was?" Aldair rested an elbow on his knee, his tone probing.

"Am?" Steele shrugged and stretched her legs out in front of her. "Either way, your father did the right thing. I've been thinking about when the guards put me on the train. They were careful about it. I was taken from the dungeon when no one was around, and they made no mention of your father. I would think if he was involved, his name would have come up."

Aldair studied her face before smiling crookedly at her. "Thank you."

She smiled back. "I wouldn't defend just anyone who sentenced me to die." Aldair laughed, and she tipped her head to watch him. "I didn't think of General Fijar initially, but I should have. When I was on the train, I thought I was heading to my execution, and I was confused when Lac mentioned heading to the camp. I still should have seen that the general would be involved."

He coughed once, adjusting his elbows around his knees. "You didn't know, and I might not have believed you until I saw it for myself."

"I was also thinking..." she began, and she bit her lip. "Since all these people are being transported to this camp, there's a chance I was being taken to the same one. And maybe my family will be there also."

"I wish we could get more solid information about their whereabouts. I'm sorry we haven't been able to yet."

Steele propped her chin on her knee. "Me too, but if there's a chance they're at the camp, I plan on turning that place upside down if I need to."

"With that determination, I'm sure you will find something."
She gave a tight nod. "I certainly hope so."

"And if you need someone to make things happen, I might know of a prince who would be willing to help you out."

"Ah," she said, biting back a laugh. "Yes, that might be very useful. Is he willing to help out for free I wonder? You'll have to let him know that I can't pay him."

"I'm sure he would be willing to negotiate something," he said with a smirk. "He's pretty reasonable from what I hear."

"Well, that's good. I make a point not to deal with unreasonable people."

The sharp, tangy smell of an orange wafted toward them, and Steele's stomach growled. Aldair raised an eyebrow at her as she peered down at her middle.

"It would seem Kaleel is not the only one who is starving," he teased.

"Apparently not," Steele agreed, allowing Aldair to pull her to her feet. "I might eat more than he does."

"Now that would be something to see. The man eats for three." Aldair said with a laugh as they followed the citrus scent back to the tent.

CHAPTER 26

After a week of following the caravan, Steele was restless. They did the same thing every day: wake up, eat, scout the train, eat again if there was food, continue to monitor the train, rotate night watch shifts, and sleep. Each day and night was the same, and while she was glad for the progress, things were moving too slow.

"Maybe I could throw a rock at one of merchants or put an escape route in the train to mess with them. At least *then* there'd be some action," she muttered to herself.

The setting sun painted the desert in vibrant colors, and the evening breeze promised another chilly night. They remained too close to the train these days for a fire to be wise, and the winds had been disagreeable.

A yawn cracked her jaw. Even though they did the same thing day in and day out, the days were long and sleep was hard to come by. As the men set up camp, she skirted the edge, knife in hand, eyes peeled for something to make into a meal. No animals caught her eye, so she threw her knife at a log in frustration. The knife hit the log, but hung limply from the wood.

"I hope you weren't aiming for anything in particular."

Steele started and turned to find Aldair watching her, arms crossed.

"It's a good thing Kaleel didn't see that," he added.

"I was aiming for the log, actually," she said, retrieving her knife.

He tilted his head, studying her. "Maybe it would be wise for Em to teach you how to use a sword. It might come in handy soon." A shadow crossed his face, and Steele frowned.

"Are…" She paused, unsure if it was her place to ask. "How are you doing with everything?" He had been so quiet the past week, and she had found herself missing the jovial side of him more and more.

He sighed as he lowered his arms. "I'm fine."

"You're obviously not." She clamped her mouth shut, immediately wishing she'd said nothing. When people pushed her, she refused to speak, retreating further into herself. Well that—or she exploded. "What I mean is that I can tell you were bothered by what we found, and I just wondered if things were any better now that you've had time to think about it." She studied his stricken face, ready to ramble on and smooth things over quickly.

"I appreciate your concern, but it would be hard for me to explain to you why it's so complicated," he replied. She thought she saw a faint smile cross his mouth as he shrugged. "It was a shock to see Fijar there, but until we know more, I don't really want to discuss it."

She frowned. "I think I could understand."

"Maybe another night." He sighed. "Let's see if Em is up for a fight."

He turned, and Steele scowled at his retreating form. On one hand, she pitied him. He was obviously distraught over what they discovered, but did he really think matters of the palace were too complex for her thieving mind to comprehend?

No, that was her pride talking. Why did she care anyway? He was the prince. He didn't have to tell her anything about his feelings. And yet…she cared that he was upset. She groaned. Sleep deprivation was muddling her brain. She let out another grunt before trotting after Aldair.

They found Emdubae and Kaleel setting up the tent. Kaleel was gripping the edge of the canvas, stretching it down for Emdubae to fasten the corner to a stake in the ground.

When Emdubae was done, he dusted off his hands on his trousers. "Couldn't have helped, eh? Just had to stand there all prince-like?" he teased.

Aldair laughed. "How would you like to teach Steele some sword fighting?"

Emdubae tucked an extra rope back into one of the packs. "I suppose there is a little light left for fencing. What experience have you with a sword, Little Thief?"

"Not much," Steele admitted. "I would spar with my brother some, but that's the extent."

"Well, that is better than no experience at all!" Emdubae said cheerfully. "I'm sure Aldair will let you borrow his saber since yours isn't with you."

The prince raised an eyebrow at her and she gave a sheepish shrug. "I promise never to be without it again."

Emdubae chuckled as Aldair handed her his saber. Her wrists dropped with the unexpected weight, and she gripped the hilt awkwardly. "We aren't unsheathing them, are we?"

"We don't want you to kill Em by accident," Aldair said, clasping his saber where blade met hilt and fiddled with a strap. "This should keep the sword encased."

He winked at her, and the flutter in her heart startled her. To distract herself, she took a couple experimental swings with the saber once he stepped away, and she was pleased to see the sheath stayed in place. She pivoted, bringing the blade downward, and yelped as Emdubae swung his own saber at her.

Jumping back, she threw her arms out and barely blocked his half-hearted attack. "That was sneaky," she grunted.

Emdubae nodded. "Yes, and you thought quickly when caught off guard. That's very good." He pushed against her saber with his, and Steele staggered back a couple of steps.

"Part of the reason I always worked so hard to be invisible was because I know I'm not going to put up much of a fight against someone as strong as any of you," she explained.

"Everyone has his or her own strengths. You just need to find yours. Try focusing on using your speed and agility against a larger opponent." Emdubae set the tip of the saber in the sand and leaned on the hilt. "Let's take a look at you, then."

Steele rolled her shoulders back, clenching her jaw as he circled around her, sparing a glance at the other two men who were relaxing in the sand and seemingly enjoying the show. "Well?" she prodded after a moment of silence.

"You're not *that* short, only a hands width shorter than I am, really. You've shown that you're quick, which will help make up for how thin you are, though with some good training and proper food, you'll fill out nicely, adding to the muscle you already have. You've already gained some weight since we found you."

She looked down at her body, but she didn't notice anything too different.

Emdubae shifted her weight to the left and crossed his arms. "As you train, you'll learn to use your size to your advantage. For example, if someone comes at you swinging their blade, ducking away from them at the last minute can throw them off-balance."

"That's how I managed to escape Lac's attacks on the train," she said, studying her grip on the hilt. When she looked up, he was smiling at her. "What?"

"Well, then, you're more advanced than I gave you credit for," Emdubae stated. "I apologize."

"I react better when I'm under pressure."

Emdubae leaped at her then, saber raised, and she braced herself for impact. It came hard and strong, and her legs buckled under the weight. Her arms shook as her saber blocked Emdubae's, and as her knees hit the sand, she propelled herself forward. He staggered on, and Steele rolled into a crouch, blade raised.

Kaleel clucked his tongue approvingly. "And if you had a knife, you could finish the job from there."

Steele spared him a quick smile before turning her attention back to Emdubae. This time when he approached, he came at her slowly, swinging his blade with precise movements. She was able to block a couple of swings but quickly found his saber pointed at her heart.

"When your opponent realizes you are quick and able to dodge an attack, he will try a new approach. This slower approach works in my favor and obviously causes you to struggle. You're at my mercy." Emdubae smiled.

She shoved his blade away and readjusted her grip. "So how do I win?"

"Depends on your opponent. Try to anticipate what my next move will be."

"How?"

Emdubae tipped his head as he considered her question. "You can't always count on this, but people tend to develop habits. For some people, they'll step out with their dominant leg before taking a swing at you. Others might always aim high or only move right." He dipped his head. "Some duck and roll out of the way, like you might tend to do because of your size. If you can find a person's pattern, exploit it."

"Emdubae, please, you know I'd probably be dead before I noticed that. You just killed me very easily if you remember."

"Follow his eyes," Aldair offered. "Most men will indicate where they will swing next, even if it's just with a flick of the eye."

"I don't really want to be that close to a person trying to kill me. Ever," she returned. She narrowed her eyes. "Okay, let's try again."

This time she managed to block more swings and was able to get close enough to cut him—that is if the blade had been uncovered. But ultimately, the fight ended with Emdubae's saber pressed against her chest again.

After a few more tries, Steele was ready to quit. "I'd rather be done while I'm improving and end on a good note. It's what I do with my horses when I'm training them."

Kaleel chuckled. "How is Em chopping your head off a good note?"

She shrugged. "I blocked more of his attacks than not. That's a positive thing."

Emdubae leaned against his saber again. "Aldair, you should test out her hand to hand skills."

Steele looked to Aldair, hopeful. "Please? Think about how sad you'll be if a burly guard picks me up and carries me off." She meant it as a joke, but none of them laughed. "Sorry. I know that isn't funny. I don't know why I said it."

"It's not funny," Aldair agreed as he approached her, "but you have a point. We would be devastated to lose you."

One moment he was beside her, and the next he was behind, one arm across her mouth and the other across her front, pinning her to his chest. Her eyes widened, and she was vividly aware of her back against Aldair's chest and his palm across her lips. *Focus!* She inwardly frowned at herself.

"Now," the prince said, breath warm against her ear, "Let's see just how good you are with hand to hand."

CHAPTER 27

Steele pushed her headscarf out of her eyes and turned to study the scene behind her. They were leaving the dunes, the ground gradually hardening beneath the horses' feet, the shifting sand replaced with gravel and the occasional shrub. They were nowhere near the end of the Nasshari Desert, but soon they'd be leaving the comfort of Solarrhian lands.

She'd never been this far from home.

Emdubae and Aldair rode in front of her. Occasionally one of them would make a comment about the area they were in, but otherwise the group remained silent, waiting for Kaleel to return from scouting the train's progress. Ever since they discovered General Fijar's involvement with the investigations, the air had been thick with tension and the pressure continued to grow with each league they covered.

For Steele, her mind kept playing games with her. It was almost as if what lay before them was taunting her. A part of her, a horrible, traitorous part, wanted things to stay as they were. This way, there would always be hope that Tazmeen and Ali were alive and well. Of course, she wanted to find Tazmeen and Ali, but there was a bliss to not knowing their fate. It had been so long since they had been taken, and she struggled to hold on to the thought that even if they had been taken to the camp, they would still be there. She ground her teeth together, refusing to let any visions of what could have happened to her family undo her.

A yawn fought its way past her lips, and she rotated her neck as they continued on. The fissures in the sand and dirt weaved throughout the land in front of her, drawing her eye to oncoming rust-tinted hills. She'd slept fitfully as the growing anxiety seemed to hold sleep just beyond her reach. She absently rubbed around the edges of the scar on her shoulder, pleased with how the cut had healed. Emdubae had frowned at the red ridges when he'd removed the stitches the night before, but she assured him she didn't mind. Scars had never bothered her.

Her eyes moved to Aldair, and she started. He was watching her. She smiled, and although he smiled back, he looked distracted. She wondered what was going on in his head. He'd been out the entire night and had barely spoken today. No one mentioned the prince's restlessness.

She didn't know who General Fijar was to Aldair, other than the fact that he was the head of the Solarrhian military. They must have a relationship because of that, but the air around Aldair exuded that this was more than treason to the kingdom. She understood the almost desperate need to move. Idleness was no friend, especially when answers were needed.

Even with this understanding, she was surprised with how disappointed she was to not have been with the prince to help him and that he hadn't wanted her by his side. It was a silly thought, and she shook her head.

A horse and rider appeared from a low point of the side of one hill, and she tensed.

Emdubae raised his spyglass. "Kaleel's back."

Still, she only relaxed once Rhub's golden body slid into focus. Kaleel slowed the palomino to a trot and circled around the group before finding his place beside the prince.

Kaleel pulled his scarf down underneath his chin. "We need to angle southeast. We'll have good coverage in the knolls, but we need to pick up pace to keep up. You will not like this."

Aldair frowned, but said nothing. He handed Kaleel a fresh water pouch and allowed the soldier to take a long swig. Kaleel's dark curls were plastered to the sides of his face, his cheeks flushed.

"We're getting close to the camp. Under thirteen leagues, I expect. I took a stroll around the caravan when it was stopped earlier-" Kaleel paused at Emdubae's cough. "*Carefully* and was not discovered. You can relax. There was mention of an oasis of a thousand trees. I think," he paused to hand the pouch back to Aldair and rubbed his eyes wearily. "I think this camp will be much bigger than we anticipated, and it would probably be wise to alert your father of our location."

"Do you think it's near The Green River Forest then? That leads right into Oakenjara territory and puts this whole business within traveling range for the southern province." Emdubae scratched sand off his cheek. "Well, mostly. I don't think many like to travel through that forest by choice."

"I wouldn't mind doing it once. It can't be as bad as people say." Kaleel shrugged.

"Your sanity is questionable on a normal day." Emdubae returned. He looked to Aldair. "What is General Fijar up to? Could he be in partnership with King Eram?"

Aldair stared ahead at the hills, not answering. Finally, he spoke softly. "How far ahead is the train?"

"Not very. I was worried you would come upon us and give us away," Kaleel replied. "Still, they've taken a route above the hills, and in order for us to remain better hidden, we'll need to keep to the low ground pathways as much as possible."

"Won't we lose them then?" Steele pondered aloud. The train would be cutting out quite a bit of ground.

"We're going to have to risk it. That, or come up with a really good excuse for following them. I'll message Father."

★☽★

Four hours later, Steele fidgeted on her saddle. They'd managed to wind through the knolls at a reasonable rate, but she didn't like that she couldn't see the train from this side of the hill.

Aldair halted the group. "We should be close to the forest. Steele, can you check the status of the train?"

Relieved, Steele slowed Kesif to a stop and hopped off him. Leaving him with the others, she scrambled to the top of the hill, keeping low to the ground and searched the area. The train moved along before her over flat, cracked beige earth. It had gained quite a bit of ground while traveling above the knolls, and from her vantage point, she could see all of the compartments of the train hovering across the open desert. How they were going to tail it without being seen, she had no idea. As she opened her mouth to call out its location, she paused, eyes catching on a burst of leafy green trees that stretched as far as she could see. She'd been surrounded by so many shades of brown for so long, the trees looked like heaven. She grinned.

"What do you see?" Emdubae called up to her.

"I had almost forgotten what it looked like to see so much green!" She replied. "Get up here! We won't lose sight of the train right now, and you have to see the view!"

The three men quickly joined her, and the four of them rested against the peak of the hill for a moment, taking it in.

"I've never seen it in person," Aldair admitted. "Only in paintings."

"It's unfortunate that we don't have time to explore down there. I'd like to take a swim in the river," Kaleel almost sounded wistful.

She focused on the train again. The air glimmered in front of it as it trodded alongside the forest. Her eyes narrowed, and she nudged Emdubae. "Did you see that?"

The air rippled this time like a heat wave as tall as the trees beside it, and suddenly two people on horses appeared from that exact spot.

Aldair grabbed Emdubae's spyglass just as the soldier unfastened it from his hip. Emdubae sighed and focused on the scene again.

The riders flanked the train on both sides at first, but instead of turning around to escort it back to where they came from, they took off toward the forest. The train continued forward toward the rippling air.

"It's a gateway," Aldair explained. He passed the glass to Steele.

Through the lens, she could see the horizon ripping open, revealing men and women roaming around, but if anyone neared the edge of the rippling air, they disappeared from sight. A bell donged in the distance. She handed the spyglass to Emdubae.

The train entered through the gateway, and just as the last box passed the barrier, the air winked and the sound vanished.

"Well, that may complicate things a bit," Kaleel said after a few moments.

"How will we get inside?" Steele asked, then turned to Aldair. "We were able to cross the magi barrier near the train. We could try sneaking in."

"The question is where to try that. Has everyone memorized where that entrance was?" Aldair frowned.

Steele looked for any markings, but there were none she could see with her own eyes. Emdubae said nothing.

"To the forest?" Aldair addressed the group.

The four descended the hill, and Steele didn't know how she was able to keep her balance. Everything in her pulsed with new energy. This was it.

"We should be able to sneak in from the side then," Emdubae added as he followed from the rear. "But who knows what we'll run into."

Kaleel chuckled. "That's the fun of it, my friend."

They jumped on the back of the horses, and as quickly and stealthily as they were able, they left the knolls behind them.

★ ☽ ★

Half an hour later, they stood at the edge of the forest, behind some tall, untamed bushes, their horses tied out of sight on a picket line. The trees were enormous, taller than anything Steele had seen before, and the birds' incessant chirping swelled beneath the canopy of leaves.

"How are there birds?" she asked, looking for one of the flying creatures.

"How is there a forest like this in the midst of a desert?" Emdubae smiled. He studied the area the camp should be in. "Aldair, I think we should head in soon. We could go two at a time, or divide into two groups."

"We may set off some sort of alert," Kaleel cut in.

"What would you recommend then?" Emdubae replied, exasperated. "There will be risks everywhere."

"Why don't we try integrating with them?" Kaleel pointed to another group of riders and wagons approaching from alongside the forest to their right.

"There's enough travelers that we may blend in," Aldair said, though he sounded skeptical.

Steele examined the approaching group. It was not moving with much speed, as there were some travelers walking. There were people on horses, a few even bared similar coloring to Kesif. At a glance, Steele thought she saw six or seven wagons. From the looks of it, the wagons were mostly empty, save a few people hitching a ride. As the new caravan approached, she saw a few people on foot besides the wagons, but she wasn't sure exactly how to blend in with them. They didn't have much time to set a plan.

"Our window is closing," she said, watching Kaleel go back to the horses. "What are you doing?"

"There are a few walkers, but plenty on horses."

Aldair nodded, his eyes on the wagons as group passed in front of them. "Steele, you should take Kesif. He'll blend in. I'll have to leave Cahya behind on this one. She's too recognizable."

She nodded, tuning out the chatting of the riders some twenty feet in front of them. Aldair sneaked to the right, aiming for behind the caravan. Emdubae followed shortly after him.

Kaleel passed Kesif to her, and Steele nodded her thanks.

"Sorry, boy," She whispered to him. "I'd hoped you were going to get a bit of a break."

Once they were both settled on their horses and the group was a little in front of them, they moved out. Steele looked for Aldair and Emdubae, worried they'd not found a way into the group, but she relaxed somewhat when she saw Aldair walking beside the back wheel of wagon, his shoulders swaying as he kept with the slow pace. Emdubae sat on the back, his elbows resting steadily on his knees. She followed their lead and pulled her headscarf over her face.

Kaleel and Steele kept their horses at a walk behind the group, easing up the pace if they were came too close. Steele glanced at Kaleel and tried to relax. She didn't know how he looked so content.

"It'd be better to pull up to the side and not be straggling behind," Kaleel spoke lowly.

"Yes, until one of them realizes they've never seen us. We're exposed enough as it is. I think if one of them spots us, we speak first about the camp." She tapped the horn on her saddle, channeling her nerves into that small action.

Kaleel pursed his lips. After a moment, he shrugged a shoulder. "That could work. Remind me to request you as my partner in the future."

Steele almost laughed.

They were nearing the entrance of the camp, and so far, no one had questioned their presence. There were, however, a few people who rode in the wagons that worried her. They occasionally looked in their direction, but seemed more focused on their conversations than tagalongs and stowaways.

The air rippled, and a breeze that hadn't been there before tickled at her cheeks. Slowly, the scenery was pulled apart in front of them, as if a curtain was being drawn, to reveal four men standing before them. Behind the men, a few tall, gray tents blocked her view of what could lay beyond. She did, however, hear a deep voice yelling in the distance. Though she couldn't make out the words he was saying, it was slow and deliberate. A bell donged again, and the voice hushed.

A low horn resounded, this time to her right, and caught her attention. The caravan slowed to a stop, pausing their trek to allow a floating gilded carriage to pass through.

"That's interesting," Kaleel murmured.

Steele squinted at the carriage, trying in vain to see inside the windows. "It looks pretty fancy. Maybe that's how General Fijar is getting around?"

"I wouldn't be surprised."

After the carriage halted its course, one of the four men on the ground gestured for the caravan to enter. Steele urged Kesif forward, keeping an eye out for anyone exiting the carriage. If the general *was* in there, he'd recognize all four of them in an instant. A horse whinnied somewhere to her right, and Kesif's ear perked. She hummed at him and reined him in before they got too close to the men greeting the group. Shouts erupted from the same direction the voice had come from.

"I know we just saw a barrier lift, but it's still strange that it was so quiet a moment before and now it's like we're in a village market," Steele noted.

Of the four men who stood to greet the new arrivals, the shortest of the crew approached the carriage door and opened it. He bowed his head slightly as a man stepped down onto the ground and smoothed the wrinkles on his pants. He was tall and broad like Aldair, though his skin was darker than the prince's, more like honey. What drew Steele's eye though were his dark eyebrows sitting on his prominent brow bone. The eyes beneath them looked hardened, like a hunter prowling for his prey.

"Well, well, Roman Lothar. I wonder what he's doing here." Kaleel surveyed the rest of the area. "We need to make a layout of this place. We don't want to get caught with no escape."

Steele nodded, dismounting as Kaleel did the same, and she looked for Aldair and Emdubae. Emdubae was on the ground now, standing beside the prince. Both had their faces turned in toward one another, but she was too far to see what they were up to.

A man dressed in very fancy linens handed his reins to Aldair, and she had to smile. The prince took the reins and held them limply for a moment, staring after the retreating man. Aldair glanced at her and shrugged.

Roman Lothar laughed loudly, clapping the shorter man on the back.

"Who's Roman Lothar?" Steele asked. "I know he's one of the members of the High Council, but I never bothered to learn much about them."

Kaleel spoke softly rubbing Rhub's neck, as if he was murmuring to his horse rather than her. "The Lothars live closest to the palace near Eastfall, and they work quite a bit with the mercenaries and various markets in the more southern region of Solarrhia. Roman's father, Aren, just passed away last year, leaving Roman in charge of the House and estates."

"Lac and Fijar mentioned him when I was in the prison. They said something about him wanting to use me as an example to the people?" Kaleel's brow furrowed, but he nodded. "Thieves don't make for good business for mercenaries or in public markets. Executing you, a well-known thief, would have scared off quite a few people with itchy fingers waiting to grab someone's purse or product."

General Fijar rounded around one of the gray tents, his face breaking out into a large grin. Both Steele and Kaleel stiffened.

"Roman, you made good time. I trust you had a comfortable ride?" The general called out.

He strode toward the carriage, passing Steele who quickly bent, busing herself with Kesif's hoof. The horse leaned into her, almost knocking her over.

"General." Roman dipped his chin. "Pleasure."

"I've just been conversing with our financier. He was pleased to hear of your upcoming visit, and I have news of your terms." Fijar looked up at the taller man, and his tone softened. "How is your mother fairing?"

Kaleel nudged Steele's foot with his own and whispered, "Lac. Behind you."

She nodded, just barely restraining herself from turning to look. Her free hand involuntarily brushed against her neck where the swelling and bruises used to be. She'd not let him get that close to her again. She stayed bent over Kesif's hoof and looked for Aldair, but she couldn't find him from this angle. Carefully, she stood, making sure to stay behind Kesif's body.

"Kaleel, we need to get out of here."

"Just give me a moment." Kaleel smiled through closed lips and nodded toward the group they'd come in with. They were in a discussion with the other three men who'd greeted their group.

Steele almost yelped when Kaleel led Rhub toward them, but she quickly followed. She wished she could stick close by to hear more about this financier, but moving as far away from Fijar and Lac as possible seemed like a good idea, too. She'd be no good with a head full of knowledge if she got caught.

One of the greeters, a lean man of medium height and a balding head, was speaking as they approached. His light and smooth voice was very pleasant. "Again, we apologize for the delay. We were not expecting you to arrive until tomorrow." He looked at a file in his hand. "You are from the Barrowlands, correct, Master Valas? Were your needs not met at Camp Four?"

A golden haired man with scruff on his cheeks nodded. He looked to the group of people around him, save for those who stayed near their wagons and horses. "A few of us are. We've been traveling near the southern border of the Nasshari for a while now. This is the closest market we were able to get the location of."

"Master Cyril did send us a message referring you, so I am glad you decided to visit. We are happy to serve you and hope you find what you are looking for. Currently, we have a meeting occurring at the Auction Stage. Sales will begin tomorrow morning. In the meantime, Ingwe will be happy to give you a tour of Camp Two. He managed Camp Four for years, so I'm sure you'll have plenty to talk about regarding the meadowlands."

The greeter paused, studying the new arrivals, and he seemed particularly curious about Kaleel's hood. He glanced at Steele, whose face was still mostly covered. He reached his hand forward, "Magnus. I did not have the pleasure of meeting you earlier."

Kaleel grabbed Magnus' outstretched hand. "Name's Ezra. A friend of Master Lothar."

He gestured to Roman and Lac whose backs were turned toward the group. Fijar was nowhere to be seen, and Steele wondered where he'd gone. Kaleel lowered his hood to reveal his face, but she didn't follow suit. Her instincts screamed at him for uncovering himself so close to Lac.

Magnus pursed his lips, looking doubtful, but the man next to him, who was peering at a paper, coughed and nodded. Magnus relaxed and smiled. "Welcome, Ezra. Your companion?"

"He's my servant. Don't mind the mask," Kaleel waved his hand around nonchalantly. "He has hideous scars that twist people's stomachs."

Steele lowered her eyes, as if ashamed.

"Pity." Magnus said. He clapped his hands and addressed the crowd. "Everyone, we have stable hands who will take your horses and supplies to your tents. If you please follow Ingwe, your tour will begin."

A few boys appeared by the guest's sides, ready to take the horses. Steele thought about going with them, and she looked for Aldair and Emdubae. Again, she didn't see them, which was probably for the best considering they couldn't risk the prince being seen. Lac turned then, scanning the crowd. As discreetly as she could, she kicked Kaleel, who bent to adjust his boot, using Rhub's body as a shield. The crowd following Ingwe were going in the opposite direction of Lac, and she sighed. She handed Kesif's reins to a stable hand, and followed the Barrowland group, watching as the hand led Kesif right passed the captain. She'd remove herself from the tour as soon as she was away from Lac's presence.

CHAPTER 28

"As you saw, we have our greeting area. We're all arguing on what to call it, so if you have any suggestions, please put a word in," Ingwe explained, ambling along the pathway between neatly kept grey tents. He was no taller than Kaleel, with chocolate skin, and a thick black hair pulled back into little braids. His voice was thick, and as he spoke, he gestured in various directions. "Soldier's quarters are on the west side of camp, the stock near the back. They're heavily guarded, as soldiers are stationed throughout the entire camp."

"We heard there were magi being kept here. Aren't they dangerous," a youth asked, his tone a little rushed like he'd been desperate to ask about them for ages. He couldn't have been more than fifteen. The man beside him, possibly his father, put a hand on the boy's shoulder.

"You are right," Ingwe responded with a small smile, "But they are no threat to you. They are under our complete command. You should feel safer with them here amongst all the riff raff."

The boy's lips twitched, but he remained silent after his father squeezed the hand on his shoulder. Steele thought of Bero and of the other magi she had seen on her train and she studied Ingwe, looking for anything that could be a pridestone. She didn't know what his specifically looked like, but she believed that if she could free Bero, the magi would help them.

Ingwe continued, "As our guests, you'll be staying near the soldier's quarters. We are going there first, so you may see if everything is up to your standard. There's a lounge area for relaxation for those of you who desire to sit for a moment. While I'm on that thought, tonight our chefs will be preparing a feast in honor of a very prestigious guest, and you are welcome to join in his honor.

The auctions and business deals are dealt with near the center of the camp. I'll be collecting more information from you regarding what it is you are looking for, so that I can direct you to where you need to go tomorrow morning."

Steele followed closely behind Kaleel, keeping in mind her timid servant persona. Thankfully, no one was trying to speak with her, and once she'd been introduced as a servant, they barely even looked at her.

She wondered if they were in the soldier's quarters. Occasionally she'd see a man dressed in black with a green colored sash, but she didn't recognize the colors. They weren't Solarrhian uniforms.

"K-Ezra, how'd you know to use that name?" She murmured, face turned toward the outside of the pathway.

Kaleel looked over his shoulder, but avoided looking at her. "I saw him hand luggage over to Em. He's newer to court, and Em's been away from the palace long enough that Ezra may not have recognized him. Figured it would be a good name to give."

A red-haired woman stepped out of one tent, her hand clutching the hilt of a saber attached to a belt on her hip. A man dressed in black but with a silver sash called out to her. "Alana, get over here!"

She paused to look at the tour, her gaze passing over Steele, before she pivoted and sauntered toward the man. "Could you be any louder?"

Steele whispered at Kaleel's back, "Did you recognize her?"

Instead of replying, he shook his head no, keeping his eyes on Ingwe and Valas, the Barrowlander who was now asking Ingwe a question about the following day.

She was curious as well, but as she turned her ear toward the two men, she spotted Emdubae disappearing behind a tent. She tugged on Kaleel's sleeve quickly before stepping to the side of the touring crowd. Dropping to the ground, she adjusted her pant leg that had come unrolled. She took off her boot and dumped sand out. The crowd continued on without her, including Kaleel.

He glanced back and nodded her along before continuing on with the tour. Shaking her head at him, she put her boot on and snuck around the tent to look for Emdubae. Kaleel would be fine on his own. She hoped.

Behind the tent was another one, their backs facing each other. The entire row of tents were like this, pushed up against one another, though there was enough room to walk carefully between each one.

She checked behind her first, and when she was sure no one had followed her, she crept forward, looking for signs of Emdubae or Aldair. She found Emdubae on the other side of the tent. He was crouched, staring at a few soldiers in the pathway, and when she stepped again, he held up his hand. It wasn't until after the soldiers left that he lowered his arm.

She crouched beside him. "Where's Aldair?"

"We were separated. He was asked to bathe a horse, and I was told to transfer a chest to the living quarters. Aldair was gone when I returned. You haven't seen him?"

She shook her head. "Where do you think he'd go?"

He was silent for a moment. "If he didn't go straight to Fijar, he'd try to find where they are keeping the most information here."

She wondered if Aldair was reckless enough to confront Fijar on his own. "We need to get closer to the center of camp, then. The tour guide said that's where all the business is done. If we can't find information there, we'll at least be able to track people."

"Follow me, then." Emdubae crept between the back of the tents, crouched low enough that his head wouldn't be seen over the tops.

She set her jaw, ignoring her dancing nerves. A strand of hair fell into her eyes and she pushed it back into her headscarf and continued forward, pressing her hand to the blade on her belt. Just in case.

They moved farther into camp, sticking to the small spaces behind the tents and swiftly crossing intersecting pathways. They paused only to duck out of sight if a person appeared around a corner. Steele allowed a sigh of relief each time they avoided someone, but her insides twisted more intensely as they neared the center.

She was in the middle of crossing a pathway between tents when she heard the pounding of multiple sets of footsteps coming her direction. Emdubae quickly pulled her back and into the tent behind them. He jerked the flap closed, and she breathed heavily, heart fluttering and hands tingling with adrenaline.

"That was close," she muttered under her breath. She turned around to see a large desk placed near the back of the tent with papers neatly stacked into six piles. A larger paper lay prominently on the middle of the desk.

Emdubae walked slowly toward the desk, trying not to disturb the fabric of the tent. Steele followed him, but when she saw the papers, all she could make of the contents were numbers and random descriptions. They were in code.

She studied Emdubae's reaction. As he scanned the papers he seemed to recognize some of the codes. "Grab a bag, please."

She looked around and found a medium sized travel bag. As quickly and quietly as she could, she dumped its contents to the ground and set it on the desk. Emdubae nodded his thanks, and she carefully made her way to the entrance to check on their surroundings.

She peeked through a rip in the fabric and saw a group of men dressed neatly in black tunics and slacks joining two lone men dressed similarly except for a forest green sash fastened across their middle. The men stood near the tent, and Steele wished that more than just the uncomfortably thin canvas separated them. She caught Emdubae's gaze and held a finger up to her lips. He quietly fitted a stack of papers into the bag.

The men finally moved away, and Steele let out a breath. She turned to Emdubae. "What do those papers mean?"

"I cannot say exactly what they are, but they appear to be charts filled with sales of products," he said gruffly. "I do not want to believe what the papers are telling me, though."

She crossed her arms, heart rate increasing. "And?"

"The descriptions seem to match people profiling." He fingered the larger sheet of paper and began folding it. "Some of this is making sense now, like you being shipped out into the desert on a train. They would not use such a force as the magi to transport one prisoner who could been easily executed on a normal gallows, so I imagine you were not the only one on your train. It doesn't look like they are bringing people here solely for the purpose of paying for their crimes. Some have been auctioned off to the highest bidder. Some...there are other notations, but I cannot make sense of them."

Steele froze. People were being sold? Now what Fijar had said about making a fortune off the prisoner made sense. "But Tazmeen and Ali aren't even criminals. Why would anyone approve of this?"

Emdubae tied the bag shut and placed a hand on her shoulder. "Aldair told me what happened with your family, and I am so sorry. But I hope these papers will help us find out what happened to them." He shook his head. "As for your question, I know King Ax wouldn't. From the years that I have worked closely with the royal family, I have never heard him speak of solving any poverty or crime issue with enslaving those affected. The question is, who *is* involved?"

He spoke firmly, but she wondered if he wasn't just trying to convince himself that his king wasn't capable of such corruption.

Outside of the tent, voices erupted. Steele tensed, wondering what was going on and how many people were gathered to make that much noise. She inhaled sharply. If a large group of people were gathering, maybe she'd be able to spot Tazmeen or Ali. She leapt for the flap and peeked through the rip again before deciding it was safe to exit. She nodded at Emdubae, who tossed the bag over his shoulder. She trotted to the safety of the next tent, every fiber taut with the hope that she would be united with her family soon.

A single voice was magnified much louder than the rumble of the crowd, and she walked faster as she neared, ears straining to hear beyond the last barrier of tents. All she could see beyond the canvas was a mass of people who faced a platform. Emdubae pulled out his spyglass and observed the scene. She crossed her arms, trying to ignore the tingling of anticipation in her hands.

Finally, he lowered his arms, quickly wiping sweat from his chin. "Aldair is in the crowd."

"How can you tell?" she asked, taking the glass in hand. She pulled back when all she could see was a man's arm and then the ground when her hand shifted slightly. After adjusting the settings of the spyglass, she scanned the crowd.

Emdubae pushed her hands in the general direction. "Look for the man in the white hood toward the front."

"Should we go up to him in that crowd?" she asked, spotting him when he had his face turned to the side. She used the spyglass to scan through the masses, praying one of them would be Ali or Tazmeen.

"If we don't join up with him now, who knows when we'll see him again? I can't chance him stumbling upon Fijar first." He strode forward, easily immersing himself in the crowd, and didn't wait for her to follow.

She reluctantly lowered the spyglass and pushed her way through people, aware of a putrid stench growing more and more potent as she weaved in and out of pockets of people. She briefly covered her mouth and nose with her headscarf, but when a boy looked at her with accusing eyes, she dropped her hand and willed herself to breathe normally.

She was now close enough to the stage to see two males on their knees, and one man dressed neatly with his hands on his hips. He was pacing behind the two who knelt, and their shoulders hunched whenever he passed by. Something about his gait annoyed her already, and she hadn't even been paying attention to what he was saying. A magi stood in the corner, and she imagined he was the source of the man's projected voice.

Emdubae stopped about three rows back from the stage beside a man in a grayish white hooded cloak. The man turned, revealing his profile and a very familiar lip scar. Steele half smiled, relieved to be reunited with part of their group. She looked around for Kaleel, and wasn't surprised that he was nowhere to be seen. He could still very well be on the tour, and she hoped he'd not been discovered as a fraud.

Aldair did not smile at her when she halted by his other side. His mouth was set in a grim line, eyes narrowed and lit with anger as he stared up at the men on the stage.

"What's happening?" Emdubae asked.

"The men up there were caught stealing food in the camp and are to be executed as an example," Aldair explained, "Apparently they were punished already this week for not being bought at an auction."

Steele studied the men closely, seeing more clearly their sunken in cheeks. These men were starving. It was no wonder they stole. And no wonder that they hadn't been bought in the first place if they had been

216

sold under the pretense of good labor. They looked like they could barely hold themselves up, let alone build something.

The man addressing the crowd unhooked a whip from his belt and waved it around grandiosely. "After today," he said in his magically enhanced voice, "if anyone is caught with food outside of the indicated mealtimes, they shall be whipped and chained to the pole for three days without food or water!"

Aldair shifted, and Emdubae grabbed his arm. "No."

The prince ripped his arm from Emdubae's grip. "We need to stop them."

"But not here. I need to show you these papers I found. This thing is bigger than we imagined. Much more advanced than just a crime ring in the kingdom like we first thought."

"These men need to be helped *now*," the prince said gruffly.

Steele nodded from behind him, and Emdubae threw her a look. She raised her eyebrows, annoyed. Surely he thought the men needed to be saved.

The man on stage snapped his whip in the air, the line cracking loudly. One man fell forward onto his elbows, but the other straightened his back. The man with the whip had a sickeningly sweet smile on his lips, as if he enjoyed this part of his job. He popped the whip onto the back of the defiant prisoner, who fell onto his side with a loud wail. She cringed, ducking behind Aldair's shoulders and stared at the ground, with gritted teeth.

"What do you suggest then? We leave these men to die?" Aldair protested quietly.

"Do you think you can waltz up there, announce you're the prince, and they will just let everyone go? There are men and women here who will not recognize your authority and will do anything to make sure their sins are covered," Emdubae pleaded, "You need to come with me, so we can make a plan."

Steele saw Emdubae's sense and placed a hand on Aldair's arm. "If we were to save them, or any of them, how could we protect them right now? Where would we take them? How would we provide for them?" she spoke dully, hating having to use his own argument against him. His blue eyes locked on her brown ones. For a moment, he looked angry, then sorrowful.

"I need to find Fijar," he said resolutely. "Now." He turned to weave his way to the outside of the crowd.

Steele watched Emdubae start to follow the prince, but she couldn't pull herself away from the men on the platform. Emdubae glanced back at her and stopped when he noticed she hadn't moved. He shook his head fiercely as she wavered, torn between what her heart told her to do and what her mind knew was better. But how could letting these men die be better?

Aldair did not turn back, and Emdubae sighed and grabbed her wrist. "We will never find out what happened to your family if you do this now."

Her eyes filled with tears, but she nodded, throwing one last glance at the man lying on his side, his face scrunched in pain. The other lay prostrate and defeated, waiting for his fate.

She picked up her pace, gripping Emdubae's hand and tuning out the murmuring of the people she passed. No one she could focus on was looking toward the stage. Their eyes were down.

The trio came upon a group of tents and did not stop walking. Aldair turned to the left, passed a few tents, then right, and continued straight until they came to a darker pathway, shaded by two trees.

"What will you even say to Fijar when you find him?" Emdubae called, though he still tried to keep his voice low.

Aldair stopped then. Steele wondered if he had just run out of purpose by the way he stood, on the verge of moving, but his feet planted to the ground. The prince crossed his arms and looked around. "You said you found papers?"

"Yes, from just a quick study, it appears they have been auctioning people off..." Emdubae broke off as footsteps sounded around the corner.

Steele found herself suddenly shielded by Aldair, and she gripped his waist to steady herself. They stood, every muscle tense until a figure rounded the corner. She found the intruder's face, and relaxed, sagging against Aldair's back, when Kaleel's wild eyes slid into focus.

Aldair reached back to steady her as he moved toward Kaleel. "Any news?"

Kaleel licked his lips nervously, and he looked at Steele quickly. "Shortly after you left, we ran into Lac's tour with Roman. I overheard a bit of their conversation, and it sounds like Fijar is recruiting the High Council to finance these camps. I think there's more to their deal than that, but without stone hard facts, I don't want to say."

"Kaleel." Aldair snapped.

"Fine," Kaleel grunted. "It sounds like there's multiple camps, from what Steele and I heard. I don't think Fijar just wants to make a fortune, and my instincts say that there's a power play in formation."

"What are you getting at?" Emdubae started to pace.

"Lothar House has always been at odds with the Zhanbolat House. Always. And I don't think they'd mind seeing your father dethroned, Aldair."

"Fijar would never usurp my father," Aldair returned quickly, but his face betrayed his tone's certainty. He looked troubled. "They're like brothers."

"I know," Kaleel said, "I hope I'm wrong, but I think it'd be wise to treat him like he's the enemy."

Aldair stared at the ground. Steele wished she could read his thoughts, but even his face was blank. He then looked to Kaleel and broke the silence. "You know where he is, don't you."

Kaleel hesitated before nodding. "I saw him, but…that was five minutes ago."

Emdubae stepped in front of the prince before the man could so much as breathe. "I'll confront him."

Aldair narrowed his eyes and set his shoulders back, straightening to his full height. He looked down into Emdubae's icy blue eyes. "This is my duty, Emdubae. I cannot send you to do the hard stuff for me, especially not when I'm the future king."

"Which is precisely why I should go," Emdubae disagreed. "You are irreplaceable to the kingdom, and you do not know what tricks Fijar has up his sleeve."

"Fijar is a master swordsman; he trained me. I may not know all of his tricks, but that doesn't mean I shouldn't confront him out of fear. Since when is being a prince an excuse to stay back and let others do my job? My first responsibility is to my people and the crown."

"And my job is protect you."

Emdubae and Aldair stared at each with equal fervor. Steele was unsure of who would win this argument, and her heart tightened. She looked to Kaleel who remained silent, his eyes worried. He kept surveying their surroundings, and she followed suit. They shouldn't stick around here for too long, especially not as a group.

"Hold your tongue, Emdubae," Kaleel warned, pulling Steele's attention back to the argument.

"You are not king yet," Emdubae said, ignoring his friend's warning. "Your father would execute me for letting you go. You're too valuable, and you don't have a brother to hide behind anymore, Aldair," he snapped.

Steele didn't think anyone could resemble a stone as well as Aldair did at that moment. Emdubae's expression quickly morphed from fury to regret, although she doubted he spoke without much thought. His light blue eyes darkened a shade when, aside from a sharp inhale, Aldair did not respond. An uncomfortable silence settled in amongst the four.

Emdubae opened his mouth several times before finally speaking. "I would like to go with you at least."

Aldair flexed his jaw but said nothing, and Steele exchanged a glance with Kaleel.

"What if we walk and talk," she suggested. "We obviously can't just leave, so in the meantime, let's do something about the magi. Bero was imprisoned when I met him, and I would bet many of these magi aren't here willingly. So, how about we walk and talk about how to free them, as well as keeping an eye out for Fijar." She glanced at Kaleel, and he gave her an approving nod.

"I think that sounds reasonable," Emdubae said slowly, his eyes flicking toward the prince.

Aldair rubbed his eyes and sighed. "Fine," he said as he turned to Steele. "Thinking of the magi is wise."

She gave him a small smile and started walking, hoping they would follow. Kaleel quickly fell in step beside her, and she heard the other two follow behind them. "Bero told me that Lac had his pridestone when we were on the train, so I'm guessing the magi's pridestones here are either with Fijar or Lac. I'm not sure how to release a magi from someone once you have a stone, though."

"Having the stone in your possession allows you to control the magi. I think you only need to speak to the stones a command, and it will reach the magi." Aldair quickened his pace so he was on the other side of Steele, and Emdubae came alongside Kaleel.

She nodded. "Good. So. We need to find Lac or Fijar or someone else who looks like they're in charge, and take the stones from them. While we're doing that, we can keep an eye out for anything else we may want to investigate or help with. Sound like a plan?"

Kaleel grinned and nudged her hard enough that she bumped into Aldair. "Yes ma'am. Maybe once we get home, the palace guard will be run by a woman."

She gave him a flat stare. "That would be ironic but maybe an improvement."

Kaleel started to chuckle but a yell from across camp cut him off. Emdubae scratched his beard. "Let's walk faster, shall we?"

They increased their pace, glancing between rows of tents as discreetly as they could. Stress prickled at Steele's insides, but she didn't try to slow down. They were already committed to exploring the camp, and the faster they found the magi rings, the faster they could get some help. They made good time, pausing only a handful of times to avoid being seen, and she was starting to wonder if they had been looking in the wrong direction when they turned around a corner and ran into a group of people.

The man at the front was the largest man Steele had ever seen, and he folded arms the size of tree trunks across his chest. "Who're you?" he asked in a guttural voice.

Before they had a chance to reply, a wiry woman jumped forward, eyes wide, and pointed to Aldair.

"He's the prince!" she cried, reaching for a sword at her side. "Get them!"

"Run!" someone cried from the back of the group, and Steele tried to do just that, backpedaling as fast as she could. But then she saw the large man tackle Emdubae, and she froze, unwilling to leave her friends in a fight. She threw her belt knife at the man, but he paid no mind to the blade as it sank into his arm. The wiry woman fought Kaleel, and they clashed together with the sharp clang of metal on metal. She turned, grabbing for her sword while looking for Aldair, and was knocked off her feet by a blow to the small of her back.

She scrambled on her stomach, scraping her elbows as she tried to crawl to her feet, but she was forcibly flipped to her back, and someone pinned her arms to her side.

"You're a feisty one," a man said, leaning down to better see her face. "It's a pity I have to kill you, but the princeling isn't welcome here. I've got a good thing going for the first time in I can't remember and I ain't about to let you ruin it. Food, a bed, people to hurt…" He clucked his tongue, planting his weight on her middle. "It's a shame though. You've got spirit, and you ain't ugly."

She tried to wriggle free, but he held her arms down with his knees. With a triumphant grin he grabbed her throat and squeezed. Panic uncurled in her gut so quickly she nearly vomited and terrified tears leaked from her eyes. Her vision darkened even as her heart galloped on, and she tried in vain to free one of her arms. She shut her eyes, not wanting this man's manic stare to be the last thing she saw, and spots danced against her eyelids.

Suddenly the man jerked back with a low howl, his grip slackened, and he slumped forward, forehead thumping against the ground over her shoulder. Her eyes flew open, yet all she saw was darkness. She tried to breath, but could only cough and gasp, and terror clawed at her insides as her lungs demanded air. Then the man was gone, pulled away by Emdubae. Not seconds later Aldair's arms wrapped around her, helping her sit. She leaned forward against his arm, dragging air into her lungs, and stared at her hands. They trembled on the ground in front of her, and she grasped them together, trying to control the tremors. She glanced over to see Emdubae retrieving his sword from the man's back and tears of gratitude burned behind her eyes.

She didn't have long to rest. The large man was down, but he was stirring, and Kaleel still fought with the wiry woman. A large group of people cowered in the pathway, and when she squinted against the sun, she could see they were chained together. Prisoners? Slaves?

"Are you all right?" Aldair whispered, blue eyes wide with fear and anger.

She nodded and moved to stand. He helped her up, and when he held out her knife to her, he froze, staring at something over her shoulder. She turned to see Fijar standing beside the tent, flanked by two guards. His jaw twitched and his eyes narrowed.

She stepped back.

Fijar turned on his heel and ducked behind the tent. His guards hesitated only a moment before following his lead.

Steele exhaled, relieved that a confrontation hadn't happened yet, but then Aldair rushed passed her after the retreating men. She swayed, gripping her knife and tried to process everything that was happening. Her throat throbbed and she gingerly rubbed her neck.

Kaleel dealt a blow to the wiry woman's head, and she dropped to the ground. He crouched over her, pressing his fingers against her neck, checking for a pulse. He nodded to himself and when he stood, Steele saw he had blood running down his face from a cut beneath his right eye. He used his shoulder to wipe some of the red away, but more trickled down his cheek. He glanced in the direction Aldair had run before moving to speak with some of the people who were chained together.

"That man is the most difficult opponent I have ever faced," Emdubae commented, coming to stand beside her.

She turned and hugged him. "Thank you for saving me," she whispered. "I owe you one now." She tried to smile, and Emdubae patted her back.

"I'll hold you to it, Little Thief. Although Aldair was only a second behind me. Where did he run off to?"

She frowned. "He saw Fijar. I think—"

"Em! Steele! Come here," Kaleel called, interrupting her. "This is Ryker," he said once they had joined him, gesturing to a lanky man with sandy hair and green eyes. "He says this group is part of a soldier unit."

"Soldiers?" Steele questioned, eyeing the wiry woman.

"Yes," Ryker answered, glancing at the burly man on the ground. "There are several groups of us being trained in fighting and endurance."

"Why?" Kaleel asked.

"We're not sure," Ryker answered, struggling to keep his footing as the people around him shifted, their chains clinking. "Most in these soldier units are happy to be here because this is a better alternative to what they were supposed to get, but some of us are here unwillingly or haven't proven our loyalty. Hence the chains."

Kaleel twirled his saber as he observed the prisoners. "Should we free them?' he muttered low enough that only she and Emdubae could hear him.

She surveyed the people bound together and sighed. They could free them, and some might help. Or they could turn against them if they thought anything like the man who had attacked her. Freeing prisoners would draw more attention to them, but Fijar now knew they were there.

"Uuungggghh," the burly man groaned and moved an arm.

"We need to do something with these guys first," Emdubae resolved with a sigh.

"There are some cages where we're kept at night," Ryker said, jerking a thumb over his shoulder. "It would take you a while, but you could drag them there."

"Can the cages lock?" asked Kaleel.

Ryker's eyes widened, focused behind the three.

Steele turned to see the burly man charging toward them, mouth twisted in a snarl. Emdubae threw his sword up just in time, yet even so, the power of the swing knocked him almost to his knees. Kaleel was quick to join Emdubae, and she darted forward, looking for a way to help.

"Go find Aldair," Kaleel said through gritted teeth. "We'll take care of this and find you, but he shouldn't face Fijar alone."

With a quick, "Be careful," she turned and ran the direction the prince had gone.

CHAPTER 29

As Steele moved along the rows of tents without Emdubae and Kaleel by her side, she suddenly felt very alone. And a little paranoid. The shushing sound of the wind turned into voices, and the rat-tat-tat of sand against a tent became footsteps. Stopping, she closed her eyes and breathed in deeply through her nose and out through her mouth. In a few moments she was calm.

The tents she passed were all empty, her disappointment growing the farther she walked. She was wasting valuable time.

Voices caught her attention. They were different from those of the shouting of men around the camp.

Holding her breath, she crept to the edge of the nearest tent and risked a glance around. Her heart jumped. Not ten paces away from her stood Aldair and Fijar, facing each other with the general's back to her. She quickly glanced around, looking for Fijar's guards, but they were nowhere to be seen.

Aldair's arms were crossed, but Fijar rested one hand on the hilt of his sword and the other on his hip, the fabric of his tunic pulled up and exposing a sash tied around his waist.

Steele squinted. The sunlight cast a muted glow on what appeared to be golden jewelry attached to the sash. Rubies, emeralds, sapphires, and other gemstones twinkled.

Pridestones!

Hugging the side of the shadowy tent flaps, she slowly scooted toward Fijar. If Aldair kept him occupied, she could cut away part of the sash and be gone before he realized she had been there. She pulled her belt knife out and held it ready in case he caught sight of her. As she edged closer, she caught their conversation.

"This is illegal, Fijar." Aldair threw his hand down in frustration.

The two men shifted their weight on the balls of their feet, their bodies tense as they watched each other from opposite sides of the pathway. Some people paused in the shadows, but they did not linger. Steele could see Aldair was tempted to look around, but he could not take his own eyes off this man. If he did, he could die.

Fijar tutted. "My prince, my prince, you are being a little hasty here." He circled to his right.

"Hasty! This is not a refugee camp. Some of these people are not even convicts!" Aldair exclaimed, mirroring Fijar's steps.

They were like two firecats circling one another before a fight, sizing each other up, looking for weaknesses.

"These people are useless to society. Beggars, thieves, murderers— poor folk who clog our cities. Some might call it…street cleaning."

Rage burst from Steele's heart, spreading like fire. The knife shook in her hand, and she took a calming breath to steady herself.

Aldair blinked, an incredulous anger painting his eyes navy. "Do you not see?" he asked. "It's not only that you took people you deem unworthy. Your *heart* is corrupt. You would have taken anyone if my father were to turn a blind eye. And for what? To make money off them? They may not be the wealthiest, but they do not deserve this sort of treatment. Do not twist this into more lies and justification. It's disgusting." Aldair paused, scowling. "You have taken advantage of a weaker people because they did not have the means to stand up to you. You are nothing but a spider, fighting in the shadows, picking on those smaller than you. Nothing but a spider to be squished."

Fijar stared at him disbelievingly for a moment. His eyes shifted back and forth, studying Aldair's face, but Aldair did not flinch. In fact, the prince leaned closer, eyes defiant, as if he knew it would irk his former confidante.

It worked. Fijar snarled and gripped the hilt of his saber more firmly. "I taught you everything you know, boy. Do not think you can best me in a contest of swords."

Aldair's gaze shifted a fraction, and Steele knew he'd seen her. His expression did not change, but he settled back and Fijar relaxed.

"There's a good prince. You are wise to obey."

Steele glowered at the condescending tone the general used; like he was bringing a dog to heel. Fueled by anger and unable to remain still, she lurched forward and slashed at the sash with her knife. It came loose, and she deftly grabbed the pridestones before they fell into the sand and slipped them into her pocket. As her momentum carried her away, she felt something slice across her ribs. Something hot. And then painful. As she stumbled to her hands and knees, she felt at an opening in her tunic and her hand came away slick with blood. Crimson drops dotted the sand, and she blinked, frustrated that Fijar had been able to cut her.

A shadow covered her then, and when she looked up, she saw Fijar's blade cutting toward her face. She tried to kick herself backward, throwing an arm up to protect herself, and flinched when a *clang* rang out near her head. She lowered her arm and saw that Aldair stood over her, and was forcing Fijar away. Their sabers scraped against each other, and Aldair managed to get the general to move back a couple of more steps.

"You won't harm her again." Aldair spat, shoving Fijar back and pointing his saber at him.

"Oh, but of course I will, dear boy. Of course I will. I'll cut her head from her neck the second I am through with you." Fijar tipped his head to the side and studied Steele with the same look a cat would give a mouse before eating it. "Or I'll make you watch as I kill her. That way you will have had the privilege of witnessing it." Fijar wiped her blood from his blade with a cloth. "She reminds me a bit of your brother. He was so weak in death, so very afraid as the illness gripped him. That weakness in the face of a challenge would have made him a poor king."

"Did you never care for us? Was it all a lie?" Aldair asked, his voice soft. He took a step toward the general.

Fijar clicked his tongue as he raised his saber. "You boys could have been great, but your father's weakness rubbed off on you, I'm afraid. And you, the one who should not be king, you're the worst of all. You could stand with the strong, but instead, you ally with the lowest of the lot. You'll be the downfall of this kingdom, if I let you rule. Your brother would be so ashamed."

One second Aldair was standing in front of Steele, and the next he was on Fijar, sabers ringing as they fought. Aldair struck at the general with hard fast jabs, looking angrier and more out of control than he did when he parried with Kaleel or Emdubae.

She tried to move, to help Aldair in some way but the wound on her side pulsed and she sank back to her knees.

Fijar snarled and stumbled back, grasping his right side. Blood pooled between his fingers and Steele saw obvious relief on his face when Aldair backed away.

The prince briefly took his eyes off of Fijar, his hand finding Steele's face, and he ran his thumb along her cheek. "You don't deserve to live, Fijar." Aldair spoke so coldly that Steele shuddered. "But when this is over, neither of us will be dead. I want you alive to face the horrors of what you have done." Aldair shifted his weight and moved toward the general, who stepped back and sneered again.

"We'll see about that." With a sharp clang, their swords met. Aldair glanced at Steele before circling around the tent, Fijar parrying the entire way, the canvas now blocking them from sight.

Steele was alone again.

★ ☽ ★

As the pain in her side flared, Steele fought down the panic that was bubbling up inside of her. She just knew that if she looked down, what should be inside would be out.

No, Steele told herself. She'd been cut before. This wasn't anything new. She would be fine. She *had* to be fine. And she still had the pridestones. She held the sash in front of her, willing herself to focus on the glittering jewels.

Next, she gingerly lifted her outer tunic over her head and examined her wound through the tear in her undershirt. The cut was long and shallow but still bleeding. After cutting a strip of cloth from the tunic, she tied it awkwardly around her torso. It didn't cover the entire wound, but it would have to do.

She recalled what Fijar had said to Aldair about the prisoners, his brother, and her. Her side burned, and she allowed it to fuel her anger and determination. She was not worthless. She jerked the ends of cloth to make sure they were secure and gritted her teeth against the stab of pain as the fabric scraped against the raw edges of her cut.

She examined the jewels again. She wasn't so wounded she couldn't follow the prince, but maybe the best thing to do for him right now was free the magi.

She cupped the gemstones in her hands. "You're free, magi!" she exclaimed breathlessly.

Pushing herself onto her feet, she set out in the direction Aldair and Fijar had gone. When each row of tents she passed brought her to no one, she moved faster and faster until she was running. Where were they? She rounded a corner and skidded to a stop before crashing into Kaleel and a grimy young man.

"Kaleel! Take these!" Steele shoved the rings into his hands. "I think I freed some magi, but I don't want to be responsible for these. Aldair is with Fijar, and he needs our help. We can..." Whatever she was about to say died on her lips.

She'd looked at Kaleel's companion, and what she saw dropped her to her knees. She would know those wide brown eyes anywhere.

Ali knelt in front of her, and Steele knocked her chin on his shoulder as she pulled him into a hug. The pain of her wound was a fading memory, and the immediate danger seemed far off. Her heart thrummed hard against her ribs and the dam she had built inside came crashing down. Burying her face in his shoulder, she burst into tears.

Ali's body hitched as he clung to her, and his fingers dug into her back. "I knew you'd find me," he whispered.

Steele pulled back and inspected him for injuries. "Are you well? Where are you hurt? Did Kaleel give you some water? When was the last time you ate? Or slept?" The questions burst from her so rapidly that Ali laughed. It was a ghost of the wonderful, joyful laugh Steele had been wishing to hear again, but the sound brought more tears to her eyes.

"I'm fine, Steele."

"All right," she breathed, pulling the collar of her undershirt up to wipe her eyes. "We're not done here, Ali. We have to take over the camp, and I need you to stay safe. Do you understand? I refuse to lose you again." She stood and pulled Ali up with her, wrapping him in another hug. Had it really been a month since she had seen him last? He was so tall now. She stepped back to look him in the eyes. "Where's your ma?"

Whatever Ali was about to say was cut off by the arrival of two camp soldiers. Before Steele could react, Kaleel threw a knife at one of them while pulling his saber free to face the other.

Another guard ran forward and Ali lunged for the saber of the fallen soldier. Steele grabbed his arm, pulling him back. "Ali, no! You have to get out of here!"

"No way, I've been dreaming of this for weeks!" He pulled his arm free and grabbed the saber.

"They're trained soldiers," she pleaded, frantic with worry. He clenched his jaw and looked at her. Without saying anything, he jumped into the fight, blocking what would have been a death blow to Kaleel by the second guard had Ali not stepped in.

"Steele!" Kaleel shouted. "Aldair! Go!"

Her voice grave, she called out, "You take care of him."

Forcing herself to turn away from Ali was one of the hardest things she'd ever had to do. She thought of Aldair and, in that moment, realized that helping him was just as important to her as finding her family. She put her trust in Kaleel to protect Ali, and without a backward glance, she ran.

CHAPTER 30

Steele rounded the corner and threw herself to the ground to avoid losing her head to a saber. The guard who swung at her staggered, lurching as he turned to face her, a sneer twisting his lips. She pulled her saber up and gripped the hilt with a smirk. While her skill with a saber still wasn't her greatest asset, her training with Emdubae had helped, and she would exude confidence until it killed her. She itched to glance around and see where Aldair was and how he fared, but she knew if she looked away even for a moment, she would be dead. The sharp clanging of metal on metal let her know that someone still fought, and she could only pray Aldair was one of those alive.

Steele feigned a lunge to the left, and the guard bought it, jumping forward and swinging his sword down. She jerked to the right, cutting across the back of his legs with her blade. He shrieked and fell to his knees, blood pooling on the sand below, and Steele watched, mesmerized as the dark red and brown seeped into the ground. She hadn't used her full force; she wasn't looking to kill anyone, but there was still so much blood. The guard glared, and she ducked as he threw a small knife at her.

She retrieved the knife from where it had landed in the sand and used it to salute the man. "I thank you for the extra knife."

She turned from the guard, and relief spread through her chest as she saw Aldair standing opposite Fijar, the pair looking less sure than they had during their earlier argument. Blood trickled down Aldair's wrist and spread like veins down his saber, and he did not look to be standing comfortably. Fijar, on the other hand, did not appear to be faring any better as he swiped at the blood leaking from the corner of his mouth, leaving a smudged trail on his chin. Coughing, he covered his middle, the front of his tunic dark and wet looking.

Several of Fijar's men had stopped to watch what would unfold, and Aldair's name spread like a wildfire among them. A few sheathed their weapons, and one rushed at Fijar. He was tackled by another soldier before he could get to the general. The ones who had put their weapons away jumped forward, but were also blocked. It looked like their loyalties were split.

Another guard raised his saber to Steele, confidence oozing in his grin. He thought she would be an easy kill. Taunting him with a wave and a sly smile, she tried the same move with the previous guard, and just like the other, he fell for it. She nimbly dipped to the right, bringing the hilt of her saber against the back of his head with a satisfying crack.

As he crumbled to the ground, a short, balding man lingering behind Aldair caught Steele's eye. Something about the way he watched the prince frightened her. The longer she watched this man, the more she felt a pull toward him, an urge to stop him and whatever he was about to do. She started in his direction but was cut off by another one of Fijar's guards. Glancing up, she felt a spasm of fear course through her. It was Lac.

"Steele, isn't it?" He leered at her for a moment before pulling his own sword out with a flourish. "Isn't this just perfect? You've found your way to your new home."

He lunged at her, blade swinging, and she threw her saber up, bracing for the impact. It came hard and strong, and she grunted with the effort of staying upright.

"I'm flattered that you've come back for more," he said, his muddy-green eyes peering into hers as he leaned into her. "You outwitted me once, girl. It won't happen again."

She quirked an eyebrow at him and spat in his uncomfortably close face.

He stumbled back with a disgusted grunt and swung his blade at her head. The blade cut through the air quickly, and she ducked, knowing she moved too slowly. The flat side of Lac's sword slapped her cheek, knocking her sideways. She recovered and faced him again, rubbing her stinging skin.

Lac twirled his saber. "Wondering why I didn't take your head?"

"Because your aim is poor?" She narrowed her eyes. Something glittered under his tunic. It looked like the pridestones she'd taken from Fijar.

Lac laughed. "I plan on taking you alive, Steele. A sort of reward for the hunt you've given me, and I would not want to mar your pretty face. General Fijar said you won't be worth much because your spirit is too fiery, but I have to disagree. Breaking you will be a highlight, worth every piece of bronze to see you give in to me."

A cold shudder ran down her spine. *Better to die in this fight than be taken alive by this man.* But if he refused to cut her, that gave her an advantage. Lac was a fool.

He raised his saber when she ran at him, and she didn't try to block his swing. The flat of his blade smacked off her arm, and she thrust her shoulder into his chest.

He stumbled back, and luckily—she thought briefly—into a wooden beam supporting a tent. His head smacked against the wood, and a swatch of canvas floated down over his eyes. Steele shoved him hard, using his imbalance and the canvas in her favor. His head snapped against the beam again, and as she pushed him a third time, she brought up her saber.

He righted himself just in time to see her come at him, blade raised. He lifted his arm to deflect her, but he was either too slow or too dazed. With a cry, she plunged the blade into his shoulder, jerking the blade down before jumping away to avoid a blow from his unaffected arm. His blood sprayed her, and she ignored the warm splatter with gritted teeth. Her blade was tinted red, as were her hands.

Lac raised his blade, and Steele ducked, somersaulting forward.

She wasn't quick enough, though, and his blade peeled into her left arm, dragging along as she rolled. Cursing, she jumped up, clamping her hand to the wound. Lac moved to approach her and blanched, peering down at the deep gash in his shoulder. It was not as long of a gash as the one Fijar had inflicted on her side—a wound that seemed to be ablaze at the moment—but somehow his wound was spurting blood. He gripped it and sank to his knees, blood leaking through his fingers. He shook his head, color draining from his skin, and barely flinched when she kicked the saber from his weakening grasp.

He lurched for her, grabbing hold of her belt and pulling her toward him. Within a second her blade was at his neck, and she stopped just before pressing into his skin. "You will release me, sir, if you know what is good for you." The anger in his eyes was terrifying, but she held her ground.

"Why don't you take the kill?" he spat.

Steele wiggled the saber against his neck, and he flinched. The thought that he was afraid of her was a little too thrilling. She held his pathetic life in her hands, and she could end it so quickly. Pulling the blade back, she held it to the side, ready to deliver the final blow, but as she swung the blade to his neck, something stopped her. She saw him kneeling there, everything incredibly vibrant for a moment, sweat dripping at the nape of his paling neck and his rasping breath. With a frustrated yell, she plunged the saber into the ground.

She could do it, but she wouldn't. Instead, she grabbed the pridestones from beneath his tunic, and delivered a well-aimed kick to the heart of his wound. He gasped and rocked back, arms waving.

"I don't think I need to do anything. You'll bleed out before long," she said, staring at the blood around them as she tied the stones around her wrist. Not all of it was his, though, she realized. Her shirt was soaked red now from Fijar's attack. The jewels reflected against her crimson-stained skin, and she held them close to her lips. "Magi, I have your pridestones and you are free. Please help us."

She pulled her blade from the ground and went to search for Aldair and Fijar.

The two men still faced each other, but they seemed to be talking now. The balding man still stood behind Aldair, but his hands were inside his tunic instead of clasped behind his back. Once again she started for him, and a commotion to her right caught her eye.

She glanced over to see Emdubae restraining another of Fijar's guards. "Watch Aldair's back," he commanded.

Roman Lothar stood beside him and blocked a sword from cutting into Emdubae's side. She frowned slightly, but didn't have time to puzzle over the fact that Lothar seemed to be helping them.

She nodded and ran on, pushing herself as the bald man strode forward, revealing a saber in one hand and a short whip tipped with barbs in the other. If Fijar noticed the man, he didn't wave him away. The general was a coward, allowing Aldair to be attacked while his back was turned. Steele dug in, cursing the sand for slowing her down, and she slammed into Aldair, pushing him down and out of the way, gasping as a few of the barbs raked across part of her shoulder and back.

Aldair landed with a grunt, and as he rolled protectively over her, Steele saw the man recovering from his miss. "Aldair, move!" she screamed.

He rolled and pulled her with him, the man's saber missing them by inches. His weapon sank deep into the sand, and while he bent to pull his sword free, Steele lurched to her feet, threw her knife at him, and it pierced his chest, just underneath his neck. She couldn't help but think Kaleel would be proud of that throw. She looked over to where Fijar stood, and she swayed, dizzy from fatigue and blood loss.

Aldair helped steady her, and she noticed his left eye was swollen and beginning to bruise. "You're hurt," she commented. Her back felt warm and sticky, but she chose to ignore it, instead searching Aldair's face for other injuries.

His eyes never left Fijar, but he pulled her close. "We all are." He clenched his jaw. "We have to stop him."

Fijar strode toward them, but even wounded, he managed to look as though he was in charge. His arm jerked, and Steele gasped as a blade lodged in her shoulder.

"Steele!" Aldair shouted.

"It doesn't hurt," she grimaced, more disgusted with the blade protruding from her skin than in pain. It burned and made her arm feel numb, but she didn't feel pain. She wondered about that for a moment. Her other wounds had hurt, hadn't they? The only thing she felt came from her back, and it was writhing. The lashes seemed alive.

Fijar held his saber out, wobbling a bit. Steele narrowed her eyes. He was clearly hurting. If she and Aldair worked together they could bring him down. She tried to raise her saber, but could not move her arm properly with the knife in place, so she gritted her teeth and yanked the blade out, groaning as it slid free. Warm blood trickled down her arm and chest, and she whimpered.

Aldair looked at her then, worry clouding his blue eyes.

His gaze moved from her face to her shoulder, and his eyes widened. "You should have left the knife in."

"I couldn't use my arm with it in," she replied, trying to sound calm. "If we work together we can overtake him. He's wounded, moving slower, and between the two of us, we can win. I know it." She glanced around to see if they would get any help. Emdubae and Roman appeared to be restraining some guards, and she didn't see Kaleel or Ali anywhere. Swallowing her worry, she turned her attention back to Fijar.

The general was eyeing them, a mocking smile twisting his lips. "What's this, Aldair? You've been reduced to taking advice from a thief? Pathetic."

Aldair growled. "This ends now, Fijar. I don't even care if you live anymore." He tipped his head and pressed his lips to Steele's ear. "I'm taking the brunt of this fight. But if you can, his left side is the wounded one. Exploit it." She nodded and heaved away from him. Her legs felt like lead.

"Only fools ignore good opinions just because they come from a commoner," Aldair added.

Fijar chuckled. "We shall see."

Aldair lunged at Fijar, and Steele blinked, attempting to clear her head. She clutched her shoulder wound, trying to staunch the bleeding. She could not spare the moments it would take to bandage it. Edging closer to the fight, she gripped her knife, ready to throw it at Fijar.

A man fell beside her, lifeless, and she gasped. Emdubae kneeled next to her for a moment. "Are you okay?"

She nodded. "Yes, but I need to help Aldair." She looked to the prince, who shoved Fijar back with a grunt. She cocked her arm back, ready to let the knife fly.

A whooshing sound gave her a pause, and a gust of wind stronger than anything she had experienced knocked her flat on her back. The sky warped and shimmered above her, and she gasped for air. A pair of invisible hands pushed her into the sand, and she struggled against the force holding her down.

As suddenly as the pressure was there, it was gone, and she pushed herself up, panting, eyes frantically searching for Aldair. Pillars of sand erupted all around her, rising high into the sky. A column exploded in front of her, and she watched it stretch toward the heavens. Currents of sand churned within the pillars, and just when she was certain she was dreaming, the sand pillars shattered with a muted *whumph*, flinging golden grains through the air. Her face and arms stung, and she weakly raised an arm to block the assault, but that didn't offer much protection.

She pushed herself to her feet, determined to escape the strange sandstorm. The sky rained sand as she waded through the gritty river, desperately searching for relief.

Defeated, she dropped to her knees, leaning forward to protect her face. Strong winds whipped the sand into a frenzy. The grains swirled faster and faster, and the wind howled around where she knelt. It was too much. The sound of the wind, the stinging sand, and the way her limbs felt like stone. She pressed her knuckles in her mouth to keep from screaming.

The wind abruptly stopped. More sand fell from the sky, blanketing her, and an eerie silence filled the air. She slowly lowered her hands from her face and sat up, sending rivulets of sand down her clothing and to the ground. The world lurched, spinning around her, and she squeezed her eyes shut, willing everything to stop turning. Aldair, Emdubae, and Kaleel needed her. Ali and Tazmeen needed her. She needed to rest. She needed to move. She needed to lie down. A buzzing in her head turned to a dull roar. Tired, so tired.

She realized she was still gripping the hilt of her saber when someone grabbed it and pulled it from her. She tried not to let go, but it slid easily from her blood slicked fingers. Then she was up. Up and moving. She opened her eyes—when had she closed them?—and looked up into Aldair's concerned face. His hand gripped her injured shoulder, and she turned into him, trying to escape the pressure. He carried her a short distance and sat himself down while continuing to cradle her in his arms. The dizziness ebbed, and the roar inside her head quieted.

She looked at Aldair and frowned. He looked so worn. "What happened?"

"I think, the magi. Whatever that wind and sand was, it wasn't natural." His voice was weary. "When the sand cleared, Fijar was restrained in a sort of bubble of air." He scooted her off his lap so she was beside him. "I need to look at your wounds. You had no business jumping in front of that whip."

Steele snorted, suddenly angry. "No business?" she breathed. "Your life is worth more than mine. You will rule a kingdom someday, and I'm just a horse thief." She paused, gasping as he inspected the gashes left behind by the whip. When she turned to face him, his gaze had softened.

"You've lost a lot of blood."

She heard a ripping sound, and cool air blew against her back. "Did you just tear my shirt?"

"Partly. I need something to cover your wounds." Another ripping sound, and a cloth was gently pressed against her back.

She hissed, jerking away. He continued to press fabric to her raw skin until the lashes were covered. When he was finished, he sat back with a sigh, and she looked to him.

Concern drew his eyebrows together. "You have to stay alive, my thief."

Stay alive? She'd been injured before. These wounds certainly didn't feel life threatening. She rolled her shoulders, but even that made her feel woozy. Her head suddenly weighed a hundred pounds, and as her neck was now too weak to support it, she allowed her head to slump forward. Aldair caught her by the forehead and guided her so she rested against his side. Looking down, she noticed that the bits of her skin that weren't stained red almost seemed to gleam white in contrast. The paleness bothered her. Her skin was usually more of a copper tone. The gems she'd taken from Lac flashed in the sun, and she weakly extended her arm to Aldair.

"I took these from Lac. Make sure Bero gets them."

While Aldair slid the gems from her wrist, a name jarred itself into Steele's mind. *Ali!* She had seen Ali! Spoken with him, in fact! She had to see him.

She lurched forward, and the sudden movement caused her to stumble to her hands and knees. She had to find Ali. If anything had happened to him she would never forgive herself. She sucked in two deep breaths and lifted her head to look around. Ali was nowhere to be seen, and she pushed herself to her feet. He *had* to be alive. She staggered forward a couple of steps, willing the blackness at the edge of her vision to fade. If Ali was hurt, he needed her, and she needed him, regardless.

The ground fell away as she was scooped back into Aldair's arms, and he carried her. She struggled weakly in his grasp but to no avail.

"Let me go please. I have to get to Ali," she begged.

Aldair tightened his grip and slid back to the ground with her. "No. You have to rest. Emdubae has gone to get us help."

"But if something happened to him he'll need me. I have to find him!" She looked at Aldair and blinked. His stained-glass eyes and freckles stood out remarkably against his own abnormally pale skin. He had also lost a lot of blood.

A small frown pulled at his lips as he shook his head. "Ali's fine. He's with Kaleel."

Steele blinked back tears. Ali was safe! He was alive! She relaxed, and as she did, she felt Aldair's grip loosen.

He cocked his head and glanced down at her. "I find you remarkable."

She slid off his lap and settled next to him. "Hmm?"

Now that she knew Ali was all right, the fatigue was back tenfold. Sweat trickled down her face, and she shivered. She shuddered again, and Aldair brushed her hair away from her face, eyes worried as he took her in.

"Come here," he murmured, pulling her back onto his lap. He raised his legs, and Steele curled against him, finding some relief in his warmth.

"Remarkable how?" she whispered.

Aldair rested his chin on her head. He shifted and tightened his grip. "I'll have to think of some fancy speech later. Right now I'm just too tired."

Steele tried to laugh as her eyes slid shut. "I suppose I find you remarkable, as well," she muttered, trying to fight the exhaustion.

Something rumbled by her ear. Thunder?

Her breathing slowed, her heart thumping raggedly within her. For a wild moment she wondered if she was at the end of her life, but she was too tired to care. With a long sigh, she allowed the blackness to take her.

CHAPTER 31

The ground crunched beneath Steele's bare feet with each step. As if pulled by the strings of a puppet master, she followed the sound of a thunderous wind. She had fallen asleep in the desert and woken up in the mountains. She pushed a branch out of her way, peering around a vine-covered tree before stepping out into the opening. The wind stopped, and everything quieted until all she could hear was her own breathing.

A dragon rested in the middle of the meadow, its blue and green scales shimmering in the sun, and while that should have been enough of a surprise for Steele, she was mystified by the unicorn from the desert standing there, appearing to be conversing with the dragon. The creatures stopped staring at each other and turned toward the intruder standing just outside the tree line. The dragon puffed smoke out its nose, flapping its wings once, but it remained nestled in place. The unicorn pawed at the ground, snorting, and let out a high-pitched whinny that faded into screaming. Steele covered her ears and closed her eyes. She crouched to her knees, folding within herself as the screams turned to wailing, laughter vibrating around the pain.

She opened her eyes to a sky the color of Aldair's dark blue eyes. Her thoughts did not make sense. Around her, shades of people danced. She blinked. No more dancing. People walked past her, their burdens chained to their backs, dragging behind them. One man limped his way by her as if not seeing her. She reeled around, calling after the man, but he continued on, hobbling into the unknown.

Her side screamed, and she clutched her ribs. Holes peeked through her middle where the barbs had peeled away her skin, and when she brought her hand away, it came away red, warm, and sticky. She stared at her hand, horrified as a drop of blood rolled from her fingertip down to her palm. The front of her desert-colored shirt was soaked crimson. The slash she'd received in the fight was infected, and it was spreading. Her breath hitched.

A boy trudged toward her. She reached for him, but he did not stop. She gasped as he walked through her. Steele held up her arms, turning with the boy as his body pushed through hers. He continued his tired hike down the camp road, an aimlessness clinging to his spirit.

Was this death? To walk in a half-life, able to see the living, but never able to touch them? If this was death, she did not welcome it, for who could desire such hopelessness and emptiness? She longed for the mountain and its peace again.

"How is she?" Emdubae's voice vibrated around her. She swirled around again, searching for her friend.

She was standing among a series of tents, and Bero stood there, not even a breath away with an aura around him glowing a bright blue. She shrunk back as he placed his hands on both the sides of her skull. His eyes began to shimmer, and the blue glow enveloped her just as she felt ice pour into her eyes and down through her toes. The searing in her rib cage opened up her lungs, and she screamed, her knees buckling. The pressure in her shoulder festered, rattling her nerves until she jerked away from the magi.

"Why?" she whimpered, not able to look at Bero. "It hurts. Please, stop."

Bero hummed, his hands steady against her cheeks, and her frosted insides began to melt, the burn simmering. When she looked up, the magi was gone. Instead of standing, she was lying down with her arms folded over her middle, her hands squeezing her sides. She was so tired. The clouds moved above her, the sky shifting colors as each one passed. Purple, gold, stained-glass blue.

She waded between the dream world and reality before the roads in her mind finally snapped together, and she followed the one that led her to the waking world.

Her eyes opened, her lids fluttering against her will, and the thought at the front of her brain was only of sleep. She didn't listen to it, though. Instead, she sat up, an action that brought on a wave of dizziness, and her thoughts jumbled again. She braced her arms against the bed to keep from falling and reoriented herself with a slow blink and a quick shake of her head. The thoughts and her surroundings shuffled back into place.

"A bed?" she mumbled. If anyone had heard her, they probably would have only heard gibberish. She squinted at the sun, and it welcomed her with a piercing glare through the opened windows just behind the pale gray columns in the room.

"A room?" This phrase came out clearly. Purple tiles blurred with shades of brown and gold.

She ripped the covers off her and swung her legs over the side of the bed. As she set her feet on the ground, the pain that burned up her leg and settled behind her kneecaps resurrected visions of blood, swords clashing, sand and metal digging in her skin… She grabbed her head, lost in the shouts of men, Aldair's voice, Fijar chuckling.

Steele jerked as a pair of hands pushed her back down on the soft mattress. She swung her arms to defend herself, connecting with flesh, but the hands did not move. She focused on them. They were soft and delicate and most definitely not the hands of a soldier.

"My lady, you must rest." The woman's voice was deep and raspy.

Steele trailed her eyes up the hands, the arms, past the golden-colored sleeves, and up to the gold-lined brown eyes that were filled with warmth and concern. She relaxed.

"Where am I?"

"You are at the palace." She had a long slender nose and inviting eyes, and Steele imagined that this woman was always the beauty in the room, even now that she had fewer years before her than behind.

Steele took a moment to study her surroundings. It looked like she was in a very expensive room with the silk blankets and an excessive number of soft pillows surrounding her. The gold in the wooden arches above the doorways and windows was not just a color accent but actual gold, and the arches melted into sturdy stone columns. She looked up and was torn between being impressed and bothered with how much time someone took etching the artwork on the ceiling. She could have eaten three meals a day the rest of her life with the amount of gold in the room.

Her companion sat beside her, her fingers delicately laced together on her lap.

"Thank you," Steele finally said, realizing she was being rude. "I'm sorry I hit you."

Lines crinkled around the woman's eyes as she smiled, and Steele's heart warmed. "It is not the first time. You have quite the strength for such a little body."

"I'm afraid I don't remember." Steele's voice faltered. She sifted through her latest memories but couldn't remember this woman. There weren't many people from the palace who she had met, unless they'd had an encounter on the streets.

The woman shifted so that she was sitting closer to Steele and patted her arm. She smoothed out the wrinkles of her golden dress. "I am not surprised. Magi healing comes with a price. They heal your wounds, but your body still works to the point of exhaustion to recuperate. Let me introduce myself. I am Raj, the Queen's Hand, and I have been tending to your needs."

Steele exhaled slowly, her eyes widening a bit.

The Queen's Hand? The queen?

Aldair's mother, the most powerful woman in the kingdom, had sent her aid to help someone like Steele?

"Thank you, Raj." She smiled weakly and then yawned. "How many days have I been here?"

"Six," Raj stated simply.

"Six days?" Steele exclaimed. She sat up and grabbed her side as a sharp pain shot up her spine. "What's happened to the others?" Try as she might, she could not remember anything after sitting with Aldair.

Raj laid her hand on Steele's shoulder and smiled kindly. "Everyone is fine and healthy. You had the worst of the injuries."

Steele was unsure if she was relieved about this fact; her pride felt seriously wounded. "Oh...Where's my family?"

A grimace passed across Raj's face, but it was gone so quickly, that Steele doubted she had seen it. "The prince has been checking in on you frequently. He seemed adamant to be the one to update you. I have already sent a maid to tell him about your waking," Raj reassured her. "If you would like, I can take you to the bathroom to freshen up."

"He's been checking on me?" Steele patted the tangled mess that had at one point been a braid. "As much as I'd like a bath, I want to know what's been happening first."

"It was difficult to get the prince to leave." Raj glanced at Steele, and she blushed at the scrutiny the queen's aid was able to convey in that fleeting look. Raj must be wondering just who Steele was to be in the company of the prince and his soldiers. She may even have been at court the day Steele had been arrested.

"The magi did a fine enough job cleaning you after the battle, but if you want to freshen up any, there's a bowl of lavender water over there." Raj motioned to where a basin sat on a table in front of a mirror. "I'll make sure the prince knows to give you some time before he comes up." She smiled warmly at Steele before patting her arm and leaving the room.

Steele waited until the door shut before pushing herself to sit all the way up. A small table sat beside her bed and her phoenix feather rested on top of it. She grabbed it and struggled to her feet with a grimace. Her body ached, but the pain was bearable if she didn't move too quickly. She had felt worse.

She made her way over to the basin and paused to study herself in the mirror. She pulled up her shirt to examine the scars that painted her body from the fight at Fijar's camp. Silvery lines crossed over her side and peppered her back and she touched the marks briefly before turning her attention to her hair. She groaned. It looked like a rat had decided to make a home on her head.

She did her best to comb the mess with her fingers before tipping her head to wet her hair in the basin. The lavender scent in the water reminded her of Kaleel and his lavender salts, and she smiled. Once her hair was wet, she moved on to the tedious process of working through the knots. While she worked through them her thoughts shifted to Aldair.

She wasn't surprised to discover herself pleased that he had visited her. In fact, she had expected him to come to her aid, to be so kind and considerate. When she thought of him, one of the first things to come to her mind was trust, and a burning in her heart that she was still unsure of. He was safety to her, and she could easily follow him on any adventure. To be apart from him would mean pain and loneliness. The word *love* bounced around in her skull, but she shoved it aside. She barely knew him, so love could not be the answer to the burning in her heart.

Yet, she did feel like she knew him and that he knew her in a way no one else did. How did he feel for her, though? There was no way of knowing that truth unless she asked, but she would never utter the question. Her heart shuddered at the thought of being so bare before another. She grunted with frustration and wondered when all this had happened.

She ran her fingers through her hair and sighed at how tangled it still felt. She grabbed a brush and set to work braiding it. Her phoenix feather shimmered against her dark hair as she tilted her head, and she half shrugged. Tazmeen could always braid her hair in the most interesting ways. Steele jerked violently as if someone had pulled on her braid.

Tazmeen.

Somewhere in her mind she had paired Tazmeen and Ali together; where one was the other was as well, but she hadn't seen Tazmeen at all during or after the attack.

Guilt stabbed at her as she tied off the end of her braid. "I should have thought to ask about her right away!" she growled. "I should never have just assumed she was safe. I know better than that. I know better."

She gripped the table and looked up into the mirror. The person staring back at her was not herself. This person looked wild, out of control, afraid. So afraid. She stared this girl down, sucking air into her lungs until she began to look like herself. She needed to be strong. For Tazmeen, if she was indeed there, or for Ali if…just if.

She unclenched her grip from the table and stalked toward the door. It opened into a hallway and in a rush, she turned a corner and ran right into someone. She glanced up, an apology on her lips, and found Emdubae smiling down on her.

"Where are you going in such a hurry, Little Thief?"

"I need to talk to Aldair—Prince Aldair, I mean. I need to ask him about Tazmeen. Did a woman come along with Ali?" she rambled, "You haven't seen her have you? At the camp, anywhere? You probably don't even know what she would look like. Silly of me to even ask, but I need to find her." She finished in a whoosh and glanced up at Emdubae, too agitated to care how jumbled her words were.

He wrapped an arm around her shoulders and gave her an encouraging smile. "I'll take you to the prince."

Steele nodded and stepped in line beside Emdubae. "I'm sorry I ran into you."

"No need to apologize. Worry over a loved one can create anxiety that overpowers your thoughts. It happens to the best of us," Emdubae squeezed her shoulders. "Even seasoned fighters like myself."

They rounded a corner, and Emdubae pushed open a heavy door. They found Aldair sitting behind a desk, his dark head bowed and pen scribbling over paper. He glanced up as they walked in, and he quickly jumped to his feet when he saw Steele. The relief she felt at seeing him was immediate and almost overwhelming.

"I ran into her in the hall. She said she needed to speak with you urgently."

"Thank you, Em." Aldair nodded. "Would you deliver these papers to my father?" He shuffled some of the papers on his desk into a neat pile before holding them out.

Emdubae took them slowly. "I can give them to someone who can. Sarai expects me home soon, and I refuse to let her keep Mathis all to herself." He gave Steele a smile, and despite her prickling anxiety, she managed to smile back. In all that had happened, she had forgotten Emdubae had a new baby at home.

Aldair gave Emdubae a quick nod and waited for the man to leave before turning to face Steele.

Grimness clung to the set of his mouth, and she knew he wouldn't have the answer she wanted. He hesitantly started to reach for her, and before he could change his mind, she grabbed his arm, and he pulled her to his chest. He rested his jaw on the top of her head and held her tight.

Steele shuddered and clung to him, and she believed for a moment that her world was not about to be shattered. But the need to know consumed her, and she broke away from that moment, stepping backward to get a better look at his face. It was time to face her fears.

Still, she tilted her head and asked with a glimmer of hope laced in her thoughts, "Tazmeen?"

Aldair's eyes were red with fatigue, as if he had yet to sleep since their return. He shook his head. "No. By the time we got there, Tazmeen was gone."

She was wrong earlier. Steele felt as if she herself was shattering, not the world around her.

CHAPTER 32

"Is she…?" Steele drifted off.

Aldair tucked a strand of her hair behind her ear as he shook his head again. "Ali said that she had been sold three days after they arrived at the camp."

Steele leaned against the desk, supporting herself with her hand. "Sold?"

"That's what those papers you and Em discovered were. It was a quarterly report Fijar was scripting. No names, though, just numbers. We found a record of the women and have been studying anything that may lead us to her."

"She's thirty-nine, a little taller than I am, and—"

"Steele." Aldair cut her off, soft and firm. She blinked and set her jaw against the sob building in her chest.

"Ali has described her in perfect detail." He paused, "This will not be easy for you to do, but you have to rest. Worrying will do nothing."

Steele nodded, the sob threatening to break through her ribs. She needed to be strong. Her eyes stung with unshed tears. They could not fall or she would break, so she scrubbed them away roughly with her fist.

Strong, strong, strong, she chanted to herself. If Ali saw worry in her eyes, he would be crushed, and she needed to protect him.

She jumped when Aldair grasped her shoulders. Her sad eyes met his concerned ones. He shifted, and she was swiftly underneath his arm with her head on his shoulder. She let him hold her as they leaned against the desk.

"Steele?"

She raised her head, dazed and staring out the window where the sun shone brightly, and somewhat cruelly, ignoring the dimness in her heart. "What?"

"Kaleel has been sent out with a group of men and magi, all excellent trackers. They've begun at the camp, containing what guards remained and helping the prisoners. They were able to gather some information that will help them find those who were sold." He turned them so they were facing the desk and he gestured at three piles on the table. "These are the prisoner records. It seems once they were brought to the camp they were given a number, a category, and a description. Leilan, one of our guards, has been reading the lists to Ali, searching for Tazmeen's description, and now that you are awake, I'm sure they would appreciate your help."

Steele nodded, peering at the lists, but she didn't move from under Aldair's arm.

Aldair cleared his throat and continued, "We're using the information Kaleel is gathering to decode who the buyers are, or who they're working for. We need to know who this type of market appeals to, and see exactly why this is so important to Fijar. He was already rich, so he could have been working toward a coup, gathering followers and soldiers. But that said, if we're wrong, we could risk the Zhanbolat reign or the kingdom itself." He breathed in deeply beside her. Steele rested her head against his collarbone and he continued quietly, "My thoughts are, if Tazmeen was categorized as being valuable to a buyer, she will be cared for."

"And at what cost?" Steele mumbled.

She felt his sigh. "I'm sorry. Please do not give up hope. Do not succumb to the darkness that grief can bring. We will find her, I promise you. Even if the trail goes cold, we will not give up."

Steele leaned away so she could look him in the eye, tears threatening to blur her vision. "I—thank you, Aldair. Prince. You don't know how much this means to me."

"I can imagine."

She swallowed the shards of her heart and breathed deeply. "Did Kaleel find anything else?"

"He's working with a man named Ryker, who I think you met at the camp?"

"I remember him. He said something about soldiers I think."

Aldair nodded. "Apparently the camp we came across is only a small part to the story. The documents you and Em found also indicate that something much larger is at work here. We think there could be a bigger camp someplace, one with a bigger market for the selling and training of people. We are working on extracting information from Fijar, but he is unfortunately incredibly self-disciplined." Aldair ground out the last few words and frowned before continuing. "Ali told us he was part of a group that were being trained like soldiers, which matches what Ryker told you. We don't know why they are being trained or who in the kingdom they're working for, but it seems like there was definitely a ranking system in place, much like you'd find in any military."

Steele dropped her forehead against his chest. "I need to leave, Aldair. I need to go back to the camp, back to where she last was, and look for her."

Aldair's arms tightened around her before he stepped back. "I understand that, but going back there now won't do any good. Give me three weeks. Three weeks to hear from Kaleel and sort through information for leads. If we haven't found anything by then, you can take Kesif and go."

Tears burned behind her eyelids and she gripped his arms. Three weeks seemed like an eternity, but she nodded. "I guess being the prince wouldn't allow for you to come with me?" she asked quietly.

"I would want to." He clenched his jaw and looked like he wanted to say more, but he remained silent.

Steele gave a heavy sigh. "So you've been talking with Kaleel and working through what he's sending you. That's fine but doesn't feel like enough."

Aldair leaned against his desk. "I've also been drawing up a plan to coordinate with the other kingdoms to put an end to the slave trade, but since we aren't certain which kingdoms were willingly involved with the trading, the planning for that is in the early stages." He looked sideways at her. "I want answers just as much as you do, and I understand feeling frustrated by taking time to gather information. I want to get to the bottom of this to not only bring families back together, but also to preserve the future of my kingdom." Steele looked at him but said nothing, so he continued. "The biggest hurdle in this plan is figuring out the amount of time it will take to travel to all of the kingdoms. I would welcome your help with looking at the different routes we could take if you're interested."

Steele nodded. "Of course. I'll help in any way I can." She wound a loose strand of hair around her finger and frowned. "Since you're still talking to Fijar I'm guessing he hasn't been sentenced yet?"

Aldair grunted. "We have been debating how to handle him. The consequences of his actions will be announced to the kingdom, but before that, we have decided to bring him before the High Council. The meeting is in three days, and you and your brother are both invited to participate. Would you like to?"

Steele bit her lip. "Yes. It'll be good to see him answer for what he's done. But I hope you know I wouldn't go to something like this for just anyone." Aldair's grin widened, and she returned the smile. "I would've thought Fijar had been dealt with by now. I was arrested and tried in a day."

Frustration flashed in Aldair's eyes at the mention of her arrest. "Other than my mother, General Fijar has been my father's closest companion, and I believe he needs this closure in giving Fijar a chance to show some remorse. Anyone else would have already been dealt with, or wouldn't have let themselves be taken alive. And we're still trying to get information from him but like I said he's very self-disciplined. We don't want to execute him while he still holds valuable information, so the actual execution date is to be determined."

Steele chewed on her thumbnail. "What are we going to do? Let him rot in his cell until he confesses?" she asked doubtfully. "Something tells me he's not one to give away his secrets."

"I know," Aldair agreed with a heavy sigh. "But we have to try everything we can before we let him take his knowledge to the grave."

She nudged his side with hers. "That sounds familiar. I had trouble understanding why you needed more and more information instead of just attacking the camp, though it makes more sense now. If someone that close to my family had betrayed us, I would want answers, too." She frowned. She had stolen horses, knowing the price of thievery was her life, but Fijar had stolen *people* and was responsible for the deaths of some of those people. "Would his fate change if he were to repent?"

Aldair sighed. "No. He committed treason against my father and endangered the kingdom's citizens. I do not think even my father could turn a blind eye to that." He fidgeted, picking up a sheet of parchment out from a nearby stack. "The training of soldiers is odd, but it's the human trading that makes me furious."

"Human trading?" she asked, frowning at the wording.

"That's what we've been calling it. People like Tazmeen and Ali who are kidnapped, enslaved, and sold to others, sometimes across kingdom borders," he explained, his tone hardening with each word. He dropped the parchment onto the desk. "As if they are supplies to be imported and exported. It is sickening to think that this has been happening in my own kingdom, and I knew nothing about it."

Steele hesitated before placing her hand on his. He wrapped his fingers around hers, and she was glad he couldn't hear her heartbeat increase. "When you *did* hear, you immediately acted."

His eyes shifted to hers, and she was almost caught off-guard by the intensity in his gaze. He tilted his chin and coughed. "I can get you out of coming to the council meeting if you really don't want to come."

She leaned against the desk beside him. "Sometimes I wish to never see any of those people ever again," she said softly, studying her hands. "Other times I want to, just so I can see them experience the pain I felt and more. I want them to see that I am alive and well despite their best efforts, and I want them to feel fear and dread as I did…and still do knowing that Tazmeen is still out there because of them. I want them to suffer." She stopped speaking, pulling her gaze to Aldair. "Does that make me a monster?" she finished with a whisper.

He opened his mouth to speak, but Steele cut him off. "If I'm being honest, all I really want is for justice to be served. Fijar was caught, and his evil deeds need to be brought to light. So, I will go. I owe it to Ali and Tazmeen to do that much. And to you. For helping me." She raised her eyes to his, and they shared a smile. "I'm assuming Ali will have to be there?"

He nodded. "If he wants to speak, he'll be a good testimony against Fijar considering his time at the camp. The other refugees have already spoken in court against some of the guards with lesser authority."

"What happened to them? And Roman Lothar? I saw him fighting *with* Emdubae before we faced Fijar."

Aldair rubbed his temples and stood. "Many of Fijar's guards had scattered by the time our reinforcements arrived, but those who were caught were questioned, and either punished or executed."

Steele blanched and Aldair gripped her shoulders. "I'm sorry," she said, lightly gripping his wrists. "I knew they would be punished, and I should have known execution was a possibility." His hands slid to her elbows and she tried to smile at him. "I shouldn't be surprised, really. What they did is worse than stealing horses."

Aldair studied her face before sitting back beside her. "Roman is currently in prison. He did help Emdubae, but we also can't ignore that he was there in support of Fijar."

"How long will he be there?"

"Just for the time being. He gave us information and has been cooperative for the most part, but I imagine he isn't happy to be in prison. Father is using his imprisonment as an example to the other High Council members. When he is released, one of our spies will tail him. He possibly has told us everything he knows, but if not, he may still lead us to new information."

Steele tipped her head, watching him. His spirit seemed to grow heavier the longer they conversed. He noticed her scrutiny and nodded. "It has been a bloody week. I'm glad you're awake."

"So you can relive the nightmare by filling me in on everything?" she asked dryly.

His disapproving look confused her. "You really cannot see?" He frowned and continued softly, as if almost to himself. "Never mind that for now. The timing is wrong."

Steele furrowed her brow, unable to track his train of thought. She leaned in closer to him. "I'm sorry, Aldair. It must be difficult to see fellow soldiers betray your trust."

He crossed his arms, and his fingertips lightly grazed Steele's elbow. "When the council meets, we are not to reveal any information regarding our knowledge of the training of soldiers, our suspicions of other camps, or the involvement of other kingdoms. Only information pertaining to Fijar himself."

"But if Roman was involved with him, don't you think Fijar would have other houses working with him?"

"I'm sure he does," Aldair agreed. "It's risky allowing them to be in the same room, but we can also see how the High Council react to him. It might give us an idea on who's involved. They would be foolish to let anything slide, but it has happened."

"Is it not—" Steele paused, standing so she faced him.

Aldair watched her, eyebrows raised. "Go on."

"Is it not too dangerous to allow someone like Fijar so close to your father?" She hesitated. "And you."

"We are both capable, I assure you. We cannot always hide behind others and trust them to get the job done. My father has never sent a General Replacement into battle before, and in many ways, this too is a war. I prefer fighting on the front lines. Battles of courts and politics can be tricky, and if we do not do this carefully, it very easily could turn into a clashing of the swords." Aldair's lips thinned. "We are not a passive people, despite the years of peace we have had locally, and we are not to be trifled with. Hopefully, both Lothar's imprisonment and Fijar's sentencing will convey that."

His eyes drifted to a faraway place in his memory again, and Steele did not interrupt his thoughts. As she moved to give him space, he grabbed her hand, and she met his gaze. "I have to finish up with these documents, but can I see you later? Perhaps give you a tour of the palace?"

Warmth spread through her cheeks, and she nodded. "I would like that very much. Can you point me in the direction of Ali? I need to see him."

Aldair smiled. "Of course."

Steele sat on a bench beside Ali, watching him whittle a piece of wood with a knife, and still couldn't quite believe he was actually with her in the palace. They were sitting in the shade of one of the outdoor courtyards, and the wind that blew down on them from the distant mountains carried the faint smell of pine.

Ali glanced up at her to smile before turning his attention back to the wood. Now that she saw him clean, he wasn't as skinny as she'd thought. He was leaner, but more muscled, and she still couldn't wrap her head around how much taller he seemed. She wanted so badly to ask him about his time at the camp but wasn't sure how to bring it up.

A group of the King's Guard jogged past them and Ali paused in his carving to watch them closely. The group stopped at the end of the courtyard and took out practice swords.

"Do they train every day?" Ali asked.

"I'm sure they do."

"Sometimes Aldair teaches me swordplay. He's really busy so it's nice that he makes time for me."

They shared a small smile and Steele shook her head. "I can't believe you're actually here. I'm so happy I could cry."

Ali huffed. "Please don't."

"I won't," she said with a laugh.

The soldiers across from them continued to spar with each other, and one man started yelling instructions and what Steele assumed were fighting stances. Ali resumed watching them, staring so intently that he didn't realize when both his knife and the wood he was carving slipped from his fingers. Steele bent to retrieve them and noticed that each time a command was shouted from across the field, Ali's hands formed tight fists. She leaned back, setting the wood and knife on the bench beside her, and gently poked him in the arm.

"Hey. Are you okay?"

He blinked and glanced at her. "I'm fine."

"Ali, I…I want to ask you about the camp. But I—"

"I'll tell you about it," he cut her off. "But I don't want to talk about it right now." His eyes slid from hers to the soldiers, and he ran his fingers over the edge of the bench.

"That's okay," she said softly. "I don't want you to have to do anything you don't want to." His shoulders relaxed and she hugged his arm. "I'm going back to the camp in three weeks if we haven't heard anything from Kaleel. I assume you'll come with me?"

He nodded, and she smiled. "Good. Now, have you sat here long enough?"

"I think so," he said. "Why?"

"Aldair said he would show me around the palace. Want to come?"

Ali smiled. "Sure. Although while you were unconscious I got a tour."

"Oh, well you don't have to. I just thought it could be fun."

He jostled her with his shoulder. "It will be. Plus I want to get to know Aldair more." He paused and gave her a wicked grin as he stood. "And see if I'm right."

"About what?" she asked, standing as well and handing him the knife and wood.

"Oh, nothing," he said slyly. "Come on."

She glared at him but followed him out of the courtyard.

CHAPTER 33

The next morning Steele was lost. Her pride spiked at the admission, but there was no fooling herself. She had somehow wandered to a section of the palace that Aldair hadn't shown her yesterday, and nothing looked familiar.

Except for you, she thought, eyeing a reddish-gold phoenix statue. Although, the bird was only familiar because she'd already passed it twice. She stopped where the hallway intersected with another and peered left, then right.

"I swear I've gone both directions," she muttered, crossing her arms. Perhaps she should just wait here until someone found her. With her luck, it would be both Aldair and Ali who came across her, and she would never hear the end of it.

"Straight it is," she grumbled, striding forward for what felt like the hundredth time.

"I know what you are doing." Fijar's voice broke the silence, echoing against the walls.

Steele froze, heart leaping into her throat. Was he watching her from somewhere? Had he escaped? She willed her heart to slow—the pounding made it hard to hear anything.

"It won't work," the general continued, his voice rising. "You forget I've led these little interrogations longer than you've been in service."

Steele followed Fijar's voice until she came to a dark archway. There was no door, so she crept through, making sure to cloak herself in shadow. The path she followed rose sharply, and she hesitantly followed it up, the air growing damp and musty the higher she climbed.

"Fijar, there is no use denying your involvement." Emdubae's voice was laced with weariness and frustration.

This must be an interrogation. A tiny pinprick of light shone up ahead, and after checking to make sure she was still alone, Steele decided to investigate. She lowered herself to her belly and inched closer, until she came upon a ledge over a barren pit. Fijar sat in the middle, looking far too relaxed for her liking.

She scooted back so he wouldn't glance up and see her, and frowned. If she had a weapon with her she could have easily targeted Fijar. The design of the room seemed foolish. Unless…she tipped her head and tentatively reached out a finger. She smiled as her finger hit an invisible barrier. The room must be enveloped in a magi created shield. Satisfied the room was secure, Steele focused her attention back to the interrogation.

"The prince himself overheard you speaking to men from Hamonsfell in the Nasshari, and we interacted with Barrowlanders at the Green River camp." Emdubae said, voice firm. "We know citizens from other kingdoms are involved, and it would be in your best interest to tell us what *you* know."

"Your precious Prince Aldair lied to you," Fijar sneered. "I have had no contact with the men of the mountains."

"We do not want to force the information out of you. You used to be one of us," Emdubae said. "Why were the men of the mountains bringing prisoners to the camp?"

"Why were the men of the mountains bringing prisoners to the camp?" Fijar mocked. "I was never one of you. I was your leader, and I still am to many."

At Emdubae's silence, Fijar sighed. "Why don't you ask King Ferdinand? He commands his people. I do not."

Emdubae grunted, then said, "Do what it takes."

Steele didn't know who he was talking to. Something, a chair perhaps, scraped against the floor, and Emdubae's shadow moved along the opposite wall.

"If you want to advance in this world, you have to be willing to do more than that, Captain. You can't expect your subordinates to do the dirty work for you," Fijar called as Emdubae's shadow grew smaller. Steele didn't know how Emdubae kept from turning back to the taunting general.

She pulled away from the ledge and headed back how she came. Following this route, she crept down the hall, halting when Emdubae stepped out some feet in front of her, facing the other direction.

"Em!" she called out, trotting to catch up with him.

"Steele!" He gave her a warm smile. "What are you doing on this side of the palace?"

"I got lost," she admitted, wrinkling her nose. "I was caught up thinking about the council, and Tazmeen, and if we'd hear from Kaleel soon, and the next thing I knew, I didn't recognize anything around me."

Emdubae chuckled and beckoned her along as he started to walk. "When I first came to the palace I got turned around more than once." He winked. "It happens to the best of us."

Steele laughed, falling in step with him. She wanted so badly to ask him about what she had overheard, but knew it was probably best she kept the eavesdropping to herself.

"Em! Steele!" Aldair's voice called out from behind them.

They stopped, and when the prince reached them he was smiling. "I've been looking everywhere for you two!"

"Kaleel found something?" Steele asked, hope swelling in her heart.

Aldair's smile slid a fraction. "Not the something you're thinking, but he did send over more information about Fijar's target market." He fished a piece of paper from his pocket and handed it to Emdubae. "I figure you could use a break."

"Thank you, yes." Emdubae said, quickly reading over it. He looked back to Aldair, "Have you had a chance to look over this, too?"

"I haven't yet," Aldair shook his head. "But Steele and I are needed elsewhere."

"We are?" Steele asked, suddenly nervous.

Aldair glanced at Emdubae before facing her. "My father has requested you attend a court meeting today."

Her eyes widened. "Today!"

"Yes," he chuckled. "The meeting is in ten minutes."

"Ten minutes?" she yelped, eyes flying from Aldair to Emdubae. "What am I supposed to wear? Or do? Or say? I don't know how to act in court! I don't—"

Aldair cut her off with a chuckle, and he shook his head. "So many questions. What you're wearing is fine, and you won't need to act any certain way."

She ran her hands down her sides and over the tops of her pants before looking at Emdubae.

"You look perfectly acceptable," he said with a warm smile. "Now if you'll excuse me, I'll leave you to your meeting and see you both later." He waved and headed down the hallway.

Aldair gestured back the way he had come from, and Steele fell into step beside him. "Why do I have to be at court? Will I be sent away again?" Her heart sank at the thought.

A muscle feathered in his jaw before he spoke. "Father would have some angry men to face if he did that."

Steele tried to smile, but nerves got the better of her. Why else would the king want to see her if not to address the issue of her sentencing? She almost stumbled—and she would have had Aldair not kept a good hold on her—when it occurred to her that despite what Aldair had said, King Ax may ask her to leave the palace or follow through with her execution. Housing a convicted thief was probably frowned upon. She swallowed, fighting down a wave of nausea.

"You never said what this meeting was for," she commented, hoping he had an answer to soothe her anxiety.

"If I knew, I would tell you."

"You don't know?" Her stomach clenched.

He shook his head, and Steele's heart sank. If Aldair didn't know the purpose of the meeting, that couldn't bode well for her.

When they reached the heavy wooden door that lead to court, Steele froze, memories of her last trip through them washing over her. Rough hands on her shoulders, shoving her forward, condescending eyes boring into her back, snide comments about her worthlessness, and then the king and Aldair looking down on her. Steele shut her eyes, breathing slowly. When she opened her eyes again, Aldair was watching her, concern drawing his eyebrows together.

"We don't have to go in this way," he whispered, wrapping an arm around her shoulders.

Steele leaned into him for a moment before straightening her spine. "No. I can do it. I *need* to do it."

A soft smile tugged at Aldair's mouth, and he squeezed her gently before releasing her. He nodded to a pair of guards Steele hadn't noticed, and the doors groaned as they opened.

CHAPTER 34

The back of Aldair's hand grazed her own, and Steele linked her smallest finger with his, allowing him to lead her into the room. In truth, she was glad he was with her. She could feel dozens of eyes staring at her, and she wasn't sure she could have made the walk alone.

Aldair stopped them behind a couple that King Ax was dismissing with a satisfied nod. Steele looked to where the king sat and was surprised to see the queen sitting next to him. Was it common for Queen Marian to sit with her husband at court? She hadn't been there at Steele's sentencing.

The couple passed by Steele and Aldair, and she swallowed as the Iron King settled his gaze on her.

"In times of distress," he began slowly, "there are people who step up to the challenges set before them, and I wish to honor those who have demonstrated great valor in dark times. Steele, would you come before the throne?"

Aldair nudged her. "Go on," he whispered.

Steele licked her suddenly dry lips. It seemed she would be facing the king and queen alone after all. Wobbly legs carried her to the front of the dais, and she stood, anxiety rankling her insides. Squaring her shoulders, she took a deep breath and summoned the courage to meet King Ax's gaze, the man who once again held her life in his hands.

This is it. She inhaled and exhaled as evenly as she could, though all she could think about was the tightness around her neck. He was going to send her to her grave. Again. The thought slammed into her skull, and she swayed, heart beating so hard the sound was overwhelming. If this was to be her last chance to stand before the king and queen, she wanted to leave with a clean slate.

She inhaled quickly and blurted softly, "Before you say anything, I need you to know how deeply sorry I am for purposefully defying the laws you set in place. I cannot apologize for the help I gave, but there could have been a better way. For that, I'm sorry. I, um—" She cut herself off.

The king studied her, and she braced herself. "Steele, you had every reason, every opportunity to turn against me and the kingdom, for we had sent you to your death. Yet despite the danger to your life, you aided my son in his quest to find the camp. When this was done, you did not abandon them, choosing instead to help them further, even to the point of putting yourself between the blade and my son." The king stood then and carefully descended the steps until he was uncomfortably close to Steele. It took everything within her to not cower back. He gently placed a hand on her shoulder and smiled. "I will be eternally grateful for your courage and quick thinking."

She held her breath, mind reeling. Of all the scenarios she'd imagined, receiving compliments from the king was not one of them.

King Ax tilted his head, continuing softly. "I do not excuse you, lady, for your previous choices, but you have come before us willingly, despite your death sentence. You have shown you are of sound character, a person of loyalty and integrity. You will have your redemption. From here on out, you are pardoned. Go and live a better life as a friend to the king of Solarrhia."

A tiny gasp escaped Steele, and she glanced around, blinking back tears.

Then the king leaned in and spoke only to her. "If only more people thought to ask for forgiveness, they might be surprised by the grace they would find."

A familiar figure caught her eye, and she started. Bero stood among the crowd, a cowl pulled over his head.

She looked back at the king.

"Thank you," she whispered. "Though I feel I must give credit to the magi, Bero. Were it not for his help on the train, I would never have escaped and met Prince Aldair in the desert. Instead, I would have ended up at the camp myself and been of help to no one. Bero gave me my freedom, knowing he couldn't follow."

"You are not the first to speak highly of Bero," King Ax said, almost smiling.

She nodded, her thoughts stuttering. Had she really been pardoned?

"Again, I thank you. I do not feel I deserve this kindness," she admitted quietly.

"Steele, your heart is in the right place, though your choice to steal was not," the king said in a low voice meant for only her to hear. "Please, take this pardon and make something of your life." He squeezed her shoulder and with a tilt of his head, gestured for her to step aside.

Aldair had a look of immense pride on his face as she came to his side, his grin stretching ear to ear. It was then that Steele noticed Ali seated behind where they stood, a disbelieving smile on his face. He glanced around before hurrying over to Steele, pulling her into a tight hug. She hugged him back, at a loss for words. When Ali released her, she glanced at Aldair.

"You did know about this," she accused in a whisper.

Aldair's eyes twinkled. "Perhaps."

She debated asking the prince if he had anything to do with the king's change of heart, but she found she didn't need to know. She was free. A sense of awe washed over her, and she gave her head a shake as more tears built behind her eyes. Just as she was going to ask Aldair if they were dismissed, King Ax clasped his hands together.

"Would Bero, Chief of the T'Klei Tribe, come before me?" Bero stepped forward, lowering his cowl with blue-marked hands. "Your Highness," he acknowledged the king with a bow of his shoulders.

King Ax held his hands up. "Please, from one king to another, call me Ax."

Steele thought Bero stood a little taller in that moment, though he remained silent.

"Bero, you are an example of the man I wish to be. Enslaved, you still managed to serve your people. We recovered these pridestones at the camp, and I trust you would know how to find their owners." The king carefully took a necklace out from underneath his tunic and pulled it over his head, holding it out to the magi.

A dozen sparkling gems on various rings and pendants glittered along the strand, and Bero fingered one of the jewels before taking the necklace. He gripped the gems in his hands, bowed his head, and exhaled in a long, meditative breath. Again, Steele found herself blinking back tears. How long had Bero awaited this day? When the magi raised his head, his blue tattoos began to shimmer, and goose bumps stood on Steele's arms as she felt something akin to delight exude from the magi to those around him.

King Ax and Bero nodded to each other, mutual respect radiating from them. Bero turned and took his place off to the side while the king looked around the room. "Now, for those of you who have come for other purposes," he said, "the floor is open if anyone wishes to present to me any questions, concerns, and petitions from the villages."

✶ ☽ ✶

Ali hugged Steele again once they were outside of the hall. "You're free, S!"

She tried to speak but words wouldn't come.

Ali released her, and teased, "Speechless for once. It's a miracle."

"I just...I don't believe it's real," she said softly.

Ali and Aldair exchanged a grin. "It's real," the prince said, lightly grasping her elbow.

She tried again to speak, but couldn't get words past the lump in her throat. Tears blurred her eyes and she tipped her head back, breath hitching. Her emotions were running wild, and she needed to compose herself. Aldair eyed her before pulling her through a doorway and into a small study.

As soon as the doors shut behind them, Steele sank into a chair, trembling. Aldair crouched in front of her and gripped her knees. "Are you all right?"

A relieved laugh burst from her, and she covered her mouth as the laughter turned to sobs. "I'm sorry," she choked out, "I'm happy, I promise."

Ali grabbed a water pouch from his belt and offered it to her. "Are you sure?" He squatted beside Aldair and squinted at her face while she took a drink.

"Yes, yes." She handed the water pouch back to Ali, though tears still tracked down her cheeks. She leaned forward, taking Aldair's hands. "Did that actually happen? Your father really pardoned me?" She hiccupped, another sob breaking from her.

Aldair pulled her from the chair and wrapped his arms around her. "It really happened," he said, amusement in his voice. "Though I admit, this is not the reaction I was expecting."

Ali squeezed her shoulder and chuckled. "This is more how I picture Ma reacting."

Steele laughed. Her tears wet the front of Aldair's shirt, but try as she might, she couldn't stop them. "I think I'm in shock," she said in an unsteady voice. She used her fingers to wipe at her eyes and gave Ali a wobbly grin before peering up at Aldair. "I can't believe you knew and didn't say anything!"

Aldair chuckled. "Father asked me not to, and I had no qualms about keeping it a surprise."

"Did you have anything to do with it?"

He gave her a crooked smile. "Kaleel and Em may have spoken on your behalf."

"And you?" She prodded.

His smile softened. "I may have spoken on your behalf as well."

Her cheeks warmed as a shudder ran over her body. She took a deep breath, relieved she could finally breathe without her lungs snagging on the air. "I hope your father understands how grateful I am to him for this," she said. "Saying 'thank you' sounds like too little. I don't think I'll ever be able to verbalize how much this means to me."

Aldair used his thumb to wipe more tears away and he smirked. "You could go laughing and crying to him now if you wish? Your reaction is unexpected, but I do not doubt your sincerity."

She laughed again, dropping her forehead against his chest. "I'd probably just frighten him, or he'd think I'm crazy and reconsider his pardoning."

"Definitely," Ali teased.

"Ali!" She glared at him and he shrugged while Aldair chuckled and rubbed her shoulders.

Another hiccup and she exhaled in a whoosh. "Thank you both for being here," she said, looking from Ali to Aldair.

She couldn't quite read Aldair's expression. He looked pleased still, but there was something deeper in his gaze. Her cheeks warmed under his scrutiny, and her eyes shifted from his to his nose and then lingered on his mouth before dropping to the floor.

"Of course," he murmured.

Ali coughed and Aldair loosened his hold on her.

She smiled before taking a deep breath. "I think I'm okay now."

"Finally," Ali said, rolling his eyes.

Steele glared at him. "I guess we could move back into your house now that I don't have to worry about being arrested." She looked at Aldair and then quickly dropped her gaze to the floor so he couldn't read the sadness she felt on her face. She was a free woman now, so why did thought of leaving make her heart hurt? When she looked back at the prince he was frowning. A quick glance at Ali showed he was doing the same.

"That's an idea," Ali said slowly, wrinkling his brow at Steele.

"Why would you want to do that?" Aldair asked, a half smile on his lips. "Annoyed by me already?"

She hiccupped a laugh. "No. I just wouldn't want to outstay our welcome. Your family has been so kind to let us stay here already."

Aldair scratched the back of his neck. "I was actually thinking it would be best for you and Ali to stay here until we've dealt with Fijar. Unless you wanted to leave? I'm sure you could—"

"No, I want to stay," she cut him off and then fought a blush, hoping she didn't sound too overeager. "I mean, I think it would be good, like you said. At least until we hear from Kaleel or we go back to the camp. Ali?"

"I want to stay, too," he said quickly.

Aldair grinned at them. "Good. Are you hungry? We have a while until dinner, and I could eat a snack."

"We're always hungry," Steele said with a laugh.

✶ ☽ ✶

After they grabbed some food, Ali headed back to his rooms, and Steele and Aldair decided to take a walk before dinner. They turned down a hall and spotted Emdubae. Steele opened her mouth to greet him, but the look on his face stopped her cold.

He quickly smoothed the anger from his face and nodded to them.

"Congratulations on your pardoning," he said, grasping her shoulder.

She glanced at Aldair. He was regarding his friend with a troubled look. "Em, are you…Is everything all right?" she asked.

Emdubae's hand slid from her shoulder, and he rubbed his eyes. "Yes, I'm sorry. Just tired from the day."

A muscle clenched in Aldair's jaw. "What did you learn?"

Steele gave Aldair a sideways look. Emdubae must have been back with Fijar again.

He grunted and shook his head. "Nothing. Nothing, Aldair. The man won't speak."

Voices echoed from down the hall, and Aldair looked around sharply. "Tell me more, but not here in the open. Here." He trotted down the hall and opened a door. Emdubae sighed but followed the prince. Steele wavered, unsure of what to do until Aldair poked his head around the door, beckoning to her. She moved toward the room and walked in.

The room appeared to be a private dining area. An ornately carved table sat in the middle, with six chairs situated around it. A cabinet full of wine bottles sat against the left wall, and on the right, glass doors opened to a small patio.

Emdubae sat at the head of the table and drummed his fingers against the surface. "I don't know what else we can do," he said once Aldair had shut the door.

Steele sat so she could look out the glass doors. A few torches flickered on the patio, but otherwise all was dark. "If Fijar won't speak, how do you get information?"

"There are methods," Emdubae said carefully. "But we don't like having to resort to them." He gritted his teeth and punched the table. "I want to just beat the information out of him, Aldair. To shake him until he cracks because we *know* he has information. But he just sits there with that condescending smile, and when he does talk, he tries to make a

260

mockery of the palace. The urge to knock that smile from his face is so strong sometimes." Emdubae's normally clear blue eyes were a storm, a raging blue-gray as he looked at them. "It might be time to try something different with him."

As Steele pondered their words, she had a thought. The idea made her frown, but she voiced it anyway. "Why don't you give him hope for life?"

"You mean like granting him his life in exchange for information?" Aldair asked.

Steele half-shrugged. "He may like the sound of that better."

"He probably would," Emdubae agreed. "Unfortunately he's been in his position long enough to know how those types of offers pan out. He himself has been on the opposite side of a deal like that. He knows it's an empty promise."

"Does it have to be?" Steele asked begrudgingly. She wanted Fijar to be held responsible for what he had done, no matter what that looked like, and she believed the world would be better without him, but if sparing his life meant gaining information that could put an end to the human trading, it could be worth it to make him an offer.

"No," Aldair said, tapping his fingers on the table. "But Em is right. Fijar knows how those offers go. He would never believe us even if we were being sincere. Plus, keeping him alive is probably a bad idea in the long run."

The three sat in silence until Emdubae cleared his throat. He stood and walked to the wine cabinet. "I think," he continued, pulling three glasses from the cabinet. "We should take a moment to focus on how wonderful it is that Steele has been pardoned." He glanced over the bottles of wine before pulling a rose-colored bottle off the shelf.

Steele smiled at Emdubae as he returned to the table, setting a glass in front of her. "Thank you, Em."

"I suppose you're right," Aldair said, spinning his wine-glass between his hands.

"Of course I am. We will get the information from Fijar." The smile he gave was almost believable, though frustration lurked beneath the surface.

Steele looked to Aldair, and he winked at her. "You know, my father never pardons people. Perhaps this day should be made into a holiday to commemorate it." He passed his wine glass for Emdubae to fill, and Steele copied him.

Emdubae chuckled as he popped the top off the wine. "That's not a bad idea." The rose wine was frothy as he poured, and when Steele took a sip, she savored the sweet, fruity flavor.

261

Emdubae filled his glass last, and settled back in his chair. "So," he said, looking between Steele and Aldair. "Happy Steele Day?"

She laughed, a blush creeping along her cheeks. Aldair grinned, holding his glass up. Emdubae raised his as well, and they both stared at Steele until she raised hers.

"Happy Steele Day indeed!" Aldair said as the glasses clinked together.

CHAPTER 35

The next afternoon Steele wandered outside, in need of a break. She had spent the morning with Ali and Leilan, and they hadn't found anything in the descriptions to match Tazmeen. She wandered over to a paddock and rested her arms against the top rail of the fence. Several horses were outside and she smiled as she watched them graze. Kesif noticed her and came trotting to the fence in search of a treat.

Steele's smile widened and she reached into her pocket to get an apple she had grabbed from the kitchens. The paint happily crunched on the fruit, and while he ate, she looked over the other horses. She spotted Emdubae's lanky buckskin, but didn't see Cahya in the herd. A dark bay gelding pricked his ears at her and two chestnut geldings stood nose to tail, swishing flies from each other's faces.

Kesif snorted, sending sticky drops of apple juice onto her, and she shook her arms with a laugh.

"That's the thanks I get?" she asked, wiping the juice on the gelding's neck.

"So Ali was right," Aldair said from behind her.

"About?" Steele asked, eyeing him as he leaned beside her and rubbed Kesif's forehead.

"I was looking for you and he said that you'd probably be with the horses since they're the only things that make you happy," he said, mimicking Ali.

She laughed. "He said that?"

Aldair chuckled and shoved Kesif's nose away. The paint was looking for more treats. "He did. He made it sound like you were in a bad mood."

Steele rolled her eyes. "Not a bad mood. Just frustrated. And nervous for the meeting."

"I thought you might be," Aldair said, pushing back from the fence. "I have a room that I want to show you because it's extraordinary and it might help take your mind off of things. Will you come?" Excitement danced in his eyes, and he held out his hand to her.

"I will. You have me curious." Butterflies danced in her stomach as she took his hand. She didn't have long to enjoy the moment because he quickly pulled her away from the fence and toward the palace, but she couldn't ignore how nicely her hand fit with his.

Aldair led her down several halls and she had to jog to keep pace with him. They reached the end of a hall and Aldair slowed so they could walk. Steele was pleased he didn't drop her hand once they slowed.

Finally, he halted. He fidgeted with the leather cuff on his wrist, the one that covered his tattoo, and glanced at her. She held her free hand up in question.

"I would like to show you something."

She nodded, eyebrows raised. "I gathered." His boyish smile was contagious, and she grinned.

"It's not too far now," he said, giving her hand a squeeze before leading her down a set of steps that quickly turned into a maze of stairs and corridors. Steele had spent any free time wandering around the palace grounds, memorizing the floor plans and where people stayed, but this was an area she had yet to visit. It seemed older here, the walls a dusty gray as opposed to gleaming white. The extremely detailed etchings in the stones, however, suggested the place had once been grand.

Aldair let go of her hand to push open a tall wooden door and a strange whirring sound came from somewhere deep in the room. Though a shadow covered much of his face, she could see his grin clearly. "I know it sounds odd, but trust me, this is unlike anything you have ever seen." He stuck out his hand.

She tentatively took it, and he guided her into the room. Once her eyes adjusted to the dim lighting, she gaped in surprise.

Above them, currents of color pulsed across the surface of a glass ceiling, like ribbons fluttering in a breeze. The rainbow streams illuminated the underbelly of the room, and Steele held out her arm, fascinated by the pink and orange lights playing across it. A green color passed over next, and a shiver ran through her, causing the hair on her arm to stand on end. She patted the hair on her head cautiously to check, but it lay in its rightful place.

Aldair laughed at her wonder, the purple and blue and pink reflections dancing across his face, and Steele could not help but stare. He looked beautiful bathed in the myriad of colors. She pushed the thought away and abruptly changed her thoughts.

"What is this place?" she asked.

"It is a sort of network room for the magi. We have fifty or so magi who work in the palace, and each of these colors represent the magi who created it." Aldair held up his hand in the lights. "I would not know whose magic was whose except by their colors, but I have been told that each magi's power leaves behind a personal imprint."

"What do the currents do?" Steele tipped her head back to watch a bright-pink stream dart past them.

"It depends on the responsibility the magi has for that week or month. I know a little about their scheduling only because I frequented this place before joining the military. For the most part, they manage themselves," Aldair admitted, rubbing his palm against the back of his neck. "Two might take care of the east side of the palace, cooling the rooms, keeping tanks of water for showers and baths warm, or lighting the torches, for example. There is a list of duties."

"They're not enslaved?" she probed, eyeing the casual set to his shoulders.

"Not in the palace, no. They are free to go whenever they please, and we pay them, though magi typically do not value the same things we do."

"So they just channel their magic through this room? Why don't they report directly to where they are needed?" she asked.

"Would you want to dash in and out of a room every time someone asked for you? Believe me, we have many people in this palace, and the magi designed this room themselves so they could be in a stationary place, controlling the environment and serving each person with less hassle. Though there are several magi who enjoy helping us directly."

"How do they know when we need help?"

"For personal favors, we send messages to them through normal means, like letters and messengers. There is a general schedule they follow. But explaining how the palace functions is not what I had in mind when I brought you down here." He took her hand again and tugged her toward a door on the other side of the room.

He stopped just before they reached it. "Hadrian and I used to visit here as boys whenever we decided it was time for a break from our lessons. Mother was never too happy when the tutors revealed that we had evaded them. No one ever thought to look here, though, and the magi never tattled," he said, his tone laced with boyish excitement. "Our faithful friends must have enjoyed that the princes could not get enough of their culture."

He pushed the door open, and Steele stepped inside. Everywhere she looked, there were magi. Some lounged while others mingled about the expansive room. Some were—Steele ducked. Some were flying!

She threw her arms over her head, but all she felt was a gust of wind as another magi flew over her on some sort of rug. "I thought you said there were only fifty magi in the palace!"

"You cannot expect us to keep them from having visitors!" Aldair laughed. "Welcome to the magi lair."

★ ☽ ★

Her eyes widened as she looked around. "Wow," she breathed. The room seemed to extend beyond sight. "This room…It's like it goes on forever in every direction!"

Aldair only shrugged. "Magic, remember?"

Steele scanned the room again. "They are so powerful. I would hate to be an enemy of a magi," she said, unable to shake the sense of awe from each word she uttered.

Another magi zoomed passed her, his guttural laughter echoing off the walls. Behind him, purple sparks shot out from the rug and then it crumpled. Steele gasped, starting for the falling magi, but before he could hit the ground, he stopped in midair, belly down and legs spread, hovering mere feet from impact. He stood and shouted at someone.

Aldair chuckled and walked deeper into the room, his arms crossed behind his back. "Thankfully they are generally peaceful and lack the bloodlust other cultures are prone to cultivate. The magi tribes that wish to be alone tend to isolate themselves if they disagree with the tribes who immerse themselves into our cultures."

The image of the chained magi next to the train, the hot desert sun weighing on their broken spirits, flashed in Steele's mind. She bit her lip. "Aldair, don't you think that could change now that dozens, if not more, have been enslaved for their power? I still feel the imprint of chains on my wrists, and I was only in captivity for a short while. And for those who have family imprisoned, I can feel their pain and the need for revenge bubbling in my own veins."

The prince was silent for a moment, his brow furrowed in thought. "That is good foresight, Steele. Maybe I should appoint you as an ambassador to the magi."

There was a hitch to her step at the word *ambassador*, but she righted herself before she stumbled. She had yet to determine what she would do after today, other than finding Tazmeen. She had assumed she would move back in with Tazmeen and Ali, and they would finally work together to provide for the household. Could there be anything else for her?

"Me? An ambassador?" She snorted, though her heart fluttered at the thought of living and working closer to Aldair. Was it possible? And why did she suddenly feel so alive? She blushed, thankful Aldair could not read her mind.

"You doubt yourself? How unlike the woman I met at the inn," he said in a teasing tone before gesturing to a magi who was mounting the enchanted rug. "Some of the magi used to entertain us with flying objects. One time Hadrian and I convinced them to let us fly on one of their carpets, and it quickly led into races and duels with our play swords. We invented all sorts of games up in the air. We loved it."

Steele looked at him, hearing the lingering sadness return to his voice, and he offered her a faint smile. She reached for his arm. "I'm sorry. I know it must be difficult. We can leave if you would like?"

She didn't want to go, so she was grateful when he smiled crookedly, appreciation in his eyes. "Absolutely not! I didn't bring you down here just to weep as I share my sorrows over events that will not change."

"You must be Lady Steele," a voice drawled from behind them.

Steele whirled around and found herself facing a beautiful magi with snowy hair and wide-set amber eyes. The magi had blue tattoos that shimmered along her shoulders and arms, reminding Steele of Bero. The blue markings climbed her neck to her face, somehow enhancing her alien beauty. Twin red tattoos curved from her eyebrows and fanned out like wings to her hairline. A sapphire sat between her eyes, held in place by a golden chain, and Steele assumed this was her pridestone.

"I am," she stammered. "I'm sorry, I don't know your name."

The magi laughed. "My name is Kismet. It is so wonderful to finally meet you." The magi's amber eyes flicked to Aldair and when she looked back at Steele, she was smiling. "I've heard so much about you."

"You have?" Steele asked, arching an eyebrow at Aldair.

Kismet chuckled. "You hear many things when you work in a palace," she said with a wink.

Aldair cleared his throat. "Kismet is a magi who likes to work directly with people in the palace," he explained. "She helps Mother out immensely when she needs something much quicker than Raj can provide."

Kismet dipped her head. "Those instances are rare. Raj is a wonderful help to your mother." She glanced between Steele and Aldair again before taking a step back. "I'll leave you two alone now," she said, giving them a knowing smile that reddened Steele's cheeks.

"Actually, I have a favor to ask of you." Aldair paused and glanced at Steele. "Would you like to fly?"

Steele watched a pair of carpets zooming above them and recalled the magi falling off the carpet. "I have flown on horses. That's enough for me, I think."

Aldair pursed his lips. "That is not the same."

"Do not worry, Lady," Kismet said airily. "You will not fall."

The magi motioned to a rug near the wall, and it snapped up at the corners before walking toward the pair. Steele's jaw nearly hit the floor, and Kismet's laugh rang out like a harmony of bells. The rug stopped, floating parallel to the ground now, rippling occasionally as if sitting upon the sea.

Aldair hopped on and sat in the middle, his legs crossed. He motioned for Steele to join, and she huffed before tentatively sitting in front of him. She flinched at a sound behind them, instantly feeling silly, and settled herself so she was facing the prince. She felt as skittish as a nervous horse.

"I will do one lap with you, but you will have to fly on your own after that." Aldair smiled deviously. "There is nothing like it!"

She smiled at the exhilaration in his voice. "I doubt it. Have you flown through the night sky on the back of a horse?"

He scowled at her briefly, but instead of replying, he nodded to Kismet, whose skin shimmered pearly blue. The rug pulled taut, and Steele stuck her hands down to steady herself as they slowly rose higher into the air. She glanced down, her head spinning to see Kismet so far beneath them, and a gasp slipped between her lips when she looked up. The rug shot forward, and she toppled over into Aldair. Muttering a curse at his laughter, she righted herself.

"I should have warned you about that." He smirked.

"Somehow I think you didn't on purpose." She spared him a glance before looking over the edge again. If he replied, she didn't hear it, as she was mesmerized with how they quickly they zipped past the magi below.

As she sat upright she heard Aldair say to turn around, so she obeyed, her movements exact and careful. Grasping onto a sliver of confidence, she leaned forward onto her hands. She closed her eyes, imagining dancing among the stars. This was not quite as good as sitting on the back of a flying horse, but it was something.

Suddenly, the rug shot upward, and she fell back into Aldair again. Shouting her apologies, she scrambled for something to hold onto again, fear twisting at her stomach, which had relocated to her heart. When she did not move from the middle of the rug, her body slackened, though her stomach felt heavy in its rightful place. She remained that way, with her back pressed against Aldair's chest as the rug slowed its pace in their approach to the lofty ceiling.

"This is the best part," Aldair's mouth was at her ear, and she shivered. "You can't close your eyes."

"I don't know if I can do that."

He chuckled, placing his hands on her shoulders. "You have to lean forward, too. It's the only way to really experience it."

She took a deep breath, knowing that no matter how high up they went, they must eventually come down, and it was going to be terrifying. This was madness. They were so far from the ground and even knowing magic was involved, she felt less secure on the carpet than when she rode flying horses. Here there were no wings to brace her legs against, no barrel of a horse to squeeze her calves around, and no mane to hold on to. At last the carpet leveled out, and Aldair pushed her forward. She stiffened, trying to resist, but he was too strong and she found herself perilously close to the edge.

He scooted next to her and lay flat. She did the same, shaking slightly as her nerves set in. The carpet hovered for a moment, then tipped and plummeted toward the ground. Her stomach dropped, and a shriek escaped her clenched jaws, but she kept her eyes open, briefly noticing that her body remained solidly pressed against the fabric.

As they neared the ground, the rug slowed and straightened, and the next thing Steele knew, they were back on the ground. She sat up and faced Aldair, who laughed deeply at the look on her face. She knew her eyes were wide, and she could feel her heart hammering against her ribs. Then she felt giddy, and she joined him in his mirth. "I have to do that again!"

Aldair rolled off the rug and into a crouch. "I knew you would like it."

"You were right," she admitted, and she scooted back to the middle of the rug. "I haven't done anything like that before."

He grinned. "You have to promise to take me riding on a flying horse someday, though."

"Deal." She nodded at Kismet, and once again the rug stiffened before the ground fell away.

This ride was different. Boldness took over her, and she crawled to the very edge of the rug, lay flat, and rested her chin on the edge. The rug flew back and forth and up and down and then suddenly shot up and back in an arc. The carpet twisted upside-down as it plunged toward the ground, and she felt a moment of panic as her body came off of the carpet before landing safely back on the fabric. Her heart in her throat, she gripped the edge, determined not to come off again. The rug turned upward and corkscrewed toward the ceiling, and just before Steele felt too woozy, the rug leveled out. She shook the dizziness from her head and mentally prepared herself for the drop to follow. When it came, her stomach still lurched, but her grin widened with pure glee. As the ground leaped up toward her, she squeezed her eyes shut and braced for impact, remembering how landing a flying horse had jarred her bones if she tensed up.

It took her a moment to realize she was still, and she opened her eyes half expecting to see she was hovering at the ceiling again. She was still floating, but the carpet had stopped waist level with Aldair. The prince was peering down at her.

"Are you all right? The spiraling ascent used to make my brother extremely dizzy. Or sick." He eyed her as if he expected her to throw up on him.

She sat back on her knees and smiled. "Yes! I think I am going to want to do this every day until I...leave." Sadness pooled in her chest as she looked up at him. She saw a similar sadness mirrored in his sapphire eyes.

His gaze held. She scanned his face unashamedly, committing it to memory. Once they found Tazmeen, she would have to leave the palace, and she wouldn't be able to see him again, at least not so freely. She didn't want to forget him. His eyes traveled her face as well, and he held his hand out to help her off the rug. She took it, scooting forward to slide off in front of him. When she got to the edge, the carpet bucked forward and up, and Steele found her lips on his.

Her eyes widened in surprise. For a brief moment, she considered pulling away, but when he did not, her confidence grew. She closed her eyes, enjoying the new sensation fluttering in her heart. He kissed her gently, pulling her toward him, and she hooked her arms around his neck. The carpet fell away from beneath her, and Aldair held her in the air before gently setting her down on her feet. Only then did they break apart.

He kissed her once on the forehead before smiling sheepishly at her. "Would you believe me if I told you I had nothing to do with that?"

She laughed once, a giddy laugh she did not recognize. "I...um..." She looked over his shoulder to see Kismet smiling a little too smugly. "Yes, actually, I would believe you."

He rubbed the back of his neck. "I am not sorry it happened, though."

She sighed, relieved. "I'm not either." She looked to the floor, her cheeks warm. "What does this mean now?"

Aldair grinned, brushing his hair away from his eyes. "We have spent too many nights with our hearts filled with worry." He traced his thumb over her cheekbone. "I have been thinking a lot about you since we returned to the palace. I've missed spending time with you every day and talking with you." His thumb grazed her bottom lip.

She smiled softly. "I never expected—" She halted, embarrassed. "I'm not good at expressing my feelings." She reached a finger toward his face and lightly traced the scar that crossed over the side of his mouth. "But I care for you. So much that it scares me."

He snapped his teeth together, and she jerked her finger back. "Well, I am quite fierce."

She scowled at him. "You know what I mean."

He tipped his head, thoughtful. "I believe so." A mischievous glint appeared in his eyes. "But we are not going to dampen the moment with fear. Instead, I would really like to kiss you again."

Her cheeks warmed and tightened with a smile, and she did not shy away as she may have before. She pulled his head down to meet hers, leaning into him to steady her teetering legs. She sighed, realizing he had the ability to kiss a smile onto her face.

A cough rang out from behind her, and when they broke apart, Aldair grunted, annoyed. Steele swiveled around to see a magi she had not seen before standing a few paces away. A very intimidating magi. He wore black trousers and a silver vest, and his dark hair hung in dreadlocks. Thick, green tattoos slashed their way across his golden brown chest, forearms, and face, and his eyes were a beautiful blue green. She stepped back, and Aldair took her hand, giving it a reassuring squeeze.

"My prince, your father sent me to inform you that there will be a small meal to celebrate Lady Steele being pardoned," the magi said in a deep voice.

"That was father's idea?" Aldair asked, sounding mystified.

The magi half-smiled. "Your mothers, actually, and she would not approve of your dining attire."

Aldair rolled his eyes, and Steele chuckled.

She whispered, "Pampered," to the prince and received a half-hearted elbow to her bicep in response.

"Steele, this is Batya. Batya, as you know, this is Steele." Aldair gestured between them.

The magi dipped his head. "I am pleased to meet you, Lady Steele." When he straightened, he raised an eyebrow at them.

Aldair sighed. "We will change before dinner. Happy?"

Batya chuckled at Aldair's tone. "There will be plenty of time later to kiss the girl, Prince. No need to take your irritation out on me. As a peace offering, I will help you this once so you are not late." He winked at Steele, and his tattoos gleamed emerald.

She shivered as a current passed over her, and when she looked down, she saw she was wrapped in a fine blue cloth. Invisible hands seemed to pull and pinch the cloth until it hugged her figure and was secured in place by a wide gold belt around her waist. Golden embroidery curled down the sleeves and fanned out from below her belt. She stared at the dress, and Batya chuckled, a deep sound that rumbled like thunder.

"Thank you," she said, awestruck.

The magi nodded as Aldair offered her his arm, looking very fine in a maroon buttoned-up jacket. "Apparently, it is much later than I thought."

Steele hooked her arm through his and they followed the magi out of the room. "Batya has been around for as long as I can remember," Aldair explained as they walked. "He was a sort of bodyguard when I was small."

"He looks frightening at first," Steele whispered.

"I think that's why my parents chose him to watch me when I was little. Hadrian's was just as intimidating."

Steele studied the floor as they walked. "I wish I had known your brother. He sounds like a wonderful man."

"I'm sure he would have loved you. Anyone who met him came away a better person. He brought the best out of people." Aldair chuckled. "He was also very charming. He probably would have won you over, leaving me to succumb to bitter jealousy."

"Don't be so dramatic. I don't like charming men," she said with a laugh.

Batya chuckled. "Imagine what that says about you, Prince," he called over his shoulder.

Aldair scowled at the back of his head, and they rounded a corner, bringing them closer to the dining hall.

CHAPTER 36

The ceiling opened up into a beautiful dome over Steele's bed. The pearl tiles slid in and out of focus as she lay on her back, staring up through the gauzy canopy a servant girl had pulled down for her. The soft mattress and feather pillows allowed her to believe she was sleeping on a cloud, though her bones protested, much to her surprise. Too many nights in the desert and sleeping on that lumpy bedroll had conditioned her back. She traced a finger along the seams of her blanket until the sharp end of a feather poked her skin. Pinching the tip, she slid it free from the fabric and held it up to her nose.

She blew it free from her grasp and watched it float over the edge of the bed. Her fingers tapped against her lips and she sighed dreamily. She felt foolish for it, but she couldn't stop thinking about kissing Aldair. A blush rose on her cheeks, and she sighed again. On one hand she was anxious to see him again, to talk with him and, yes, kiss him again. One the other hand she was afraid any future interaction could be awkward. He hadn't kissed her goodnight, and though she understood why with his family around, part of her wished he had anyway. A sharp knock at the door grabbed her attention, and she pushed herself onto her elbows.

"Um, come in?" she called, unsure of protocol.

The door cracked open, and Ali's head popped through the opening. "Can I come in?"

Steele sat upright and beckoned him closer. "I just said you could! Come here!" She made a move to stand, but Ali bounded as quickly as a stag to the middle of the room and jumped beside her onto the oversized pillows with a loud "*mmph!*" Loose feathers exploded from the fabric and danced along the sheets until they settled along the sheets and lazily drifted over the floor.

The grin dropped off his face as he glanced at her. "We see Fijar soon. I didn't think I'd be so nervous."

She sighed. "Me neither."

"That man needs to die. It scares me how much I hate him," Ali spat.

A dozen questions threatened to break from Steele's lips, but she stayed silent, hoping he would continue. He did.

"When Ma and I arrived at Camp Two, they split us up, and I was thrown into the middle of a ring with a group of prisoners from the train and told to fight. Whoever won would get dinner and a bed for the night."

Steele frowned, unsure of how to respond.

"I lost. Pretty quickly actually. I tripped over one of the guys and broke my arm." He held his forearm out and rotated it so she could see a silvery jagged line etched into his skin. "They sent a magi in to heal our wounds, but I slept outside, chained to another prisoner named Kel. The next day, we were thrown into the ring again and told the same thing: if we won, we'd get food, a bed, and sometimes other rewards. Every day was like that, and you either learned how to win, or you didn't eat. I wasn't very good, but I did win some. Kel was a more natural fighter, and he and a couple of us shared our food with each other. Kel was moved to another group before you came."

Steele thought about the prisoners she'd come across with Kaleel and Emdubae, and how Ali had chosen to fight beside Kaleel even though he'd never had formal training. "How exactly did you learn? Were they teaching you hand to hand or swordsmanship? One of the prisoners said something about training soldiers."

"I wasn't very high on their list for them to tell me much. They did call us soldiers, and I got a few tips from some of the other prisoners, but otherwise, my training was fight or die. A few did die before magi could heal them, and some people were moved to other groups when they won a lot."

Ali trailed off, staring down at the ground. Steele rested her hand on his arm, rubbing her thumb against his scar. "You said you were split up from your ma on the first day?"

"On the second day, I was able to find her once near the market area when I wasn't chained to another prisoner. She seemed okay at the time, although I keep running the scene over and over in my head, and I think that was more her trying to be strong for me. I found her tent a few days after that, but she was gone. Twenty pieces of gold," he spat bitterly, leaning forward so his head hung close to his knees. "That's what she sold for."

Steele swallowed a lump in her throat. "Did you hear anything about the person who bought her?"

Ali shook his head.

Steele chewed on her thumbnail. *What a mess.*

Ali took a deep breath and turned to face her. He looked so incredibly young. "I always knew we were poor, but I never thought we were nothing until now."

Anger spiked in her heart and she sat straighter. "Never say that again."

Ali stared blankly back at her and she took a breath to calm herself. She succeeded on the surface, but her insides were boiling. As she looked at Ali, she briefly considered storming into Fijar's cell to confront him, saber in hand, damning the consequences along the way.

Just as quickly as the thought came, it vanished, and she gave her head a shake, surprised by how strong the urge had been. She drummed her fingers on the bed. "They've done this to you, but you don't have to believe them. Don't let anyone strip you of who you are."

"And what is that exactly?"

Frustrated, Steele was at a loss for words. "You're my brother. My family. And that's everything."

Ali dropped his gaze, but the corner of his lips turned up in a half-hearted smile. "Thank you. But you didn't see what they did to make sure a man was broken, Steele." He pulled at a thread on his tunic. "Do you think we'll find her?"

"Yes," she said automatically, desperate to say more. She had so many more encouraging words to say, to repeat, but she couldn't. It was as if a wall stood between her heart and her mouth, keeping her from speaking the faith Aldair had preached. She couldn't believe Tazmeen was dead, but doubt found her an easy target. The prince had been right, though. It wouldn't make sense for people to go through so much trouble to buy Tazmeen just to rid themselves of her within weeks. Yet, she was gone, and Steele found it hard to stay positive without genuine proof of Tazmeen's whereabouts.

She looked upon her adopted brother, mourning his loss of the simplicity of being a child. She could no longer call him a child despite his sixteen years. Life had not been kind to her, but she would never wish for others to relate to her in that way. She ruffled his hair gently. "Will you tell me more about this Kel someday?"

"Of course. From what Aldair has said, Kel's working with Kaleel at the camps." He said with a cough. He flicked a feather at her. "How can you sleep with all these feathers floating around? I think someone has given you a broken pillow." He laughed, then cast a sideways glance at her. "I never expected to like Aldair so much."

"Prince Aldair, Ali. He deserves his title," she instructed matter-of-factly.

Ali raised an eyebrow. "Since when did you care about titles?"

Steele's thoughts flew to the magi lair, and she punched his arm, her cheeks warming. He responded by smacking the back of her head with a pillow, and she gasped, indignant, and tried to grab it from him.

He jumped up on the bed and held the pillow high. Steele growled and shoved him, taking advantage of his imbalance. He fell back into the excess of pillows with a muffled grunt. Their fluffiness seized him, and he struggled to free himself from the feathery cushions.

"I give up! I give up! Your bed is attacking me!" His cries were muffled by the pillows.

"You know better than to turn against me!" She stood on the bed and placed her hands on her hips triumphantly.

"It's a good thing Aldair will be around to protect me from you from now on," Ali exclaimed.

"Great, now I will have two overgrown children messing with me," she responded dryly, shaking her head as she silently pondered Ali's statement for a moment. *Would* she have Aldair—Prince Aldair—around from now on?

Her thoughts were interrupted by a knock at the door. She called out her permission to enter, and Kismet walked inside. Steele hopped off of the bed, and noticed that Ali sat a little straighter.

"Hello, Steele. Ali," the magi drawled, strolling closer to the pair. "I am here to help you dress for the meeting, if you would like." She smiled at Steele.

"Wow," Ali breathed, and Steele elbowed him while nodding at the Kismet.

Another magi, with hair like fire and orange tattoos stuck his head in the door. "Ali, if you will please follow me..."

Ali mutely slid off of the bed and staggered over to the magi. "What's your name?" he asked as he followed the magi out of the room.

"You may call me Ramla," the magi said as the door clicked shut behind them.

Kismet studied Steele and nodded before gesturing for her to follow. "I don't want you to think I don't believe you capable of readying yourself," she said over her shoulder. "But I wanted to offer."

"I appreciate it," Steele said with a whoosh. "I have no idea how to act or what to wear or anything."

"I can help you with what to wear," Kismet said, stopping before a massive dark-stained wardrobe. "As for how to act, your prince can help you with that. He informed me that he will meet you at the eastern servant's door outside the Council Chamber, and I don't want to keep him waiting." She gave Steele a grin before opening the wardrobe doors.

CHAPTER 37

Steele shifted in her seat and glanced at how Ali was fairing. He sat beside her quietly, as stiff as dried out leather. She reached for his hand underneath the table and gave it a gentle squeeze. He gave her a tight smile before he returned to surveying the room. She didn't blame him. She'd been doing just that since they sat down fifteen minutes before, waiting for the king to begin the meeting.

This room was smaller than the Hall, but large enough to accommodate the seven houses that made up the High Council of Solarrhia. King Ax and Queen Marian sat at a head table. There looked to be room for others to sit beside them, but today, they were alone and in a deep discussion. The other houses sat behind long curved rectangle tables on each side of the king and queen. Steele counted three tiers, of which most seats were filled today.

Ali and she had been introduced as guests of the royal family. So far, everyone had left them alone, but Steele could feel the weight of more than a few curious glances. That answer wouldn't satisfy them for long, she didn't believe, especially because she sat next to the prince in the front row and closest to his parents. She ran her hands down the top of her thighs, finding the feel of the silky light-blue pants surprisingly soothing. The outfit was much finer than anything she'd ever worn, and the silk top showed off the muscles along her shoulders and arms as well as the silvery scars she had acquired from the battle at the camp.

Across from her, she observed Roman Lothar. He kept his eyes forward, looking only at the king, and his mother only spoke a word or two to those around them.

"Lothar may suffocate under your stare," Aldair said, gently taking her left hand. He gave her a crooked grin and leaned in, his breath tickling her ear. "Did I mention you look breathtaking?"

Steele's heart quickened, and she took a deep breath. She pursed her lips, trying to keep her own smile from taking over her face. "Stop trying to distract me."

"All right," he replied, winking at her, but when he tried to take his hand away, she squeezed it tighter.

"Remind me about it later." She laced her fingers in his, and he nodded, relaxing back into his chair.

"Now, onto the reason you are all here." At the sound of King Ax's voice, everyone focused on him, a hush falling over the room. He gestured the houses. "You have been told that Fijar has been imprisoned. You were also made aware that Roman Lothar has been kept here, having been linked to Fijar's activities. Marian and I have long debated how to handle this...situation." He looked to his wife, seated next to him. She reached for his hand, her pale arms standing out against the cropped shoulders of her black gown.

Her cat-like blue eyes moved from her husband to the crowd. "We have decided to accept your requests to see Fijar for yourselves. We all have a responsibility to our people. Therefore, you need to know what we've uncovered, and you will have the truth."

There was a slight buzz as the council members talked quietly among themselves.

King Ax spoke above the chatter and the room became silent. "While Prince Aldair was in the Nasshari, he, along with the help of several others, uncovered a camp managed by Fijar. We have yet to uncover the truth behind the entire operation, but what we do know is that it involved the buying and selling of humans, as well as some sort of military training. As you can imagine, this is troubling to us for many reasons and will not be tolerated. After today we believe your questions will have been answered."

A knock sounded and all eyes cut to the door.

"Enter," the king called in a loud, strong voice.

The door groaned open, and Aldair stiffened beside Steele. She briefly touched her shoulder to his and squeezed his hand as four soldiers stepped into the room. Fijar was bound in chains in the center of them. He looked haggard and worn, like one of the men he had unlawfully sold. How ironic that he would become exactly what he thought was beneath him. Emdubae followed a short distance behind the group, his eyes hard and set forward.

One of the soldiers stepped away from the group to grab a chair, and when he returned, he set it between the front rows of the High Council, facing the head table. Fijar took a seat. The room was so quiet Steele was sure everyone could hear her heart pounding. Aldair was still as a stone on one side of her, and Ali shifted in his seat on the other.

She had expected Fijar to sit tall before the king, but instead he slouched in his chair. Those slumped shoulders could easily be mistaken as the posture of someone who was defeated, but to her, he appeared to be a beast lurking in the shadows ready to pounce on anyone he considered weak. His head hung low to his chest, and he peered at the king with a predatory grimace.

Steele bit the inside of her cheek, anxious for this to begin. Fijar's presence in the room was settling into her skin as though she had slept in a bed of poison ivy.

"It is good to see your face, Your Highness," said Fijar, his words slicing into the silence of the room. His voice dripped with oily superiority, and he smiled at the king.

Steele tried to read the king's expression as he leaned forward. "General Fijar, you have been accused of treason, of working with those who wish to harm our kingdom, and of unlawfully arresting citizens to sell them across borders. You have abused your position as my advisor and the leader of my guard. In your own words, tell us what you have been doing."

Fijar inhaled as he rolled his shoulders back and slowly cracked his neck with a disturbing sense of ease. He scanned the people in the room, laughing quietly as he saw Roman. "It's good to see you again," he said, chains clinking together as he shifted in his seat. "I had hoped you had gotten away."

Roman stared at Fijar, jaws clenched, but said nothing in return.

Fijar chuckled to himself and looked at Steele and Aldair before turning his attention back to the king. "Everything I have done will make this place better, more…livable, and more prosperous than ever before." He held his wrists toward King Ax and clicked his tongue. "You would find that every person in that camp had a hand in bringing the communities in the kingdom down; they were trash littering the streets." Fijar surveyed the room again. "This issue has been discussed in this very room many times before, and until now, no one had the courage to actually do something about it. I have that courage and the desire to see our kingdom thrive. Think on the past months my friends and I think you will agree that the state of our towns have been much improved."

Ali grabbed Steele's hand, anger pulsing through his grip. "He's talking about my ma," he whispered harshly.

Aldair gave her a concerned glance and she realized she had been gripping his hand just as hard as Ali had grabbed her own. She loosed her fingers and leaned toward Ali.

"If we react, we'll be playing into his hands. His whole argument is that the towns are better off without us. We have to prove him wrong. We don't want the High Council to sympathize with him." It was a thought that just came to her, and her heart broke as Ali set his jaw, fire flickering beneath his silence.

"He's a monster," Ali muttered, though his breathing had steadied.

"While many were recorded to have offended the law, their sentencing was not carried out according to it," King Ax countered.

Fijar started to wave his hand, but quickly set his wrists down in his lap again. "You are correct. There were people destined to rot in a cell who were given an alternative. Others, well, to others, I gave life." He threw Steele a punctuated stare. "Am I not right, Steele?"

Silence pulsated through the room. Steele's heart thudded as bile bubbled in her stomach. Was he really insisting he was her savior? Her thoughts lay frozen, unreachable, her tongue like an unyielding anvil.

"If no one has recognized her yet, let me educate you," Fijar announced to the houses, projecting so that everyone could hear. "This girl on the prince's arm is the same girl who stood in my position less than two months ago, charged with horse thievery and sentenced to death. Tell me, my friend," he said, looking to the king, "am I so evil to have let the girl live when you did not?"

"From what I hear, death would have been better than the life you gave at your camps," Steele spat, unable to stay silent. "I am only here now because I outwitted your guards and escaped your train."

A tense silence followed until Tedric Palidin cleared his throat. "Fijar is right though, we have talked for years about cleaning up the streets."

"And we have also seen a decline in crime," Birdy Katauren added thoughtfully.

Aldair sat back in his seat, but Steele could feel the anger rolling off of him. "But at what cost?" he asked evenly. "Fijar says he gives life, an alternative to people who supposedly have nothing better." He looked at Tedric and Birdy as he leaned forward. "Can you not hear it? Can you not see what he is actually saying? Fijar does not value anyone he thinks will not further his influence. He has taken advantage of his post to further *his* gain, not the kingdom's, no matter what he has justified to be his excuse. He has proven where his loyalty lies, where his heart endures."

Fijar sucked on his teeth and sighed. "An impassioned speech by your prince," he said. "But think about it, is it bad to give people a second chance at life? People who were destined for death now have a chance to work for something and earn a living. I don't see why I should be punished for helping people."

"Helping people?" Ali blurted, anger flushing his cheeks. "You call raising the taxes behind the king's back helping people? You knew people like my ma couldn't pay what you were asking! You made sure we'd be arrested."

"Ah, one of my soldiers," Fijar said fondly. "You had such potential as a fighter. We taught you skills you would never have learned otherwise, boy. Someday you will thank me for my tutelage."

"Thank you?" Ali said, incredulous. "Thank you for what? For being held against our will?" He cut off abruptly, looking to the king, but King Ax nodded, so he continued. "And I'm sure the women will thank you for letting your soldiers abuse them."

"Are you finished?" Fijar asked, sounding bored.

Ali's cheeks reddened, but before he or Fijar could continue, Tobiah Beringer spoke. "You did not authorize the raise on taxes?" he asked, directing his question to King Ax.

"Out of everything he just said, the taxes is what you're worried about?" Steele said, disgusted. "In case you didn't understand what he was saying, people at those camps were being violated. And you're worried about taxes."

"They were raised without my permission," King Ax affirmed, brown eyes glinting with anger. "We had discussed raising the taxes as you are all aware, but I did not sign off on the proposal. Fijar went behind my back and passed the raising anyway. Which led to the circumstances Ali described."

"We saw the camp," Aldair said, squeezing Steele's hand. "The conditions people were kept in were unlivable. There were cages. Whips. You should be concerned about the taxes being raised but not because of the money. You should be outraged that in doing so, the actions of Fijar were paid for and he was able to continue working against our kingdom."

"I agree with the king." Danissa Dunraven said heavily. "Fijar's actions are treason."

"I also agree," Sage Wymare said, nodding. "Fijar you have overstepped your position and abused the power given to you."

Fijar glowered and scanned the council. "You see where trying to help the kingdom will get you? Thrown in chains and, unless I am mistaken, a death sentence."

The room was quiet, all eyes on the king, waiting to hear his response.

"You are not mistaken," he said firmly, the words ringing with a sense of finality. "I can only assume you acted against the kingdom to gain power for yourself. You have never been satisfied in second place. You lust for control. Even now I know your thoughts. You think you can sway the council to your side, you think you are in control. But you are not."

The slightest flicker of unease flickered in Fijar's eyes as the king spoke.

"The only reason people listened to you is because of your title. Something I gave to you and will now take away. From this day forward, you are no one in this kingdom. You will not be able to speak with anyone without them questioning the authority you hold. You know what happens to people who cross me, Fijar, and now you will experience it firsthand." The king stood, hand on his sword, and walked around the table toward Fijar.

Fijar shrank back in his chair. "You sent Kalman to his death!" He said, voice wavering with barely suppressed emotion.

King Ax paused, and the tension in the room deflated slightly as he hovered a few paces from Fijar whose eyes were trained on the king. His mask had slipped, revealing a deeply injured man.

"You still blame me for that?" The king took another step toward the general. "This is what all this is about? You'd destroy thousands of lives for the sake of revenge!"

"For my son." Fijar swallowed and clenched his jaw. "The one you thought expendable."

"We've discussed this! You're a soldier. You know there's a risk with any mission. He knew that!"

Steele didn't know what to think. She'd not been told Fijar had a son. She cast a questioning glance at Aldair, but he only responded with a slight shake of his head.

"You didn't let me go with him." Fijar's hands were clenched in his lap, knuckles white with rage.

The king smoothly dropped to one knee and looked straight into Fijar's eyes. "Your fight was with me, but you knew you wouldn't win a challenge against me."

He stood and turned away from Fijar. "You are stripped of your titles and your lands, and you will be executed for your crimes." He looked to Emdubae. "Captain."

Emdubae and another soldier pulled Fijar to his feet, and the former general inclined his head at the king. "Always a pleasure, your majesty."

Everyone remained quiet, as if they were hesitating. The king returned to his seat, and finally, a small buzz filled the room.

The king sat back, allowing them to talk, so Steele leaned over to Aldair. "Now what?"

King Ax held up a hand and the room fell silent. "As you are all aware, Roman Lothar has been in our care since Prince Aldair returned from the Nasshari. Roman had been visiting the prisoner camp Fijar was running and seemed to be in support of the operation." The king paused and then focused his attention on Roman. "Your actions on the day, and your actions since then show that you are willing to work with this kingdom instead of against it. However, your decision to partake in the camps at all reveals that you are not ready to be the head of your house. From here going forward you will be suspended and the house will be run by Vara Lothar. I will finalize any decisions made by your mother, and the actions of your house will be closely monitored until further notice."

Vara Lothar placed her hand on Roman's forearm and looked to the king. "It will be as you command."

"I hope this meeting has been informative," Queen Marian said. "We are glad you were able to join us today."

King Ax stood, a stern look on his face, "Rumors spread easily in times like these, whispers in the shadows turning people toward a certain way of life, and I believe it is best that I, as your king, uphold my duty to communicate to you what has happened behind the curtains." His gaze hardened as he took in the members of the houses. "If anyone else is involved, let it be heard today that we will uncover you, and you will held accountable as the former general has been. If you know anything, it is in your best interest to come forward." He held out a hand to his queen and she stood beside him. "The council is dismissed."

"I don't think I have ever been so stuffed before in my life, Aldair," Steele sighed, leaning in her seat to rest her head against the back. The torch-lights flickered in the kitchen's side room. She'd spent the evening after the Council Chamber in her room, sleeping, and she'd missed dinner.

Aldair propped his elbows on the table, and he carefully peeled an apple with his short knife. He laughed, not taking his eye away from the shiny red fruit. "Truthfully, I had no idea you could eat so much."

Steele lazily flopped her arm down, slapping the table, promptly startling him. He expertly caught his knife as it slipped off the apple. She hugged her stomach with her other arm, and he chuckled as he resumed peeling the fruit.

Their silence was comfortable, but she wanted more. Surely Aldair could feel the energy between them.

"So." She began, not sure what to say, but wanting to say something.

He flicked his gaze to hers. "So?"

She narrowed her eyes. "Are we going to talk about what happened in the magi lair?"

"About flying on the carpet?" he said with a grin. "Sure, we can talk about that."

"Don't make me say it." She groaned, dropping her forehead to the table.

Aldair chuckled and she heard his chair scrape across the floor. When she raised her head, his chin was propped on the table beside her, blue eyes sparkling.

She sat and he mirrored her. "Can we agree to talk about it after tomorrow?" he asked, reaching out to cup the side of her face. "You should know that I'm not trying to do anything to over-complicate your life. I like you, Steele. I like having you in my life."

She leaned into his touch and closed her eyes. She wanted nothing more than to figure out where they stood, but she understood wanting to wait until after Fijar's execution to figure things out. When she opened her eyes, Aldair was watching her, a slight smile on his lips and she leaned forward, tipping her face toward his.

His lips barely brushed hers when a bell sounded from somewhere overhead. It was a low sound, one that soothed her, but he perked at the noise, raising his head to the ceiling as if deciphering the bells location.

The door burst open, and a short sturdy guard tumbled into the room. Steele instinctively shot forward as Aldair turned, the blade spinning in his hand. He must have recognized the guard, whose hands had shot up in defense, for the prince's shoulders relaxed. "Siek! A little warning!" Aldair exclaimed.

"I am sorry, Your Highness," the man apologized, panting. "I ran straight here. The queen sent me."

"What is it?" Aldair stood up, dropping the half-peeled apple. Steele vaguely saw it roll across the table, falling off the edge and landing on the ground with a soft thud. She straightened, pushing the chair next to her out of the way.

"The palace is under attack! There's been an attempt on the king's life!" Siek brushed a rebel hair behind his ear.

Aldair quickly glanced at Steele before squeezing between the shorter man and the door and sprinting up the stairs. Dark eyes wide, Steele breathed, staring disbelievingly after Aldair as he quickly disappeared from sight. Siek gulped and took a deep breath before turning on his heel. She followed suit and dashed after the prince.

CHAPTER 38

Steele reached the top of the stairs to find an entirely different place than when she had descended to the kitchens. Before it had been peaceful, but now that she was above ground, the bell in a tower across the outdoor courtyard resounded, its echoes vibrating against the walls. She swiveled around, looking for sign of the prince and saw him already across the square and disappearing through an archway.

As she darted after him, Ali scampered past her, sliding to a halt once he recognized her. "Steele!"

She grabbed his hand and pulled him along. "I need to catch up with Aldair!"

Ali did not have trouble keeping up with her pace, but he had never been one for endurance, preferring the rush of a dead sprint. He sucked in air and grunted.

"Have you seen who has attacked the palace?" She broke the silence, trying to steady her breath. She clambered up another flight of stairs, hazily remembering where Aldair had described the location of the king's and queen's chambers.

"I saw one man scaling a wall, but Emdubae took him down," Ali explained between breaths.

"Is Fijar…?" Steele trailed off when she heard a scream of a servant girl in the distance, then a loud thud. She winced, hoping that the girl was still well, but Steele continued forward.

"I'll check on her, you go!" Ali cried, darting off to help the girl as Steele reached a four-way crossing.

She stopped, suddenly at a loss. If she picked the wrong way, she would waste so much time. She looked left and right, hands balled into fists in frustration. Which way?

Footsteps slapped the floor behind her, and she whirled to find Ali trotting up to her. "The serving girl is fine," he panted. "They were sending guards down to make sure Fijar's contained." He grabbed her arm and yanked her to the right. "This way!"

"Do you even know where we are going?" she shouted after him.

"Aldair went to find his father, right?" he called over his shoulder.

She nodded and sputtered. "Yes!"

"This way!" Ali rounded a corner ahead, now turning left. Steele pumped her fists, trying to keep up with him.

A man came crashing down the hallway. Steele almost called out until she recognized his face. Lac. Her heart lurched in horror as his eyes flashed in recognition. She tried snatching his wrist as he barreled past her, but he was much too large to bring to a stop. His momentum pulled Steele off her feet and sent her flying into the back of his legs. She threw her arms out to catch her fall, grunting as she hit the ground. Lac stumbled slightly, but he recovered frustratingly quickly and continued running down the hall.

Steele hopped up and tore after him, fury bristling in her veins. Ali called after her, but she did not stop or check to see if Ali was following her.

She noticed an arrow embedded in Lac's shoulder as she chased him, though from his speed, it may as well have not been there. He turned a corner and sprinted to the end of the hallway, stopping abruptly. Steele realized it was a dead end, more of an enclosed balcony than a hallway, really. He rested one foot on the railing, pausing to look her direction. His eyes met hers, and he swayed back onto his planted foot as if he was choosing to confront her. Cursing, she skidded to a halt, unhooked her belt knife from her trousers, and clenched her jaw, ready to face him for a third time.

"What, are you afraid I'll best you again, Lac?" she taunted, balancing on the balls of her feet.

He glowered. "You should have killed me when you had the chance. You will live to regret the moment."

"How did you even survive? You lost so much blood." Steele frowned. Now that she was facing him again, she wondered if she had made the right decision to walk away from him last time. "I'm just a harmless little thief who no one cares about. Killing me will be the only way to hurt me, and that'll not be so easy for you to accomplish." She raised her eyebrows, daring him to make a move.

"Steele!" Ali called out from the end of the hall, concern coloring his cry.

If Lac had charged her then, she would have been satisfied. She could easily kill him in defense of Ali. Instead, a horrifyingly peaceful look settled into his features. He bared his teeth in a menacing smile and tipped himself over the edge of the railing.

Steele sprang forward with a shout. She fully expected to see Lac lying crushed on the ground below, but when she braced herself against the railing, she saw his figure running across the courtyard in the torchlight before disappearing into the shadows. A mixture of disappointment and trepidation simmered in the pit of her stomach.

Curious as to where Lac had been, she turned and followed the blood spatter he had left behind. Ali followed silently behind her as the drops led them in the direction of the prison cells.

Steele rounded the corner and just managed to stop before tripping over someone's leg. Ali slammed into her back, and she staggered forward, stumbling over the person with a grunt. She looked down, and a young serving girl stared back at her blankly. Quickly, Steele scrambled back to her feet and pulled her belt knife free.

The rest of the room was in chaos. More people lay on the ground, dead or dying. A few guards were fighting, including Emdubae across the way. Two magi dueled in front of Fijar's cell, a female with black hair and a male with golden, but they moved so fast that Steele didn't know if she would recognize either. Golden light shot toward Fijar's cell, but an inky wave washed over it before it could reach its target.

They paused for a moment, and Steele recognized the magi woman from when she was arrested. The two magi studied each other for a moment before releasing a ripple a power toward the other. The gust of magic flared out from the magi, and Steele struggled to stand against it. She looked for a way around the duo so she could get to Emdubae. He appeared to be fighting off two soldiers on his own.

"Look at Fijar," Ali muttered in her ear, and she tore her gaze from Emdubae to look at the cell.

Fijar paced behind the bars, his dark eyes watching the fight intently, though a small smile traced his lips. A dead soldier lay outside of his cell, neck torn open, and his blood oozing toward the former general. He barely blinked as he stepped right into the blood-trail.

"He doesn't look too worried," Steele said, eyes narrowed.

Ali nodded and started forward, but was quickly knocked back by another blast of magic. Steele pulled on his arm and leapt to the ground just as another burst of light whizzed above them. The male magi slammed wave after wave of golden light into the female, and while she continued to throw up inky barriers, she looked to be weakening.

"That magi is trying to free him," Ali growled. He pushed himself to a crouch. "I won't let that happen." He gripped his sword and eyed the two magi. "If we can get close enough to them, I bet we could injure the yellow one."

"Maybe," Steele said uncertainly.

More people entered the room across from them. From their dress, they were not Rhian soldiers on their way to relieve them, and they paused only a moment before rushing to Fijar's cell.

Emdubae tried to cut them off, one man against six, but he didn't appear like much of a threat, hunched over, unable to put weight on his right leg. A man turned and kicked Emdubae in left knee. Emdubae shouted and fell to his right leg, the color draining from his face as he made contact with the ground. He blocked another assault from the man with his sword, but he looked spent. Before the man could overpower her friend, Steele threw her knife behind the magi, hitting the soldier in the side. He wobbled, reaching back to his wound, and Emdubae surged forward to finish the man off.

Steele exhaled, relieved. She reached for Ali's hand, but he wasn't there. She wheeled around, frantically looking for him. She spotted him tackling a man trying to sneak up on the magi woman. A woman struck at him with a saber, and he rolled away from her, hopping up with his own blade drawn.

Steele searched for anything to help the fight now that she'd given up her knife. A sharp clang brought her head around, and she gasped.

The other four people, including the man Ali had tackled, focused their attack on the magi woman, blocking her attacks with swords and shields, taking turns to wear her down and draw her attention from the golden-haired magi. He had his hand on the lock of the cell, and golden light weaved around the metal and up the bars. Fijar stood just on the other side, his hands clasped behind his back, waiting.

"No," Steele whispered, panic seizing her heart. The cells were warded with magic, but it looked like the golden threads where undoing what was in place.

She sucked in a deep breath. Emdubae was on the ground, the other soldier next to him, motionless. Ali was preoccupied. She had no weapon. She felt completely useless. A torch hung on the wall, and she grabbed it, grunting as she hefted it from its hold.

"Magi! Here!" She shouted and turned, wishing she knew the female's name.

Steele hurled it toward the golden magi. A flare of black light enveloped the flame of the torch. With a pop, fire exploded, catching the robe of the male magi on fire. The torch smacked against his back, and he whirled, golden eyes bright. His weave on the bars of the cell held, and the bars began to melt. He reached a hand to Steele, and she tensed, ready to jump.

The magi woman screamed, and the air around her warped, blazing the room with a light so bright it pierced through the eyes and into the brain, before plunging the room in darkness. Steele floundered, eyes squeezed shut and she fell forward, palms pressed against her eyes. Her skull pounded and tears leaked out from her eyes. Her hands slid down her cheeks and paused below her ears. Her skin was sticky and wet, and she pulled her hands away, trying to see them.

She blinked, trying to clear her vision, and slowly the blackness of the room began to lift. It rose and vanished like fog, and when Steele could see her mouth fell open.

Both of the magi lay on the ground, along with everyone in the hall. Pieces of the bars from the cell stuck in the walls like spikes, one dangerously close to the Fijar's prone body. The former general was flat on his back, eyes open as if with shock.

Steele sat up and turned, searching for Ali, and she found him leaning against the wall, rubbing his eyes. She glanced down. Her hands were stained red, and she checked her ears again, stomach twisting as more blood came away. The room was so still, so silent that she was afraid she had lost her hearing.

She licked her lips.

"Emdubae?" she called out, relieved when she could hear herself. She sounded muffled, but she could hear. "Em!" she called louder, as she struggled to her feet.

Ali was beside her then, helping her to stand.

"Are you okay?" he asked, voice too quiet.

She nodded. There was a slight ringing in her ears, and she shook her head. "I can't hear you very well. You?"

"I'm fine." His eyes cut to Fijar. "Is he dead?"

"I don't know. Check the magi. But don't get too close, please."

He either didn't argue, or she didn't hear him. She willed her legs forward, keeping her eye on the male magi as Ali checked for a pulse.

"He's dead," he said.

She moved into the cell, picking up one of the pieces of a bar just in case, and she approached the general's body. Blood trickled from Fijar's ears, mouth, and nose. His chest remained motionless. She nudged his leg with her foot. Nothing. His dark brown eyes were vacant, his face slack. Slowly, she crouched beside him and placed a finger to his neck. His skin was still warm, but there was the blood had stopped flowing through his veins. His pulse was gone.

"Steele!" Ali's muted voice cut through the silence.

She turned, the bar ready in her hand, and found him kneeling by Emdubae. He was sprawled on his back, alive but deathly pale. He, too, was bleeding from his ears, and blood seeped from a long gash in his thigh. The relief she felt at seeing him alive brought tears to her eyes, and she fell before him. She ripped his pant leg away from the wound to get a better look, and used the bottom of her shirt to wipe away the blood. Ali tore off his shirt and handed it to her. She pressed her full weight onto the makeshift gauze and into the wound.

"Ali, call for help," she cried, eyes flying to Emdubae's face. "Hey, Em, hey, it's Steele. Wake up!"

Ali took off up the staircase behind them, and Steele could faintly hear him calling out for help.

Emdubae's eyes fluttered, and he tried to smile. Ali's shirt was already soaked.

"You are not allowed to die," she said, sitting back to pull off her shirt. The blood she'd wiped from Emdubae's gash had soaked through to her undershirt. She placed the clean part of her shirt top of Ali's and pressed down on the wound again. Emdubae shouted. She hummed to him, shivering against the chill in the room.

"I may need to tie your leg off, Em," Steele finally said. Her hearing had cleared some. That statement sounded sharper than before. "The bleeding isn't stopping."

He looked at her, but didn't say anything.

Footsteps sounded in the hall behind them, and she grabbed Emdubae's sword. Kismet ran into view, followed closely by Ali, and Steele exhaled in a whoosh. The magi spared Steele a quick once-over before dropping to Emdubae's side and placing her hands on his temples.

Emdubae gasped and stiffened as Kismets tattoos flared blue. Steele took his hand, eyes jumping between his face and Kismet's. The red tattoos around Kismet's eyes glittered like rubies, and the blue markings pulsed, growing brighter and brighter until the magi sat back with a light sigh.

"You may remove your shirt from his leg, Steele," she said tiredly, looking around the room. "He'll keep the leg, but he may have a limp..." she trailed off, amber eyes, filling with tears. "Oh, no." She lurched to her feet and hurried to kneel beside the dark-haired magi.

Steele's heart sank at Kismet's sorrow, and she turned her attention back to Emdubae. He struggled to sit, and Ali knelt beside him, bracing an arm around his back.

"How do you feel?" She removed the shirts from his leg and peered

290

at the wound. A thick, silvery line curved down his thigh to his knee.

"Tired," Emdubae said, his voice heavy.

Ali nodded and helped Emdubae lean back against the wall. "What was all that?"

"I will tell you what I know," Emdubae said, eyes sliding closed. "In a moment."

Steele nodded. "I'll be right back."

She slowly walked to Kismet and crouched beside her. Kismet stroked the magi woman's dark hair, her amber eyes heartbroken. "She was my friend."

"What is her name?" Steele asked.

"Laiken."

Steele squeezed Kismet's arm and looked at where Laiken lay. She blinked with surprise. She hadn't been mistaken earlier. Laiken had been the magi to meet her coming to the palace when she had first been captured. The magi looked like she was asleep, though the inky black of her tattoos were tinged with gray and her raven hair had dulled, almost as if when she'd breathed her last, her magic exhaled with it, drying her out.

"She saved us all." Steele said and gestured to the male magi. "He was trying to get Fijar out, and she somehow managed to take everyone down except the three of us. I don't know how she did it."

Kismet studied Steele for a moment. "There is blood coming from your ears."

The magi cupped Steele's cheeks between her palms, and her tattoos radiated. A current of magic washed over Steele's body, and her head cleared. She hadn't even realized how foggy it had been.

"Thank you," she smiled softly, her voice sounding piercing to her freshly healed ears. "Wow."

"I will heal your brother as well," Kismet said, looking behind Steele to the male magi. A sneer curled her lip.

"Do you know him?" Steele asked, also turning to look at the magi. His golden hair had turned brassy, and his tattoos had lost their luster.

"Not well." She quickly turned away from his body. "His name is Kaspar. He lived with Bero's tribe when he was young, but had become something of a nomad. I hadn't seen him in a while, but I remember he was powerful. And very opinionated and impulsive. I did not care for him." She motioned to Ali. "Come so I may heal your head as well."

Ali trotted over and jolted as Kismet's healing passed over him. When he sat back he exhaled sharply. "Thank you."

Steele remembered Fijar and checked for his body again, just in case she'd been wrong earlier. "Kismet, will you examine Fijar? He's dead, but I want you to double-check me."

As Kismet strode over to the former general's body, Aldair burst into view, his blue eyes wide with concern. He took in the sight of Emdubae sitting against the wall. The captain's eyes were closed, and the prince rushed over to his friend.

Emdubae peeked open one eye. "I'm alive, friend."

He searched the room, his gaze settling on Steele. She walked over to him, and his eyes traveled down to her middle. His face paled and he reached for her.

Steele walked into his arms, and he hugged her to him for a moment before stepping back, fingers moving to graze her cheekbones. "Where are you hurt? You shouldn't be on your feet." His hands gently ran along her arms and down her sides, before he gently examined her ears.

"Aldair, we're okay," she said, finding his hands and squeezing them in her own. She met his eyes. "Kismet healed us. We're okay."

She realized his hands were shaking, and she kissed his knuckles.

"Are you all right?" Emdubae asked the prince.

Steele gripped his hands. "Is your father—"

"He's alive," Aldair said hoarsely. "Someone dressed as a soldier tried to assassinate him. Father took him down, but he was stabbed in the process. Thankfully, Bero healed him." He looked at Steele a moment before pressing a kiss to her forehead. "I thought…when I saw that blood on you, I thought you were gravely injured."

Steele hugged him again. She gripped his back and realized just how devastated she would be if something had happened to him. Relieved didn't quite cover how she felt. Tears gathered in her eyes, and she hesitated only a moment before rising on her toes to kiss him. Her heart thudded against her ribs, and when they parted, she pressed her cheek against his chest.

"The general is dead," Kismet said from behind her.

Aldair tensed. "He is?"

He released Steele and jogged to the cell. Emdubae struggled to stand, and Steele and Ali quickly helped him to his feet. They supported him as they followed the prince. Emdubae leaned heavily against the wall next to Fijar's body. Ali's lips parted and his brows drew together. Aldair sat down, hard. Steele stared at the corpse, trying to accept what she'd already known to be true.

"What happened?" The prince finally asked.

Emdubae grunted. "One minute, we were preparing for a change of guard, and the next, the room was in pandemonium. That golden magi appeared and attempted to blast the bars open, but Laiken's magic enforcements on the cell were too intricate for that. She did well. So did my men." Emdubae looked outside of the hall, his eyes welling up with tears. Steele followed his gaze. Several Solarrhian soldiers lay on the ground, including the serving girl she had tripped over. "I tried to help Laiken." He stopped, closed his eyes, and took a couple of deep breaths. His skin was still pale, but when he opened his eyes, they were clear. "We managed to get the golden magi distracted, but reinforcements for Fijar came down, and my focus was on them. That's when Steele and Ali showed up."

"They were trying to break Fijar out, Aldair. Kaspar was almost successful, before Laiken took everyone out in one blast," Steele explained.

"She was a good soldier." Aldair examined the magi on the ground. "We need to tell my father this wasn't just an assassination attempt." He turned to Kismet, his eyes softening. He placed a hand on the magi's shoulder. "I am so sorry. Do you need anything from me?"

"Will you ask Batya to meet me down here? He knows Kaspar more intimately than I do, and I don't recognize the magic he was using. It feels darker and more ancient than anything I have experienced. And I will need help with...with Laiken."

"Kismet, you are in charge of Fijar's body until Batya joins you. I'll send a few trusted guards to move the bodies. We need to return the soldiers to their families."

"Yes, your highness." She dipped her chin and headed over to Laiken's body. She sat beside her and began to speak softly.

Steele felt for the magi. She seemed shattered. She considered asking Aldair to demand Kismet take time to grieve, but she didn't think that would be received well by the magi.

Aldair stood up. "The rest of us will go to my father's chamber."

"What will we do with the assailants?" Emdubae asked, struggling to his feet. The two men started for the hallway, slowly for Emdubae's sake. Steele and Ali fell in line behind them.

Emdubae and Aldair stopped beside Kismet.

The captain looked down at Laiken. "You will be missed, my friend." He gave her a small salute before heading down the hall.

"Who do you trust to manage the bodies, Em?" Aldair rested his hand on the hilt of his sword. "We've been observing our soldiers for weeks, and anyone we found questionable, we suspended from duty. We can check the assailants for any of our own, but I don't know how we would know friend from foe. If they had any Rhian allies, we can't be sure they'd be dressed in the same black uniforms these people were in. And any Rhian allies may have only let them in the door. That could be difficult to track."

"I think Orlo and Tase will be up to the job. Simone, too, if she's available."

Aldair nodded as they walked, and placed a hand on Emdubae's shoulder. "I will speak with Tase and place him in charge. You need rest my friend."

Emdubae grunted but didn't argue, and Ali stepped forward to help him up the stairs. Steele paused before following them, turning to look once more back at the body of Fijar. A hand slipped into hers, and looked up at Aldair. They studied each other for a moment before Aldair bent to kiss her forehead, and together they turned away and followed Emdubae and Ali out of the room.

CHAPTER 39

The next morning, Steele found herself in the king and queen's personal lounge room. The king had been too exhausted from the healing Bero had given him, so they had waited until the morning to discuss the events of the day before. Ali had stopped by for a moment, but had left to practice his swordplay with the soldier named Tase. Steele hadn't seen Emdubae, so she assumed he was still at home recovering from his own healing.

The Zhanbolats appeared relaxed on the outside, but there was an almost tangible tension in the air Steele could not shake. King Ax had been stabbed, and although Bero had healed him, there was a weariness that clung to his eyes and a stiffness to any movement he made. To Steele, he also seemed frustrated they hadn't been able to meet sooner.

Queen Marian hovered at his side, trying to spoon food into his mouth.

"I really can feed myself, Mari," the king protested, disgruntled with how much additional attention he was receiving from his family and servants.

"You say that, but you have yet to see yourself in a looking glass. Your beard is covered in sauce." His wife clicked her tongue, wiping remnants of gravy off his chin. He ran his forearm against his mouth, but Steele thought she saw a small smile play across his face, which was quickly replaced with a determined frown. His hand rested on his abdomen where the wound would have been had Bero not been there.

"Father, you were stabbed. Let her care for you." Aldair kicked his leg back and forth against footstool in front of his seat, which Steele happened to be sitting on. The motion knocked a page to the ground, and she bent to retrieve it.

King Ax raised an eyebrow. "Bero healed me."

"Correct, and he also said to take it easy because you lost too much blood and should have been dead by the time he reached you." The queen adjusted her dress with one hand and shoved a spoon in her husband's mouth with her other, her lips turned downward. "I should not have left you alone."

"Mari, you did nothing wrong," he replied, resting his hand on hers, more husband than king in this moment. His wife smiled sadly.

Steele fidgeted and glanced at Aldair. He gave her a small smile before looking back to his parents.

"I left the veranda door open," the queen said softly.

"As we always do," he reminded her.

Queen Marian nodded, fire flashing in her eyes. "And what a stupid thing to do! How many years have we been on the throne? We have grown too used to people loving us, and we have been so naive."

King Ax sighed. "I think it would be wise to assume this was more about freeing Fijar than killing me. That would have been an added bonus."

Queen Marian paled. "Who would even want him freed?"

"I saw Lac," Steele volunteered. "He escaped out a window, but from what I remember, he and Fijar were pretty friendly."

King Ax readjusted his position in his seat. "I'm not surprised. Fijar is like a father to him. He was close to Fijar's son, Kalman, before he died. They did everything together."

The king cleared his throat and Aldair glanced up at his father.

"Who were Lac's friends in the palace?"

"He had a few," Aldair said, rubbing the scruff on his cheek, "We thought we were keeping a close eye on those people, but I'll make sure to tell Simone to be extra vigilant."

"Maybe because Fijar was running Camp Two, they wanted him back for management?" Steele suggested, pushing thoughts of Fijar's son from her mind.

Aldair nodded and scooted to the edge of his seat. "We know he had a lot of influence based on what Roman Lothar told us."

The queen's mouth tightened. "I hate that we were so deceived by men under our own roof."

Steele wet her lips. "Who would want Fijar to be back in charge badly enough to break into the palace?"

"Maybe he was part of a council," Aldair offered with a shrug. "It would make sense that they would risk so much to free him if he was that powerful to them."

King Ax nodded thoughtfully. "From what we have gathered, we know these camps weren't new creations. They have been developed over a period of years, cleverly disguised by the use of impoverished people or criminals. The types of people whose disappearances would not raise questions."

Steele frowned. "That's not true." All eyes turned to her and she took a deep breath before continuing, "People noticed. They questioned. Before I was brought to the palace, the behavior on the streets was shifting. People were scared to say anything because no one who had the power to stop it was doing so."

"No one meaning everyone in this room," Aldair commented.

Steele shifted to look at him, ignoring the king and queen. "I'm not blaming you or anyone else, but I think it's important to point out that no one said anything because they thought no one cared. And plenty of people, Tazmeen and Ali included, thought that they were being arrested." She looked back at the king and queen before facing Aldair again. "I know now that you do care, though. It took working with you in the desert for me to see that, but I grew up thinking the opposite. Even before I was a thief," she added with a smile, hoping to soften the bluntness of her words.

Aldair smiled back, although his eyes were thoughtful. "You said something similar in the desert, remember? You mentioned how it was easy to lose hope in the system because there isn't any follow through on promises that are made. I can see how you would start to feel like we didn't care about you or your situation. And," he added with raised eyebrows, "I seem to remember you making a very good argument that even liars make promises?" He rubbed his arm for emphasis,

Her smile widened and she shook her head at him before looking back at the king and queen. "I don't want to offend you," she said, slowly, "but with everything that has happened I think you deserve the truth of how other people view the royal family."

The king stroked his beard and Queen Marian smiled. "We appreciate your words, Steele. You and your family are just as much a part of this kingdom as the higher houses, so we value your opinion."

"When did you start noticing the shift on the streets, Steele?" King Ax asked, trying to cover a wince as he shifted in his chair.

Steele closed her eyes, recalling her journey with Snap. "People were always cautious, and I didn't stay in one place too long, but a week or two before I was arrested, people in Azubah, Falu, and Asha mentioned either people missing or things being off in the towns."

Queen Marian tipped her head in thought. "I wonder why it only recently became so noticeable."

Steele half shrugged. "I guess if you're doing something like that where it involves taking people from their homes, I think it's only a matter of time before you're discovered. With Tazmeen, it came across like taxes were raised and she couldn't meet them, so she was arrested. Maybe that happened in other places and more honorable people were taken, and that's how word spread?"

The king grunted. "That could be true, but there is probably more to the story."

"Maybe he was more desperate?" Aldair suggested.

"Perhaps. That could indicate that he was working toward something and he was under pressure to meet a goal or deadline."

"Being rushed usually results in making mistakes," Aldair agreed, "I wonder what will happen now that Fijar is dead?"

The room was silent, and Steele thought back to Kaspar. If a magi had been brought in to free the former general, she was afraid to think about what could happen next. She leaned back against the arm of Aldair's chair with a sigh.

The king risked a glance at his wife. "We should also look into other people of power," he said carefully.

The queen straightened. "My father? He was never one for such secrecy. He would send you a letter about how he was on his way to break down your door and kill you himself."

The king placed his hand on Queen Marians arm. "I agree it doesn't seem his style, but we mustn't single anyone out at this point. Frankly, this seems more like something Queen Evelind would support."

"Over King Eram? And with…" Queen Marian's voice caught, and she coughed. "And with the marriage agreement?"

Steele's heart panged at the grief on the queen's face, and she risked a glance at Aldair. He was watching his parents intently, jaw flexed, and she moved over so her back pressed against his knee. His gaze flicked to her and he gave her a small smile.

"Evelind could have been playing us, Mari, and Hadrian died, breaking all bindings. A second marriage alliance was never agreed upon, and maybe Fijar is the reason why. As for King Eram, we can't count him out, either. The relationship between our kingdoms has been less than cordial since we defeated him all those years ago."

"That's true," the queen agreed. "But what would my father stand to gain from this?"

"Nothing, I believe, but I trusted Fijar, and look where that led us."

Queen Marian was silent for a moment and then her blue eyes narrowed. "I will go see him myself," she said. "I haven't seen my home in too long as it is."

King Ax nodded slowly. "Very well."

The queen patted his hand. "I will send a message to my brother today, and I will leave at the end of the week."

"Can Brandt be trusted to relay the information?" The king asked dryly.

Marian cut her husband a sharp look, but her eyes softened as she looked at him. "The two of you need to settle your little boy's feud before you start a war with your insults. You lost a bet thirty years ago. He may cross you, dear husband, but he'd never cross me." She leaned forward to help him settle more comfortably in his seat.

"Do you have trustworthy guards to accompany you?" Aldair asked. "I'm sure Emdubae would go."

The queen arched an eyebrow at her son. "Raj and I are more than capable. We're women of the mountains."

Aldair chuckled and held up his hands. "I believe you. I just thought that I would ask."

Steele bit her lip. Since the intruders from the night before had either escaped or been killed, they didn't have anyone to question about who they were working for, and she wondered if working so freely with another kingdom was such a good idea. King Ferdinand might not know anything, but like the king himself had pointed out, Fijar's corruption proved no one's loyalty should be trusted. No one should be overlooked.

The king shifted, pushing himself onto his elbow. "Regardless, what happened last night makes me think that in some ways we have grown too used to peace. My father never knew peace in his lifetime, and I have been too proud to see what is going on right in front of me because I did not want to rule a kingdom like him, with paranoia and death looming around every corner and an expectation that every relationship will lead to a betrayal."

"I think that's a noble thing to hope for," Aldair said slowly. "A king who wants peace for his people is someone who has their best interests at heart. But people are flawed and driven by greed or a lust for power, and betrayals happen. What will set our kingdom apart is how we respond to this betrayal. We won't sit back and let this corruption happen. We've already taken steps to bring an end to it." He paused and Steele felt her heart swell with pride and admiration for him, and a quick look at his parents showed a similar pride shining in their eyes.

Steele felt him looking at her, and when she met his gaze he continued. "It will be good for the all the people in our kingdom to see that we notice those who feel unnoticeable. It shouldn't have taken us this long to do that, but I think," he looked to his father, "it will be crucial for us to do so going forward." He flinched and reached into his pocket, and when he pulled out his somenstone, it pulsed with a silvery glow and he looked at Steele. "It's from Kaleel!"

She gasped. "What's he say?"

Aldair pressed the side of the stone and Kaleel's voice burst into the silence of the room.

"We found the location of Camp One. It's fifty miles southwest of Camp Two, and much bigger and more advanced than we anticipated."

Aldair paused the message and began scribbling on a piece of paper. When he finished writing he pushed on the side of the stone again.

"Their leader was tipped off that we were coming and had fled with most of the paperwork by the time we got there, but we will be running interrogations on location. I will send you all more information within the next couple of days."

The message cut off, and the only sound was Aldair's pen scratching against the paper. When he finished he looked up. "Well, that's something."

"It will be interesting to hear what Kaleel can glean from them," Queen Marian said. "I wonder if Fijar was in contact with that camp at all."

"Probably," Steele muttered, fighting back a wave of sadness. The news from Kaleel was encouraging, but it wasn't the news she was so desperate to hear.

"When you message him back, ask him if he would like for us to send him more reinforcements," King Ax said. "And tell him we anxiously await any news he can bring us."

There was a knock at the door and a short, robust guard stepped into the room. "Your Highness, Bero is here to attend to you."

"Thank you, Orlo," King Ax acknowledged, and the magi entered the room. Orlo bowed his head and stepped from the room.

Bero quickly assessed the king's abdomen and said. "The healing is complete, Your Majesty. If you have no further use for me, I will be leaving in the morning."

"Will you not stay and regain your strength?" Aldair interjected, seeming surprised. "The healing you gave my father was extensive."

"My business here is finished," Bero declined. "I need to focus my attention on the magi. There are…pressing matters I must attend to."

Steele looked up. "Kismet and Batya learned something?"

"We believe so, but because no other magi was there, we can only make deductions at this point."

"Kismet said something about how Kaspar's magic was dark and ancient. What did she mean by that?" Aldair asked, leaning forward. His forearm brushed against Steele's shoulder as he placed his arms on his knees.

Bero folded his arms, a faraway look in his eyes. "Our land was destroyed during the Magi Wars by those who executed a dark practice. They severed pridestones from magi and leached the power from it."

Steele straightened. "What did they do with it?"

"They absorbed it into themselves and became more powerful."

"And you think that is what happened here?" King Ax asked, struggling to sit up.

Bero let his arms drop. "Laiken's pridestone was still intact, but Kaspar had two on hand. If there are magi who have begun practicing this act again, we must find out who and stop them."

"Can we help you in any way?" Aldair asked.

Bero looked to the king, and Steele thought she caught a hint of a smile on his face. "You continue with what you are doing. I will handle the magi. If I need help, you will be the first I come to."

The king pursed his lips together, and stood, warily at first, but he seemed to hold his balance well. "I pray that you find your people soon. Thank you, Bero, for your assistance. If you ever need me, do not hesitate to send word."

Bero bowed his head. As he turned to leave, the king called out to him. "May the sun and moon shine brightly over you and your people."

"Thank you," the magi paused before adding, "Ax." He closed his eyes, and his skin began to glow, a shimmer of magic pulsating around him. Steele held her breath, watching as the magi cupped his hands together. In Bero's open palm, a handful of gems appeared. "If ever you come across a magi, show him this somenstone, and he will know you are a friend." He placed one in each of their hands, leaving Steele for last. He knelt before her. "What a time this is, my friend, that a girl and a slave become interconnected and find their freedom together. I wish we could have spoken more."

Steele gripped the somenstone in her hand, whispering her gratitude for more than just the gem. She knew she was fond of him because he had saved her, but she hadn't expected to feel an overwhelming sense of loss when he walked out the door to begin his journey home.

The door closed behind him and she exchanged a look with Aldair. "Did you know magi could do that?" What Bero had said about the magi had frightened her. She'd had no idea they could actually steal power from one another.

"I'd heard stories as a child," he said, looking from her to his parents. "But I didn't know if they were true or rumors."

The king opened his mouth to speak but a sharp knock at the door cut him off. Orlo came back into the room and hurried to the king's side. He whispered in King Ax's ear, and whatever he said pulled the king's mouth into a hard line.

"Thank you, Orlo," he said after the guard stepped away. "Tell her we will meet with her this afternoon."
Orlo nodded and strode from the room, shutting the door firmly behind him.

"What was that about?" Aldair asked.
King Ax looked at his wife. "Breigha is here."
Queen Marian paled. "For the body?"
The king nodded and Steele looked at Aldair. "Breigha?"
Aldair slid his hand into hers. "Fijar's wife."

★ ☽ ★

Three hours later, Steele and Aldair strolled slowly, hand in hand, down the hallway, taking their time before meeting up with the king and queen.

"How did I not know Fijar was married?" Steele asked. The thought of him being in love seemed contradictory to his recent focus in life. He was the last person she could see being vulnerable or compassionate toward someone, let alone a woman. "It was strange enough to learn he'd had a son."

"I guess it wasn't the first thought in our minds," Aldair said, giving her hand a squeeze. "She hasn't lived in Rhia for over four years." He stopped and ran his free hand across his eyes.

"Aldair, what is it?" Steele asked, peering up at him.

"Just...death. I'm tired of death. Even Fijar. It's what he had coming anyway, but it doesn't erase the fact that the man was a second father to me. And Hadrian." Aldair sighed, and Steele stepped closer, wrapping her arms around his waist. His arms rested on her shoulders, and he looked at her. "I'm glad you're here with me."

Steele smiled softly at him before rising on her toes to kiss his cheek. Her gaze slid to his mouth, and her cheeks warmed as she drew her eyes back to his. "All I know of Fijar is what I have seen. I can't say that I like him, but I don't have the history with him that you do. I think if I were in your shoes, I'd be very confused right now."

He didn't respond verbally, but he stepped back to take her hand and smiled appreciatively at her.

She rubbed her thumb over the back of his hand. "What should I expect in there?"

Aldair half-shrugged as he held over a door for her. "Breigha didn't leave Solarrhia on good terms with my mother. They were close once, not as close as my father and Fijar, but they did a lot together. Kalman's death put a strain on their relationship, and then Breigha up and left for Oakenjara one day."

Steele glanced at him. "So do you think I shouldn't be here? If it's going to be tense, how is adding another person to the mix going to help?"

"I want you with me," he replied simply.

That was a good enough reason for her. "I'll just hang back then, and if you need me to do anything, let me know." She paused, thinking about Breigha and what she must be going through right now. Hearing about Fijar's death must have been a shock to her.

Steele tugged on Aldair's hand, and he turned toward her. "Before we go in there, I have a question. If she left, does that mean they weren't together anymore?"

"Fijar never spoke about her once she was gone. I guess they needed to grieve differently. Why?"

"It's nothing. I had a thought or two." She chewed on her lip. "Oakenjara is really far away, and he died yesterday. She must have been in the city already to get here so quickly."

Aldair reached out to tuck a strand of her hair behind her ear. "That's a good thought. I do know that she comes to Rhia to visit with her friends she has in the city, so it's not a complete surprise that she's here. If Fijar saw her when she came to visit he never said, but I know Mother tried to contact her when she knew Breigha was here." He glanced down the hall. "Are you ready?"

Steele squeezed his hand and took a deep breath. She could faintly hear the voices of King Ax and Queen Marian ahead of them. They appeared to be alone in front of a narrow wooden door, but a quick glance showed four guards standing in the shadows. The hallway was dark and cold, and an involuntary shiver snaked down Steele's spine.

"Ah good, you're here," Queen Marian said, smiling at them. If she thought it was odd that Aldair had brought Steele along, she didn't say anything. "I expect Orlo and Breigha will be along shortly."

While Aldair stepped forward to speak with his parents, Steele licked her lips and tried to ignore the door. She was happy to be there for Aldair, but she was a little bit jealous of Ali. He'd given her a grim smile and wished her luck when she explained where she was going before bolting to help Leilan do more research on camp prisoners.

The hollow sounds of footsteps on stone pulled her from her thoughts. Orlo stepped into the torchlight first, and the woman who followed him was not what Steele had been expecting. She was striking, with skin the color of coffee, and honeyed brown hair that hung in loose waves around her shoulders. Her green eyes were large and bright, and she pinned her gaze on the king and queen.

Queen Marian took a step toward her, hand raised, and Breigha stiffened. The queen stopped, and she lowered her hand with a sigh. "If you'll follow us," she said quietly.

Breigha nodded, eyes moving from the queen to King Ax, before settling on Aldair. She tipped her head as she studied the prince, and Steele drew herself nearer to him. There wasn't anything hostile in her gaze, but when the woman turned away, Steele realized she had been holding her breath.

Breigha followed the king and queen into the room, and Steele, Aldair and Orlo brought up the rear. The room smelled sterile and was lit by orbs of floating light. There were several bodies stretched out on cold marble tables, but Steele kept her focus on Fijar.

His eyes were closed, and the blood had been cleaned from his too-pale face, and had she not known he was dead, she would have merely thought him to be sleeping. King Ax and Queen Marian stood back while Breigha approached the body. She started at Fijar's feet and circled around him until she came to his side. She carefully straightened his collar, her mouth pinched, and when she blinked, a tear dropped onto the former generals overcoat. She hesitantly reached out her hand to cup the side of his face.

"Breigha, I am so sorry," Queen Marian said softly, voice heavy with suppressed emotion.

Breigha's hand curled into a fist, and she looked up at the queen. "My son, my Kalman, is dead because your husband needlessly sent him into a petty skirmish," she said coldly, looking at King Ax. "And now my husband is dead while in your care."

Aldair's grip on Steele's hand tightened, and she stepped closer to him, pressing her shoulder against his arm. The room was silent while Breigha studied the king and queen, eyebrows raised as if she was challenging them to contradict her.

Queen Marian looked to her husband before stepping toward Fijar's body so that she stood across from Breigha. "I know that nothing I can say will make you believe my sincerity, but I am truly sorry for your loss. I want to help you."

Breigha scoffed. "All I needed to say to you, I said the day I buried my son. Do you really believe a few words will undo all that you're responsible for? We are finished." She looked past Queen Marian to the king. "I will collect his body at first light. Have him ready. I expect no delays."

"It will be done," King Ax said firmly.

Breigha nodded and bent to kiss Fijar's forehead. When she straightened, she turned and strode toward the door without looking back. Orlo hurried to follow her, and when the door shut behind them, King Ax moved to his wife's side.

Steele couldn't hear what they said to each other, but her heart went out to Queen Marian as Aldair led them from the room.

Aldair was quiet as they walked, and she let him think. They found their way into one of the smaller gardens, and Aldair motioned to a bench. Steele sat beside him, taking in the small garden. In front of them, a young willow tree grew along the bank of a shallow pool covered in dark green lily pads. The willow's slender branches dipped lazily into the water.

Finally, the prince sighed and faced her. "I knew that would be difficult, given their history, but it's good to see how my parents handled her. I'm sure I will be dealing with similar issues when I am king." He looked at his hands and twisted a heavy golden ring on his finger.

Steele clasped his hands in hers. "Was it what you expected?"

He half-shrugged. "From Mother, yes. But I was surprised that Father didn't speak up, even though I know it wouldn't have helped the situation."

"Sometimes staying quiet is the wise thing to do," Steele said, resting her cheek against his shoulder.

Aldair turned to kiss the top of her head, and they fell into a comfortable silence. Steele reflected on what Breigha had said. It was true that Fijar had died while in their care, but it wasn't a death that was meant to have happened.

"Is what Breigha said about Kalman true?"

"About Father being responsible for his death?"

Steele nodded and stretched her legs out, scaring a frog that sat on a lily pad. It quickly disappeared into the water.

Aldair traced patterns around the back of her hand with his thumb. "I was traveling at the time, and I don't know if I've heard the full story or not. Around five or six years ago, Father sent a group of soldiers to take down a gang of criminals in Asha. I know Fijar disagreed with the tactics, but he went along with Father's orders. The entire mission was botched though, and we think someone had discovered the plans to take them down because the group of soldier were ambushed. Kalman was one of the many who died." He rested his arms on his knees and leaned forward. "My father gave the orders, but he wasn't the reason the plan failed. I think that's part of the burden of being a leader, though. Sometimes there's success. Sometimes there's failure, and you have to learn to live with both."

"It would be very difficult to make those decisions. I don't envy anyone having to do it." Steele scooted closer to him. "What are you plans for the rest of the day?"

"Oh, I have many things to do, but I think I would rather sit here for a while. The weather is nice and the company isn't so bad."

Steele snorted softly. "It's always easier to be in the company of someone you can only tolerate when the weather is nice. That's the only reason I'm still here."

Aldair laughed, and when he tipped his head to look at her he was grinning. "I *do* have things to get to, but I would like to sit here with you a bit longer. Despite what I said, I think you know I enjoy being around you. Will you sit with me?"

Her heart skipped a beat at his smile, and she turned her head to kiss his shoulder. "I enjoy being around you, too. So yes, I'll stay."

Aldair's smile widened as he wrapped his arm around her shoulders. She breathed in deeply, content to watch the lily pads bop up and down on the water. Outside of this garden, Tazmeen was still missing and Solarrhia was crumbling, but right then and there, she was happy to be still in the moment with Aldair.

CHAPTER 40

A few days later Steele sat on the edge of the fountain and pulled her knees to her chest. The day was warm, and mist from the fountain sprinkled over her shoulders and arms.

Aldair's sword, which was lying next to her, caught the light of the sun, and she blinked, momentarily blinded by the flash. When she closed her eyes, the afterimage of the sword burned in her eyelids. A thud resounded from where Ali and Aldair were sparring with wooden blades, and Ali let out a triumphant whoop.

Steele opened her eyes to watch them. Ali parried Aldair, twisting to his right, and brought his sword down on Aldair's blade, which disappeared before contact was made. Aldair kicked Ali's feet out from underneath him, easily knocking the sword from him.

"You are getting better, my friend," Aldair said. "Don't ever lose the balance in your stance, though, or you will find yourself gutted before your brain can catch up."

They had been knocking each other around for hours it seemed, though Steele had arrived long after they had begun, taking a break from her reading Kaleel's reports. So far there were four women who fit Tazmeen's description, from her size and skill level to the approximate time she would have arrived at the camp. Each woman had been sold and displaced, scattered throughout The Four Kingdoms. And they had not even reached the end of the list.

That morning, Kismet had revealed to her with regretful eyes that magic had limitations after Steele had begged her for help, to transport the two of them to wherever Tazmeen was and back to the palace in a blink of an eye. Kismet had explained that making a person vanish and reappear was virtually impossible, even with magi.

Magi were able to manipulate the elements like what Steele had seen at Camp Two with the sand, and they could cause inanimate objects to vanish and reappear. Kismet had used a dress as an example. Dissolving a dress and then having it reappear can't harm the dress because the dress isn't alive. Doing that to a human would kill them unless there was a way to do it with powerful and dark magic. Kismet also explained that magi could also use their magic as an energy source, making them stronger and able to travel much more swiftly than normal human beings, so if they knew where Tazmeen was, she could get Steele there quickly. But without that information, Kismet couldn't help her.

She had been disappointed, but she supposed she was also a little relieved that the magi could not do everything they wished with magic.

She sighed and rolled onto her side, facing the fountain. A sense of urgency pulsed through her limbs, telling her she needed to keep moving. She was getting too comfortable here when there was a mission to be after, especially one with such an important goal.

Be still, she coached herself. At any moment Kaleel could send word, carrying with him a lead, an idea of where they should begin their journey to retrieve Tazmeen. She cupped her hand in the fountain and trickled the water across her other arm, the droplets cool and soothing against the hot, suffocating air. She awkwardly splashed her face, rubbing the moisture into her roasting skin.

Aldair tsked at Ali for trying to use both hands on the sword. Steele lay flat on her back, and debated asking Ali if she could take his place, but he was enjoying himself too much for her to interrupt. He had been quietly suffering, turning into himself after he had initially opened up to her. His smile readily returned when he was here with Aldair, the sword in his hand beating the pain away. Aldair's tips were laced with patience and encouragement, and Ali was obviously fond of the prince's presence. She could even say he was attached.

Just like you are, Steele chided herself.

Aldair had been busy all week and she was surprised by how much she had missed him. Stretching out her legs, she shut her eyes, enjoying the cool misting from the fountain. She lazily swirled her fingers around the surface of the water, occasionally lifting her hand to feel the droplets jump from her fingertips to the rippling pool below.

The rhythmic thwack of wood on wood and the warmth made her drowsy, and her thoughts drifted. Fijar's death and her worry over Tazmeen pressed against her mind. She pinched the bridge of her nose and pushed the thoughts away as she turned her head to watch Ali fall to the ground, and Aldair reach for the boy's arm to pull him back up. He was proving to be a quick learner.

She closed her eyes again, orange and yellow spots twirling around in the blackness. She threw her arm over her eyes. The time to leave was coming. It was inevitable.

Soon she would be off to find Tazmeen, or Tazmeen would return with Kaleel, and she would go home to be a normal commoner in the village, not...whatever she was while here with Aldair. She could not imagine his parents would be proud to call her their daughter, so a future with them together was not possible. No, she would have to walk away from this, and her heart ached to even think about it.

Steele knew loneliness. It had been her constant friend, accompanying her in her nomadic lifestyle, shadowing her whenever she said good-bye to Dal, Spar, and Twitch. Somewhere deep down everything in her wanted to forget the idea of leaving Aldair behind, but she couldn't see where she fit in this world.

Still, somehow she had grown to care for him in a different way from anyone else she had come across. She was not even sure when exactly it had begun. Again, the word *love* flitted through her thoughts, reverberating until it settled nicely in the center, satisfied at having made its presence known.

Love. Do I love him? she shouted in the caverns of her mind. Would her mind be able to answer? She didn't know how to recognize the feeling seeing as she had never been in love before. She didn't think his feelings for her were fleeting. She believed him when he said he liked being with her, but a part of her wondered if they were just wasting time. It seemed silly to waste this emotional energy on something that couldn't be.

She grunted and rubbed her eyes, wobbling a bit on the edge of the fountain as she adjusted her shoulders. The sound of sword fighting had stopped, and she couldn't hear Aldair or Ali. Just as she moved to make sure all was well, hands grabbed her and pushed her toward the water. She shrieked and lashed out, looking for something to grab onto. The moment she accepted she was going into the water, she was pulled back off the ledge and onto her feet. Ali had a grip on her arm and was grinning at her mischievously. Aldair stood behind him trying to hide his amusement behind his hand.

She shoved Ali's shoulder.

"You are a pest!"

"You were asking for it." He shoved her back, and she glared.

Aldair laughed weakly, and Steele looked to him. He was far away from her right then, living in some other world, but the moment passed quickly. He caught her eye and smiled. "I will admit, when he told me his plan I may have encouraged him."

Ali snorted. "No, he told me to actually push you in, and that you deserved it for having your guard down."

Aldair scoffed, and she arched her brows. "Oh, he did?" she said flatly.

"Yep," Ali said with a nod. "But experience has taught *me* never to do that."

"That was wise."

Ali turned a smug smile at Aldair. "I told you."

The prince shrugged. "I have my doubts that she could remain mad at you for long."

Steele rolled her eyes, but it was true. She would not let anything drive a wedge between them.

"So, Ali, what do you think your mother will say about the palace?" Aldair asked as he picked up the wooden swords from the ground, placing them on the ledge. He gave his actual blade a couple of small swings before sheathing it. "Do you think she will enjoy it?"

Steele shot him a grateful look. Tazmeen's absence screamed at them daily, but Aldair's positive attitude was infectious and encouraging for the pair to hear. Even if they couldn't stay at the palace forever, it was nice to know Aldair thought Tazmeen would see it someday.

Ali kicked a pebble. "She'll love the gardens the most I think." He threw a look and a smile at Steele. "And your parents. Steele and I used to make fun of the royals and their pampered ways, but you aren't anything like we thought."

Aldair cocked a victorious smile at Steele, who feigned ignorance. "Did you ever stop?" he asked, amused.

Ali gave Steele a quizzical look, and she ducked, avoiding both their gazes. "Is it dinner time?"

Ali nodded. "I think I just heard my stomach rumbling. The cooks told me they would have a special dessert waiting for me today."

"Of course they did," Steele replied dryly. She moved to follow Ali, but Aldair grabbed her wrist lightly. She paused, raising an eyebrow at him.

"We'll catch up, Ali," Aldair said, sitting down beside the fountain. Ali grinned and backed away from the couple.

"Your loss, then. The cooks never let me down, and I doubt I will be able to restrain myself from eating it all."

"I thought Tazmeen taught you better manners than that," Steele teased.

He shrugged, his grin turning crooked as he pivoted around with a quick, "See you later!"

Steele sat down beside the prince, wondering if he had a new thought on Tazmeen's whereabouts. "Yes?"

Aldair swallowed. "I'm sorry to take you away from your brother, but I haven't seen you alone very much since the palace was attacked."

"Well…" her heart jumped, and she twisted her body to face him, tucking her left foot underneath her right leg. "We're alone now. What do you want to talk about?"

A smile played across her lips as Aldair rested his hand on her face and leaned in to kiss her. Her eyes fluttered closed, but after a moment, she pulled away, completely aware of their exposed position in the courtyard. "Aldair, as much as I enjoy this, we'll never have any conversations if this is all we do when we're alone. Even though your talking gives your mother a headache, I shockingly miss it."

His disappointed look pleased her more than it should have, and she cupped her hand around his neck, brushing her thumb over the groove of his jaw. She kissed him softly, scooting in closer, and though she could not see it, she felt his lips stretch into a grin.

This time, he pulled away. "Steele, there has been something on my mind I want you to know."

She froze and laughed nervously. "What?" Her heart seemed to stop beating altogether before racing off, crashing against her ribs.

He paused, running his fingers along her phoenix feather, before his gaze flickered up to meet hers. The intense light pulled pale blue flecks out of his eyes. "I love you," he finally said, as if deciding that was enough.

Her head twitched, lips parting with surprise. Heat shot through her body, and she shifted her weight off her foot. She realized he was watching her reaction, hope fading into acceptance.

"Love?" she finally repeated. It was a proclamation that needed a response in some way, but the words died on the tip of her tongue. The warmth in her heart at the sound of those words made her want to tell him she loved him as well, but how did she know that what she felt was real?

"Yes. Please say nothing you don't mean." He paused. "We have always been honest with each other. Well, no, that's untrue, but we shouldn't feel the need to keep secrets from each other any longer. I know I love you, and you deserve to know, as well."

Steele's jaw hung completely open now. Even as she searched his face, she knew in her heart he was sincere. She nodded, cheeks warming before tightening against her smile. She grabbed his face and pulled him to her, crushing his lips with her own. Taking a breath, she tilted her head back. "What did I do to deserve you?"

He cocked his head to the side, lips twitching. "Well, you aren't quite there yet, I suppose. You've helped uncover serious corruption in the kingdom, sure, but you've yet to completely eradicate the problem. And I haven't tasted your cooking yet."

A quick punch to his shoulder shut him up with an "Oof!"

Steele grinned as he rubbed his muscle.

"Save the kingdom. I'll get right on that. As for cooking, I can make a meal out of most things-benefit of being a nomad-but *you* have yet to prove yourself worthy of such efforts, Prince," she said, mimicking his tone, and added, "Sure, you've helped me find my brother and probably had a part in my pardoning, but I am not completely satisfied with the conditions of this palace."

"Oh, you aren't?"

"Why, no. My pillows are far too soft, and the room is incredibly drafty." She swiped her finger across the fountain ledge and inspected the grains of dirt on the tip. "And this? This is unacceptable."

As she wiped her finger off on his shirt, she raised an eyebrow, daring him to protest. She received a wide smile as he glanced at the dirt streak now adorning his chest like a badge. He laughed, eyes twinkling in the light.

"Oh, I do apologize. I will immediately inform Mother of your disappointments. She'll make sure the staff is extra diligent."

"Good," Steele said, a smirk playing on her lips. She folded her arms, stuck out her chin and closed her eyes. "I expect nothing less."

After a few heartbeats of silence, she opened her eyes again and gauged his reaction to this banter from the corner of her eye. He was looking back at her with a small smile.

"Really, though. I should start making a list of all your faults or your ego will be too big for the palace with all the compliments people send your way." Steele patted his knee.

"Please, don't. The list would be too great," he pleaded, catching her hand before she could remove it.

Her gaze dropped to their intertwined fingers, and she traced a sprinkling of freckles across the back of his hand. His hands were much larger than hers, though they both were equally rough and callused. Hers were not the hands of a courtier or a princess.

She bit her lip. Her heart twinged.

"Aldair, how can this work?"

He sat up straight, his shoulders tense. "What do you mean?" he asked, the playfulness gone.

"I don't see how I can fit into this world. Look at me. Beneath all these fancy clothes, I am still a girl from the streets, who until recently, was a wanted thief." She pulled her hand out of Aldair's and turned it over, studying her palm. "I've always worked with my hands to make ends meet, and I'm not comfortable with being pampered or waited on."

"I can always tell the servants to leave you alone. Let you clean your room or prepare your own meals," he jested, bumping her shoulder with his.

Ignoring him, she continued, "What happens after we find Tazmeen? You say you love me, but for how long will that be true once life settles down into normalcy? You'll be disappointed because I won't conform to how you're used to palace courtiers behaving, and I'll be angry that I'll be expected to change. You said I could be an ambassador for the magi tribes, but we both know I would be a terrible choice. I'm too impulsive and follow my own way too often, and you'd probably be worried whether I would follow protocol or step out of line. Not to mention your parents, who must think of me as some raggedy riff raff and most definitely not a match for their son."

Aldair shook his head during her speech. "Steele, my father pardoned you. Do you know how often that happens? He sees something in you. Maybe something you cannot see yourself yet. As for my mother," he paused, throwing her a look for emphasis, "she has been talking about my marriage for a while now, and when we arrived with you in my arms, she looked practically gleeful."

"You carried me into the palace?" Steele halted on the image, her heart warming.

Aldair threw her another look, this time annoyed. "Yes. You were still passed out from the combination of your wounds and Bero's first attempt to heal you. He used all the energy he could spare but had to save some to get us back to the palace. As for me being disappointed with you because you are different, that is exactly what attracted me to you in the first place. I have never come across someone who speaks her mind even if everyone else in the room might disagree. I already know you are impulsive and sometimes bullheaded—"

"Bullheaded!" she cried out.

"Sh! Yes, sometimes. But if you were perfect, I'd be incredibly bored and maybe a little jealous."

"With that description, I wonder why you would find me attractive at all."

"I'd rather work through differences with you for the rest of my life, knowing you have my best interests at heart, than have you sit back and agree with everything I say just to keep me happy."

"Thank you," she said softly.

The annoyance faded slightly from his countenance, and he half smiled. "Would you like to take a walk after dinner?"

He pushed himself away from the fountain's ledge and stretched his hand out to her. She laced her fingers in his as she followed him out of the courtyard, the wooden swords forgotten.

CHAPTER 41

The following dawn, Steele lay on her back, her eyes wide with pent-up energy and the covers kicked off the bed. She desperately wanted to sleep, but it seemed she was destined to wake every hour until it was time to rise for the day. She groaned and banged her head against the pillow, finally admitting defeat.

The nightdress Kismet had set out for her was hanging on the screen, untouched, and Steele eyed it as she pulled a robe over her underclothes. It seemed strange to have a wardrobe for sleeping, as well, and while she had been wearing the daytime clothes Kismet had picked for her instead of her preferred trousers and shirt, the nightgown would remain on the hook.

The balcony outside her room beckoned to her. She shivered, the air reminiscent of the cold night, and pulled the robe tighter around her middle. As she leaned against the railing, she studied the mountains in the distance, grateful for the clear orange and pink sky.

She remained where she was as the sun climbed into the sky, content to think about Aldair. Their walk had lasted most of the afternoon, him showing her around some of the gardens and talking about his dreams for the kingdom. He had spoken candidly, but she had not contributed much to the conversation. As he'd been talking, she had realized that while she hadn't thought she would always be in the business of stealing horses, she had no idea what she wanted her future to look like. It could be different now that she had been pardoned, but was that what she wanted? Or would she return to the life she once led? She doubted it, considering how much more insulted King Ax would be if she were ever caught again. Still, how else could she help the horses who had no voice for themselves? And how many people would be willing to take a chance on a former convicted horse thief?

Before she'd had time to consider these thoughts, Aldair had pulled her into a garden with magnificently tall and wide trees. They had climbed them immediately and swung from their vines. Steele couldn't remember the last time she'd laughed so hard as when his vine snapped mid-swing and he landed in a thorn bush. Perhaps she shouldn't have found it so funny, but his reactionary hollering made her fold over in laughter, grasping onto the branch she'd been sitting on for fear of falling to the ground herself. She had never thought one could suffocate from laughter, but yesterday she'd found it a definite possibility. She smiled.

A cough interrupted her thoughts. She yelped and almost ducked beneath the railing until she saw Aldair standing on the grounds below looking up at her with a wry grin. He knew he had startled her and was not sorry for it.

"It's fairly early to be lingering beneath people's balconies, Aldair," she scolded.

He managed to look sheepish and rubbed the back of his head, ruffling his hair. "Honestly, I wasn't lingering anywhere. I woke early and decided a walk was in order. Care to join me?"

"Will we be swinging from any vines today, or do you have something else up your sleeve?"

He chuckled. "No, I don't think my back can take another fall like that. I know of the perfect place."

"I'll be right down. Don't move!" she said, going inside. She threw on trousers and an oversized shirt, hastily tying a sash around her waist. Stopping halfway to the door, she bit her lip and whipped around, a crazy idea forming in her head. She strode through the balcony door and climbed over the edge near the wall before Aldair could protest. Thankfully, the stone had multiple footholds and a vine plant to grab onto. Adrenaline masked her fear of heights, and she laughed as she dropped the last few feet to the ground.

Aldair shook his head at her, though his smile contradicted any scolding he might have given.

"Where to?" She asked ignoring the arm he held out for her. Instead she slipped her hand into his, lacing their fingers together.

"The magi created another beautiful space we didn't get to explore the other day. It's said to be a replica of a favorite spot from their homelands," he explained as they walked. "I was heading that way."

"Oh the magi, again? Do you use them as an excuse for when you want to kiss me?" she teased.

He stopped, pulling her against his chest with a chuckle. "You think you're so clever," he said, ducking his head to quickly kiss her.

She laughed when they parted. "I stand corrected."

"Does the courtyard not count?" he asked as they resumed walking.

"I'm fairly certain we kissed there, too."

"Yes," she admitted, smiling faintly at the memory. "I stand doubly corrected."

They walked mostly in silence back to the magi's lair, allowing her the time to memorize the path and to think. Even though she hadn't said anything to Aldair's declaration that he loved her, she respected him all the more for not avoiding her for it.

They reached the entrance of what Steele was starting to call the recreational room, and a magi she didn't recognize nodded at them as they stepped through the door. A few others napped on the pillows spread across the floor. Kismet lay across a hammock, reading a book, and Steele wondered if the magi had yet to go to bed or if they even needed sleep at all.

"Will the magi mind that we're invading their space so early in the day?" Steele whispered.

"If they do, one will say something. They're usually not shy with me," Aldair said, giving her a quick kiss on the top of her head, before leading her through a small opening at the far end of the wall.

Steele had to duck low to fit in the dark tunnel. She stumbled behind Aldair, who had to crouch even lower to move through the space. Too quickly, she righted herself, smacking the top of her head on the ceiling. Aldair peered back as best he could when he heard her hiss.

"Are you all right?" he asked.

She nodded, one hand on her head, the other on the wall. "Go on."

An odd sound, like a crackling or a pattering of water against the rock, bounced off the walls, growing stronger as they moved until she wondered if it was raining in the room they were approaching.

The throbbing in her skull dulled some when the tunnel opened into a large cavern. Beams of light poured in through various holes in the ceiling, revealing a waterfall that twisted and turned down the rock until the water met the ground, forming the pool in the center of the room. Steele would have expected a cave to be barren of any plants, but the magi must have charmed the place. The cave looked—and *felt*—more like an enchanted forest, save for the lack of trees and the rocky walls around them.

She pulled off her shoes and stepped into a bed of wildflowers, the cool grass squishing between her toes. Two birds sang above them, and one planted itself on a perch in one of the roof openings.

Aldair followed her example and removed his own boots. He rolled his pants to his knees and strode over to the pool. "What do you think?"

"It's wonderful! This is a reminder of their homeland?" Steele turned in a slow circle, soaking it all in.

"That's what Batya says."

"Why do they not return there?" she pondered aloud, more a thought than an actual question.

"I believe it was destroyed in a war, but you'll have to ask Kismet. They don't speak of it often."

Steele wandered around the cave while Aldair waded in the pool. She halted at a vine-covered stone archway leading out of the cave and into what Steele suspected to be the personal quarters for the magi or more reminders of their origins. Words and runes she couldn't read were etched into the stone. Around the words, a meadow scene had been sketched, showing a stag leaping into the trees as a wolf chased him. Below, the stag stood his ground, his head reared for battle against the wolf. The scene continued on down the stone, but the vines had overgrown their space, covering the art.

Near where Aldair stood knee deep in the water, Steele found a moss-covered rock to sit on. "Could you not sleep?" she asked him.

"I slept in the study. Emdubae and I were working on the lists, trying to find out who else Fijar was working with."

She sat taller. "Did you learn anything?"

He shook his head. "He was very careful. Though I wonder why considering he didn't expect anyone to discover his endeavors." His eyes widened a bit, and he grinned, plunging his arm into the water. He peered closely at something in his palm before he waded toward her, holding his hand out to her. "Here."

She took the medallion-sized object from him and held it in a beam of light in front of her. It was a turquoise stone with swirling champagne veins that shimmered in the light as she twisted it between her fingers. "It's beautiful. What kind of stone is it?"

Aldair shrugged. "You never know what you may find here."

Steele reached to hand it back to him, but he denied it. "You keep it. Kismet can possibly turn it into jewelry for you."

Blushing and not entirely sure why, she tucked the stone safely in a pocket of her trousers. "Thank you."

"Fijar wouldn't work with just anyone," Aldair said abruptly, pushing himself out of the pool and sitting on her rock. He scooted back until he was beside her.

"Well, let's look at what we know. The train we followed was from Hamonsfell, and the nomads thought they saw Barrowlanders. Just because we didn't *see* anyone who was obviously from Oakenjara, doesn't mean they weren't there." She hugged her knees to her chest. "And we know Fijar was in contact with the Lothar house about financial backing for the camp. But Roman didn't know if Fijar had talked to the other houses?"

"Right. So who could we trust to contact next? If Fijar could infiltrate our High Council, who's to say he hasn't contacted others within our court as well as generals or nobles from other lands..." Aldair trailed off.

"Other kings, queens," she added, knowing he was avoiding it. He threw her an exasperated look, and she returned it in kind. "I'm sorry, Aldair. We can't ignore the possibility."

"Regardless of who is involved, for anyone to think that the trading of humans is acceptable is despicable." He grunted. "I don't believe Grandfather is guilty of that."

Steele rested her chin on her knees. "Is your mother still going to visit him?"

"Yes, still at the end of the week."

Steele tilted her head to study his face. "You remember I'll also be leaving then?"

He nodded, but remained silent.

She gently nudged him. "I think when we leave here, I'll go to the study. Will you come?"

"Yes, after I check to see if Kaleel sent anything." Aldair picked up a few smooth stones, throwing them into the water one by one. Steele watched as they skipped across the pool and to the other side of the cave. One rogue stone disappeared beneath the waterfall.

They sat in silence. Steele lay back against the moss, captivated and lulled by the pitter-patter of the waterfall.

"Steele, are you awake?" Aldair's voice pulled her back into consciousness.

"Yes?" She blinked and stretched her back before sitting up. "But I might have dozed off. The sunlight seems brighter."

"I don't think you were out for more than ten minutes."

"Did you want to say something?" She leaned into him, pulling her knees up to her chest.

Wrapping his arm around her, he took a deep breath and exhaled slowly. "I want to ask you a question, but I'm not sure how you will react."

Steele stiffened but remained where she was snuggled beside him. "You have to know that starting a conversation that way isn't a very good decision."

He chuckled softly. "Yes, you're right, but don't worry."

"Aldair, get on with it." She pushed into him with her shoulder, tilting her head so he could see her wink.

"Do you think you could grow to love me?" he asked after a few moments.

Her lips parted, heart tripping within her. She was startled, yes, but a little thrilled at the thought.

He sighed. "I'm not even sure I want you to answer that question, actually. I'm sorry I said it."

"Don't be," she started, but he cut her off.

"It's not an easy life, being royalty, and one I would never force someone into." He watched her from the corner of his eye as he continued. "You say we're from different worlds, that you wouldn't fit in, but that's not how I see it. We're from the same world, no matter the background we come from. Whatever this is that I've found with you, the life we could have together, I want it. I think it could work if we're both willing."

He paused. She considered saying something but waited to see if he was truly finished. He wasn't.

"And if you could—grow to love me, that is—would you even want that, to grow through this life with me, as my wife?" His tone was pensive. He wasn't looking at her now, which she thought might be for the best because she wasn't sure if she looked as calm and collected as she wanted to.

Yes. She licked her lips, taking a deep breath. "Aldair, I," she began, but the words would not come. "Is that a proposal?"

Marry him. Her heart pounded, thrill intermixed with fear.

"It doesn't need to be. I want you to be ready, not taken aback. If you find me in your heart, I will ask you again when you tell me that it's okay for me to do so." Now he was staring at her, his blue eyes burning into hers.

"Thank you." She shut her eyes. The sun really had gotten brighter. "I need a moment to think."

"That's fair," he replied.

She smiled faintly, her thoughts buzzing. "It's all so much, so fast."

He chuckled quietly. "I know, I imagine I may be scaring you. I'm terrified of pushing you away." He paused, brow furrowed.

Steele let him think. His words both terrified and delighted her, and she wanted to hear him out before doing any thinking of her own.

"I can hardly find the words to say it right," he said after a moment. "After the attack here, and I saw you covered in blood and thought something had happened to you...I just knew that I would be..." His jaw clenched and he closed his eyes. When he opened them and looked at her, she could feel how badly he wanted to get these words right. "The thought of losing you is too horrible for me to imagine," he continued. "I've realized I don't ever want to be parted from you. You've made yourself too important to me to just let you go without telling you how I feel, and that I would like you to stay with me from here forward."

Her heart swelled as he spoke, and she found it hard to breathe. She thought she could understand what he was saying. When she pictured leaving him forever, a choking sadness filled her heart. But she also couldn't ignore the he was a prince, and if she chose him and his life, she would be queen someday. That thought made her want to lose her lunch.

"I can't answer you right now," she said quietly, holding his gaze.

"I don't expect you to," he replied. "Like you said, it is so much so fast."

She believed him and the goodness of his heart, but she knew he must be disappointed. She knew she would be if the situation was reversed. "I don't want to make your life more difficult," she said, mirroring what he had said to her before. "I promise I will give you an answer soon."

Aldair opened his mouth, focused on something behind her, and then smiled one of those smiles that spread deep into her bones and settled somewhere close to her heart. "Take all the time you need."

They were silent for a few beats, until Aldair shifted. "Do you, do you want me to leave you now?" he asked, the usual confidence in his tone wearing thin.

Steele shook her head and he looked at her with a mixture of emotions she couldn't quite figure out. Sympathy. Impatience. Understanding. Frustration?

In a moment, they were all gone, replaced with a careful smile. He cocked his head, then carefully disentangled himself from her and stood. Holding a hand out, he asked, "Are you hungry? We can grab a bite to eat before you go to the study."

Her heart calmed, and she silently thanked him for his understanding before she took his hand.

CHAPTER 42

Aldair proposed to me. The prince proposed to me. Steele paced her room, hands on her hips. *I need to think.*

She sat on the bed and lay back. Sunlight streamed in through the windows, blinding her, and she held her arm out to block the sun. The light winked in and out between her fingers as she flexed and wiggled them around, fascinated with the changing shadows across her skin.

Aldair loved her. He wanted to marry her. Her heart thumped. It was strange that marriage was even something she was allowed to consider now, since before that life had seemed far away. But now...now she was pardoned and Aldair loved her. A smile tugged at her lips. She always knew that Tazmeen loved her, and that Ali loved her like all little brothers love their sisters, but this feeling was something completely new. Someone who wasn't her family had seen her at her worst, had loved her and wanted to be with her in spite of that. That thought had her halfway off her bed to search for Aldair to tell him that of course she would marry him. She caught her reflection in the mirror and gave herself a sheepish smile. Her reasons for needing to think logically about what he said were still valid. Just the thought of being queen someday caused panic to seize her heart.

It was too easy to lie to herself and pretend those reasons didn't exist while she was in the palace. She needed to get out, to put some space between herself, the palace, and even Aldair. The man muddled her thoughts.

She slumped back against her pillows and thought of Tazmeen. She and Ali slept comfortably in lush beds while Vlaar only knew where Tazmeen was and if she even had a blanket to keep her warm at night. A sudden ache of homesickness swelled in her heart and she sat, kicking her legs over the side of the bed. Maybe a walk would help her think.

She roamed the halls, her thoughts reeling, until she turned a corner and stopped. Ali stood just ten paces from her, studying a portrait of a young King Ax and Queen Marian. She coughed, and he glanced her way. With a smile, he waved a hand at the painting.

"How long do you think they had to stand there in that pose before the painting was done?"

Steele laughed and came to stand next to him. "Probably a lot longer than I would be willing to stand for." She prodded his arm. "Want to go on a walk? I want to get outside of the palace for a little bit."

He nodded and they headed in the direction of the palace gates. "Is this going to be hard for you, having to walk past vendors and know you can't take anything?"

"Ali!" She shoved him, and he snickered.

"Does your *sweetheart* know that you're taking a walk?"

"What does that even *mean*?" Her cheeks burned.

"You know exactly what it means, Steele." He grinned, shaking his head.

She ignored him as they walked, thoughts turning back to Aldair. Ali joked about Aldair being her sweetheart, but she knew the endearment wasn't entirely wrong. Aldair was dear to her, and she would be lying to herself if she tried to pretend her feelings for him were fleeting.

"It's not something to be ashamed of, you know," Ali said, gave her a sidelong glance.

"I'm not ashamed," she protested. She considered his words for a moment. "I've had boys like me before, so this isn't all new to me...but me liking someone back?" Her nose wrinkled. "I've never even had a long-term friendship before. Well, sort of. I have friends, but I rarely see them. How do I know I could marry him and then live—?"

"Marry!" Ali exclaimed, an incredulous look in his eyes.

Her eyes widened, and she dropped her head, mumbling, "He may have proposed to me."

"He did what?" Ali yelped. "What did you say?"

"I told him I needed to think." And then she added firmly, "As any girl should before making such a big decision."

Ali opened his mouth, but she held up her hand. "Can we talk about this later? Maybe when we're not *in* the palace?"

He eyed her but nodded. "Fine."

They walked in comfortable silence until they got the front gates. Steele started to explain what she and Ali were doing, but the guards only smiled and let them pass. As they stepped out onto the main street, Steele's hand instinctively reached for her headscarf to cover her face so close to the palace. She stopped. Tears pricked at her eyes, and she let out a deep breath, her hand dropping to her side. She no longer needed to hide from the vendors or guards roaming the streets.

Ali glanced between her and the people mingling around the booths that lined the street before smiling slightly and pulling her along. "I'm happy for you, S, but I don't want to spend all our time out here watching you stare down every single person who walks by."

Steele laughed and fell in step with him. "Do you remember when I first moved in with you and your ma?"

"Yes. How could I forget?"

"You were so young, that's how."

He grunted. "A girl from another house was moving into my house and becoming my sister. You also took my bedroom."

She snorted. "You still haven't forgiven me, even though you have it back now?"

"I had to live in an old storage room," he protested, though he smiled.

"Those first few weeks were rough," she said softly. "My parents were gone, but Tazmeen was so incredible with me. I know I didn't deserve her patience with all my outbursts. Do you remember when she helped me build that wooden cross for them?"

"Yes, and she bought some flowers from the market and made a wreath for it."

"She spent the whole night making that wreath just to help me grieve. What woman already bringing up a child would want take in an angry orphan?"

Ali chuckled softly. "She's amazing, that woman. She's got a heart of gold."

Steele nodded, eyebrows pulling together in determination. "She'll make it through, Ali. She always has."

"I know," he said quietly. "The women were sold for all sorts of reasons. I feel wrong wishing a good outcome for her when I know other women are suffering."

"Don't feel wrong about that," Steele said, pausing before they turned onto the busy market street. "I understand what you're saying, but it's not wrong to hope that she's okay. When we move forward, we'll do what we can to take care of those people as well. No one is deserving of what happened to you."

Ali nodded and then cleared his throat. "I never thought I'd see the inside of the palace, let alone be a guest," he said, stepping down another the vendor-lined street.

Steele laughed, accepting his change of subject. "It's definitely not something I ever expected."

As they walked, Steele noticed fewer people crowded the streets than what she was used to. She'd usually avoided this particular market, as it was close to the palace, but in the times she'd been brave enough to visit, the street had been full of people. As she scanned the vendors she picked out three right away that would be easy to steal from. An accidental bump here and a trip there and she'd have enough fruit for a meal.

She paused. It surprised her how quickly and easily those thoughts had come. Surprised her and scared her. What if she couldn't adapt to this new life? Could she even choose a different path? Did she have any skills other than stealing?

"Steele, you look like you're thinking very serious thoughts. Stop." Ali tugged on her arm.

She glanced at Ali and was about to respond when something soft glanced off of the back of her head, knocking her forward. When she looked around for the assailant, a very perturbed Spar stepped in front of her.

"I can't believe you're alive!" Spar dropped her satchel to the ground. "We'd heard you'd been arrested." She pulled Steele into a crushing hug and whispered, "I thought for sure you'd been executed."

Eyes wide, Steele spat Spar's hair out of her mouth. "I—"

Spar pushed her an arm's length away, cutting her off, and gripped her shoulders. "You didn't respond on your stone for weeks, and when we came to check it seemed the rumors were true." She smacked Steele's shoulder. "Me and Twitch had to admit that you were at least a decent thief since news of your arrest made it to Azubah," she finished dryly.

Steele snorted. "Thanks."

Ali coughed, and Spar looked at him. "And who is this?"

"I'm Ali."

"Your brother! Oh, hi! It's nice to meet you. My brother and I stayed with your mom once, but you weren't around. I think she said you were with the blacksmith?" Spar threw him a quick, apologetic smile.

"Yeah, Master Lorne."

Steele gestured to the small blonde. "This is Spar. She's friend of mine."

"Nice to meet you."

"Anyway," Spar turned her attention back to Steele and pulled her hood up over her head. "I'm only here because I wanted to get some Rhian-made jewelry, and I wanted to see if Tazmeen was around. But yeah, like I said, it was just so crazy. You'd have thought you were the greatest thief in the world with the way the news traveled." Spar frowned. "Really that title should be given to me, but no one even knows about me."

"So you're upset that I was arrested and not you?" Steele asked with a laugh.

"Well I'm torn. On one hand, I'm the only one out of you, me, and my brother who doesn't have her face on a poster, but on the other hand, what's a girl gotta do to get noticed?"

Steele laughed and threw an arm around Spar's shoulders. "Horses are generally harder to miss than some jewelry here and there," she said. "So if you want people to notice you, you need to steal something a little more noticeable. Not that I'm saying you should," she said quickly.

Spar eyed her thoughtfully, green eyes narrowed. "Mmm, no. I don't think I'll switch to horses. Twitch doesn't like them very much and people would probably accuse me of copying you. Can't have that. I'll stick to my jewels and very carefully make sure people notice when things go missing."

"And the fact that I really was going to die for my crimes won't convince you not to?"

Spar shrugged. "I'll be fine."

Steele shoved her friend lightly. She decided not to tell Spar she was only recognized because she had been trying to help Tazmeen and Ali. It was so nice to just banter with Spar that she didn't want to ruin any of the fun. "I wish I'd been able to tell you I was okay. I know if I'd heard something had happened to you or your brother or Dal I would've been worried sick."

"We were. Like I said, we tried contacting you on your stone until Twitch decided we should come here to check the story out for ourselves. We heard all sorts of stories, but the one we heard the most was that you'd been sentenced to die." Spar swallowed, eyes bright. "I'm so glad those stories weren't true."

"Me too," Steele agreed emphatically. "Is Twitch with you now?"

Spar grinned an incredibly smug grin. "My dear brother, who thinks so highly of himself and his sneaking skills, almost got caught when we were here."

"What! What happened?"

"I don't know everything because he was too embarrassed to say, but I know he was trying to steal some jewelry off a street vendor and the man saw him. He only got away because your friend Dal helped him out."

Steele gave her head a shake. "Why was Dal here? How'd you even know who he was?"

"Because he heard you'd been caught, too. People care about you, silly. So Dal helped Twitch get away, but Twitch is hesitant to come back so soon because unfortunately he's got a pretty detailed wanted poster hanging around this town. I've tried to tear up or mess up any that I can, but the vendor was pretty angry and I guess wants his revenge because the posters are *everywhere*. And I guess when Dal helped Twitch and they realized they were in the same area looking for information on you, they just connected the dots. I don't know for sure; I wasn't there."

Steele gave a bewildered laugh. "I'm glad he got away."

"Me too. As much as he annoys me, he *is* my brother."

"Were you able to meet Dal?"

Spar shook her head. "Once he and Twitch heard that you had in fact been tried and sentenced they went their separate ways." She sighed. "I left my stone with Twitch, but I'll be sure to get a message to Dal that you're okay."

"Thank you."

"So what did happen to you?" Spar asked.

Steele linked arms with Spar and they followed Ali as she strolled from vendor to vendor. She relayed her story as quickly as she could, beginning with meeting "Ardeth" at the White Horse and ending with her pardoning. She considered telling Spar that Ardeth was actually Aldair, but decided against it, his proposal ringing in her brain.

As the story progressed, Spar adopted a look of wonder that left Steele feeling uncomfortable. It sounded like a grand adventure, but really it had been downright awful in many ways. She had never been so physically and emotionally broken in her adult life, no matter how many forests she'd slept in.

"I'm sorry about Tazmeen," Spar said quietly once Steele was finished. It must be hard to just wait for information before you can look for her.

"You have no idea," Steele said with a laugh.

"I'm proud of you, practicing your patience. Normally you'd be halfway to nowhere by now just to keep moving."

"That got me wandering around the desert half-dead the last time. I'm no good to Tazmeen dead."

"Also," Spar continued, "I can't believe you're pardoned! That's amazing! I was actually wondering why you didn't have your face covered out here."

"It feels so strange to not have my scarf," Steele said, glancing at her friend.

Spar chewed on her lip. "If you don't have your stone, how will we contact each other?"

"Actually," Steele reached in her pocket to pull out her somenstone. "Bero, the magi I told you about, he gave me one, and another magi named Kismet showed me how to use it correctly! We can still use our code, but I need to teach you how to use the other functions. And apparently they're called somenstones. Who knew?"

"Just how many other functions are there?" Spar raised an eyebrow.

"I'm not entirely sure," Steele said, shrugging. "I think some stones are different."

She quickly showed her friend what she knew about the stone, stopping when Spar asked, "Can we send a message to Dal?"

"Not with this one because it isn't linked to his. And unfortunately, even if you had your stone, I couldn't link them together. A magi has to be the one to do it. If you had yours, I'd bring you back to the palace with me. I'm sure Kismet would link them for us."

Spar wrinkled her nose. "Of course the one time I could actually meet a magi, I can't because I don't have my stone. Which is probably a good thing because I need to leave today. I told Twitch I'd be back by the end of this week, and I can't tell him there's been a change of plans."

Steele frowned but she understood. "Well, when things get back to normal, promise you'll come visit and then we can get them linked?"

"Promise! This is honestly the only time I would ever pass up meeting a magi. Pesky, worrisome brother."

They caught up with Ali who had stopped to admire leather wrist cuffs. Steele smiled to her herself. Aldair may be her sweetheart, but at least she didn't buy clothing to match his.

"Do you have any idea who else is behind what happened besides…you know…?" Spar trailed off, wisely keeping Fijar's name from the conversation.

Steele rubbed her temples. "No." She lowered her voice. "*He* was important, of course, so he could be the mastermind, but where did he pull all his resources from?"

"He was definitely in charge," Ali said, finally moving on from the leather cuff. "People came and asked him about people for sale and what to do with people they were training."

Steele sighed. "We have a long way to go before this is all settled since whoever he was working with were taking people from all over and using them as soldiers or for manual work."

She fell silent as they walked. The part about the training still confused her. Both Ali and Ryker had mentioned people being trained to fight, which made her think that someone wanted soldiers. And the only reason she could think to build an army was for war, but if that was the case, using people from different regions didn't seem to promote unity. If Fijar had been wanting to overthrow Solarrhia with a personal army, she was relieved even more-so that he would never again have the chance to terrorize the kingdom.

"That's sickening," Spar spat.

"Just," Steele said firmly, "keep safe out there."

"We'll be careful," Spar promised, pulling them into an alley. "This is probably where I should stop," she said with a tiny frown. "But I'm not ready to say goodbye to you yet."

Steele grinned. "We'll see each other again soon. Especially since you're coming back when all of this gets settled."

"That's true. And you'll have to let me know how things go with Ardeth." Spar wiggled her eyebrows.

"What?" Steele sputtered. "What are you talking about?"

"Oh come on, Steele. I could tell from the way you were talking about him that you like him," she teased.

Ali chuckled. "I like you, Spar. You pick up on things Steele herself doesn't see. Apparently *Ardeth* wants to marry her."

"What!" Spar exclaimed. "You left that out earlier. What did you say?"

Steele glared at them. "I said I needed to think. I don't know what would be best."

Spar grunted. "Why? If he was horrible, then obviously the answer would be no. If he's so great, which from your story I gather he is, what exactly is holding you back? Do you think you're not good enough for him?" She glanced at Ali who shrugged.

Steele bit the inside of her cheek. Was that part of it? "We've only known each other for two months though," she pointed out, looking to Ali.

"Hey, I've known him a lot less, and I've got no objections to you marrying him."

Spar nodded. "I've heard of people falling for each other in less time. And you aren't like a lot of girls, Steele. You wouldn't even be considering this if he wasn't someone of good character. There's a difference between being rational and being afraid. You could be running from something great just because it's scary and different."

Steele sighed and leaned against the alley wall. "I wish Tazmeen was here. She would know exactly what I should do."

"She might, but she shouldn't make the decision for you. This is your choice." Spar adjusted her satchel. "But if you begin to think, even for one moment, that you aren't good enough for him, I want you to remember how ridiculous that sounds."

"Thank you," Steele said, her heart warm. "I could probably get you a horse, if you'd like," she offered.

"You've just been pardoned and you're offering to steal a horse for her?" Ali retorted.

"Hey, I'm touched by the gesture," Spar teased. "Means a lot."

Steele gave them a flat look. "I meant a palace horse. I know people I could ask."

"As much as I appreciate the offer, you know I'd never make it back to Azubah. No matter how hard you try, I can't seem to get horseback riding to stick. I will, however, take this apple." Spar bent to grab an apple from where it had rolled into the alley and waited to see if anyone was coming to claim it. The alley stayed empty, so she pocketed it with a grin and turned to leave. She tossed the hair out of her face. "Ali, it was good to meet you finally."

"You too."

Steele pulled Spar into a tight hug. "Stay safe and give Twitch and Gemma hugs for me."

Spar leaned back just enough to look Steele in the eyes. "Hey, you too. You'll be in the thick of things, it seems."

Stepping back, Steele nodded. Spar gave them a little wave before turning around and strolling down the alley.

"So that was Spar?" Ali asked, as they resumed their stroll.

"That was Spar," Steele confirmed with a laugh.

"Nice to know you didn't just make your friends up so Ma and I wouldn't feel sorry for you."

"Hey!" She shoved him. "I may be a loner but I'm not crazy."

Ali only shrugged before showing her a man selling birds. The animals were marked with vibrant blues and reds and some seemed to mimic the people speaking around them. While Ali tried to get a bird to talk to him, Steele considered what Spar had said about her feeling inferior to Aldair, and gave her head a small shake. That wasn't it. She didn't have a clean record, but she liked who she was. She liked being strong and independent and was proud she could provide for herself and help others. There were things to be sorry for, but who she was as a woman wasn't one of them.

Even though she and Aldair easily fell into teasing each other, they seemed to work well together. They could be good partners. But could she be a princess? And then a queen? She swallowed. Who in her right mind would want that kind of responsibility if she wasn't born into it?

"We should probably head back to the palace," Ali said, turning away from the cage and glancing at the sun. "You said we'd talk about Aldair's proposal."

She sighed, nodding. "I did. But doesn't that talk with Spar count?"

"Nice try, but no. If you think it's too soon, just tell him that," he suggested. "Or if you think you're over-thinking things, look ahead. You could tell him yes, you love him and would like to marry him. You'd get to spend the rest of your life with someone you love and respect, and who seems to love and respect you back. Or, you could say no. You'll leave, maybe move back in with us and help with Ma's crafts or get a job with Master Lorne. Aldair will be betrothed to a foreign princess for political reasons, and you'll have to watch them be together the rest of your life."

That last one sounded like a terrible scenario, and she threw him a flat stare. "Are you manipulating me?"

He laughed, raising an arm in defense. "I'm just trying to help."

"Well, manipulation makes me want to run the opposite direction." She thought of Aldair and Ali's time together and softened. "You really like him, don't you?"

"Yeah. He's nice, treats me like an adult, and seems to be a good judge of character. What's not to like?" Ali grinned.

She pictured Aldair, allowing herself the freedom to imagine a future for them together. He complemented her, and challenged her to be a better version of herself, and she respected him for that. She liked who she was becoming, and while she was responsible for her growth, she knew some of the credit went to Aldair. He had earned her trust, and she knew she could talk to him about almost anything. She could depend on him to work alongside her instead of over her. They were a team. Maybe even a family, someday. Her cheeks warmed. Having a family with Aldair seemed nice. He would be a good father someday. It was evident in the way he interacted with Ali. As she imagined Aldair holding their child, she saw her own parents being proud of the family she would be leading.

She did not want to leave this man behind.

"What if his parents don't want me around? They are the king and queen, after all, and probably *do* want Aldair to marry a princess."

"Unless they've kept it a secret all these years, there's no law against him marrying a commoner," Ali pointed out. "And King Ax pardoned you, so he obviously sees something in you."

"Aldair said the same thing. But what?"

He rolled his eyes. "I love you, S, but I can't force you to see yourself from my perspective."

"What do *you* see?"

"Someone people like us would want to follow." He looked at her as they walked and shrugged a shoulder. "I don't know how to explain it other than that."

Steele didn't know how to respond. She wasn't sure others would agree with him, but the words still warmed her heart. Her mind wandered to what life would be like if she did return home for good. She would have to adjust to following the laws to the strictest degree because the guards would, no doubt, be closely watching for her to slip up. She probably wouldn't go to court, which meant she probably wouldn't see Aldair very often.

She chewed on her lip. She could move someplace where her face wasn't as well-known which would give her some freedom. Yet if Tazmeen was in fact gone, though her heart squeezed at the thought, she didn't think Ali would want to leave his home. He was old enough to have a job, and she had some blacksmith training, so they could scrape out a living for themselves. But staying in Rhia also meant being near the palace.

Her thoughts moved to Aldair and the possibility of a royal marriage. Prince Hadrian had been betrothed, so it wasn't farfetched to think Aldair would end up the same way if she turned him down. She cringed at the thought of seeing Aldair and some woman, his wife, touring the village, walking past her as she scrubbed pots or cleaned smithing tools.

"What's going on in that head of yours?" Ali asked. When Steele looked at him in surprise, he added, "You look like a caged lion."

She loosed a deep breath. "I was just thinking of what life would be like if Aldair was with someone else."

"And that has you spitting fire, ready to pounce on the next woman who looks at him?"

Steele glared at his amused smile. "It's not funny."

Ali had the decency to cough and look chagrined. "Of course it isn't."

"I think…" She started and then stopped, taking a breath before continuing. "I do love him, Ali. I want to be with him. But I can't say I want to be queen. How can I tell him that?"

Ali threw an arm over her shoulder and hugged her. "I think he'd be happy with just your love, S. He's a good man. He'll give you the time you need."

She sighed.

Ali grinned, and they resumed walking. He jostled her shoulder. "So when are you going to tell him you love him?"

She ignored him. "Let's pick up the pace. I'd like to make it to dinner."

"The sooner the better to see your love," Ali teased.

Steele laughed in spite of herself. "Yes, yes, now come on."

CHAPTER 43

The moment they entered the palace, Steele rushed to her room to wash up. She didn't really feel like walking the halls of the palace having not bathed since they left. And it would be nice to feel refreshed before she saw Aldair again. *And beautiful,* she admitted.

She opened her wardrobe, looking for something to wear, and saw five or six outfits hanging there. She stared at the clothing, perplexed. She had never had an issue picking out what to wear before. She'd never really had choices, though, or bothered to purchase another outfit when she had extra coin. Tazmeen had always been her seamstress and made the choices for her. She dropped her forehead against the edge of the door and grunted.

Half an hour later, three dresses lay on her bed, taunting her. She sat naked on the floor, ignoring the outfits and twisting the turquoise and champagne stone Aldair had given her in her hand. Wet hair clung to her back, and she used her free hand to pull her hair over her shoulder. Water dripped to the floor.

Aldair had looked so delighted when he saw the stone resting beneath the surface of the pool, and without a second thought, he had given it to her. He had called her remarkable once, but it was he who was the remarkable one.

She thought back to their first meeting and how he had debated with her about people and horses. Then, in the desert, he had accepted her into their group as one of them-not a convict, not a female, but another partner. She remembered his face, etched with grit at sewing her torn stitches back together when she hadn't been able to do it anymore.

Steele understood a little better what her heart had been saying for weeks. She might have known all along, really, but now she felt ready to admit it. She loved Aldair. He happened to be the prince, but she loved *him* and would not give him up just because she was terrified.

A light breeze blew through the room, and her skin prickled. A knock sounded at the door.

"Hold on!" she cried, leaping for her robe, which was hanging on the screen. She threw it on.

"It's only me, Lady Steele," Kismet's voice was muffled.

"Come in!" Steele hollered, securing the belt around her robe.

"Thank you for agreeing to help me, Kismet." Steele smiled, a little embarrassed. She wrung some more water out of her hair.

Kismet tilted her head. "I am grateful you thought to ask. What do you need?"

"I wanted some help with this stone. Can you somehow make it into jewelry?" Steele had made jewelry before but not with a stone this fine. She had never made anything for herself, either, and she had no idea what she would like most. It was too large for a ring, but maybe it could do well as a pendant or a piece of a bracelet.

The magi concentrated on the stone in her palm. "This is beautiful. Where did you get it?"

"Aldair found it in the magi pool beneath the waterfall, actually." Steele's cheeks heated, and a thought occurred to her. "Oh, is it all right for me to even have this?"

Kismet's lips turned up slightly, her eyes amused. "What you find in the pool is yours. Magi do not concern themselves with material things."

"One of the benefits to having magic?" Steele pondered aloud.

Kismet shrugged, pursing her lips and humming as she studied the stone. "I know just the thing."

Her blue markings shimmered down her arms.

Steele watched, amazed, as a gold band wrapped around the stone, and branches the color of champagne burst forth from the sides intertwining to make a wreath circlet.

The magi smiled at Steele's awed, "Wow." She held out the circlet for Steele to take.

But she didn't move. "Is it not too much like a crown?"

333

"When I fashion it in your hair, it will look more like a headband. No one will think you are trying to dress above your station." Kismet shook her head. She observed the dresses on the bed. "The cream will look lovely with this."

With the magi's help, Steele was ready much more quickly than had she tried to attempt dressing up alone. The circlet did indeed look more like a band to keep her long waves away from her face, but Aldair would be able to see the stone sitting prominently on top of her head.

The women separated just outside of the study, and Steele suddenly felt a little silly for having dressed up only to check on any new reports. She reassured herself that dinner would be soon after, but her heartbeat quickened as she pressed against the door and her hands began to sweat.

Aldair's voice cut off at her entrance. He stood at the desk, holding a piece of paper before Emdubae, but he was looking at her, surprised. He smiled the easy grin she loved and she relaxed, entering the room.

"Steele!" Emdubae nodded. "It's good to see you. We were just discussing some consistencies we found between Camp Two and one that Kaleel has discovered farther west."

She moved so she could see the paper. "Another one?"

"Yes, it was smaller. Do you remember what that man Ryker said about the group of people he was with?"

"That they were soldiers?" she asked, absently rubbing her neck.

Aldair frowned but said nothing, allowing Emdubae to continue.

"Yes. Kaleel came upon some similar issues. It was easy to just assume they fought against us as a way to earn favor in the eyes of Fijar, but there seems to be more to it than that." Emdubae pointed a large list of men's names. "They were all men who were convicted for murder. And these are men and women who were charged with extreme violence. They were all transferred to the same place."

"Where?" Steele asked.

"We haven't broken the code yet, but it does appear to be a location somewhere in the Gilded Alps near Oakenjara," Aldair pointed to the range on a map sitting on the desk.

"Why would they gather all these men in one place?" she wondered aloud, but the men didn't answer. She looked around the room, which was slowly becoming more organized as papers got sorted into separate piles indicating gender, age, and which lands they had gone to. She grimaced. There were so many displaced people to find.

She sat down next to a stack of papers she had been sifting through the week before and reviewed the pages. She glanced up at the prince and froze when they made eye contact. Throwing a quick look at Emdubae, who was now comparing the map and the documents, she brushed some hair behind her ear and returned her own attention back to the papers. She smiled. If she were in Aldair's shoes, she would be bursting with impatience, especially since she was wearing the stone he had given her just before a very intimate confession. She didn't want to be cruel, but she would say nothing until they were alone.

They all worked in silence for a while longer, and the more she read, the more she wished she could write. While her pace and vocabulary was improving the more she pored over the documents and Fijar's journals-carefully not including who he was working with-she had yet to learn how to draw the letters on the page. The last time she'd tried, the lines were large and wobbly. Recording all her thoughts would be so much easier than having to relay them to Aldair, who then wrote her ideas on their list of possibilities.

"Should we call for dinner to be brought here?" Aldair interrupted the comfortably silent atmosphere.

"Sarai would have my head," Emdubae declined.

"When will I get to meet her, Em?" Steele asked, straightening the edges of her dress. She still couldn't believe she had dressed up to sit on the floor. She would have rolled her eyes if the men weren't looking her way. "And your children. I haven't even thought to ask you about Mathis. I'm sorry."

"Don't apologize, Steele. There has been much to occupy your mind."

"You should bring your family to the palace. They haven't paid a visit in too long as it is," Aldair suggested, leaning against the desk and crossing his arms.

"Sarai would be very grateful, but as wonderful as the baby is, he keeps us awake most of the night. Once we've settled into more of a routine, we'll come visit. Sarai *does* ask about you often, Little Thief. Maeya, on the other hand, believes she should be a princess already. In her mind, she is betrothed to you, Prince." Emdubae laughed.

"Oh really?" Aldair smiled warmly, his eyes locked on Emdubae. Steele noticed his shoulders and forearms tense, his hands in fists against his middle, betraying the casual curve to his lips.

"It's all she has been talking about in the evenings." Emdubae straightened the desktop before making his way to the door. He turned to Steele. "If Sarai doesn't want to make the trip to the palace, I'll ask if she would mind having you and Aldair to the house. She is just as anxious to meet you."

Steele smiled and nodded, and Emdubae waved as he left. The door shut behind him.

His absence left a cavernous hole in the atmosphere, and she took a deep breath, staring at the blurring words in front of her. She'd never felt awkward with Aldair before, not really, and she found she did not like the feeling at all.

"How was your day?" he asked after some time, his knee bouncing.

"I went into town, actually," she said. "A friend surprised me Or, I think I surprised her. She'd heard I'd been executed."

"You should have invited her to the palace," Aldair said, turning to look at the map. He took a pen and marked something.

"You may have ended up missing a couple of jewels if she'd come back with me," Steele said with a laugh,

Aldair chuckled. "Oh *that* kind of friend."

She nodded and stood to get a look at what he was doing. "Aldair, I want to learn how to write."

He paused his writing to look to her. "All right. Do you want me to teach you?"

She shrugged. "You can, but I know you might not have the time with everything else going on."

"I'll make time," he said. "It's not too difficult once you get the hang of it. Practice is key. It's reading that proves to be more challenging."

She nodded, the orange and blue of the evening sky catching her eye. "Do you want to step outside? The sky is showing off today."

The air was cooler than usual, Steele noticed, as they sat on a stone bench, but a blanketing warmth where the sunlight hit her skin helped. She studied Aldair as he watched the sky transform above them.

"I was able to think while I was out," she announced, feeling him shift beside her. His deep-blue eyes caught the light.

"You asked me if I could grow to love you." She paused. "And the answer is no."

Aldair visibly wilted, dropping his gaze to his hands. Steele hesitated before hooking her fingers in the crook of his elbow. "I can't grow to love you, Aldair, because I already do."

His face whipped toward hers, eyes wide, mouth curling into a wondrous grin. "You do?"

She cupped the side of his face. "I love you so much it frightens me. I want to run from you because these feelings are so strong, but I realize that I could never leave you behind without leaving a part of me behind, as well." Heat flushed through her body at the confession, and she shuddered.

Aldair pushed his face against her palm before leaning toward her and pressing a sweet kiss to her lips. She sighed, her hand sliding from his face to his hand, giving it a squeeze when she pulled away.

"I don't know what to say to your proposal, though," she acknowledged softly. "I love you, but I don't think I can be queen of Solarrhia. I've been turning the thought around and around in my head."

"If you were to agree to marry me, there is nothing that says we have to be married straight away. We could wait a year or more if you wished." He wrapped an arm around her shoulders and pulled her to him.

"Would you run away with me?" she joked. "We could disappear in the desert and join a nomadic tribe. I can be very thrifty, and I'm sure you can manage to pull your own weight."

"If running away was the only way to have you, I would leave right now." Aldair chuckled and kissed her temple. "The thought is too tempting, but you've caught me on one of my responsible days. You make sacrifices for those you love, but so does a prince for his kingdom."

Her jaw slackened, and when she realized her mouth was hanging open, she snapped it shut. "I would never seriously ask you to make that kind of sacrifice for me."

"I know," he said.

"I think I would like to marry you eventually," Steele murmured, grunting as Aldair's grip on her tightened. "But even saying that has me wanting to run away as fast as I can. Not because of you. It's the idea of becoming a queen, or even a princess, that is overwhelming."

He ran his thumb along her cheekbone before tipping her head up. "You don't have to commit to anything right now. I said I would ask you again when you told me it was all right, and I meant it."

"I'm sorry I can't give you an answer right now," she added quietly, leaning into his shoulder.

Aldair shook his head. "Steele, I'm not going to pretend that I will never get frustrated with people who are more cautious than I am. A few years ago I would have stormed off, but time away from the palace has taught me much about life. You and I are different. We come to decisions differently. Patience has always been a virtue I've needed to work on, and," he took a breath and scratched at his chin, "I think you are worth the wait."

Steele's breath caught. "Again. I don't know what I've done to deserve you."

"I don't believe it is about deserving each other," he countered. "More that I should work to be someone you want to love, just as I need to work to be a good king someday. Take the time you need."

She smiled softly at him. "Ask me again sometime."

CHAPTER 44

A few days later, Steele wandered around a corner, halting in front of two massive wooden doors she had passed before but had yet to go through. The queen had asked for Steele to meet her at this garden, and now that she was outside the doors, she felt nervous. She tipped her head back, taking in the detail of the golden designs inlaid into the wood. Two large gold firecats were affixed to the front as handles, their gleaming backs arched out for one to grab.

She glanced to her sides, seeing no one, and pushed one of the doors open. The sunlight blinded her, and she had to blink a few times before her eyes adjusted. On the other side of the door was a grassy pathway leading into a large garden. The tip of a sword stopped just before her neck, and she barely refrained from jumping.

She stiffened, eyeing the two guards with white sashes, who appeared from behind the wispy vines hanging from a tree planted near the doors. Shame and a hint of fury resounded alongside her pounding heart. She hadn't noticed their presence. "I'm sorry, I thought this was where I was meeting the queen."

"Let her pass," Queen Marian said. She stepped around a tall hedge and into Steele's line of sight, holding a bouquet of purple flowers in her hand.

Both guards tipped their chins toward her and, with a bow, retreated behind the vines again.

Steele smiled appreciatively at the queen. "Thank you. I didn't realize this was a private garden," she said uncertainly.

The queen's eyes crinkled as she laughed. She set the bouquet down on a bench nearby. "You look like a chastised pup. Come with me."

They turned down the pathway, where two serving women stood, sprinkling water onto the plants and giggling together. For part of the walk, they were completely canopied by archways of vines of foreign flowers. Steele had never been one for gardening or learning about the different plants and flowers, but she could not deny their beauty.

"People from all over the world have donated flowers to this garden," Queen Marian explained.

"They're beautiful."

"I must admit, I used to have a gardener, but I've recently decided I like the way the garden grows when I leave it be," the queen whispered as if they weren't alone.

Steele nodded, overwhelmed with a spark of self-consciousness. The path, except for the sound of trickling water and the occasional chirping bird or insect, was very quiet.

The queen lightly touched Steele's arm and smiled at her. "I hope we will have the chance to become good friends, Steele. I look forward to getting to know you better."

Steele smiled, a little taken aback. "Me too." She took in the variety of plants around her, and brushed her fingers over the leaves of a bush with peach-colored blossoms. "Do you garden for food, too?"

The queen nodded. "In another garden on the other side of the castle. The magi make this land more suitable for gardening, fortunately." The queen turned her head, not a hair slipping out of place in her intricate twist. Steele's own hair, she was sure, was not so obedient.

The queen led Steele to a marble bench where three books were stacked. A stream trickled behind the bench, and she closed her eyes, imagining the streams in the woods between Rhia and Azubah.

"Aldair informed me that he is teaching you how to write," Queen Marian said, taking a seat and patting the marble beside her.

Steele frowned as she sat, but she nodded. Did that lessen the queen's opinion of her?

Queen Marian gently touched Steele's forearm. "I would like to teach you, too," she said with a kind smile, her cat-like eyes soft and encouraging.

"You would?" Steele asked, bewildered. "Aren't you leaving soon?"

"Yes, I leave tomorrow, but since I am sure I will be seeing you again, I want you to know I plan on helping you when that time comes. In the meantime," she turned and picked up the books, holding them out to Steele, "take these with you whenever you leave. Hadrian and Aldair used them to help with their writing when they were boys, and while they won't teach you everything, it is a good start for practicing the shapes of letters."

Steele exhaled deeply, a smile forming on her lips. "Thank you." She took the books and rubbed a finger over the leather covering of one.

"Education is something I have taken for granted, I fear. I should be thanking you for bringing to my attention that not everyone is as blessed as I was to have received one. We need to work on creating a system where more people can read and write," the queen said, her tone growing more passionate as she spoke.

Steele felt a sudden rush of love for the woman sitting beside her. "I'm sure I'm not the first person you have come across who isn't educated."

"No, you aren't," the queen agreed. "But you are the first to show a desire to change that. Publicly, at least."

"I never really needed to know how until now. Symbols and basic words were all I needed, but it will be nice to be able to read a book or write letters to my friends who know how to read," Steele admitted.

Queen Marian chuckled. "Like I said, these books won't be able to teach you everything, but they will help. I know that when you leave, you will not wish to pack much, but the books are thin enough that I think you can make room for them."

Steele opened one and flipped through it, pausing to smile at the childlike scribbles on the pages.

The queen looked over Steele's shoulder. "This is Aldair's book. I hope that you will make him read you some of what he wrote while you travel. It will embarrass him very much."

Steele laughed and closed the book. "I promise that I will. And thank you, again, for this. It means a lot to me."

The queen gave her a warm smile. "You are welcome, dear. While I am gone, Aldair can help teach you as well, but I'll take over once we are all together again." They were quiet for a moment, and then the queen turned to study Steele. "Will you tell me about your family?" she asked. "Aldair mentioned that your parents are no longer with us."

Steele tilted her head, thinking of where to begin, and drummed her fingers on the books. "Yes, that's true. They were killed in an accident while returning home from one of Pa's smithing jobs. Ma always went with him on the long trips, but they never allowed me to go."

While the ache was duller than it had been when her parents first died, she didn't want to talk about them long. Still, the stories produced their faces in her memory, and she smiled wistfully.

"They were good people. I miss them both so very much," she said, staring into the stream, following the ripples of the light. "But I am grateful for Tazmeen. She deserves more than I can ever repay."

"A mother never feels the need to be repaid when it comes to her children," said the queen. "Thank you for sharing that with me. Your parents would be proud of the woman you have become. As should Tazmeen."

Steele smiled faintly. "Thank you," she said softly.

The queen reached over to squeeze Steele's hand. "Now I must leave you to prepare for my journey in the morning. Please feel free to stay here as long as you like. This garden is large and there is much to see." She stood and walked back in the direction that they had come.

Steele, feeling lighter than she had in months, watched the queen leave with a growing sense of gratitude and affection in her heart.

CHAPTER 45

"Did your brother love anyone when he died?" Steele asked Aldair a week later. She leaned against the railing on the balcony outside of the study, lower back rejoicing. She had been sitting on a bench all morning, pouring over maps and lists, and after noticing her shift and stretch several times, Aldair insisted they take a break outside. She had brought a paper and pen with her so she could practice her own letters, and while she appreciated Aldair's help, she looked forward to a time when she could work with his mother.

Steele sat with her legs extended across the bench, the sheet of parchment propped against a book resting in her lap. Her hand paused after drawing a curvy *S*. "Like that?"

Aldair braced his arm on the railing behind her, and she looked up at him, tilting the paper so he could see.

"The more you practice, the less shaky it will get, and yes. A wonderful *S*. Now what is the next letter of your name?" He twiddled her phoenix feather before moving to sit on the ground in front of her. He tipped his face toward the sun and closed his eyes. "To answer your question, not when he died, no. However there was a girl from his past whom he loved very much, but I'm unsure of their feelings for each other when he died."

She bit her lip as she carefully drew a *T*. She added the rest of the letters and threw a triumphant smile at Aldair. He was watching her and her joy waned slightly at the troubled expression in his blue eyes.

"Did she refuse him?" Steele prodded.

"No, they were together for years." He hesitated. "And while they loved each other she was not royalty. My brother was intended to marry Princess Reagyn Rose of the Barrowlands, and he was too disciplined for his own good. Since he was the heir, his thoughts were Solarrhia first, himself second."

Steele half smiled at him, setting her pen down on the page. Aldair propped his elbows on his knees. "I guess I am more selfish than he is, but I will happily be selfish if it means having you. I mean, if that's what you want."

She stared down at him, his words ringing in her heart. She wished at that moment she were better at speeches and freely able to express her feelings. Though her heart was full, her mind was blank. Aldair was watching her intently, and he cheeks warmed. She held the page up, pretending to study the name. She lowered the paper and frowned. "Will you look at this? I think I wrote this part wrong."

Aldair got up and sat beside her, nose wrinkling as he studied the parchment. He turned to face her, and Steele kissed him soundly. He grunted, surprised, before gently raising a palm to her cheek and kissing her back. She smiled when she sat back, pleased her plan had worked.

"Clever trick," he said with a laugh.

She grinned and leaned against him, thinking about Hadrian and the woman he had given up. She wondered how the woman had felt when she learned the prince had died. Her smile slipped. "I have a question," she said, sitting up to look at Aldair. "But it's about your brother and his death."

"You may ask it," Aldair said, shifting on the bench so he faced her.

"Bero healed your father of his wound, he healed us in the desert, and Kismet healed Em, so why couldn't a magi heal your brother of his illness?"

Aldair exhaled and adjusted the leather cuff around his wrist. "They tried. When Hadrian first got sick, it didn't seem very serious, but as he worsened, the magi tried everything they could to heal him. He would seem to get better and then he would get much worse. I don't know why the healing didn't work." He clenched his jaw and anger flashed in his eyes. "What Fijar said about him, that he was weak and afraid in death, that wasn't true. We were all frightened because we didn't know what was happening to him, but to me, he seemed very brave."

Steele's heart went out to him and she cupped his cheek in her palm. "If I've learned anything about the Zhanbolat's, it's that they don't let fear overcome them. I never believed what Fijar said about him. It was a coward's way of trying to make you angry."

The anger faded from Aldair's eyes, and he pressed his forehead against hers. She was still, very aware of how near his lips were to hers.

"Thank you," he said finally, raising his head to look at her.

She gave him a small smile and began to doodle a horseshoe on the side of the parchment. Aldair cleared his throat and she looked over at him.

"I know you'll be leaving soon," he said. "In a few days, correct?"

Steele nodded. "In three days. I haven't even started to gather my things together," she admitted.

"Ah. Well, don't get mad, but I have one more thing for you to pack."

"I hope you don't mean yourself, Prince. I don't think you'd fit in my saddlebags."

Aldair chuckled. "Unfortunately no. But I do have this for you." He held out a compass to her. "It's mine and I would like for you to take it with you."

She took the compass from him and ran her fingers over the phoenix that was etched onto the back. "It's beautiful," she said, raising her eyes to meet his. "Thank you. I'll take good care of it." She studied his face for a moment before leaning in to gently kiss him. "I'll miss you," she said quietly, sitting back and pocketing the compass.

Aldair brushed her hair behind her ear and rubbed his thumb along her cheekbone. "And I'll miss you. But since we have our somenstones linked, we can be in communication and when the time is right, we'll meet again. Just hopefully this time you won't be in the sun half-baked to a crisp." He gave her a wry grin.

She rolled her eyes and opened her mouth to speak, but her retort died on her tongue as the door leading from the study to the balcony swung open to reveal Emdubae and King Ax.

Steele pulled the book and parchment to her chest and hurriedly stood.

"Emdubae." Aldair said, pushing himself up to stand. "Father? What is going on?"

"We were in the king's study looking over some codes when we received a message from Kaleel," Emdubae said, motioning them forward.

Steele hurried forward, heart racing. As her eyes adjusted to the darker study, she could make out Batya standing with a group of guards. Aldair shoved several books to the side of one of the larger tables, and the king laid a map flat across it, pausing to rub his chest.

Once everyone had gathered around the table, Emdubae tapped the map and looked up at Aldair. "The camp has been cleared, and everyone has been thoroughly questioned before they were transferred home."

"We have a list of fourteen towns that you can go search," King Ax said, taking a pen and circling names on the map. "From what both Kaleel has found and what your mother has sent, it will be more profitable to start the searching and questioning to the south. When you arrive at a town you will see if you can free anyone who has been sold and you will question anyone you can to get information about who is involved." He looked at his son. "Carefully, of course. Bear in mind, some of these towns are in Oakenjara."

Aldair nodded and bent to study the map. "You would have us go through the Green River Forest?"

Steele looked from the map to Emdubae. "Does that mean we can set out?" She was so anxious to be moving. And while Emdubae hadn't said anything about Tazmeen, she would much rather be out looking than stuck at the palace.

Emdubae nodded as the king traced a line to the south. "It will take you longer to travel that way," King Ax said. "But your chances of being seen will be lower. We can't risk our actions being known to anyone outside of those we trust."

Emdubae pointed to a spot on the map along the route the king at traced. "Kaleel said to meet him here, at the town of Tuliu, a few leagues away from Valuis, And," he continued, a smile tugging at his lips as he looked at Steele, "he said that of the fourteen towns, eight have women who match Tazmeen's description."

Tears blinded Steele, and she fiercely wiped the heel of her hand against her eyes. "Really?" she asked, voice thick.

Emdubae smiled fully. "Really."

"When can we leave?" Aldair asked, looking to his father. He took Steele's hand, lacing their fingers together.

"Dawn," the king replied. "You will take Batya and Kismet with you, along with six of our soldiers" He looked from his son to Steele. "While I am happy that you have news of your Tazmeen, you must realize that this mission is much larger than just finding her."

Aldair's grip on her hand tightened for a moment, but she nodded. "I do, Highness. I am not the only person to have lost someone, and I am thankful for the chance to bring people home. And to help the kingdom."

She was a little taken aback by the king's abruptness, but the words she spoke were true.

Aldair let go of Steele's hand to pick up a pen and blank parchment. "At each location we will locate people who were sold and those who did the buying," he said to himself, writing quickly on the paper. "Depending on the city, we'll have to do this creatively."

Emdubae scratched the back of his neck. "I agree. We will have to be prepared to steal people back, buy people back, manipulate the masters of the house for intel…" he trailed off as Aldair continued to write.

Steele didn't like the idea of buying people, but she saw the logic in it. If people were being treated as objects, a sympathetic outsider would raise questions. But taking the time to ask questions and get information would take time. When she rescued a horse, she never stayed in the city very long. It was in her favor to get in, get the horse, and get out quickly. She gave her head a shake and returned her focus to the map. She understood the need for caution. She just preferred to be cautious quickly.

Aldair glanced at her and grinned. "Are you ready for sleeping in tents and on bedrolls again? We'll likely be gone for months, and I know you've gotten used to sleeping in a luxurious palace bed."

"Yes," she said rolling her eyes at him. "Very much so." She looked at Emdubae. "Does Ali know?"

"Not yet. We got the message and came straight here."

"You should go tell him," King Ax said kindly. "All we have left to talk about is what you'll need to pack and other minor details. Your plans and schedule will change depending on what you find in the towns, so you won't miss much by leaving us now."

Steele nodded her thanks and, with a quick smile at Aldair, left in search of Ali.

Steele lay in her bed, staring up at the ceiling. It was still an hour until she was supposed to be at the barn. She pushed herself into a sitting position and grunted. Her eyes burned with exhaustion. She knew she needed all the sleep she could get, but her body hummed with energy.

With a sigh, she kicked her legs free of the covers and got out of bed. She quickly pulled on her clothes, grabbed her satchel, and straightened the blankets.

The barn was quiet save for the occasional snort or sigh from a horse, and she hooked her arms over Kesif's stall door. The gelding pricked his ears at her and gave a breathy whicker as he approached. She set her bags down beside the tack room door and grabbed a brush from the bucket.

Kesif was groomed almost daily, so only a small amount of dust and loose hair came free. Still, she took her time, enjoying the way he leaned into her brush. After she picked the dirt and sand out of his hooves, she collected his saddle, pad, and bridle from the peg on the wall of the tack room. Her jaw dropped when she walked inside. There were at least a hundred saddles set on stands hanging from the walls. She inhaled deeply; the scent of leather would always remind her of home.

Kesif watched her, brown eyes inquisitive as she hung the bridle on the stall door. She placed the blanket across his shoulders and set the saddle on top of it. She circled around the horse, checking the entire saddle meticulously until she was satisfied everything was as it should be. Kesif sighed heavily as she tightened the cinch, and she chuckled.

"You, my friend, have had too much time off." She scratched his ear, and he tipped his head toward her, enjoying the rub. "This trip will be different. We are looking for someone special, and I am not coming back until I have found her."

"I hope you aren't implying that he's fat," Aldair said from behind her.

"Of course not," she said, turning to find him leaning against the stall door. "Couldn't sleep?"

He shook his head. "You?"

"I tried," she said, covering a yawn with her fist.

He laughed quietly and let himself into the stall. "I'm happy for you," he said, wrapping his arms around her.

She buried her nose in his chest and exhaled. "I'm happy for me, too."

"I know we talked about this a little yesterday, but you know that if something comes up or we discover something that would have me go in a different direction than what was planned, I'll have to do that." His thumb rubbed her shoulder blade.

"I know," she said quietly, looking up at him. "It's not what I want. Selfishly I want you with me the whole time, but I do understand that the future of your kingdom is at stake."

"I'll travel with you for as long as I can," he assured her. "I'm hoping that actually being out and among the townspeople will give me some much needed insight. It will be good to talk to people."

She nodded and then pulled his head down to kiss him. "I'm a little afraid of what we might find," she admitted.

He pressed his forehead to hers. "I am, too. But good or terrible, this is something that we have to investigate until we have answers that will allow us to put an end to it. Someday this kingdom will be mine, and I have to protect that future."

Steele cupped his cheek as she leaned back to look him in the eyes. "Solarrhia is lucky to have you as an heir. This drive you have to keep your people safe is admirable." He leaned down to kiss her again, and when they parted, she grinned. "You should go get Cahya ready. If you take your time, someone will do all the work for you and you wouldn't want to be coddled."

He gave her an easy grin as he backed away. "You're right. I'm so lucky I have you to keep me humble." With, a wink he slid the stall door open and disappeared down the aisle.

Steele laughed and turned to rub Kesif's neck. The paint nosed at her pockets, looking for a treat, and she batted his nose away. "You have to earn that," she chided, reaching for his bridle. "Otherwise you'll become coddled, too."

She slipped the bridle over his ears, and he opened his mouth for the bit. After buckling the straps around his face she secured her saddlebags against the back of the saddle. She ran her eyes over his body and smiled at the comforting familiarity to the routine.

She led Kesif out of the barn and mounted up, scanning the area for Ali. He'd yet to arrive, and she hoped he hadn't overslept. Emdubae caught her eye from across the stable yard, and she tossed him a grin before observing the rest of their group.

Six others would be joining them at first, until they found Kaleel in Tuliu. He had a band ready to help them in their travels, for protection and transport of prisoners.

Kesif shifted beneath her, and she turned him in a circle, strangely pleased that he had not lost his quirks since being back at the palace. He was as impatient as ever. His brown ears swiveled back and forth, taking the sounds in, and she ran her hand down his gleaming white neck.

Emdubae began talking to the men and women at the front of the group, and Steele strained to hear what he was saying. The wind snatched most his words before they reached her.

"He's just explaining how important this mission is," Aldair said suddenly from beside her, and she started.

"How long have you been there?"

He smirked and patted Cahya on her dark-gray neck. "Only a moment, but it was entirely too easy to sneak up on you."

Steele rolled her eyes. "Where is Ali?"

Aldair motioned over his shoulder, and she twisted around in her saddle, a grin lighting up her face as she watched Ali trot up to them on a brown gelding named Stretch.

"I'm going to ride at the front with Em," Ali announced when he pulled up between them. "I want to be able to tell Ma that I was first out of the gate when we set off for her."

"She would expect nothing less. You remembered to pack everything, right? You have water? Your saber? Extra scarves?"

Aldair chuckled, and Ali rolled his eyes. "Yes, *Mother,* I have it all."

"You better get up there," Aldair said, patting Ali on the back. "I think Em is ready to lead us out."

Ali nudged his horse back into a trot and disappeared between soldiers.

Steele sighed. "Were we right to allow him to come?"

Aldair squeezed her knee. "There's always a risk involved in these missions, but I will do everything in my power to keep him and you safe."

"If you remember correctly, I do believe I was the one who kept you safe last time," she said wryly. "I can fend for myself."

Emdubae suddenly wheeled his horse around, and they vanished in a cloud of dust. The rest of the group followed, and Kesif bobbed his head, anxious to catch up. Aldair leaned over, a challenge in his eyes, but before he could speak, Steele grabbed the front of his tunic and crushed his lips to hers. Just as she pulled away, she loosened her hold on Kesif's head, and the gelding did not hesitate a moment before galloping away.

Aldair's startled laugh rang out from behind her, and she grinned. She did not need a head start to beat him, but she would take advantage where she could. She eased Kesif into a comfortable canter, angling him to the group's flank to avoid the dust and kicked up sand.

As the Solarrhian palace grew smaller behind them, she set her jaw in determination, her mind fixated on Tazmeen's smile, her hands, her long dark hair pulled back in a braid. Steele would not return without her.

Her next great adventure had begun, and she was more than ready.

· ✷ ·